MINDSTORM

CINDY KOEPP

LUMIN ANIME
CITRON CONCASSÉ
ABERDEEN, WASHINGTON, USA

MINDSTORM

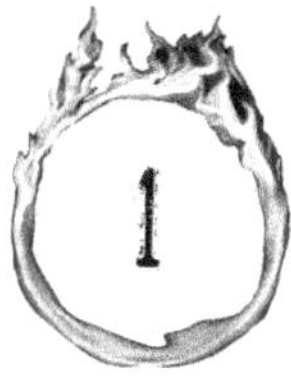

Thomas McCrady scooted his chair back and mentally recited this week's mantra. *Bored, bored, bored!*

He stood, careful not to touch the plywood held up by rocks in each corner. The last time he'd jiggled the makeshift table, his partner had threatened to skewer him with the rusted gardening tools littering the Cordilians' sacred garden.

"Don't go too far." Angela flipped the page she was reading to the back of the pile.

"I won't," he said mid-stretch.

Thomas walked along the one path that hadn't been overrun by unruly plants. If the treaty negotiations were successful today, perhaps the gardener-priests could get busy without causing riots when one faction objected to the other's idea of beautiful.

He reached the end of his path and admired a blue flower on a spiny shrub. Meiko would love one of those. The locals wouldn't appreciate him plucking one, and these local blooms weren't available in Haidar's stores. He'd have to settle for the next best thing. His fiancée was overdue for her next installment of tulips.

Thomas took a deep breath to enjoy the vanilla and cherry scent before he turned around and paced back the other way.

Angela still sat in the garden's center. Her long hair was drawn up into a tight bun on the back of her head. Her black suit and ruffled blouse were out of place among the flowers. She sat on a folding chair and reread the peace treaty for the five millionth time since they'd arrived this morning.

Angela's thoughts touched his. *"Thomas, time to begin."*

He nodded and walked back to the table. *"What do you need me to do?"*

She glanced up at him. *"Sit and observe."*

"I really am capable of doing more than weighing this chair down." He settled into the chair next to her.

"As I told Joy before we left, I don't need your help."

He rolled his eyes and kept his thoughts to himself. *You could try humoring me and giving me something to do.*

At one end of the garden, steel doors twice the height of an average man swung open with a cacophonous sound like a guitar out of tune. Was the mess of noise meant to be musical, or was it in dire need of adjustment like the rest of the garden?

The Cordilians slunk in on their multi-jointed legs. Each one looked like an odd cross between opaque glass tubes and half-meter tall centipedes. Although they moved slowly now, earlier in the week, when faced with a possible threat, they'd put racehorses to shame.

In the crowd outside the wall, Thomas sensed a flare of psionic power that resolved into a group of people. He narrowed his thoughts on the area. A Haidarian female's signature stood out like an LED lightbulb among the almost two dozen human, male tealights.

What's this about? He leaned closer to Angela. *"Did you invite some—"*

She glared at him. *"Hush. I need to focus on the meeting."*

He turned to face her. *"Look, someone just tele—"*

"Be quiet, will you! When we're done here, I'll be more than happy to explain away your worries."

Thomas sighed and left his warning unspoken. He reached out with his thoughts to identify the newcomer and hit a wall of psionic force.

A combat shield? He scowled.

No one from home with a legitimate reason to be here would come looking for a fight.

Readying his own mental protection, Thomas stayed still as he sought for other signs of danger. The crowd was full of searing anger and blunt-edged resentment. Were those the normal feelings of people who disagreed with the current plans? Were there violent protests in the works to stop the treaty before the delegates could make their marks?

He grabbed Angela's arm. "Listen to me—"

"Thomas, quit!" She shrugged away from him.

Angela reeled back as if she had been kicked in the head. Thomas tried to catch her, but his fingers brushed past the sleeve of her shirt. She hit the ground hard and stayed still.

"Angela!"

The garden's gate burst open a second later under the weight of several Cordilians. The first hit on his mental shield came a second after the gate fell. His protection wobbled but held. Gunshots echoed off the garden's wall. Bits of rock from a planter struck his thigh.

He yelped and dove under the table, even though the thin wood would never stop a bullet or a blaster bolt. He clapped his hand over the wound. If he were lucky, the snipers wouldn't see him.

Shrill screams split the air. The sense of pain and terror from the delegates sickened him. He could do nothing to help them directly, but if he could reach Angela, he could teleport them both home, get her to a doctor, and send back more experienced help for the delegations.

As he inched toward her, a female presence shoved against his shields. Thomas bolstered his defense and pushed her back.

The second attempt battered at his mental shield and bored through. Before he could reset his guard, his attacker thrust into his mind like a spear. Thomas clenched his eyes and focused inward.

You want a fight? You got one.

A dark, curvaceous image bearing a pair of fiery knives appeared in his mental perception. Her hand covered her mouth. *"Ooo. That didn't hurt, did it?"*

Thomas mustered every scrap of power and focus he could pull together. *"Not half as much as this will."*

His own personal image formed in the shape of a huge wolf. He launched himself at the shadow woman and tackled her, tearing into her with a mouth full of sharp teeth.

After he had scored a couple good hits on her, her psionic knife tore into his wolf's chest causing a new surge of pain that convulsed his physical body. On the mental battlefield, the unknown warrior threw Thomas off, the knife still stuck in his ribs. He levered himself back onto his feet and growled at the shadow-woman. Foam boiled from her wounds. She staggered back but kept her footing.

Brandishing her remaining knife, she came closer. *"You're dead!"*

How could she keep going? The considerable damage he'd done, combined with the added strain of battling on his turf should have taken her out. Whoever psycho-woman was, she had to be either impressively powerful or highly trained.

Thomas gathered himself for another attempt. Before she could reach him and renew her assault, he charged. His wounds slowed him. She sidestepped and threw her remaining dagger. It cut a line across the wolf's shoulder.

His internal vision blurred. His wolf avatar struggled to his feet again and faced the shadow-woman. She limped toward him, wounds still gaping. Twice, she faltered but kept coming. The edges of the image darkened. He couldn't black out. She'd kill him for sure. He bared the wolf's teeth and growled. Her silhouette raised a dimly glowing hand. He backed up a pace and tripped over his own feet. She collapsed and vanished, leaving him alone in his own mind.

Dismissing the images, Thomas forced his eyes open. Gunshots and hollered commands in multiple languages created a ruckus he couldn't sort out. The world randomly blurred, doubled, and righted itself over and over as he blinked hard to focus his sight. He pressed a hand to his forehead in a useless effort to ameliorate the report of his mental injuries.

He had to get out of here and call in help for the Cordilians. Angela lay unmoving out of arm's reach. Blood stained her blouse, and he prayed he still had time to help her. His sense of her mind showed her still with him but weakening by the moment.

His head swam in a haze of pain and disorientation. Terror, rage, and agony assaulted his thoughts. Thomas crawled on his belly and made his way toward Angela. Bullets ricocheted off every hard surface around him. Thomas gritted his teeth and stretched. He locked a hand around Angela's wrist and focused his mind on home.

Dr. Calla Geisman poured herself a glass of ice water

and stared out the porthole at Earth spinning below the station. She turned away before her brain started replaying her last visit to the planet and looked around. Her new apartment would tolerate company. A floral print couch with fraying cloth on the armrests faced a solid black recliner across a wooden coffee table. A box served for an end table and held a tarnished metal lamp with a faded blue lampshade. Nearby, a card table and four folding chairs made up her dining room. The door to her bedroom was closed, blocking the view of the boxes that made up her dresser and the sleeping bag on the floor that worked for her bed.

Obligations had kept Calla too busy to clean up in over a week. She hadn't inherited her mother's cleaning obsession, but she did want the place to be presentable when her teacher arrived for the catch-up lesson.

After a little tidying up, the place felt more like the Med Ward break room than a home, but she was glad enough to be alive. The fire in her apartment a month ago had robbed her of everything she'd owned, and replacements came as slowly as the insurance money, which might arrive some time prior to eternity. Maybe that was just as well. The unknown male who had attacked her and set fire to her place might try again. Many who survived one attempt fell to the second one. Friends and family were keeping an eye on her place now, but after five years of searching, the police were no closer to figuring out who was going after the disabled.

She put her glass in the sink as someone knocked on the door. That would be her teacher. Sean Zagruder had aged gracefully into his late fifties. His dark hair had been ever so lightly salted with gray. In ten years or so, he would make a kind, old, grandfatherly sort. His eyes glittered brightly in spite of the strong lighting in the room, a testament to the power he controlled. After admitting Mr. Zagruder, Calla gestured for him to sit at the table.

He set a black case no bigger than his hand on the table and sat in one of the folding chairs. "Good morning."

"Hello. Thanks for coming." Calla offered him something to drink. "What did I miss?"

"We worked on basic, short-distance teleportation for the rest of the hour." He pulled out a practice target. "You and I need to back up a little more than that. I checked your training record, and you're further behind than I thought."

Calla handed him a glass of water. "The hazards of the job, I'm afraid. Am I too far behind to stay in the class?"

"No." He took a sip. "We can do this. You'll need a few sessions outside regular class time and a good deal of independent practice, but it'll work out. Now, do you remember how to light a target?"

Calla frowned. "I remember the steps you described, but I also remember failing miserably."

He adjusted the settings on the device. "Let me see what you're doing."

The fist-sized cylinder had a light on the top and a couple switches and dials on the side.

Staring at the target sitting on the table between them, she focused her thoughts and pushed outward. The light stayed dark.

Mr. Zagruder looked from the target to her. "Hmm, all right. This works the same way as throwing a basic psionic punch. Do you know how to do that?"

She leaned back in her chair. "I'm afraid not. I don't know much that could be used aggressively."

He smiled. "Oh, I don't know about that. I once had a student who was a paramedic. He responded to a call in a rough part of the space station. His patient came under attack by a thug with an ax to grind. To save the patient's life, the paramedic reversed one of his stabilizing procedures and caused the assailant to have a heart attack."

Calla snorted. "Pity that didn't occur to me when that lunatic started the fire in my apartment."

Recollections strutted into her thoughts, reminding her of the shadow-warrior avatar coming after her in what had to be the most lopsided fight ever. The maniac had stood over her battered avatar and brandished his flaming sword. *"Useless! Syndromers like you are a drain on our society."*

That's enough of that. She visualized a storage box and slammed those memories back into it.

"You were a little preoccupied. Anyway, back to this." Mr. Zagruder pointed to the target. "Watch what I do."

As he demonstrated, she observed the flow of his powers. He marshaled his raw strength like a capacitor then let it flare out at once. The light on the sensor burned with his success, casting deep shadows behind her hand.

Her power didn't amount to half of his, but she wasn't going to give up without trying. Calla gathered her strength and hurled it at the target. When the target refused to give her so much as dull glimmer, she sighed.

"Are we sure this is within my power level? I've run into other things Power Deficit Syndrome won't let me do."

Mr. Zagruder shrugged. "Your disability will keep you from doing some of the things the class will get to later on, but this is more about control than strength. Ultimately, you should be able to teleport, but you won't get the fantastic interstellar range some folks do. You've never used your mental abilities for anything like this before, but you can do it." He pointed to the cylinder. "Again. Concentrate."

Squinting, she focused her attention on the small cylinder on the table. She tried to pinpoint her efforts to a single spot and projected mental energy.

"No, you're going too slowly." Mr. Zagruder leaned toward her and pinched his thumb and forefinger together. "Gather the power and release it all at once in a single, big burst." He flicked his hand open.

After closing her eyes for a moment, she gave her attention to the target again. Building up power felt like an odd pressure against the inside of her forehead. When the sensation changed from pressure to a dull pain, Calla released the energy, causing a faint glow in the indicator light.

Mr. Zagruder pointed to the device. "There, you see? You did it!"

Exhaling the breath she'd been holding, Calla smiled at him, but when she picked up the target and looked at the glow, her elation faded. "Why so dim? When you showed me, I could have read by the nova you produced from this miserable little sensor."

Mr. Zagruder chuckled as he looked at the cylinder. "Either you focused in the wrong place, or you didn't put much power into it."

"The effort gave me the start of a headache." She hoped she didn't sound petulant.

He put the target between them again and regarded her curiously. "Maybe your control is a little off. This skill isn't supposed to cause you pain, even with your limitations. Try again. I'll go into your head with you and watch from the inside this time."

Calla closed her eyes and opened her mind. His presence was a soft touch, as if he were resting his hand lightly on hers. Her memory dredged up recollections of the attack she'd faced a month ago, but she associated Mr. Zagruder's non-invasive contact with her rescuer, not her assailant. Mr. Zagruder, in many ways, reminded her of an older version of her boyfriend, Matt.

"If at some point you want me out, say the word, and I'll break the connection," he thought.

She nodded. *"I will."*

"Now show me what you were doing."

Calla stared at the target.

The communicator looped over her ear beeped for attention before she finished her preparations. She jumped, almost collapsing the folding chair she sat on.

"Go ahead and answer that." Mr. Zagruder withdrew from her mind.

Calla tapped the talk switch. "This is Calla."

"Hello, Dr. Geisman," Matt said.

She scowled. He only addressed her as "Dr. Geisman" when he called for something official, not unlike how Mom had called her "Calla Marie Geisman" only when she'd been in trouble.

"What do you have for me, Dispatch?" Calla matched his formal tone.

"Emergency in Medical Ward Seven. They need someone who can deal with psionic injuries."

While looking for her shoes, she frowned. *Don't shoot the messenger.* "Matthew, I haven't had a day off in two and a half weeks, and I'm in the middle of a lesson with Mr. Zagruder to make up for the class I had to skip out of the last time you paged me for an emergency. I'm not even on call today."

"I know. Believe me, I know. We haven't had a date in so long I'm half-afraid I'll forget what you look like." He heaved a sigh. "I'm sorry. I went through the whole list. You're the only one available."

If I'd gone for a different specialization, maybe I wouldn't get called out so much. Calla shook her head. "Ward Seven?"

"Yep."

She grabbed her shoes and slid them on. "I'm on my way."

"I owe you a big one, Callie," Matt said.

"Yes, you do. How does dinner sound?" Calla grabbed her purse and slid it over her shoulder.

"I won't get off work until late tonight. How 'bout tomorrow?"

"Fabulous. See you later, Matt." After turning off the communicator, she looked up at Mr. Zagruder. "I'm so sorry."

"Hey, at least you got a date out of it." He patted her shoulder. "We'll pick up the lesson again next time and try to move on to teleportation. Speaking of which, Ward Seven is on the far side of the station from here, isn't it?"

Calla put the target back in the case and handed it to him. "Yeah, couldn't be much farther from here and still be on this donut."

"I'll take you." He pocketed his target. "When you get a chance, get in touch with me again, and we'll arrange a new time."

"Thank you, and I really am sorry about this."

He rested a hand on her shoulder. "Duty calls."

With a bullhorn.

She took a deep breath. Her apartment distorted into a swirling mass of colors.

When her surroundings righted themselves again, Calla found herself in a waiting room. She barely had the presence of mind to notice the red-and-purple-checked carpet of Ward Seven before she doubled over and fought back the urge to retch. Breakfast had not been interesting enough that she wanted to see the pancakes again.

Someone, Mr. Zagruder she assumed, helped her to a chair and sat next to her with a supporting hand on her back.

"Tell me you get used to that," she mumbled.

If not, she could learn to live without ever finding out how to teleport.

"I don't know." He rubbed her upper back. "Never had that effect on me. My last student with Power Deficit Syndrome didn't have that problem either, but another one I know about only had problems as a passenger. As long as she controlled the teleport, she was fine."

"Great." She groaned and sat up. "At least that's an incentive to get that silly target to light up."

"Are you okay?" Mr. Zagruder asked.

No, but this is an emergency call. She nodded. "I'll be fine. I'd better get in there. I'll contact you when I know more about my schedule. Thanks for the lift."

"No problem. I'll see you soon."

As Calla turned away, Mr. Zagruder vanished. Keeping a hand near the wall to steady herself, Calla ran past the receptionist and wove her way back to the emergency room. The air was thick with the smell of antiseptics and lemon-scented cleaning products.

A flurry of activity near one of the beds drew her attention. She reached out to that area. The tension in the medical staff and the agony of the patients made her previous protests feel terribly petty. She had to help.

While covering the remaining distance to that part of the ward, Calla studied the mass of multicolored scrubs to identify who she'd be working with. One nurse wore the pale purple of intensive physical care, and the other wore the pale green of surgery. Neither of the nurses looked familiar, but from behind, she recognized the doctor, Nikk. No one else in the medical staff had platinum blond hair like that.

Although a few years older, he had graduated a year after she had. In addition to being a specialist in treating the victims of biochemical warfare, he also had considerable skill as a trauma doctor. He liked the color blue and—

Calla gritted her teeth and stopped the flow of trivia her mind dredged up. There were other, much more critical things to worry about.

She speed-walked over to the beds. There were two patients. The male had wavy red hair and a freckled face. Blood oozed through the hastily applied bandage on his leg. Dirt streaked his dark slacks and blue dress shirt. The smell evoked mental images of the arboretum on the upper level of the station.

The blond female dressed much more formally in a black pinstripe suit and ruffled blouse. Nikk had her shirt open and was inspecting what looked like bullet holes. People still used weapons like that?

Calla moved to where she could see Nikk's face without interrupting his efforts. "What are we looking at?"

Nikk aimed a portable scanner at one of the bullet holes. "Two patients, both in their twenties. Appeared in the waiting room unconscious. Female was shot twice in the chest with an old-style projectile gun. Both patients have psionic injuries, but I'm not sure how severe. Check the male first."

"I'm on it." Calla hurried to the male patient and perched on a stool next to a portable vat of pseudo-amoebic growth accelerator.

She reached into his mind. Visualizing his mind as a maze of glass panes, she took a moment to survey the mental landscape. Areas of blackened, broken panes stood out against the others near them.

For such a young man, he'd had a troubled life. Discounting the obvious damage, years' worth of panes bore witness to endless tribulation.

Childhood, usually marked with brilliantly colored support poles and almost cartoon-like images, looked oddly muted. An illness couldn't have caused the problem. The panes would have been thin and brittle if that were the case.

Calla had seen the dull, lifeless color scheme associated with feelings of isolation, often from absent parents or a perceived lack of security. The boy she mentored had a similar run in his maze between the time his mother had left and a month later when Calla had met him and taken him under her wing.

Adolescence showed a dramatic change to a blindingly bright scheme marking fear and hypersensitivity. More reds and oranges appeared, and the supports now bristled with spikes to keep people at a distance. Some of that could be normal, but Calla rarely saw such an intense anger.

That span lasted a short distance before the real tragedy reared up. In the space of a few weeks, the maze changed from garish to monotone. Images were blurred and warped, and the frames were twisted and frail. Some pictures were too grayed out to discern. Chemical dependence. Judging from the severe degradation, she supposed drugs rather than alcohol had been his poison of choice.

Then, some seven or eight years ago, there had been a gradual change. Colors returned, first the hot colors of anger and fear, and then in time the cooler colors of happier times until the images looked like photos in an album. The supports showed the change by becoming straighter and melding their colors and materials to provide a pleasing match to the images they held.

He'd righted his life again, and the depressing monochromatic drug addiction hadn't returned even once. An admirable achievement, given how many patients she'd seen who had never made the journey or had tried, only to lapse back into the old, destructive ways.

She completed her general overview in less than a minute, and then she returned to what damage there was.

Calla shifted her attention. A sense of pain and weakness from teleporting with injuries stood out in her perception. Her natural sympathetic reaction threatened to pull her down, but she kept her focus on the patient.

Two collections of the glass walls lay in sharp pieces, one in the monotone addict phase of his life and the other more recent. Scorched or cracked single frames and short runs were scattered about.

One of the cracked panes in his drab childhood broke apart and fell. A nearby one darkened and splintered moments later. The floor in this area looked uneven, marking damage to a deeper level of his mind.

Although the male patient's condition would slowly

decline, Calla could afford to leave him for now and come back later, provided she didn't wait too long. From the other bed, the pain and instability in the woman's mind demanded more immediate attention. Calla hated to leave her current patient, but the woman's physical and mental injuries might compound each other.

With a promise to return, Calla pulled away from the young man and spun one hundred eighty degrees to the other victim.

Shielding herself from the distraction the woman's injuries would cause, Calla formed a connection with the second patient's mind and summoned the glass maze. She whistled.

Obsidian shards and broken, mangled supports were strewn across a ragged, uneven floor. Deep crevices and wide sinkholes further disrupted what should have been a smooth, level plain for the rest of the structures. Of a maze that should've held hundreds, only a couple dozen panes remained standing, but they were so badly burnt, she couldn't even guess what part of the woman's life they belonged to.

Debris plugged the stairwell leading deeper into the patient's mind, so Calla went to one of the sinkholes. Changing her personal avatar from herself to a bird, she flew down through the hole and then shifted her form back. The pillars of this level were cracked and crumbling. Many had already fallen. Here, as above, the jagged floor spoke to more severe damage.

Calla winced. The lower level held the most basic life functions. Problems that far down were not always correctable. Matt wouldn't be the only one working late tonight.

"Talk to me." Nikk's strained voice aimed away from her. "Whatever you're finding in there, it doesn't sound good."

"Male is not stable, but the progress of his decline is slow enough that I can leave him for now." She paused and drew a breath. "The female has severe trauma. I'm still assessing the extent. I'll keep you apprised as I go."

Calla found the ladder to the third level of the woman's mind and descended into the veritable web of biological wiring. Nerve fibers crisscrossed the space. Electric impulses carried along the axons illuminated the area with their zipping lights. The section associated with pain flickered like a psychotic strobe.

Some parts of the visualized network remained dark, which wasn't unusual. Those suffering from critical wounds wouldn't be engaged in philosophical thought or many other activities.

Ferreting out the damaged sector took less time than getting there. Calla wove her way through the three-dimensional web. She came across shriveled dendrites and bruised cell bodies. For each, she stopped and imparted restorative power to heal the injuries. In the worst of the damage, several axon-images had been severed, and their dangling ends spewed sparks like high-voltage power lines. Matching the jagged ends and sealing them with psychic glue took seconds.

Back in the middle level, Calla confirmed her previous work successful by examining the now even floor. "Nikk, innermost level is healed. Starting on the midlevel now."

"Excellent. I'm working on the second bullet."

She nodded once. "Understood."

Calla's next task would be fixing the pillars that held up the outer level. With the deepest region repaired, some of the middle area had recovered spontaneously. A few columns needed a little tweaking. A bit of mental effort sealed over a handful of cracks.

Of the collapsed ones remaining, Calla started with

the center and spiraled outward. She mentally fitted the large disks atop each other, healed any surface damage, then went on to the next.

While assembling the pieces, she learned about deep-seated preferences. Brilliant purple swirls outlined a vivid image of a jazz band. A collage of romance novel covers decorated another section of a column. The things she enjoyed were contrasted with the dull, flat icons of things she hated: children, tomatoes, and insects. What sort of interesting story linked those together?

Calla set the last piece in place and then took a quick tour to make sure she hadn't missed anything. "That's two. Only the maze to go."

"Good. Keep at it," Nikk said.

With a nod, Calla rose up to the most superficial region. Shattered panes in expansive groups left few memories standing. Where to begin? She blew out a breath and picked the nearest set of burnt but steady panes.

No real fire had caused the wreckage, but the scorched appearance sent Calla back one month to the fire in her own apartment. Her brain conjured recollections of the burning smell and the intense heat. Smoke had all but choked her. If Matt hadn't come—

Calla shook her head. She would not allow the distraction of her own problems to interfere.

Starting at one end of a short run of standing panes, Calla rested her image's hand on the damaged glass. A soft white light radiated from her hand. When the light faded, the cracks had sealed and the glass had cleared to show the cartoon-like pictures of a child's party. She didn't have time to admire the happy kids running around before going on to the next one in the chain.

A baker's dozen later and she was out of standing panes in the short group. Next came the more time-consuming part of constructing the rest of the maze from pieces scattered about the floor. She knelt among the debris of random shards and sought two pieces to put together. No sooner had she selected a couple than the psychic equivalent of an earthquake hit.

The wail of a nearby heart monitor signaled arrest. Calla zoomed back out to see the overall maze again. Another group of damaged but still standing panes fell one after another like huge, ponderous dominoes.

Calla rushed to that area of the maze. After getting ahead of the cascade, she used every scrap of power she could to push back against the falling pane. The rate slowed enough to notice, but picking up a rhinoceros one-handed would be easier.

"Nikk, I've got a collapse going on in here, and I can't stop it alone." Calla kept her voice level. Panicking helped none of them.

"Do the best you can." He spoke fast and clipped some of his words. "When I get her heart and lungs going again, I'll help."

The tone of his voice had clearly indicated he would not be swayed. If the woman's mind collapsed, reviving her body would be useless. She would go into a coma and stay there. All the same, if he couldn't resuscitate the woman, putting her brain back together wouldn't do any good, either. She would still be dead.

In spite of Calla's best efforts, the collapse continued at a rate that would render their efforts unnecessary in a minute, maybe less. Not for the first time, Calla cursed the genetic quirk that limited her telepathic power levels.

At least her efforts bought Nikk a little time. That would have to do.

Seconds ticked by while Calla listened to him working through the protocols. When a second group of panes started a new domino effect, she grabbed the leg of the stool with a white-knuckled grip and grimaced as she tried to slow down each of the collapsing sets. The extra effort made her head hurt with the throb of her pulse. She needed support, and she needed it now.

"Nikk, I'm losing her," she said through clenched teeth.

The remaining parts of the woman's mind fell into a scrap heap of shattered glass images. Calla's visualization vanished as she found herself alone in her own mind again. When she relaxed, the headache subsided to a tolerable level.

Sighing, she let go of the stool's leg and opened her eyes. "Never mind. She's gone."

Nikk tore off his gloves and hurled them into the trash as he held back the curses written on his face.

Calla glanced at the patient and then looked at Nikk. "I'm sorry."

He shook his head and ran his fingers through his sweat-dampened hair. "Not your fault, Calla. I should have sent someone to help you, but I don't think that would have helped." He indicated the man lying behind her. "You've got another patient. I'll notify the family."

Calla nodded and turned back to the other bed. She had lost one, and sometimes that happened in this job, but she would have to find time to mourn the woman's death later. Someone else still needed her help.

She looked at the young man. What had happened to him and his friend? Why had she been so grievously wounded while he had few injuries? Her curiosity would have to wait. The slow collapse in progress would speed up if she didn't get to it soon. Better to deal with the deterioration while she could still manage alone.

After brushing the man's wavy hair away from his face, Calla laid a hand on the side of his head. With her eyes closed, she reached out with her thoughts.

Structures of a glass-walled maze appeared in her mind's eye.

Surveying the damage, she confirmed that the two areas lying in pieces hadn't changed. The slow collapse in the patient's dull childhood had grown some but not as much as she had expected. As she watched, one glass wall darkened and crumbled, and then the next one in the line sported a small, thin crack.

Calla exerted a stabilizing influence to stop the decline and then took the stairs down to the next level. After careful inspection, she concluded the floor was even, which translated to no inner level damage.

Once she had oriented herself to match the memory maze, Calla went in search of the underlying damage causing the problem in the level above. A little ahead of where she expected, she found the one pillar that had shifted.

The column hadn't fallen apart like Angela's had, but some of the symbol-etched disks had slipped out of alignment. Calla went to the pillar and eased the dislocated pieces back into place. A brilliant image appeared. Thomas McCrady would now enjoy chocolate cake again.

"Calla, talk to me," Nikk's voice sounded clear but distant while she worked.

"He has some mild midlevel damage. That's what's causing the decline." Calla spoke in a dull, monotone voice.

Nikk's hand landed on her shoulder. "Do you need me to help support the patient?"

She shook her head. "Not at this time. Unless something unexpected happens, I should be able to handle this one on my own."

"Good. I've seen to his physical injuries, so I'll leave you to it. His next of kin is in the waiting room. Send for me if you need me."

She nodded, and his footsteps retreated.

Taking a last look around the midlevel, Calla confirmed her work finished then returned to the more superficial area to ensure no further collapses were in progress.

Okay, now to get those broken segments back in order.

Calla chose one and assembled the pieces like an obsidian puzzle, then lifted it into place. Resting her image's hand on the pane, light emanating from her drove out the obscuring darkness. She went to the next one.

Only the growing stiffness in her back marked the passage of time. Calla surveyed the mental landscape and found it well-ordered with all structures intact.

That's got it. After taking a deep breath, she opened her eyes.

Sometime while she'd been busy, someone had covered the unconscious patient with a blanket. A plastic bag sitting on his chest contained a watch and a simple gold ring.

"All set, Dr. Geisman?"

Calla turned to the voice and smiled at the nurse, whose light blue scrubs marked her as psionic care. "All set. Where's his chart so I can enter my notes?"

The nurse handed her an electronic clipboard. "His fiancée is in the waiting room when you get a chance. She's listed as his next of kin."

Calla nodded and watched the nurse wheel the patient away.

Filling out the chart for Thomas McCrady went quickly. His physical injuries had amounted to one wound on his leg and quite a few scratches, bumps, and bruises, all of which would heal within a few days. Nikk had already entered the relevant data, so Calla only needed to enter her part, which took much less time than the actual treatment had.

On the way to the waiting room, Calla dropped off Thomas' chart at the nurse's station. The only person in the antechamber was a young Japanese lady sitting in an unyielding vinyl chair and looking at a magazine, too distracted to be reading it. The tension in her facial muscles and the rate of her breathing gave away the fear and worry. Her hands trembled as she flipped from one page to the next. At least Calla would be able to deliver good news.

Thoughts echoed in Thomas' head, making sleep difficult. He didn't feel like waking up yet, and shutting them out would take too much effort. The dull pain in his leg didn't help. He rolled over to distance himself from the intrusion and struck something cold and metallic.

He opened his eyes and gasped. The small room was about half the size of his bedroom and painted pale gray. A picture of the starfield from inside the arboretum dome graced the wall across from him. He lay on an elevated bed with metal rails.

A hand gently rested on his arm. "Hey, Thomas, it's okay. We're here."

Thomas sighed. "Meiko."

The gentle reassurances she sent his way washed over him, dispelling the initial shock of fear. Thomas relaxed and kissed his fiancée's hand. She looked more beautiful than ever. Her braided hair reached her knees, coming a centimeter or two short of the hem of her jade green dress. He could lose himself in the sparkle of light in her eyes.

After the disastrous mission he had been on, the sound of her voice, the feel of her touch, and the sense of her thoughts reassured him. How could things have gone so wrong? That trip should have been straightforward and easy as peace negotiations went.

A nearby toilet flushed and a door opened with a swish. Thomas craned his head back and caught August's eye. His pal had dirty blond hair and a diamond stud in his left ear. He had on blue jeans and a black T-shirt that read "And why would I WANT to know what you're thinking?"

August walked around to the opposite side of the bed. "Hey, hey, none of that mushy stuff. You two can do all that romantic crud later."

"You're just jealous." Thomas slugged August's arm. "Thanks for coming."

"That's what best friends are for. So, what happened to you out there?" August leaned on the bed rail. "All the doctor could tell Meiko was that you and your partner appeared and got well-acquainted with the carpet."

"Didn't you say this one was a cakewalk?" Meiko clasped Thomas' hand tighter.

Thomas sat up. "That's how it was supposed to work."

"Hold on, now." August held up one hand. "Is this one of those stories that I'll need popcorn for?"

Thomas chuckled. "Yeah, and get me a box of rock candy while you're out there."

August patted the pockets of his jeans. "Ah, man. Forgot my wallet. Anyway, this walk-in-the-park mission wasn't?"

Thomas shook his head. "No, but it should've been. According to the mission briefing, we were supposed to be able to teleport in, make the already agreed-upon treaty official, then 'port out. In a perfect universe, it would've been a day's trip at most."

Meiko leaned her elbow on the rail and her chin on her palm. "So what happened?"

"Nothing went right." Thomas blew out a breath and ran his fingers through his hair. "We got to the rendezvous site to find no one. That happens sometimes, so not a big deal."

August shrugged. "Yeah, I mean, someone has to get there first if you didn't synchronize your watches or something."

Thomas nodded. "Right. So, ten minutes later, a messenger showed up to tell us the delegates had been delayed a half-hour. We decided to wait. Two hours later, one representative arrived."

Meiko's eyes widened. "Two hours?"

"Umhm. The other one put in an appearance an hour after that."

August snorted and waved his hand dismissively. "Me? I'd've left."

"I wanted to, but Angela wouldn't have it, and she was in charge." Thomas paused to gather his thoughts. "Anyway, when we finally went to the place the neutral third party had offered us, they informed us they'd had a change of heart and told us to go somewhere else."

August rolled his eyes. "Oh, nice. So, where did you go?"

"To the garden in dispute," Thomas said.

"You're kidding." Meiko leaned away from him. "Didn't that make the delegates a little irritable?"

"To put it mildly. I suggested a restaurant or somewhere really neutral."

August rested against the bed rail. "So, you got to the park, and..."

"First one party, then the other wanted to change one point, and one thing led to another, and before we knew it, Angela had to arbitrate the whole thing from scratch again."

Meiko rolled her eyes. "So, when did the fight break out?"

"Much later. Hang on, I'll get there." Thomas patted Meiko's hand. "So, things were going along okay until about midweek. Some idiot violated the cease-fire. They caught the guy, and he said it was an accident."

August squinted and looked away for a moment.

"How do you 'accidentally' violate a cease-fire?"

Thomas shrugged. "I don't know, but that's what he said. Anyway, we had all we could do to prevent another all-out war. Angela stayed behind with the delegates to keep hammering away on the new treaty while I went to address the leaders of both governments."

"Lucky you." August snorted.

"Yeah. I still hate crowds." Thomas' guts turned crosswise thinking about those meetings.

Meiko gripped his hand. He'd already told her his whole sordid history. When their relationship had become serious, he'd told her how his fear of crowds had led to a doctor prescribing Minum to block the mental noise of so many voices he couldn't silence on his own.

The aid had turned into a crutch and from there had become a full-blown addiction. He hadn't been able to break the habit until a dealer had psionically and physically beaten him half to death after Thomas had stolen a small vial of pills.

Stephanie, a negotiator who'd volunteered in a soup kitchen on Level Nine, had rescued him and taken him in. She'd helped him through rehab, and he'd become her apprentice. She'd turned into the replacement for the family that had disowned him. A year ago, old age had caught up to her, and Thomas still missed her.

"Yeah, well, did you ever get the treaty figured out?" August asked.

"What?" Thomas shook his head to clear his mind of the encroaching grief. "Oh, yeah, yeah. By the time I got back from calming down both governments, Angela had worked out the situation to a point that all parties could tolerate."

"So, what happened?" Meiko looked down at Thomas' leg. "How'd you get hurt?"

His hands shook. "Well, today was the last day. All

we had left to do was sign the treaty and make everything nice and legal, then go home. When we got to the park, there were crowds gathered. Most weren't ecstatic about some of the concessions that had been made, but they went along with it. Then I noticed the power surge of someone teleporting in and next thing I knew, shots were flying, and some psycho-woman attacked me telepathically."

August crossed his arms on the bed rail. "You remembered what I showed you about defending yourself, right?"

Thomas nodded. "Yeah, and it worked."

"Good. What'd you use for your avatar?" August asked.

"A wolf."

August smiled and nodded once. "Excellent choice. Nice and maneuverable, reasonably strong, and not too hard to maintain."

"Who was it?" Meiko asked.

"I don't know." Thomas shrugged. "She used a shadowy humanoid form armed with flaming knives."

"Huh. Must be a former student of Joseph's. He uses a similar avatar," August said.

Thomas looked up at the clock on the wall. "Aren't you supposed to be helping him teach a class right now?"

August checked his watch. "Not on Saturday."

"Oh, yeah."

Meiko smiled and ruffled his hair. "Lost track of Haidar time?"

Thomas swatted her hand away. "Cordil has a thirty-two-hour rotation. That makes for some long days."

August smacked Thomas' arm. "Well, I'm glad you made it back. Else I'd have to find a new target to pick on. Like Meiko, maybe."

She squinted and leaned closer. "I retaliate."

August recoiled and trembled. "Ooo. Is that supposed to scare me?"

"Just a friendly warning."

Thomas chuckled. "Hey, have either of you heard anything about Angela?"

August glanced away and sighed. "She, um, she didn't make it. She was too far gone. I couldn't get the straight answer from anyone, but from the stray thoughts I've been picking up, her heart stopped and after that her brain fell apart."

Looking at the wall behind them, Thomas shook his head. They hadn't agreed on much of anything for this trip, but most of the time they got along well. Her choices had paid off, as a general rule. Would she still be alive if she had listened to his warnings about the sudden arrival of more telepaths? Had he done enough to save her? Could he have protected her better? Been a little more persistent about leaving when his instincts had warned him?

"Y'know, if you wanted to scare us, you could have teleported in behind us and yelled 'Boo!' That would've been enough." August gestured to their surroundings with a sweep of his hand. "This was not necessary."

Thomas smiled and looked up at his friends, grateful that they were around to keep him from dwelling too much on his failure. "You needed more excitement in your life."

"Are you all right?" Meiko combed her fingers through his hair.

He gripped her hand. "Better than I was earlier. I'm a little stiff is all."

August shook the bed. "What? Hospital beds aren't as comfy as you like?"

"Hey, the way that mission worked out, I'm glad to be just a little stiff."

Meiko leaned over him and hugged him as much as she could with the rails in the way. Thomas embraced her, reveling in the smell of her cherry blossom perfume and in the compassion he sensed in her.

August groaned. "You're doing it again. I told you, no mushy stuff."

There was a light knock at the door. Thomas scowled and let Meiko go. "Yes?"

A short, chubby man walked in wearing a lab coat and carrying an electronic clipboard. "Hi. I'm Dr. Andy Hale. I need to check you out. If all goes well, you can go home."

Thomas yawned. How could he be tired after sleeping for so long? "That would be great."

"We'll wait for you out here." Meiko indicated the door with a nod.

The doctor read through the notes on the electronic clipboard, nodding from time to time. "How are you feeling?"

Thomas propped himself up on his elbows. "I'm okay."

"No headache? No ringing in the ears? No dizziness?"

Thomas shook his head.

"Good." Dr. Hale set the clipboard on the small table by the bed. "I need to look in your head for a moment to make sure everything is where it should be. Is that all right?"

"Okay." His pulse accelerated.

Recollections of some of the more embarrassing things he had done lurked in his mind, but he could tolerate doctors if he needed to. Laws required them to keep whatever memories they saw confidential.

Dr. Hale squinted, and Thomas felt a pressure in his mind. The contact didn't hurt but carried more force than he had anticipated. The doctor's presence remained for a few seconds, and Thomas found himself alone again.

"Everything looks good to me." Dr. Hale picked up the clipboard. "I'm going to give you a prescription for a regenerative salve to use on that hole in your leg. Apply it twice daily when you change the bandage. It should heal fine in a couple days. Other than that, you can go home, but if you get dizzy or if you get a headache in the next forty-eight hours, I want you to come back."

Thomas nodded. "I'll do that."

The doctor left. Thomas found a change of clothes on a chair.

Once he had showered and dressed, he left the little room and joined his friends. "Have I told you guys how much I hate hospitals?"

Meiko slipped her hand into his. "Um, yep. Last time you were here."

August looked both ways down the hall then leaned closer. "Y'know, this is getting to be a habit with you."

Thomas pointed to his chest. "Me? Last time that wasn't my fault. You're the one who dropped that box on my head."

August shook his head. "You said you had it."

"No, I said, 'Wait, I don't have it.' Don't. D-O-N-apostrophe-T. Don't."

August drew a breath to continue the argument.

Meiko interrupted. "How about we blow this joint and get some dinner, or is it too early for that?"

August shrugged. "I'm hungry enough."

"When are you not hungry?" She rolled her eyes.

Thomas looked first at August then at Meiko. "Dinner? What happened to lunch?"

"You slept through it," August said.

Meiko shook her head. "Actually, I think the doctor

was still fixing your brain. It took a while."

Walking hand-in-hand with Meiko, Thomas let August lead the way. After a quick argument about who wanted to eat what, they stopped in a restaurant that served dishes from a variety of cuisines. With the number of times they ate there, they should get an automatic discount.

When August opened the door, the spicy odor of sausages and tomatoes wafted out. Thomas' mouth watered thinking about the wiener schnitzel he usually ordered. He ushered Meiko in ahead of him.

A half-dozen tables were scattered around the little place. Each had a green polyester tablecloth and bundles of silverware wrapped in white paper napkins. The chairs were simple plastic molded to look like dark wood, and light fixtures shaped like fake candles flickered in sconces around the walls.

Except for one other lady, they had the place to themselves. They found a table, and Thomas pushed in Meiko's seat as she sat down.

"Hey, that's Dr. Geisman!" Meiko pointed to the lady across the room. "She's the doctor who healed you this morning."

"No way." August twisted around.

"Yeah, really, it is, unless she has a twin sister."

"Then it wasn't Dr. Hale?" Thomas studied the dark-haired woman.

"Not until you left ER," she said.

August shuddered. "Can you believe the Magistrates let Syndromers be psych doctors?"

"She's a Syndromer?" Thomas' skin crawled.

August nodded. "You betcha. Look at her eyes. If there's any hint of glitter there, I'll eat this tablecloth, and it's not like the lights are all that bright in here."

Thomas looked again and noted the obvious telltale

of the genetic anomaly. "Oh, yeah. I guess she is."

"Syndromers should be shot out the airlock." August aimed his thumb back over his shoulder.

Meiko scowled. "August! That isn't very nice!"

He sat back in his chair and turned both hands palm-up at the ceiling. "What? They're never as good as a normal person. All they do is suck up resources."

Meiko's eyes narrowed and her jaw clenched.

Okay, guys, ease off. This supposed to be dinner, not the Haidarian Independence War. "Oh, I dunno if spacing them is the right answer, but they shouldn't be allowed into some occupations."

"Okay, if not out the airlock, then they should be sterilized." August scooted forward in his chair. "Every time they reproduce, they weaken the gene pool."

Meiko glared at them both. "You guys are so mean! I can't believe you'd say something like that."

She and August kept going at it, but he tuned them out. An argument with her now would mean a cold shoulder later. For himself, Thomas couldn't be sure which of the two were right. Intellectually, he knew he shouldn't blame a whole class of people for the actions of one. Emotionally, however, he remembered that the drug dealer who'd pounded on him so many years ago had been a Syndromer.

Had this Syndromer doctor treated Angela, too? Could Angela's death be related to that treatment? Nothing could bring Angela back, but if her death had been unnecessary, maybe he should report the problem to the Magistrates to keep Syndromers from practicing medicine and killing patients with their lack of power.

Thomas turned to Meiko and tapped her arm. "Did that doctor treat Angela, too?"

"—no reason to—What?" Meiko turned her hard stare on him.

"That woman who treated me. Did she take care of Angela?" he asked.

Meiko's eyes narrowed. "Um, I dunno. Maybe. Why?"

He pushed away from the table. "I'll be right back."

Meiko caught his arm as he stood. "No, Thomas, she's trying to eat her dinner."

"I have to know." Thomas pulled away from her.

"Why? What difference does it make?"

"Angela may not have been the best partner I've ever had, but she was my partner. I owe it to her to find out if she died because of an incompetent doctor. I'll be right back." He started for the other side of the room.

"Next time I'll keep my big mouth shut," Meiko mumbled.

"Be careful, man." August waved Thomas closer. "Wouldn't want you to catch the Syndrome from her."

A little over the top, maybe? Thomas backed away. "Bad genes aren't contagious."

Calla swallowed the last bit of her manicotti, reached for her water glass, and tried to think about anything but the conversation two tables away. She hadn't meant to eavesdrop, but the volume of the discussion between Thomas McCrady's friends had allowed her to hear every word about what they wanted to do to "Syndromers" like her. Any one of them could be carrying the Power Deficit Syndrome genes, but that probably didn't occur to them.

Thomas started toward her table. He limped, favoring his injured leg but would've looked much more comfortable in jeans and a polo shirt if he didn't radiate tension like a potent stench.

So, you really think I had a hand in your partner's death, do you? Her jaw clenched as she pushed back from the table.

Angela had appeared with two bullet holes in the middle of her chest. How could McCrady and the others find her death a surprise, and how could anyone except the shooters be at fault?

Logic rarely had a place in this sort of confrontation, though. Irate family and friends of people who died during medical procedures were to be expected in her profession, but they annoyed her slightly less than patients who refused to cooperate. Maybe the intrusion wouldn't be so bad. The diplomatic corps had trained Thomas after all, and hopefully he would remember that part of his education.

"May I have a word with you?" he asked.

What would he do if she said "no?" Would he respect her wishes and leave? She didn't get to find out. He sat across from her without waiting for her invitation.

She shoved her aggravation into temporary confinement. "I'm glad to see you up and around so soon, Mr. McCrady. How are you?"

"Fine, thanks." He sat straight and folded his hands on the table in front of him. "What happened to Angela?"

Calla crossed her arms over her chest, much happier than she had ever been before about the privacy laws. "Without the permission of her family, there's not much I can say."

"Anything, please. She was my partner."

Calla sighed. "She died of her injuries after two doctors and two nurses did everything they could do."

He leaned forward. "You were one of the doctors, weren't you?" His eyes narrowed, intensifying the glitter of his powers. "Before you went mucking around in my head, you were working on her. She died because you couldn't take care of her."

She pointed her index finger at him. "Look, Mr. McCrady, you have no grounds on which to base such an accusation. Physical and psionic injuries took a toll on Ms. Caseman, so instead of being mad at me for trying to help her, save it for the guy who hurt her in the first place. Dr. Petrov and I and the two nurses assisting us did everything we could. I'm very sorry about your friend."

Next, he would start hurling names at her: freak, Syndromer, space waste. She had heard them all, and she had no intention of waiting around to hear them again. Dropping enough money on the table to cover dinner and a fair tip, she stood up and grabbed her purse.

"Best wishes on your speedy recovery, Mr. McCrady." She walked away.

"How do things like you get psych doctor licenses?" August asked.

How do such irritating bigots like you survive? She turned halfway toward him but stopped.

Even if she bothered answering him, she wouldn't fix anything. Such narrow-minded people weren't likely to change, and reshaping society at large didn't fit into her schedule today.

A few steps out the door, she stopped and turned to go back in. Was she overreacting? Should she go back and apologize for snapping at Thomas? Grief for a friend's death could make anyone say stupid things. Maybe he hadn't realized the impact of his words.

No, he and his buddies had made their opinions clear. Walking back through that door now would open her up to more harassment, and she hadn't gotten around to hand-to-hand combat training if they decided taunts weren't enough.

Calla checked her watch. If she went to the gym now, she would be early for her catch-up lesson with Mr. Zagruder, but that would work fine. A few minutes to deal with her anger and frustration before he arrived would do her some good.

Thomas' alarm clock beeped. He groaned and smacked the snooze button. Instead of the days off he needed, he had to report to work for a meeting. Maybe the meeting would be nothing more exciting than a debriefing. Although physically and psionically healed, emotionally he could not handle another trip so soon. The last one had been too taxing, and he wanted at least a day or two before he headed out again. An assignment here at home wouldn't bother him one bit. When he had kissed Meiko goodnight a few hours ago, she had hinted about feeling neglected lately. For both their sakes, he needed the time off.

The alarm rang the second time. Thomas rolled over and sat up. If he didn't roust his sleepy butt out of bed now, he might not get to Joy's office in time.

"All right, all right, I'm up. Sort of." He turned off the alarm and flipped the switch for the lights.

If he ever found out who was responsible for setting morning so early in the day, he would have to give that person professional-quality noogies. Seven o'clock didn't count as a civilized hour.

Aside from a pile of clothes in the corner, his room looked no different than it had the day he'd left for Cordil IV. The dark brown and red quilt Meiko had made covered his bed, which was flanked by a fake wood dresser on one side and a nightstand on the other.

After a quick shower, he dressed in a white shirt and navy blue slacks and decided to forgo a tie, as if he'd ever wear one by choice. He looked at his watch as he slipped it on. Breakfast would have to be last night's two A.M. nachos. Anything more interesting would make him late.

Thomas called up a mental image of his cubicle and teleported. At such a short distance, the queasiness didn't hardly register. Gray half-height cubicle walls enclosed him on three-and-a-half sides. A desk surface attached to the left wall held his computer, file box, and a few knickknacks from his successful trips. A picture of him and Meiko in the arboretum graced the wall next to his computer. After a quick look at his space, he headed down the corridor among the cubicles to Joy's office at the end of the row.

Thomas entered his boss's office. Her desk, real wood imported from Earth, looked heavy and indestructible. The chairs were the more common faux wood with fuzzy cloth seats and armrests. Shelves around three sides were crammed with an assortment of souvenirs brought back by various arbitrators over the years. The Verulian Ivy had grown. Using the frame of her diploma for a support, one green limb had stretched almost a meter closer to the door in the last week. Judging from the sturdy odor of honey emanating from the plant, the growth spurt had started days ago. If she didn't get a caterpillar or two in here to get that thing under control, it'd take over the whole station.

Joy looked up at him and smiled. She wore her usual gray suit with a pink shirt. Her black hair hung in spray-stiffened curls.

"Thomas, welcome back." She gestured to one of the chairs. "I'd ask how the Cordil trip went, but I heard."

How could she be so nonchalant about this? A woman, one of their coworkers, had died out there.

"It ended up being a tough assignment." He planted himself in one of the chairs. "We could have used more warning about the other factions."

Joy shook her head. "I'm sorry about that, but we were assured that all other groups were too small to pose a threat. Include all your observations in your report, please. The war is back on, but Cordil IV may call us again when they're ready."

He nodded and stared at the dark gray rug. "I'll take care of it."

"I'll need the report before you leave."

Thomas sighed. *Which will be a week from Tuesday, I hope?* "When will that be?"

She sorted through a set of disks on her desk. "This afternoon."

He cocked an eyebrow and stared at her. "This afternoon? You can't be serious. I could really use a couple days, Joy."

"The emergency room doctor who put your head together again recommended a short leave of absence, but the doctor who released you marked you fit for work."

He scrambled for some sort of response. How could he get back out there so soon? When he closed his eyes he could still see the Cordil fight in his head and hear the cries. He remembered Angela lying on the ground, bleeding freely from her wounds.

Joy came around the desk and perched on the edge. "I realize this is a fast turn-around for you, Thomas. Unfortunately, you have experience related to the assignment, and the situation is too urgent to delay. I'm sorry, but you're going. This one comes from higher up."

He scowled. "How far up?"

"The Magistrates. Rumor has it they checked a few records, talked to a couple instructors and put this whole thing together. They didn't even ask if I had an opinion about it. Everything has already been arranged. You'll be the lead on this one."

Thomas shook his head. Would his assistant be able to take over more than the usual number of responsibilities? Could his destination be an easy trip for a change?

He ran his fingers through his hair. "Where am I going?"

"When your partner gets here, I'll fill you both in." She moved back around to her desk chair.

"Okay, so who's my partner?"

Telepathy in use nearby buzzed faintly in his mind. Moments later, a knock at the door frame drew his attention.

Joy looked past him. "Come in, Doctor. You're right on time."

Thomas twisted around and frowned. His partner was Calla Geisman? Oh, how perfect was this addition to the disaster?

He glared hard at Joy. "You're joking, right?"

"Apparently not." Calla crossed her arms over her chest and rested against the doorframe. "When I walked into work this morning, my caseload for the next week was being shuffled off onto other doctors or rescheduled. I was told to report here."

Joy gestured to the empty chair. "Please have a seat, Dr. Geisman."

Thomas glanced at Calla and then turned to Joy. "She has weak powers, and she's not a negotiator." He winced. *That was crass.*

Calla nodded before he could apologize.

"True enough all around." She settled into the chair next to his. "I know very little about this sort of diplomacy."

"Don't sell yourself so short." Joy beamed a smile that would disarm most normal people. "You deal with uncooperative patients and family members on a daily basis. That takes more diplomatic charm than you may be aware of."

"That's not the same thing." Calla's tone approached absolute zero. "Wars don't start if I fail."

Joy shook her head. "That doesn't matter. Thomas will handle that part."

Thomas indicated Calla with a nod of his head. "Then what's her function on this trip?"

"We need a physician there with you to help you make sense of what we think may be happening."

Calla blew out a breath. "Depending on the circumstances, that could be understandable and prudent, but there are doctors who have training in conducting negotiations and full command of very strong powers. Any one of them would support Mr. McCrady better than I ever could."

"You don't look old enough to be a doctor," Joy said.

Calla swiped that idea away with a quick motion of her hand. "What difference does that make?"

Thomas shook his head and leaned forward. Clearly Joy wouldn't or couldn't change the team's composition. "Never mind that for now. Can you tell us what corner of the galaxy you're sending us to and why?"

Joy picked up a piece of paper. "Two races, who have been at war on and off for most of the last century, have requested our help with a treaty to end the fighting, for good this time we hope. Both sides claim the other is in violation of the GATBAC Warfare treaty."

She'd avoided the whole "where" question.

"GATBAC?" Calla shifted in her seat and crossed her legs. "I'm not familiar with the acronym."

What, don't you ever watch the news? Negotiating that treaty was a royal mess about three years ago. Still in medical school with your nose in a book? "Galactic Agreement for the Termination of Biological and

Chemical Warfare."

Calla looked off into the corner of the room for a moment. "Dr. Nikolai Petrov has infectious disease specialization. He worked in a clinic in an area where the inhabitants had been hit hard with biochemical weapons. Even better, he recently graduated, too. He's older than I am, but he doesn't show his age. With his specialization, he's much more qualified. My primary field is psionic medicine."

Joy shook her head. "That doesn't matter."

"I see." Calla regarded Joy with a glacial stare.

"Because of the cultures involved, we need a female on the team. That's you."

"Where are we going?" Thomas enunciated each syllable.

"Ologo." Joy handed him the paper.

Thomas frowned. He had been to that system as an assistant to his mentor during the last part of his internship. That trip had been a treaty negotiation, too, attempting to stop a war caused by some question about a boundary line's location. One side had claimed a tract of land about half the size of one level of the Haidar Station as ancestral holdings, and the other had claimed it on religious grounds.

That sounded easy, but all the posturing and bad blood had caused the negotiations to drag with constant interruptions for such childish things as name-calling. What was the problem this time?

He scanned the paper. Words like plague and betrayal jumped out at him. "If you're sending us to Ologo, this will never work."

Joy held up her right hand to pause him. "Now, Thomas—"

He scooted forward in his chair and leaned on the edge of her desk. "The Gotrians place too much stock in an age-wisdom correlation. Dr. Geisman and I are both too young to be taken seriously by their delegation, and the Olvians are so strictly matriarchal that they'll try to bypass me and deal with Dr. Geisman, who admits that she has no idea how to handle this situation."

"Oh, I agree with you completely." Joy sat back and pointed at Calla. "Calla would still be going because the Magistrates are concerned that if someone out there is in violation of GATBAC, they'll go even further underground if they suspect that we've sent a scientist or a physician. That's why they want someone who looks too young to be either."

"That's ridiculous." Calla rolled her eyes. "I can think of several other ways to camouflage a doctor's credentials."

Thomas nodded.

Joy continued. "The lead negotiator should be an older woman so both sides will work with her. I'm not being given a free hand in choosing the people for this. The Magistrates arranged it all for us with the help of Joseph Pearce."

"The psionic self-defense instructor?" Thomas asked.

He hadn't met the man, but August frequently spoke of his boss.

Calla squinted and sat up straighter. "What's Pearce doing making assignments in the diplomatic corps? His only other training is as a paramedic, and he hasn't used that for years."

"The way I understand it, he was there when the call came in and made some recommendations." Joy frowned and pointed at the paper in Thomas' hand. "Look, I'm not keen on this either, and I was given as much say as you two. You're going."

"Wonderful." Thomas scratched over his ear. "Would you excuse us, Doctor?"

She nodded and stepped out into the hall.

He closed the door and turned his attention back to Joy. "I'm not ready for this."

She sighed. "I know this isn't an ideal first lead for you, but you'll do fine. You're very talented, and you were trained by one of the best we've ever had. Trust your partner and your abilities. You need to be there at one o'clock our time." Joy handed him a disk. "On that disk is a summary of the mission details and an image of the rendezvous site so you can teleport to it. A Terran company with offices on Ologo has agreed to provide a neutral meeting place. A Pharmacorp representative should be there to meet you. I'll see you when you get back."

When Joy turned away from him and started typing on her computer, Thomas took that as the cue to leave and met Calla outside the door. Since he had no choice but to work with the freak, he wanted her to have some sort of a clue about Ologo's history. Personal feelings aside, he would not leave her in the dark. The less she pestered him with inane questions, the better.

He walked down the hall toward his office and gestured for her to follow. "Come with me."

Thomas took her to his cubicle and sat down in his chair. Calla leaned on the half-height wall, which slid under her weight. Wide-eyed, she shifted to regain her balance. In spite of his mood, he chuckled, remembering all the times he had done the same thing.

"Please tell me you know something about Ologo." He started digging through computer files for the record of his last mission to that world.

She moved the cubicle wall back to its original position. "I can treat illnesses and injuries for both races and even do surgery if I need to, but culturally? I know the Gotrians fast from midnight to noon as part of a religious rite, and that can play unholy havoc with some medical tests. Senility and other age-related disabilities are practically unheard of. Olvians are matriarchal and color-change with their emotions. They're sexually dimorphic to an extreme and have a peculiar life cycle involving a gender change at adolescence. That is my entire cultural knowledge of the planet."

He sighed. *That's not going to be half enough.* "Well, I'm sending you the account of my last trip there. Read that, and then see what else you can dig up on those races."

"I'll do what I can. I'll also check with Nikk about biochemical phenomena."

Thomas turned to face her. Recalling his last misadventure, he sought a diplomatic way to pose his next question. "I don't know how to ask this politely, so I'm just going to go for it."

She nodded. "I'm properly forewarned."

"How are you set for self-defense?" Thomas asked.

"Physically, I've watched Dillon, the kid I mentor, prepare for his tests." She looked past him for a moment. "That's as close as I've gotten."

"And psionically?" *Dumb question. With your power level, I doubt you could manage anything with training.*

She shook her head. Fear spiked in her thoughts, reminiscent of the twinge he felt when his memories churned up the day Stephanie had saved his life. Much like he so often did, Calla buried the reminder in a hurry. What had happened to her?

"Are you anticipating trouble?" she asked.

He leaned back in his chair and laced his fingers behind his head. "No, but then I wasn't expecting anything to blow up in my face on Cordil IV, either."

"Good point." She patted her pockets and frowned. "I do have an anti-psionic generator. I'll put it in my trauma kit."

"That could be handy. You might want to keep that easily accessible."

She nodded.

He rummaged through his desk and pulled out a well-worn journal with a fake leather cover. "Bring a notebook and a couple pens, too."

She glanced at his journal. "What for?"

That should be obvious, Doc. "Notetaking. A lot of things come up during these meetings."

She shook her head. "I don't need a notebook for that."

He glared at her. *Stop fighting me on the little stuff.* "It's standard procedure. If something happens to one of us, the other can pick up all the pieces and keep going if we keep good notes. That'll be particularly true since I don't have half your medical training and you're not a negotiator."

Calla shrugged and sighed. "Fine. Any particular parameters?"

"It doesn't have to be a fancy journal, but something more official-looking than some stapled together papers." He plugged the mission disk into his computer. "Where are you going to be at one o'clock?"

"My office is in Medical Ward Eight. I'll make a point to be there by one."

"No, we should be a little early. I'll be at your office at twelve-thirty."

"I'll be there, Mr. McCrady." She turned to leave.

He reached for her. "Look. We're going to be working together for a while, and every time someone calls me 'Mr. McCrady,' I keep thinking my dad's around. Call me Thomas."

"I'm Calla."

He nodded. "See ya in a bit."

Thomas watched her go and then returned to the computer. Why had the Magistrates engineered this mission to fail? If he wanted to succeed anyway, he would have to find a way to work with Calla for the duration of the trip, Syndromer or not.

Calla leaned over to kiss the top of Dillon's head before she pulled away from the kid she mentored. Tears marred his cheeks and left his eyes ringed in red. His brown hair hung in his face, and he looked so much younger than his ten years. Seeing him so distraught hurt like an open wound, but she couldn't take his pain or her own away with a simple procedure.

He flopped onto one of her folding chairs. "I don't want you to go."

She handed him the box of tissues. "I know, sweetie, and I really wish I didn't have to. The Magistrates didn't say, 'Calla, would you like to go?' They said, 'Pack your stuff. You're going.'"

He sniffled and wiped his nose with a tissue. "You're coming back, right?"

She sat in the chair next to him. "Of course, silly."

The question wasn't silly in his eyes. Not three years ago, his own mother had left on a business trip and then sent back word she wouldn't be returning. She hadn't bothered to mention why, and speculations ran the gamut from she had a new boyfriend to she didn't like being one of the few non-telepaths on the station. Her kid and her husband were not enough reason to come back, apparently. Calla's mind flew back through the various conversations they'd had about his mother's sudden departure. She stopped the information flood and refocused on Dillon.

She had taken him under wing after he'd shown up in her office as another victim of Joseph Pearce's overzealous self-defense classes. Dillon now studied under a much more humane teacher.

Dillon wiped his eyes. "You'll really come back?"

She nodded and rubbed his back. "I came back from the medical conference, didn't I?"

"Yeah."

She tipped his chin up. "I'll be back."

He shrugged away from her. "When?"

"They tell me this shouldn't last a week. You'll hardly know I've been gone."

He crumbled up the tissue and threw it at the trashcan, missing by more than a meter. "I know now."

Calla kissed his forehead. "Come on, sweetie. I have to go. Let's get you home."

"Can I go, too?" Dillon asked.

She grabbed her bag and ushered him out. *Oh, yes, take a ten-year-old into a war zone in which there might be biological or chemical warfare. Great idea.* "Not on this one."

He wiped his nose on his sleeve. "How come?"

"You'd be bored out of your wits." Calla wrapped her arm around his shoulder. "No kids to talk to. No games to play. No pools to swim in. All you would get to do is sit in a bunch of boring meetings with me all day long."

"Oh."

She ruffled his hair. "Besides, I need you here. Someone needs to water that nifty flower you gave me. I hoped you could do that. Can you?"

He smiled. "Well, yeah. Sure."

After she dropped him off at his apartment, Calla breathed a sigh of relief. She'd been afraid he would ask her about her destination. If he didn't already know about Ologo, he would've looked up the planet and read all about the war and diseases there. He'd worry even more.

"Dr. Geisman?"

The woman's voice sounded familiar, and Calla's brain whizzed through its catalog of female acquaintances. It landed on Meiko Sakamura by the time Calla turned and found Thomas McCrady's fiancée coming toward her. The lady was almost shoulder height to Calla. Black hair hung nearly to her knees in a tight braid over one shoulder. Her eyes glowed brightly even in the well-lit corridor. The taut muscles in her face would result in a tension headache later.

The fracas with Thomas over dinner last night replayed in Calla's head at high speed. Ms. Sakamura had tried to ward off August, but she'd had more time to think over her friend's position. Maybe she'd changed her mind about what to do with people who had PDS.

At least Calla had a valid excuse for cutting this discussion short. Thomas would be coming to her office in forty-five minutes or fewer, and too many things were left on Calla's to do list.

She waited for Ms. Sakamura to catch up.

"I wanted to apologize for August and Thomas." Meiko studied her shoes while she spoke. "Sometimes they're cute when they're stupid. Sometimes they're just stupid."

Calla smiled. "Thank you, Ms. Sakamura."

"Just Meiko."

"Thank you, Meiko. I hope you didn't catch too much trouble for arguing against your friends."

Meiko sheepishly looked up at Calla's face. "Thomas didn't bring it up again, and August thinks I'm naïve."

"Well, I appreciate your efforts." Calla took a step

back. "If you'll excuse me, I have a million things to do to prepare for a trip."

As she turned away, Meiko caught her arm. "Doctor, wait. Can I talk to you for a minute? I need your help."

"I have no time for an appointment now." Calla paused and turned toward Meiko. "If you'll check with the receptionist, she can set you up with someone else or arrange an appointment for after I've returned."

"Please, it won't take a minute, and it's something I'm not sure anyone else can help me with." Meiko's lower lip quivered, and her eyes threatened to flood with tears. "Can I walk with you?"

The young woman clenched her jaw and looked away. Calla sighed. She was a sucker for people in distress.

"I'm off to Medical Ward Eight." She indicated that direction with a nod. "If you're headed that way, I don't see why we shouldn't keep each other company."

As they walked, Calla tried to sort out the jumbled emotions she sensed in Meiko's head.

After several steps, Calla slowed her pace. "I have a feeling this has to do with last night's confrontation with your friends."

"Partly." Meiko sniffled and withdrew an embroidered handkerchief from her purse. "Is there any way to know for sure if I have the Power Deficit Syndrome gene?"

Calla frowned and held up her hand to stop the discussion. "I'm not a geneticist. All I can do is speculate based on general information. A specialist could tell you more."

"I know. You said you were a psionic specialist, but you know what PDS is like."

Calla blew out a sigh. "Okay, well, I'll try to address your question, but for a definite answer, you're going to have to talk to someone who has more training in this area. In fact, there might be a test to find out for certain. For now, does anyone in your family have PDS?"

"My dad."

"Well, that makes this easier. You have one PDS gene." Calla looked down at Meiko. "It's a recessive trait, so your dad couldn't have given you anything else, in theory."

An intense wave of Meiko's despair brought a tear to Calla's eye before she could slam her defenses closed against the intrusion. What was the big deal? Power Deficit Syndrome genes were annoying, not fatal. She'd lived with a pair of them in every cell of her body for her whole life. Then again, considering who Meiko had eaten dinner with last night, maybe the reaction wasn't so bizarre.

There's a light to offset the shadow. "You also have one normal gene from your mother. The non-PDS gene masks the other, which is why you don't show any of the signs."

Meiko nodded and brushed her eyes with her handkerchief. To help her collect herself again, Calla focused feelings of peace and reassurance toward the beleaguered woman. With that help, she regained her composure after a few more steps.

"I wish I could've told you what you wanted to hear," Calla said.

Meiko blew her nose. "Should I tell Thomas?"

Calla winced and drew a breath through her teeth. "Now that's much further out of my range of expertise. When's the wedding?"

"In two months." Meiko dabbed at her eyes.

"Hmm. I understand why you're afraid." She switched her bag to her other hand and flexed her stiff fingers.

"What would you do?"

"Me? It's not an issue for me." She tapped her lower eyelid. "I can't exactly hide PDS. My eyes barely show any light in pitch black rooms."

"I know, but..." Meiko bit her lip.

Calla sighed. "This is my personal, not professional, opinion and remember that free advice is worth what you pay for it."

"Okay."

"People in general make too much of Power Deficit Syndrome." Calla paused and gathered her thoughts. "It's a trait, like blue eyes or curly hair or any of a thousand others. Unless you two are making a point of disclosing every bizarre genetic oddity you have, I wouldn't bother with this one. On the other hand, I think foreseeable matters of contention should be out in the open before you exchange vows, especially concerning an issue you both have such strong feelings about. Then again, until a year and a half ago, I was so busy studying medicine that the word 'date' had no meaning beyond the calendar showing my next exam."

Meiko smiled and chuckled.

Calla stepped ahead of Meiko, turned toward her, and stopped. "Does that help?"

She nodded and looked down. "Thank you."

"Who knows, maybe by the time Thomas and I get back, he'll have changed his mind." Calla continued toward Med Lab Eight.

"You're going with him on his next assignment?" Meiko asked.

Under duress. "It'll be just the two of us."

Meiko frowned and shook her head. "I hope he minds his manners."

Calla nodded. "I'm sure things will be fine. Tense, maybe, but fine."

"Please don't tell him I talked to you about this." Meiko spun and grabbed Calla's arm. "Promise me you won't."

Calla patted Meiko's hand. "We'll consider this doctor-patient confidentiality. You're safe."

"Thanks, Doctor." Meiko tried on a smile that Calla didn't quite believe. "I know you're busy, so I'll let you go."

"Take care, Ms. Sakamura. I'm sure everything will work out fine." *If it doesn't, there are plenty of great guys out there who don't care if their girlfriends have undesirable genes.*

Calla wouldn't trade Matt for anyone.

Meiko disappeared.

Calla looked at her watch and frowned. Too bad telepathy and the related ancillary skills didn't include a way to alter time.

Thomas walked from the door to Meiko's apartment to the rear of the kitchen and back again, over and over. Unlike his apartment, which looked like someone's attic leftovers, Meiko had decorated her place in a consistent theme. A red futon and black beanbag cushions surrounded a low black table with a simple fake flower arrangement in the center. The wall opposite her couch showed off some of her artwork, paintings of waves and flowering trees in an old Japanese style. Another wall was loaded with photographs of her family, which now included him. The immaculate kitchen no longer smelled of last night's nachos. Canisters Meiko had made herself from clay fired with food-safe glazes occupied one corner. A porcelain tea set decorated with cherry trees in bloom sat in another corner. He could personally vouch for it being used regularly. The first time she'd led him through a tea ceremony, he'd been totally clueless, but now he knew how to comport himself.

He looked at his watch. *Come on, honey. Where are you?*

Thomas parked himself on the red-padded futon. Pacing would get him nowhere, but if Meiko didn't show up soon, he'd have to leave without telling her goodbye. Given her recent comments about how he had to be gone more than she liked, he needed to see her before starting off on this soon-to-be-a-disaster of a trip.

Of all the people he could have pulled, why Calla? A rank newbie right out of school would've been better. Just his luck.

He drummed his fingers on his knees for what felt like an eon and then heaved a sigh and went to the wall of pictures. Some showed her parents, with or without her. Her dad must have been one of those light-sensitive types. He was never without dark glasses, and her mom's smile was mostly in the eyes. They looked happy, genuinely happy, unlike the forced joy Thomas remembered in his family.

He shook away those recollections and returned to the images in front of him. A random spectator at the arboretum had taken his favorite shot. Although they hadn't planned the effect, the picture had been taken in front of a fountain, and a frame of water surrounded them. He was glad he'd decided against giving Meiko rabbit ears that time.

A glance at the clock on the wall brought a frown to his face. Quarter past noon. Fifteen more minutes was about all he could spare before he had to pick up his Syndromer tag-along and get hopping. When he'd contacted Meiko a while ago, she'd sounded like she'd been only minutes away, moments if she'd teleport. What could the holdup be?

At one minute left on his countdown, the door opened. When Meiko entered her apartment, she wiped her eyes and kept her gaze on the floor. Aside from her weeping, she looked stellar in a pink floral skirt and blouse.

She sniffled, and Thomas opened his mental perceptions to see if he could get some clue about why she was crying. Aside from the obvious sadness, he couldn't single out any other emotions from the maelstrom. Whatever had caused this had to be more than simple loneliness.

Thomas led her to the couch and pulled her close. "Hey, what's wrong, honey?"

She brushed her eyes with a well-used handkerchief. "Now is not the best time. You're supposed to leave soon."

"Ologo will keep." He brushed her short bangs away from her face. "The world won't explode if I'm a little late. So, come on. What's happening?"

She leaned on his shoulder. "I, uh, I miss my dad."

There was more to it than that. There had to be. True, with the pending wedding, they both missed those who'd been dear to them, but every time she got grumpy, she blamed her mood on grieving for her dad.

Thomas kissed her cheek. "Wish I'd met him. He must've been an incredible man."

Meiko nodded but said nothing for a long time.

Say something already. How can I help you work through things if you clam up? He checked his watch. "I'd stay if I could, but I have to go to Ologo with a Syndromer."

Jaw clenching, Meiko shoved him away so hard he almost rolled off the end. "Get out!"

He picked himself up. "What's gotten into you?"

She stood and pointed toward the door. "Get out! And don't come back until you lose that attitude."

He shook his head. "Excuse me? What attitude?"

Meiko looked everywhere but at him for what felt like minutes. "That's no way to talk about the woman who saved your life. Show some gratitude."

He scowled and started making a fist before he caught himself. "I wasn't that bad off, and she killed Angela with her incompetence."

"Dr. Geisman wasn't the only doctor working on Angela, or are you also upset about that other guy, Dr. Petrov?"

Thomas glared at her. "Not the point."

She stalked a step closer. "Yes, it is. Neither one of

them could save Angela's life, so why are you so hard on Dr. Geisman?"

"She's a Syndromer!" *Okay, cool it. Yelling won't help.* He blew out a breath and continued at a lower volume. "She botched the job and cost Angela her life."

Meiko shook her head. "You're not mad at her for Angela's death. You don't like her because she had the misfortune of an inherited disease like the dope dealer who beat you senseless. Stephanie would be proud of you, wouldn't she? Prejudice in a negotiator. It's good she's not here to see it."

Thomas stared laser bolts at Meiko. His mentor held a special place in his heart. Stephanie had accepted him and taken him in when his family had disowned him. Her death had ripped him apart. How could Meiko be so cruel? She'd hardly even known Stephanie.

He paced a couple steps away from her and squeezed his eyes closed until he had himself under control. "That was uncalled for."

"No less so than what you said." Her staccato cadence cut through him.

The nagging voice in his head, which sounded creepily like his former mentor, told him she had a point, but he shut the voice up with a reminder of the Syndromer drug dealer. They were all bad news.

"I have to go." He grabbed his travel bag. "I'll contact you later."

She grabbed a tissue from the box on the end table and wiped her eyes. "If you can't lose your bigotry between here and Ologo, don't bother."

If she'd shot him in the heart, he might have been hurt less. He was a negotiator! Prejudice should be beyond him, but with that Syndromer's sneer haunting him, he couldn't let it go. Some things were rooted too deeply.

"Meiko, I ..." He faltered, uncertain how to set things right again. Perhaps time and distance would help by giving both of them a chance to cool off. "I'll contact you later."

Thomas focused his thoughts on Med Ward Eight.

Calla's office was small, almost half the size of the typical exam room. The holographic image of her degrees glittered, hovering in place over her computer screen. Aside from a serviceable desk a half-meter longer than her keyboard, she had a pair of chairs, one of which supported a somewhat precarious stack of the things she'd take for her trip.

Blowing out a weary breath, Calla flopped into the chair at her computer. She needed a few more hours to get ready. With all the red tape and surprise visits she'd attended to, she hadn't made half as much progress as she would have liked. Thomas would be here soon, and she hadn't been able to do more than read the summary of the report he'd sent to her.

She shuffled her remaining tasks by priority and opened Thomas' medical file. If she needed to treat him on this trip, the information there would be critical, so the medical record ranked highest. She could follow his lead in dealing with the races of Ologo if necessary. She tapped the icons on the screen and found his record.

What amazing twist of fate had sent her out on a mission into a war zone with a man who had already professed his deep and abiding hatred for her? As far as he was concerned, she didn't deserve the air she breathed, and this trip had more than enough other problems. Hopefully, he was professional enough to put his personal feelings aside for at least the duration of their forced time together. Later, when they were safely back home, he could have the luxury of his discrimination.

"Dr. Geisman?" the secretary called through the communicator over Calla's ear.

Calla pressed the talk switch. "Yes, Laris."

"Thomas McCrady is here to see you. He says he's expected."

Calla groaned and rubbed her forehead. "Yes, thank you. Send him on back. I'll be leaving for Ologo in the next few minutes."

"All right. Good luck, Doctor."

"Thanks." *I'll need it.*

Well, Thomas would have to wait until she finished reading the file. She had already come across an allergy to a commonly used drug and a resistance to a whole class of others. In the wrong circumstances, those two surprises alone could have been deadly.

A knock banged on the door.

She kept her eyes on the record. "Come in."

The door opened and then closed again.

He exuded tension and keen sadness. That couldn't be about the meetings, could it?

Without turning, she pointed to the open chair. "Have a seat. I'll be with you in a moment."

He dropped into the chair. "You're not ready?"

If I had a couple more days to prepare, maybe. "Almost. Let me get to the bottom of your medical file."

"My medical file?" He bolted to his feet and looked over her shoulder. "What are you doing with that?"

"Preparing for the mission. I need to know your medical history in case I have to treat you." Calla turned to face him.

His jaw muscles were tight, and the brilliant glitter in his eyes masked the color of his irises. "What right do you have to go digging in my records?"

"I'm a doctor, and you have a significantly unusual medical history. If I have to treat you on this trip, I need to have an idea of what to expect."

"I don't want you in my records." He reached for the screen's off button.

She batted his hand away. "You want me to keep a journal I don't need. Fine. Waste of paper and ink, but I'll go along because it's standard procedure. You're going to have to put up with me knowing the rest of your medical history for the same reason. Standard procedure says I have to know the medical background of anyone I go on a mission with. I have to read your record."

He looked away for a moment. "Do you have any idea how quickly you can wreck my credibility? There are lots of people who would see that I was once an addict and would ignore that I've been clean for seven and a half years by my own choice."

How could he be against her because she had been born with the two recessive genes for PDS when, according to the record, he had taken drugs because he didn't want to deal with being telepathic anymore? At least he had fixed his problem. She couldn't do anything but live with hers.

She leaned back in her chair and folded her arms across her chest. "I know that kind of information about a lot of people, and I'm well aware of problems that come up from people who refuse to see beyond their blind hatred."

This argument could go on forever, and he still wouldn't hear her. She turned back to the computer to read the rest of the record. The awkward silence elongated her task by making concentration harder, but she finished and shut down her computer.

He sat down, put his elbows on his knees and rested his forehead on his palms. "Did you read the log of my last trip to Ologo?"

She glanced back at the computer. "I didn't have time to get far."

He frowned. "I'd really hoped you would have at least a little background on Ologo by now. These things are hard enough when you know what to expect."

Calla leaned forward. "I realize that."

"Then what have you been doing for the last four hours?"

"We don't have time to go through a litany describing my day." She stood and shrugged out of her lab coat. "Suffice it to say that it was all essential to the mission or otherwise unavoidable."

"All right." He ran his fingers through his wavy red hair. "Well, I guess I'll have to feed you information on Olvians and Gotrians as we go."

She draped her lab coat over her chair. "I know we don't have many options right now, but I can't say I'm real keen on this lack of prep time. The Magistrates seem to be in a hurry to get us out of here. Is that normal?"

He shook his head. "Not at all. We usually have a couple days to get ready. I'm as concerned as you about why this is a rush job." He looked up at her clock. "We'd better get moving."

"Right." She pulled her communicator off her ear and dropped it on the desk. "Won't need that for a while."

Thomas indicated the communicator with a nod. "What's with the antique? Don't all you people have telepathy?"

She scowled. "Psionic medicine is a delicate balancing act. Unexpected intrusions can be devastating, so, yes, all psionic specialists and the nurses who work with them use this antique."

Calla stood and looked around her office. Was the tension in her gut a reminder that she'd forgotten something or a simple case of nerves? The number of times she had been away from Haidar could be counted on the fingers of one hand leaving fingers unaccounted for, and two of those trips had been family vacations more than a decade ago.

Once on Ologo she would be at Thomas' mercy. Mr. Zagruder hadn't had a chance to teach her the rest of the steps for teleportation yet, and she didn't have the power to communicate telepathically over large distances. What would she do if something went wrong and Thomas couldn't or wouldn't help?

She rubbed her forehead. *Fretting over all this will do no good.*

Calla grabbed her new leather jacket off the peg on the back of the door. She'd gotten it a little over a month ago for the medical conference to ward off the cool temperatures on the planet and in the conference halls. It still smelled brand new. For all she knew winter had settled on that part of Ologo.

Thomas picked up his bag. "Good idea. Wish I'd thought of that."

"Do you want to get yours?" Calla slipped the backpack containing her trauma kit over one shoulder.

He shook his head. "I'll come back if I need it. Have everything?"

"I think so." Calla picked up her duffel bag. Her stomach protested as if she'd stepped into a zero-G environment.

Thomas cautiously reached his hand toward her like she had some communicable disease and then shook his head and gripped her arm more forcefully than he needed to. Calla's guts lurched as her office turned into a colorful cyclone, then righted itself as somewhere unfamiliar when they came out of the teleport. With her hand pressed to her stomach, Calla staggered, held up only by Thomas' too-firm grip on her arm.

She struggled to get her bearings and forced herself to stand on her own again. He didn't need yet another reason to give her grief. Maybe the rest of the trip would go better.

Thomas shrugged off the dizziness and drew in a deep breath of sea air. He smiled. They'd arrived on the target he'd been aiming for. The large, elevated parking lot was almost empty at this hour. The few vehicles that remained were scattered around under lights bright enough to illuminate the night to sunlight radiance.

Calla wobbled. He tightened his hold on her arm to keep her from falling flat on her face. She tried to make a good show of standing without his help, but if he was a little woozy after traveling that distance, she had to be feeling horrible. Right now, when he needed her to be able to concentrate, she had trouble even staying upright.

If she had mentioned having teleport problems, he could have tried to do something to ameliorate the effects. At the very least he would have been better prepared to catch her.

I spent the last ten minutes grouching at her, and that was only the most recent installment, and I expect her to level with me about her weaknesses? "You could have warned me teleporting makes you sick."

She swallowed hard and pressed her arm across her gut. "I'm all right."

He took her black backpack and set it on the pavement and then put her other bag next to it. "No, you're not. I've been there."

There had been no other options. On the tight schedule they had been given, there had been no choice but to teleport to Ologo. Even if he hadn't been able to sense Calla's queasiness, she couldn't possibly be "all right." They were a few minutes early, and that would give her some time to recover.

He helped her sit down away from the puny rail and the three-meter drop to the swampy ground. He preferred high tide. The sound of the water lapping against the pylons was relaxing.

"I'll be okay." Calla hugged her knees to her chest. "Don't you have enough to worry about?"

"Yeah, and one of those things is a partner who won't be honest with me. I get sick when I don't teleport myself, too." He crouched next to her. "If it affects the mission at all, I need to know."

As much as he didn't care for her company, they had a job to do, and the real work had begun. Thomas hoped she had the good sense to leave their personal problems back at the station.

She clenched her eyes and ran her fingers partway through her short, black hair. "It's never been this bad. It usually passes pretty quickly."

"Congratulations. You came halfway across the galaxy instead of halfway across the station."

Calla looked past him. "Company."

He followed her gaze. Two Terrans came out of the building nearby. They had to be the Pharmacorp representatives coming to offer their hospitality or, if things went as well as last time, declare that they'd decided to stay out of the affair altogether.

Thomas stood up. "How are you feeling? For real, this time."

"Still dizzy, but as long as I keep my eyes open, I'll manage." She pushed off from the ground.

"Fair enough." Thomas pulled her to her feet. "These folks will be from Pharmacorp. Let me handle them. That'll give you another minute or two before the real delegations arrive."

"Pharmacorp? Where'd I miss that we'd be working with them?"

"That came up in the mission br—" He caught himself. Joy hadn't mentioned Pharmacorp until after Thomas had asked Calla to wait in the hall. He rolled his eyes. "I forgot to relay that to you."

Her already pale complexion went a couple shades lighter. "I hope we don't run into someone I met at the conference. They'll know I'm a doctor."

"We'll deal with that if it comes up. For now, you're a negotiator."

She nodded.

Thomas took a few steps toward the representatives to get a first impression of them. The woman wore a bright red business suit with a black blouse, but her attire didn't seem to hang right on her. She appeared to have borrowed a heavier person's clothes. Had she been ill, or had she enjoyed some diet success? A muscular man walked a pace behind her. His tan slacks and green shirt looked out of place with his companion.

When Thomas reached out with his thoughts, he ran into the tight voids of personal anti-psionic generators. His muscles tensed as he remembered the years he had wasted blocking his own powers by getting high. At least the device's sphere of influence had been set too low to affect him at normal speaking proximities.

Calla's thoughts reached him. *"Are you okay?"*

He shuddered and drove away the revulsion of the Syndromer's thoughts in his head. Since he would have to communicate with her privately, he'd have to tolerate the contact. She was not the guy who'd tried to kill him.

"Yeah, I'm fine." He glanced at her. *"I don't like generators much."*

"They can be unnerving." She reached a hand toward his shoulder but stopped and retreated a step.

"Hi, welcome to Ologo," the woman said from too far away to make for good conversation.

Asserting control won't work, chicky. He delayed answering until they were close enough to converse at a civilized volume. "Hello. I'm Thomas McCrady."

She spoke over him. "I'm so glad you made it." She clutched her trembling hands in front of her.

Thomas smiled and waited for her to speak again. A war of who had the next word wasted more time and effort than he wanted to expend on these people.

"I'm Patina Faulks, your liaison to Pharmacorp, and this is my assistant, Kevin Lithos."

Bodyguard more likely.

When Ms. Faulks offered her quivering hand, Thomas steeled himself and then exchanged a brief handshake, crossing into and out of the anti-psionic field's influence without flinching for a change. He introduced Calla next, remembering to drop her title at the last second.

"We'll be providing a room for your meetings in our corporate office building." Patina pointed over her shoulder.

"Thank you." Thomas smiled and looked past her at the building. "We're grateful for your hospitality."

"Anything to stop this, um, this—this ridiculous war these people have going on." Patina cast a nervous glance to Kevin. "Right?"

Thomas had met plenty of people who were antsy around telepaths, but what did she think he would do to her, especially with that generator armed?

She fidgeted with the buttons on her suit jacket. "Will you be able to resolve the matter quickly?"

Thomas nodded. "We'll work toward a quick resolution, but a lot of it depends on the delegations. They have to be willing to work with us and with each other."

"Oh, they're anxious for the war to end." Patina looked around for a moment. "I mean, they've been losing a lot of their beings to disease lately."

Kevin cleared his throat.

"I imagine their sanitation must be failing as the war drags on." Patina's words tumbled out at high speed.

"What's wrong with her?" Calla's thoughts came to him.

"Some people get the jitters around telepaths." He kept his eyes on Patina.

"Yes, I know that, but this is more than a mild case of nerves, Thomas. She's scared."

"I'm telling you, it's not that unusual. Let it go."

Patina pointed off to the side. Thomas followed her hand. The silhouette of an enormous stiff-winged bird, a Gotrian plane, approached. Fascinating how they kept up the natural motifs in the midst of the war.

Her smile spoke more of relief than happiness. "That would be the Gotrians."

Thomas projected his thoughts to Calla. *"How are you doing?"*

"I'm fine. Seriously."

"Good, because we're on for real now, and I'm going to need you for this part."

"What do I do?"

A mild flutter in her thoughts registered an understandable uncertainty. Not surprising. She'd spent her prep time dealing with whatever medical matters had kept her busy.

"Follow my lead. I'll direct you as much as I can."

When the Gotrian transport crossed into the light, it looked like an awkward conglomeration of mismatched parts. Unintentionally done up in slum camo, the doors and hull panels were all different colors of dented and repainted rust. Perhaps they'd kept their natural forms because they had nothing else to build from.

At the distant edge of the parking platform, the craft hovered on its jets for a moment and then settled gracefully on its landing gear. The rear door opened and a Gotrian stepped out. The blue tunic's hood shrouded his face, but Thomas recognized the unique mental texture of Brachi, the same ambassador who had represented his people last time. Their familiarity might help overcome the age issue.

Brachi took a few steps toward them, threw his arms up, and boarded his craft again.

Thomas frowned and shook his head. *Came close enough to see that neither of us are all that old and gave up. Terrific way to get started.*

Thomas projected his thoughts. *"Brachi? Leaving without even saying 'Hello?'"*

He forged a light connection to pick up the response from a non-telepathic mind.

"Thomas? Is that you?" Brachi's voice echoed as he spoke aloud. *"I didn't know you from so far away."*

Thomas even heard the guttural sound, like hacking up a hairball, Gotrians used to indicate a question. *"Yes. I was looking forward to hearing your wisdom again. Will you deny me that chance?"*

Brachi disembarked and shed his hood as he walked over. His short legs seemed shorter and long arms seemed longer than last time. Gray hair lightened what had been a solid black mane and the rings of fur around his wrists, ankles, and tail-tip.

Have you aged that much in the last few years, or are you graying your hair on purpose?

Coming toe to toe with Thomas, Brachi came up to his full height and had to crane his neck back to allow them to see each other's eyes. Thomas' guts tensed. They were too close to one another, and he had all he could do to keep himself from stepping back. Worse, Brachi hadn't taken care of dental hygiene between dinner and this meeting. What had he eaten? The local equivalent of a skunk?

"What are you doing here?" His tone was slightly warmer than zero degrees Kelvin.

"What do you think I'm doing here?" Thomas mimicked Brachi's coldness.

Brachi clapped a huge hand on Thomas' arm as he reopened the distance between them. "They sent you to help us make a treaty, of course." Brachi pursed his thin lips in his race's version of a smile. "Tell me, where is Stephanie?"

A wave of grief threatened to wash over him. Thomas sighed and pushed it away. He picked a Gotrian euphemism to convey his feelings. "I carry the wisdom of Stephanie Davilla in my heart."

Feelings of reassurance came to him from Calla, and he made an effort to keep from recoiling. She was trying to be nice, but he didn't need that kind of help, not from her.

"How long has it been?" Brachi ended with his rough-sounding inquiry cough.

Thomas looked away for a moment. "A little over a year."

"I'm sorry. The Ancient guided her every word and action."

Thomas nodded once in acknowledgment of Brachi's high praise. The delegate turned away and approached Calla.

You were paying attention, right? "Don't move. Answer his question with a question."

When Brachi closed the distance with her, and one of her hands balled up into a fist, then slowly reopened, but she stayed her ground. Brachi didn't take notice of her hand. So far so good.

Brachi craned his head back to see Calla's face and trilled his initial "r." "You. Do you think you can rreplace one like Stephanie Davilla?"

Thomas tensed as he waited for her answer, praying she would use the right format.

Calla's eyes narrowed for a moment. "Should you speak of the dead that way?"

Brachi stepped back and pursed his lips in a Gotrian smile. "No harm is done. She is safe in the palace of the Ancient, so says the Book of the Ancient. I am Brachi, the Speaker of my people."

Thomas projected his thoughts to her. *"Introduce yourself. No last name. Only the dead get a family name."*

"I am Calla, sent by the Haidar Station to help with the negotiations."

Thomas released the breath he had been holding. He would have used a different challenge, but she'd done fine. If Calla could keep this up, they might be in business.

"Did you also have the benefit of Stephanie Davilla's wisdom?" Brachi ended with the hairball hack.

Calla delayed her answer. "Did I miss a great deal by not knowing her?"

Brachi's brow furrowed.

Thomas inwardly cringed with the memory of how he'd done the same thing on his first trip here. He should have warned her. *"Don't over-generalize. Only the initial question is answered with a challenge question."*

"Sorry."

Brachi huffed. "Yes, you missed a rrare opportunity."

Calla shook her head. "I regret that I was so engrossed in other studies at the time that I never had the chance to meet her."

"You will have to earn your wisdom elsewhere, and perhaps Thomas will share what he gleaned from her."

Calla fixed her gaze on Thomas. "He's older than I am, so I don't doubt that I'll learn much from him during our stay here."

She couldn't be that much younger, but Brachi turned his back on her and stepped away.

Thomas met her gaze and nodded once. *"You're*

doing fine. He'll think you're a kid who still needs to be taught a few things. Little mistakes will be excused as ignorance for now. I'll do better about keying you in. Next time, though, if you're not sure, ask. They can't hear us unless we want them to."

Thomas and Brachi reminisced about the experiences of the previous meeting. Establishing credibility was the most pressing concern now. Stephanie's reputation would only carry Thomas so far. Once the official negotiations started, Brachi would be all business, and the fond remembrances of Thomas' teacher would no longer factor in, at least not officially. For now, he played up the connection as much as he could.

They were running short on neutral topics when a low rumble grew steadily. A tracked amphibious vehicle with a rusty propeller on the back crawled up a ramp into the parking lot.

Patina clapped her hands once and interlaced her fingers. "There they are."

Thomas startled. *You're still here?*

Brachi looked at her as if she were an intruder in a private conversation. Thomas smiled. The crow's feet around Patina's eyes gave her greater age away.

When the Olvians crawled out of their vehicle, the two females, one half again the size of the other, frog-hopped forward on long, muscular legs and smaller, webbed, almost wing-like arms. After a few hops, both drew themselves more upright and loped toward the rest of the group. In their more vertical form, they looked more like pear-shaped blobs with four appendages. As they came nearer, the lead one slowly blinked her large eyes. Her translucent skin darkened. Why was she so unhappy? With Calla here, they should feel neutral at worst. Was the problem with the Gotrian delegation?

He exchanged a quick look with Calla. *"They'll try to ignore me and deal with you."*

"Should I redirect them to you or handle it myself?"

Even as the thoughts formed, he could sense her doubts warbling in her thoughts, which suited him well enough. The thought of hanging any non-medical part of this on her with her limitations didn't sit well with him, but she had done well enough with Brachi aside from that one minor blunder. The Olvians would be happier dealing with a woman, too.

On the other hand, if she blew it, this mission could turn ugly; and she had been clear that she felt out of her league. If not the inexperience, then her own lack of confidence could make her do something stupid.

"Send them to me. Let me do as much of the talking as possible."

As Calla acknowledged his instructions, the Olvians reached them. The assistant returned to her more natural crouch, while the leader sat back on her haunches and raised her webbed, wing-like arms off her body a few inches.

"Well. We send to Haidar for help and they don't even have the decency to send a woman to help us? Are we that unimportant?" the leader croaked in a gravelly, decidedly not female-sounding voice.

What do you mean, there's no woman here? Calla may be a Syndromer, but she's a little girly.

Thomas let his eyes blur and tried to see what the Olvians saw. To their dim sight, Calla's unusual height and short hair made her look more masculine and the leather jacket would hide anything they could learn from her figure. Her voice, however, should end all concern.

Brachi smirked. "They're blind!"

Thomas projected his thoughts to Calla. *"They don't see well in the air. Say something. Try to sound offended that they mistook you for a man."*

"I am here from Haidar." Calla's voice had the same icy tone she had taken with him during their argument in her office. She propped a hand on her hip and wagged her finger at the Olvians. "I assure you I am as female as you are."

The leader shrank back for a moment then rose again. Her color shifted from the black of unhappiness to mottled confusion while she approached Calla. When the Olvian's hands reached for Calla's face, Calla shifted her foot back without actually taking a step.

Thomas took a step closer. *"Stay right where you are. Don't react."*

"I understand what she wants, but I still need to keep my balance."

One of the Olvian's webbed hands went around the back of Calla's head while the other studied her face.

Finally, the ambassador stepped back, and her patchy coloring faded to a medium gray. "My apologies. You wear the fur on your head much shorter than I expected and I did not know that females of your people could be so tall."

Thomas nodded once. *"Accept the apology gracefully."*

Calla settled her weight on both feet again. "I am somewhat unusual for my race, so such a mistake is understandable and easily forgiven."

The leader introduced herself and her assistant with croaks that Thomas could not tell the difference between. Producing the noise himself would have been impossible without a computer.

"You may call me Rana and my assistant will answer to Pipien."

Although Rana's color had lightened some, Pipien remained an inky black.

He had to get the heat off Calla, but to do that he had to somehow shift the focus onto himself without downplaying her role too much.

Thomas stepped forward. "I'm Thomas McCrady, and this is Calla Geisman."

Rana darkened again and turned to address Calla. "Given the hour late, I might suggest that we postpone our meeting until morning tomorrow."

Brachi chuckled. "Do you fear the dark?"

"Not at all!" Rana darkened and pivoted toward him like a gear needing oil. "Our visitors have traveled a distance great and should have the chance to sleep the rest of the night before we tell them of our troubles. Would you deny them that? I thought not. We would only be too glad to provide a place appropriate for them, of course."

Brachi squared his shoulders. "Nonsense. We have arranged their sleeping quarters with us. They are land-dwellers and will be more comfortable in our city."

Pipien grumbled something in her native language before speaking the tongue they had in common. "Why would dwellers land be more comfortable in the trees?"

"Air is more breathable than water."

"Parts of our cities are not filled with water, treeswinger." Pipien made an emphatic downward swipe with her left hand.

Racial slurs already? They'd hardly been in the same space for five minutes.

Thomas stepped between them. "Hey, now, there's no reason—"

Rana turned to Patina before he could finish. "You said we should prepare space for them, and we have."

"Don't be rridiculous." Brachi rose to his full height and stalked closer to Patina. "Why would Patina ask you to set aside such inappropriate quarters when she had already told us to make a place of honor for our guests."

Patina stammered and backed up a couple steps. "I apologize for the confusion. Maybe it would be best, Thomas, if you and Calla stayed with us. We have plenty of room in our corporate living quarters. The rooms are very comfortable, and it wouldn't be any trouble at all. That way, no one's feelings would get hurt."

Now that's a plan I trust.

Corporations doing things out of the goodness of their hearts were only slightly more common than a human building a house on a star's surface. This apparent confusion was too convenient.

Why would Pharmacorp want to keep them away from the delegates, though? They couldn't gain anything. Every instinct Thomas had told him to decline Patina's offer, and he always listened to his gut, especially after Cordil.

Now he had to figure out where to stay. Choosing one race over another would start rumors of favoritism. Even if he and Calla alternated hosts, someone would make the wrong assumption about where they stayed first. They'd have to split up.

Was Calla up for the challenge? Where should he send her? He knew Brachi would take care of her in an almost fatherly way because of her youth, but Rana had already expressed concern that her people weren't being taken seriously.

At least with Rana, Calla would only have to worry about minding her manners and deciphering what appropriate behavior looked like. With Brachi, there would be religious taboos to deal with, too. The Olvians would forgive ignorance of manners, but wars had started over the smallest breach of religious expectations in some cultures.

Thomas smiled politely. "Thank you for your kind

offer, but I would be honored to accept Brachi's generous hospitality." He looked at Calla and projected his thoughts. *"Your turn. Accept Rana's offer."*

Brachi struck his chest and gave Rana a smug look that her bad sight would fail to make out.

Doubt flooded Calla's mind as her thoughts came to him. *"I don't like this, Thomas. I don't know anything about their behaviors, and I'm still figuring out the color change meanings."*

"No choice now."

Brachi looked back and forth between them as if watching a tennis match. He couldn't possibly hear them, but his race wasn't known for enduring patience.

Thomas held up his hand. "Just a minute. We need to sort something out."

Calla stared at him with narrow, dark brown eyes. *"Why not stay with Pharmacorp?"*

"I have a feeling that Patina set us up."

"Thomas, that doesn't make sense."

"I don't know. Something bugs me about this."

"All right, then, what about a hotel?"

"Get real, Doc. You think this is a tourist spot? There's nothing here. I was told everything was covered, and we would get details when we arrived."

"What problem would we cause by staying at home and teleporting in every day? Certainly not pleasant from my perspective but better the nausea than being separated."

"That shows distrust on our part. It has to be this way. Don't worry. If you have any questions, you can still ask me, and if something goes wrong, I can be there in a flash."

"That doesn't go both ways. I don't know how to teleport!"

That was rich. Did she really think he would need a

Syndromer to rescue him?

He squelched a smirk. *"It's too late. We're committed. We'll have to make this work. Now get to it. They can't hear what we're thinking, but they sure can tell we're not just enjoying each other's looks. We'll have huge problems later if they think we're not in agreement."*

"I think this is a colossal error, but fine." Her movements were a little stiff as she turned to Rana. "Rana, if I might impose upon your—"

The lead Olvian sprang forward making Calla retreat a step. "You are no imposition, Calla. I am only too happy to have such a guest special."

Patina's smile looked painted on. "Well, good. I'm glad that's settled. Shall we meet again at, say, an hour after daybreak?"

Thomas tipped his head down and looked up at her. *Shut up!* "I don't th—"

Brachi growled and rounded his shoulders. "No. That hour is saved for our morning devotions according to the word in the Book of the Ancient."

Thomas shot a stern look at Patina and stepped between her and the delegates. "Of course, I would not presume to interrupt your services. Would two hours after daybreak be acceptable?"

Pipien paled. "Either hour will be fine, since we have no such superstitions."

"Belief in the Ancient is not superstition!" Brachi struck his chest with a fist.

Thomas sighed and shook his head. *Can't any of you play nice?* "Two hours. Will that be acceptable, Brachi?"

Brachi nodded. "That will do fine."

Patina clasped her hands in front of her. "Excellent. I'll meet you in the lobby."

Thomas nodded and picked up his suitcase.

Calla's thoughts came to him. *"Have I told you how much I don't like this idea?"*

"Yes. It'll be okay. You can do this." I hope.

He followed Brachi to the little plane. This plan expected a lot from a Syndromer.

Being separated from Thomas this early in the trip rated phenomenally high on Calla's list of bad ideas. She understood why going home wouldn't work, but staying with Pharmacorp couldn't have been as bad as all that. For some reason, they had been maneuvered into this division, and Thomas had fallen for it.

Did this mean he trusted her now, or would he spend their time apart sweating blood and praying she didn't start an intragalactic incident?

Calla picked up her bags and followed her hostess to the squat mini-sub that waited nearby. She ducked to look inside the cramped compartment. From floor to ceiling the space was knee-high. A small, forward compartment housed a driver. The rear compartment, separated by a half-height partition, had no seats. Squashy, plastic-covered cushions were scattered around. The inside smelled damp and mildewy.

Ugh. I'm supposed to fit in here?

Rana and Pipien both folded themselves neatly into place, but Calla knocked her head on the ceiling on the way in and couldn't sit down even with her knees drawn all the way up to her shoulders. The best she could do was sit cross-legged and hunched over facing the rear of the vehicle. Fortunately, she had the flexibility to do that without injuring herself.

"You don't look very comfortable at all." A vague chuckle burbled through Pipien's voice.

Calla smiled. "Well, I'm sure you didn't design these to accommodate taller than average Haidarians. I'll be fine."

Rana croaked instructions to the driver and the sub lurched as it got under way, pitching Calla forward. She caught herself with one hand on the floor.

Her hostess turned dark gray, leaving Calla to figure out what that meant. She understood black for anger, gray for happiness, and splotched for uncertainty, but she hadn't seen dark gray before. After a moment's hesitation, she decided not to contact Thomas for more information.

Since neither she nor Thomas were thirty yet, he would be up to his ears with calming Brachi's worries. When a real mess came up, then she would bother Thomas. For the time being, she had other tools and opened up her mental perceptions to see what they registered. Fear jittered in her thoughts. What was Rana afraid of?

The color of Rana's skin muted into the splotched pattern. "I am troubled that you let the male speak for you."

"Yes." Pipien grew darker. "Bad enough that the Gotrians sent a male to do the job of a woman, but why do you have to let Thomas have so much control?"

How could she answer the question without losing the Olvian's confidence in her while focusing their attention back on her partner?

She projected her thoughts outward. *"Thomas, I have a situation here."*

"So do I. Stall. I'll be with you in a minute."

She didn't have a minute. The silence had worn on too long already, and every passing second increased the tension. The Olvians watched and waited for an answer, and Calla had to tell them something. Maybe the truth would work if she cast it in the right light.

Calla took a deep breath before she spoke. "Well, part of this mission is being used for training."

One thing was certain. Calla would know much more about arbitration by the end of this trip. Most of her education would be by fire if things kept going this way, but if they misinterpreted her words to mean that Thomas learned the ropes from her, that would suit her fine.

Rana's coloring paled slightly. "Oh? We occasionally have some males who show an intelligence almost feminine early on. Is he such a creature?"

Calla nodded. *Perfect.* "He has shown remarkable skill as a negotiator. I wish to encourage him."

"How sweet of you!"

Pipien harrumphed. "What if he runs into trouble, though? If he's still learning, he might make a mistake."

A pins and needles sensation in Calla's foot protested the pressure her position put on it. "I am here to assist him as needed."

"If he fails, would you take over?" Rana asked.

She shifted to relieve the growing discomfort. "Well, I am part of this team."

"And how often does he consult with you?"

"Our abilities allow us to stay in pretty much constant mental contact, if necessary. I am available to him whenever the need arises." She wished she could say the same for him.

"Well, I feel better." Rana lightened further to a neutral gray.

Pipien stayed dark. Did she have some kind of pigmentation disability permanently relegating her to such a somber hue?

Calla reached out with her perceptions and read the dull-edged warmth of aggravation from Pipien. "I'm glad I could allay your fears."

"I still don't like him." Pipien huffed.

"I understand your concerns, but—"

"Do you? Truly? How can you?"

Calla waited until she was sure Pipien wouldn't continue. "You're worried your interests won't receive the attention they deserve."

Rana glared at Pipien while turning black. "I'm sure he won't be an issue. Calla is the one who's actually in charge. She can step in if the male proves too slow to function. I'm content enough with that. She must be very proud of Thomas. Males rarely show intelligence true."

Pipien turned somewhat lighter and shrank away from her boss.

Calla's concerns ebbed away. Her ploy still needed Thomas' official stamp of approval, but she'd managed to capture Rana's trust.

Not quite a minute later, the amphibious vehicle crossed from land into water and bobbed along the surface before submerging.

Joseph sat in a tan, padded chair in Pharmacorp's lobby. Employee of the month pictures graced one wall. Another showed off customer service awards and posters for some of their key products. Many showed weak and sickly children being treated by Terran doctors with crates marked "Pharmacorp" in the background.

From the lobby, Joseph could watch the introduction to the negotiations. The anti-psionic generator in his pocket protected him from detection. He hated the things. They left him feeling mentally blind, deaf, and dumb. Better that, however, than to risk discovery.

After several minutes of conversation, Thomas walked off with the Gotrian, Calla left with the Olvians, and Kevin and Patina returned to the main building.

Joseph snorted and shook his head. *I give you one simple task: get the negotiators to stay here, and I even tell you how to go about it, and you can't even manage that much?*

The bodyguard arrived first, threw the door open, and stormed in, leaving Patina to fend for herself.

Kevin checked his advance well outside of arm's reach. "Your plan didn't work."

Joseph laced his fingers across the head of his cane. "Are you certain you arranged everything correctly?"

"Yes, of course." Patina faded back a pace. "I—I—I did exactly what you said to do, but instead of coming here where we could keep an eye on them, th—they decided to split up."

Joseph smirked. *Do I make you nervous, dear?* "I

don't see why you're so worried. They'll never be able to negotiate the treaty. The Gotrians won't trust either of them, and the Olvians will demand to deal with Calla who has no experience in these matters. That's why I had the two of them paired up for this."

Kevin stepped closer. "We paid you to do a job, and you failed."

Joseph rolled his eyes. "Hardly. They'll never figure this out. Calla is useless on this trip, and Thomas has never led a mission before, so he'll be trying to figure out what to do while cleaning up the messes Calla is bound to create. He won't have time to decipher your role in this world's troubles. Even better, they can't stand each other."

"That's not good enough." Kevin balled up a fist and quivered. "I want them gone. Pull some more strings and have them removed."

"That won't happen until the mission is completed unless something goes hopelessly wrong, so do whatever you can to create an inconvenience. Continue trying to play the races off against each other. This planet is too hostile to keep up peaceful overtures if you keep reminding them of their long-standing feuds."

Kevin tipped his head down and looked up at Joseph. "Oh, that'll work real well."

Joseph shrugged. "Then kill them."

Patina gasped. "Kill them? But you can't just k—"

Kevin silenced her with a look. "That'll raise too much suspicion."

Joseph shook his head. "No, it won't. These arbitration missions can be dangerous. You do have to be careful enough to make it look like something beyond your control, however."

"To make that sort of arrangement, I need more information than I have."

Ah, the smell of money in the afternoon. If you're so willing to part with your cash, I'm accepting donations. "Breaking into the computer databases will be difficult. I'll have to include someone else, and he'll need to be paid." Using his cane and the arm of the chair for support, he pushed himself up and grimaced against the surge of pain in his knee.

"Fine. Just bring me the information when you have it." Kevin backed off a pace. "Depending on how good it is, I'll compensate you for your efforts."

Joseph nodded once and disabled the generator in his pocket. The welcome background noise of feelings and, if he concentrated, real thoughts freed him from the silent prison of his own solitary mind.

He focused his thoughts on home. Pharmacorp's foyer whirled and faded only to be replaced moments later by a different jumbled mass of spinning color that resolved into his own living room. The post-teleport queasiness passed after a couple moments. He grinned. Teleporting into his living room facing the door gave him the best view.

The real, black leather sofa and chair imported from Earth dominated the room. The paintings around him were original works by Gorde, the Haidarian who simulated the teleportation spin on canvas. True works of beauty, all of them.

Joseph reclined on the couch. With his eyes closed, he sorted through the hundreds of people on the station, comparing them to his star pupil's unique signature. August was not only a powerful telepath, but also a wizard on the computer. The boy's unwitting help in previous jobs had allowed Joseph to relieve the Haidar Station of dozens of Syndromers, cripples, junkies, and alcoholics.

Those undesirables only weakened the station, and

in a universe where Terrans outnumbered telepaths, weaklings had to be culled. Survival of the fittest should be any race's motto if they wanted to continue to live in the hostile environment of interracial coexistence.

After finding his student, Joseph projected his thoughts. *"August."*

"Yes, sir?"

"The Magistrates asked me to find someone to test the security of the medical and training databases. You were the first one to come to mind. Are you up to it?" Joseph thought.

"Yes, sir. I can do that."

"Wonderful." Without the boy's help, this task would have become monumental. *"I'll be right over."*

"Now?"

Of course, now. There's money to be made. "Yes. They want it done soon. There's some outside group threatening to crash our system. Better if we find the holes than if they do. You can help me, can't you?"

"Sure, now is fine. I'll postpone my other plans."

"Excellent. I knew I could count on you." Joseph paused for the effect. *"And August, this is a matter of internal security. If anyone learned of the potential weaknesses in the system..."*

"I understand, sir."

"Excellent. Good lad."

As he broke the connection, Joseph shook his head. When the day came for August to become a full partner in preserving the station's limited resources, Joseph's first order of business would be teaching the boy to recognize when he was being manipulated.

Grabbing a slip of paper and a pen, Joseph jotted down Calla's and Thomas' names then added other unnecessary members of Haidar Station to make the request seem less unusual. August wouldn't see the connections. Thomas and Calla would become an unusual coincidence.

After concentrating on the hallway outside August's apartment, Joseph appeared there and knocked on the door. The young man would never know that he had provided the information used to kill his own friend.

Thomas followed his host down a short flight of stairs to a wooden deck in front of a single door. Brachi produced a key from inside his tunic and unlocked the guest quarters. He ushered Thomas into the room. The space was the size of his entire apartment on the station. A large collection of red and orange pillows lay flat in one corner near the ankle-high pole that a sleeping Gotrian would perch on. Wooden chairs surrounded a chest-high table to the left of the door. Much of the right wall was an open window. A curtain fluttered in the wood-scented breeze. A door in the left wall led to a restroom much like any that would be found on the station.

Brachi set the key on the table. "This will be sufficient, I trust?"

Thomas put his suitcase down. "It's excellent, Brachi. Thank you."

"I rrecalled that your kind sleep horizontal." Brachi pointed to the pillow pile.

"That looks comfortable. I appreciate you making the arrangements."

He stood more erect and pounded his chest with his fist. "Will you be joining us for devotions?"

You remembered to arrange a bed but forgot the

loud argument you had with Stephanie about why we wouldn't join your devotions? "Thank you for the invitation, but my own religious beliefs forbid partaking in other ceremonies."

"Hmm. Unfortunate. Much wisdom could have been yours."

"Then the loss is mine."

"I'll come get you after morning devotions." Brachi turned away without further benedictions.

Thomas closed the door and walked over to the mass of pillows making up his bed. After a few minor adjustments, he stretched out on the squashy pile. The pallet was more comfortable than he had expected. Calla's bed, he supposed, wouldn't be half as nice. Olvians slept in pools, so anything she would be sleeping on would be even more makeshift than his pillow pile.

Calla! She'd had called for information earlier. Thomas sat up. He had forgotten all about her. By now, the crisis would have passed, but he had to know how bad the damage was so he could be ready to put out any fires tomorrow.

"Calla." When she didn't answer, he pushed his thoughts harder. *"Calla!"*

Did Syndromers have problems receiving telepathy, too? If that had been why she'd been so reluctant to split up, he would have to gripe at her tomorrow for not filling him in on the details again.

"Thomas?" Her thought voice sounded hardly more than a whisper.

He sensed a haze of fatigue in her mind. *"Were you asleep?"*

"Yeah. It'll be morning soon."

He looked at his watch. *"It's mid-afternoon back home."*

"True, but people don't just get sick or hurt during

normal business hours. On Haidar, doctors have learned to sleep when possible. What's wrong?" Now her voice was a touch louder and less fatigue-ridden.

How did she come up to speed so quickly? When someone woke him from a deep sleep, he needed some strong coffee to get going.

Thomas pressed his fingers against his temples. *"I'm having a hard time hearing you. Can you project louder?"*

"With my power level, this is as loud as it gets with us this far apart. I'm all but hollering now. It's that whole inverse square law thing."

Inverse square law? What was an—? Oh, whatever. He'd worry about that later.

Thomas shook his head and returned to the matter at hand. *"You called for me earlier while I was dealing with Brachi. I forgot all about it until now. What happened?"*

"The Olvians were worried that I let you make all our decisions. They demanded explanations."

Thomas drew a breath through his teeth. *"Sorry. I should've seen that coming and given you something to placate them."*

"It's all right. I don't know if I gave them a good answer, but Rana was happy with it. Pipien isn't satisfied, but Rana told her to drop it."

He relaxed and sat cross-legged. *"Can't be too bad, then. Let's hear it."*

Calla related the conversation to him in the most precise word-by-word details. She had to be making some of this stuff up, except that he felt no trace of deception in her mind. How could a Syndromer have committed a whole confrontation to memory with such accuracy?

However she managed it, her solution itself sounded

pretty reasonable, and she'd come up with it on her own. He might have taken a different approach, but hers had worked out well enough. If the Olvians wanted to think she was secretly telling him what to do, he didn't mind that one bit. At least professionally he didn't mind. Personally, he found it somewhere between offensive and amusing.

He lay back on the pile of pillows and stacked a couple fuzzy ones under his head. *"Anything else come up?"*

"No. They were awfully sleepy. Once they were happy with the way they think we operate, they dozed off for the rest of the trip back."

"Good. Don't forget to record the notes in the journal."

Her aggravation bled through the connection. *"But I just told you all about it. If these notebooks are supposed to give you information on what's going on in case something happens to me, then why do I need to record things both of us know?"*

Thomas glared in the direction of the Olvian city. *"It's standard procedure, Calla. Sometimes when rereading a record, patterns become more apparent."*

"Fine. I'll take care of it."

"How are the accommodations?" Thomas picked up a hint of a wry giggle.

"I feel like a giant. It's a good thing I'm not claustrophobic. I have to keep my head down and duck under door frames. My room is so small I can sit in the middle and touch two of the walls. I have a cot to sleep on, if I curl up on my side, and I'm glad I brought my jacket. It's pretty chilly here."

He looked around his comparatively extravagant quarters. *"Better you than me. If I can't stretch out, I can't sleep."*

"You would hate being here, then. So, what was your crisis about earlier?"

"Brachi gave me all the gory details on the current situation." He paused for a moment and dredged up the particulars. *"A disease they've never seen before is wiping out his people. Hey, what precautions do we need to take to keep from being a statistic in their body count?"*

"Nikk, I mean, Dr. Petrov assured me that our body chemistry is significantly different from theirs. We'll be fine. If we are exposed to some pathogen, I have a case full of different sorts of antibiotics and antivirals. We shouldn't need it, though. The geneticists who altered our ancestors hyped up our immune system while they were at it, so that it could take on biological agents."

"Okay, but your genetics are weird. Do I need to get you out of here before you catch something?"

"No. I have a couple recessive genes, like the way you have blue eyes and red hair. My immune system is unaffected, and actually, I'm more resistant to some chemicals than you are because of the PDS genes."

"No kidding?" Did he need a genetics lecture now?

"And there are—" She brought herself up short. *"Well, we can talk about genetic quirks and the effects of PDS some other time. The important part is our own bodies protect us."*

Thomas went to the window and looked in the direction of the Terran city. *"If Pharmacorp personnel can live here, whatever plagues there are must not affect the Terrans, either. Training new staff and paying off the families of the deceased would get pretty expensive after a while, and if they had a vaccine, it could've been adapted for Olvians and Gotrians, right?"*

"Possibly. That would depend on the agent responsible."

"All right. That's good to know." He returned to his makeshift bed. *"Well, this planet rotates every twenty hours, so morning will come awfully fast."*

"Good night."

"You're doing fine so far, Calla. See ya in the morning."

After tossing and turning on his pillows for a while, Thomas propped himself up on his elbows and reached outward again. *"Meiko?"*

"Hi, Thomas."

No joy colored her voice, but at least she wasn't yelling at him.

He projected sincere concern with his thoughts. *"How are you feeling?"*

"All right, I guess. Look. I'm sorry for the quip about Stephanie. That was a low shot."

"Yeah, but you're right. She'd spit blaster bolts to hear me talking like that. It's just—I—" He stopped and blew out a deep breath. *"Well, you know what happened."*

"But Calla wasn't even there. You can't hate everyone who has Power Deficit Syndrome because one guy was an idiot."

"I know, and I agree, but it's not that easy. Not when I can still see him gloating while I lay there with broken bones and blood everywhere and major psionic damage." He rubbed the puckered scar on the side of his head, hidden under his hair.

Her compassion washed over him. *"I understand."*

"I am trying."

"How are negotiations so far?"

He blew out a breath. *"Rough. The folks from the neutral party who offered us space keep trying to be helpful, but all they succeed in doing is starting fires for me to put out. It already degenerated into name calling* once."

"*Grand. Those people don't have to be there when the real discussions start, do they?*"

Thomas shook his head. "*No, thankfully.*"

"*Well, good. So, are you on a break right now?*"

He looked at the billowing curtain that flipped up enough to reveal the darkness. "*It's nighttime here.*"

"*Oh. Shouldn't you be sleeping?*"

"*I wanted to make sure you were okay. You were upset about something earlier, even before I spewed stupidity.*"

"*A doctor gave me news I didn't want.*"

He sat up and twisted toward Haidar. "*A doctor? What's going on?*"

"*Nothing,*" she thought too quickly. "*Nothing. I'm not sick or anything.*"

"*Then why were you crying?*"

"*Like I said, it wasn't what I wanted to hear.*"

There was more to it than that. He could tell that from the tone and the feel of her thoughts, but pushing for the answer would either upset her again or cause her to go annoyingly silent.

Thomas's brow furrowed. "*You'd tell me if it were something serious, right?*"

"*Yes, of course, I would. I'll fill you in when you get back.*"

"*I could come back for a little while now.*"

"*No, that's okay. Morning's going to come soon enough there. You need to catch at least some sleep.*"

True enough, but he wouldn't be sleeping much. "*All right. Take care, okay?*"

"*You, too. You're the one in a war zone.*"

"*I love you.*"

"*I love you, too.*"

Worries about Meiko's mysterious medical issues

and anxiety over the mission kept sleep at bay. Although he had been a part of dozens of arbitration teams, he had never been the one in charge. If he failed, the two races would keep right on fighting over something trivial until they wiped each other out. He wasn't ready to have such an uncomfortable weight on his shoulders.

The sun filtered in through the treetops to light the room a couple hours later. Thomas sighed and left his bed. He moved around, trying to shake the weariness as he got ready to go. In the distance, the Gotrians' morning chants in their temple high overhead filled the air like a weird bird chorus.

When Thomas was as ready to leave as he could be, he stretched out on the pillows to rest for a few minutes. Sometime later, a loud knock on the door jolted him awake. Heart pounding, he sat up and wiped the sleep from his eyes. That would have to be Brachi. Grabbing his notebook and pen, Thomas got up and went to the door. He still couldn't get over how much older Brachi looked from a few years before.

"Aren't you rready to go yet?" Brachi coughed.

Thomas looked down at his clothes. "Do you think I dress like this for bed?"

Brachi pursed his lips. "You do look like you haven't slept in a month."

He looked at his watch. "Oh, well, on Haidar right now, it's nighttime."

Brachi straightened his tunic. "You'll get used to the time change about the time you leave for home."

Thomas snorted. "That would be about the speed of things."

The city looked more interesting in daylight. Suspended walkways connected platforms to each other, and stairs and elevators provided the means to go between the different levels. Some of the platforms had pillars of woven branches holding up a roof, but no walls.

Within each of those pavilions, a silver-haired Gotrian sat on a dais surrounded by small children. There were no older kids, but Gotrians wouldn't be the first to employ their teenagers as sentries in the military or workers in factories to free up adults for combat duty.

Bulletin boards suspended above the walkways bore advertisements, assuming he correctly translated the smattering of their language he knew. Others looked like war propaganda.

How had the city looked been before the war? Now, large sections were cordoned off with brightly colored ropes. Some walkways had broken planks and ropes that appeared to have been burnt. Platforms carried the scars of fire and some walkways hung precariously from a single rope. The tree canopy had holes with blackened branches in the most unnatural places.

Someday, when the war was over and the diseases had been cured, he'd return and see the city in the trees restored to its full glory.

Brachi led Thomas across a few walkways to an elevator that took them to a higher platform where the planes were parked. As he climbed into their craft, Thomas' stomach growled. At least he had never been able to sleep on an empty stomach, and that could help him stay awake today.

On the way to Pharmacorp, Thomas managed to steer the conversation to harmless topics to give his mind a chance to come up to speed and throw off the fatigue. The drone of the engine threatening to lull him to sleep didn't help.

Calla stepped out of the chilly stonework bath and shivered. If the Olvians had a way to adjust the bathwater's temperature, she hadn't found it. Calla grabbed a thin, fuzzy sheet from the shelf near the pool and dried off. She wasn't a fan of cold baths, but at least any vestige of fatigue had fled down the drain with the water.

She snatched her clothes from the knee-high square rock that served for a table and dressed before she could shiver herself to pieces. She'd fastened the first button on her shirt when the door opened. Calla spun away from the door and reached out with her thoughts to identify the intruder.

Ever hear of knocking? Calla glanced back at the senior Olvian delegate in her red tabard. "Rana, I'm not dressed yet."

"Take your time. I'll wait." Rana closed the door from the inside.

Calla rolled her eyes. *We are both female, I suppose.* "Rana, among Haidarians, it's customary to let a person dress in privacy, unless you happen to be married."

"Married? You mean to have a mate permanent?"

"Yes, exactly."

"Oh, I do." Rana settled back on her haunches. "Well, that is, until he is old enough to undergo his metamorphosis."

Calla finished fastening her shirt and tucked it in. "I'm not married."

"Oh, well, that's okay. You're a negotiator like I am,

so among us, you and I have the same rank. I'm sure your people won't think you're presumptuous if I choose to treat you as my equal."

Calla smiled. She'd have to get up earlier from now on and make sure she was ready before she expected Rana. Calla grabbed her shoes and socks.

The door opened again, this time to admit Pipien in a mustard yellow tabard. The two Olvians spoke to one another in their native, gravelly language. Pipien turned a light gray and grunted something that could have been a laugh.

Uh-huh. Can't you guys find a harder target to laugh at?

As soon as she was ready to go, Calla piled everything back into her duffel bag. At least there was a lock on that, for whatever good that would do. Someone armed with a pair of scissors or a knife could bypass the lock.

She shrugged into her jacket and shouldered the backpack hiding her trauma kit. "Shall we?"

Rana and Pipien led the way out, loping along on two feet. Once out of the claustrophobe's nightmare, Calla arched her back and reached up toward the clouds. A couple joints popped, relieving the pent-up tension. She took a deep breath of the salty sea air.

A turquoise and gold, open-topped hovercraft waited for them. The whole contraption was hardly hip high. A driver occupied a front compartment, separated from the rear by a low wall. The back compartment was a meter-and-a-half square with plastic cushions scattered about. Calla stepped in over the side and sat with her back to the forward compartment. Rana and Pipien hopped over the side and squashed into their frog-like form facing Calla. Rana gave the driver instructions, and they set off across the surface of the artificial, floating city.

Rana tugged her brilliant red tabard down. "Would you like breakfast?"

Calla turned away from the scenery. "Sounds good, yes."

Pipien snorted. "I think we should take our breakfast to go and eat when we get there."

Rana darkened.

Calla furrowed her brow. "No, I won't allow that, Pipien. Brachi would take offense."

"So what if he does?" Pipien sat straighter.

"These are negotiations, Pipien. We all need to make an effort to get along."

Rana fluttered her wing-like arms. "We can't afford for these negotiations to fail. In two generations, there won't be any of us left! If you care that little about compromise and forging peace for the survival of our people, you can be excused from these meetings."

Pipien went light gray, mottled, and dark gray in rapid succession. "No! I have to be part of these talks!"

"Then put an end to your behavior male." Rana glared at her junior partner.

Pipien scrunched down into her cushion.

Rana paled. "It would be best, however, if we did have our breakfast packed for travel. We're running late."

Calla nodded. "We can eat on the way. I'd like to pick up something for Thomas, too. He'll have to sneak off somewhere to eat it, but I'm sure he can figure out something."

Pipien looked about to speak but stopped herself. The fierce heat of her anger had an undercurrent of fluttery fear.

The car stopped at a small building made of pitted bricks with crumbling mortar. The front door was no more than a tattered sheet hanging over an opening.

"Wait here. It will be quicker if I go in alone." Rana sprang over the top edge of the vehicle and frog-jumped into the shop.

Calla looked around while Pipien brooded.

Perhaps there were better parts of the town, but this area looked like Calla's vision of a recovering battlefield. Some buildings had been turned to rubble. Others had been damaged and patched, more than once in a couple cases. At the furthest edge of her vision, one building sported blackened bricks near each of the windows.

Hover car passengers and pedestrians passing them didn't make eye contact with anyone, but considering that terrestrial Olvians used hearing more than sight, that wasn't so odd.

The natives wore loose tabards on land, leaving most of their bodies visible. None of them had scars or missing limbs. Olvians didn't have regenerative powers, and they couldn't possibly escape these battles unscathed.

Were the wounded relieved of service and housed elsewhere? Ostracized? Killed, even? "Come back with your shield or on it" had been the motto of an ancient Terran culture, but that warrior mentality didn't fit what Calla knew of the Olvians. Perhaps she could ask Thomas later.

Rana returned bearing three bags made of some dark brown plant fiber and a clear, sealed, plastic bag. She handed one bag to Pipien, kept a second for herself, and offered Calla the rest. "The bag clear is for Thomas. I forgot to ask if you allow him to eat meat, so I assumed not."

Calla nodded and put Thomas' breakfast in the main pouch of her backpack, wedging the dense foam cup upright among the other contents. "I don't know if Thomas is a vegetarian or not, but I'm sure your choices will be fine." She pulled out her wallet. "I brought some local currency. What do I owe you?"

Rana turned obsidian. "You are our guest!"

Calla shrank back against the cushion in the same way Pipien had done when an apology was in order. Apparently, guests had privileges in this society.

Rana paled. "If ever I visit Haidar Station, then I will accept your hospitality."

Calla sat straighter. "I did not mean to offend."

"Of course not." She croaked at the driver, and they were underway again.

Calla opened her bag. What constituted breakfast for Olvians? Whatever it was had an odd, spicy odor. Best to eat now rather than in the sub while she did her impression of a pretzel. She didn't relish the cramped ride waiting for her, but she would feel much more comfortable with this part of the adventure when she could turn all the diplomacy back over to Thomas.

As the pilot landed in the vacant back half of Pharmacorp's parking lot, Thomas surveyed his surroundings in the clearer light of day and listened to the waves crashing against the pylons holding the platform up. No great architect had designed the box-like building, but some artistic soul had designed the colored glass pattern on the front. The stylized "PRx" with a ring around it matched the company's logo.

As he left the plane, the Olvian sub pulled into the other side of the parking lot. Calla and the Olvians piled out like clowns from a too-small car. Calla took a moment to stretch and then tucked her pale blue shirt back into her black pants. Rana and Pipien went inside, but Calla walked toward him and Brachi. Thomas had a sinking feeling something had gone horribly wrong.

He projected his thoughts. *"What is it? What's happened?"*

She shook her head. *"Nothing. At least, nothing serious."*

"Fill me in."

"Olvians have no locks on their doors, so I had an awkward moment when Rana walked in while I was dressing. Weird for me but it didn't bother her. Then Rana groused at Pipien for suggesting we all eat in front of Brachi to make him mad. Something's wrong with her. She doesn't seem at all interested in the success of these meetings but panicked when Rana suggested excusing her."

"Hmm. Definitely something to watch." Visions of Cordil IV exploded into his memory. *"Anything else?"*

She adjusted her backpack on her shoulder. *"Yeah. I caused offense when I offered to help pay for our breakfast."*

"Oh, okay. Guests never pay with them. It's the host's obligation to take care of everything the guest needs. That's minor in the grand scheme of things. Did everything work out well enough?"

"Rana grouched at me, but I'd seen Pipien scrunch up in the seat as something of an apology, so I mimicked her and Rana calmed down."

Thomas nodded once. *"Excellent observation. Occupying less space is the correct way to acknowledge fault."*

"On the matter of breakfast, I have a care package for you. Gotrians don't eat in the morning, as I'm sure you've rediscovered. I brought something for you so you don't starve between now and lunch. In the main section of my backpack, you'll find some interesting tea

and a bizarre veggie and leaf taco concoction. If you can get past what it looks like, the fish and veggie leaf taco Rana got for me wasn't half bad, but drink the tea first. Your job will be to find some creative way to have to take my backpack from me, then go somewhere away from Brachi. I'll stay with the delegates and try to keep the fisticuffs to a minimum."

Thomas smiled. His part would be easy. Surely, she could keep them from killing each other for a few minutes anyway.

"Good morning." Calla joined them. Her thoughts projected into his head. *"You look exhausted."*

"I am," Thomas thought then he said out loud, "Good morning."

Brachi stood toe to toe with Calla. "Did you think we couldn't find the building without your help?"

She frowned. "Do you find my company that unwelcome?"

He opened the space between them. "Not at all. I hope your stay with the Olvians wasn't too wet."

She stepped aside and gestured them on ahead of her. "Oh, a bit chilly but the accommodations weren't disagreeable."

Thomas took hold of her backpack's strap. After all, gentleman shouldn't leave a lady to carry something when his own hands were free. "Here, I'll get this for you."

"Keep it upright or your tea will spill." She lifted the pack off her shoulder and handed it over. "Thank you. It does get heavy after a while."

When they reached the Pharmacorp lobby, there was no sign of Patina and her bodyguard, so Thomas excused himself and went to the restroom. There he opened Calla's backpack and found his breakfast.

The spicy drink, packaged in the heavy foam cup,

brought tears to his eyes. The concoction might give him heartburn later, but the brew beat two cups of the strongest coffee he had ever tasted. He wouldn't have appreciated the drink if he hadn't been so tired.

A paper napkin held a spongy, brown leaf wrapped around what looked like dried, black and gray strips of unidentifiable plant. He didn't find it at all appetizing to look at, but he would have to trust Calla's assessment or go hungry, so he took a tentative bite out of it. The sweet, almost sugary leaf offset the more bitter taste of the chewy vegetables and thankfully put out the fire in his mouth. He rinsed out the cup in the sink and chased down all the dry food with a glass of water. He hurried in case Patina showed up and offered her "help" again.

Thomas arrived in the lobby on time. Patina stood near the steps facing Calla.

"So, has Pharmacorp been involved in the local affairs at all?" Calla stepped between the local delegations and Patina.

The Pharmacorp rep stuttered until she saw him. "Oh, Thomas, you're back. Let's get everyone to the conference room. Okay? This way, please."

She led everyone upstairs through a convoluted path of hallways to a room marked "Conference." A screen set into the wall showed that the Haidar Station had reserved the room for the day.

"Here you are." Patina unlocked the door and stepped back. "If you need anything, let us know."

"Thank you." Thomas smiled and shook Patina's hand, squelching a flinch as he crossed into and then out of the range of her anti-psionic device.

When he opened the door and looked into the room, he frowned. "Conference Room" was a generous name for this closet. A beat up, square table and a mismatched collection of chairs took up most of the space. There was no window, which wouldn't sit well with Brachi, who preferred large open spaces. Then, to be an equal annoyance to the Olvians, the room was too warm. Anyone with even a rudimentary olfactory sense would be offended by the musty smell.

Thomas turned to ask Patina if other rooms were available, but she had disappeared. If she hadn't been Terran, he would have sworn she could teleport. What they needed to discuss had to stay private, or else he would have pulled the chairs into the hallway or even moved the whole troupe back downstairs to the lobby.

"Pull the table out?" Calla walked past him and turned to examine the room. *"That would at least give us room to breathe. Or, you could get the meeting going while I go hunt down Patina and Kevin to see about other space."*

"That won't work. The Olvians would go ballistic because you wouldn't be there to guide me." He handed her the backpack. *"I'll get the table out of there. We can use part of our lunch break to find a better place."*

He flipped the table up on its side. A recent weld locked the rickety old table's hinges into place.

"How did they get this thing in here?" He compared the narrow door to the table's dimensions.

However they'd done it, he could undo the job with a minimum of fuss. Thomas focused his concentration and then summoned his powers. The microscopic conference room faded and reformed as the lobby. Leaving the table in this place would draw attention, and when they came to investigate, he would request a more appropriate room.

He reappeared in the center of the conference room. Calla stood on the side furthest from the door and directed the Olvians to one side and the Gotrian to the other while leaving the door side open. The delegates moved to their places, but none of them sat. Her frustration warbled in his mind. This wasn't her fault, though. Sometimes, full-grown delegates could act like two-year-olds.

Thomas sat with his back to the door to prevent any sudden departures. "I realize that the accommodations are far from perfect, but if you'll have a seat, ladies and gentleman, we'll get started. I'll check into other arrangements when we break for lunch."

Still, neither delegation made a move.

Calla met his gaze. *"Okay, so it wasn't just me."*

"No, they're posturing." Thomas pulled out his battered faux leather notebook and flipped open to the first blank page. *"Gotrians consider height to be an advantage, so in the absence of a tilted floor or dais, the last person standing is the most important. The Olvians know that."*

Calla opened a side pocket on her backpack and withdrew a small, cardboard-bound notepad. *"So they won't let a male stay standing after them, and Brachi will refuse to let someone younger than him continue to stand."*

"You got it." Thomas nodded and put the date on the top of the page.

"But earlier, Rana gave Pipien a dressing down about compromise."

Thomas shrugged and projected his thoughts back. *"The difference between theory and practice."*

"How do we resolve this impasse?" Calla jotted something on her notepad without looking at her hand.

"We don't. If we draw attention to it, they'll keep looking for ways to annoy each other. They'll hear and speak just as well standing or sitting. The Olvians will probably give in first." Thomas suppressed a sigh. Even that small of a reaction could be enough to keep them

egging each other on. "Calla and I were sent by the Magistrates of the Haidar Station at the request of your governments to help you resolve the problems that started this most recent war." By the time he finished, the Olvians had found a seat. *Uh-huh. Standing upright isn't too comfy on webbed feet, is it?* Once Brachi had settled in his seat, Thomas continued. "We received some background information related to the issue, but I would like to hear your perspectives. Brachi, what brought your people to war, and why do you now seek peace?"

Rana hopped from the chair and landed in the middle of the room, arms quivering at her sides to send the web membrane fluttering. "Intolerable! A male will not speak before me!"

Calla's thoughts came to him. *"And if you let Rana go first, Brachi would have been upset because he's the oldest."*

"Yep."

Turning to Calla, Rana drew herself up to full height. "Don't you want to hear the truth first?"

Thomas projected his thoughts. *"Get her to cooperate."*

Calla flipped her pen out of writing position and rested her chin on her hand and her elbow on the armrest of her chair. "If your words are true, they do not lose veracity in the order of their telling."

She had chosen more stilted language than he would have liked, but Thomas appreciated her cooperation. They could work on her word choices later.

Brachi's lips pursed as Rana turned blacker than Brachi's original fur color and returned to her seat.

"Oh, sure. Let the male decide what to do." Pipien harrumphed and flattened in her chair. "What an idea wonderful."

When Calla looked ready to answer the challenge, Thomas bit his lip. *"Let it go. Better to insult us than each other."*

Calla looked at him and nodded.

After waiting several seconds, Brachi began. "It is written in the Book of the Ancient. Before all else, there was the Universe, which has always been and will always be without beginning or ending. Naturally, with great age comes wisdom, and the Wisdom of the Universe is the Ancient. Like any other being, the Ancient seeks to elevate those like itself, and so the Book of the Ancient came into being to instruct us."

Thomas plastered on his well-practiced this-is-fascinating look. Brachi had given the same "In the beginning…" speech when Thomas had been here with Stephanie a handful of years ago. Had Thomas been in better spirits, maybe the account of the Gotrian creation myth would have been more interesting. As it was, even with the Olvian tea to help him out, Thomas fell closer to dreamland.

"Stay with me." Calla's pen wrote furiously as she took notes.

He projected his thoughts to her. *"You wouldn't happen to have intravenous coffee, would you?"*

"No, but if you let me farther into your head, I can make some temporary adjustments to keep you going for a while." She kept her eyes on her work. *"In a few hours, you'll feel like you haven't even seen food for a few days and you'll crash pretty hard tonight, but you'll stay awake for now."*

He considered the offer. A few hours from now would be lunch, and he had plenty of money with him if he wanted to get a large meal. With her help, he could keep from dozing off, and sleeping soundly tonight would be a real bonus, but her plan had a down side. He would have to let the Syndromer go far into his mind and change things. Then later, he supposed, he would have to let her in again to undo whatever shifts she had made.

She was a doctor. Letting her into his head shouldn't bother him, but even simple communication with Calla made him feel unclean. Anything more went way past his comfort level. As tempting as her offer was aside from that, he would have to find another way. He didn't need her help that badly.

"No thanks. I can do this."

9

Thomas had no sooner broken the connection with his partner when Pipien turned to Calla.

"Is the Gotrian's history skewed really all that important?" Pipien asked.

"How can you know where you are going if you don't know where you've been?" Brachi's fur bristled. "Even a child like you should know that."

Pipien raised her arms and fluttered the wing membranes. "But you're making this stuff up!"

Brachi bared his teeth. "It is all rrecorded in The Book, and every word is inspired by the Ancient."

"Which is something else you made up."

"You rridiculous little frog! How typical of the Olvians to send a child to do such an important task."

"You're just a male. What do you know?"

Thomas' eyes drifted closed then snapped open. The delegate situation had degenerated further by the time Thomas caught up to the exchange.

Calla's offer came back to mind. If he took her up on it, he might do better at his job, but he didn't like how she had to do the procedure. Meiko and his regular physician were the only two who had been so close to him outside of an emergency. Calla had been too inept to save Angela, and Thomas had no desire to give the Syndromer the chance to make the same sort of mistakes with him. Far better for him if he could keep her at arm's length.

He sighed. The glorified playground spat among the three locals wasn't going to burn itself out. Thomas put his fingers in the corners of his mouth and whistled. The loud, shrill tone echoed wonderfully in the room, and all attention returned to him.

He glared at both delegations before he spoke. "Rana, Pipien, you will have your chance to tell me anything you want later. Right now, it is Brachi's turn to speak, and I don't want another interruption from either of you."

When Rana looked at Calla, his partner ignored the delegate and nodded approvingly at him. In her mind, though, disappointment thrummed. Did she think she could do better? Maybe he should let her try. Then again, he supposed he should be grateful that she still hadn't challenged him publicly. This wasn't his finest hour.

He yawned and gestured for Brachi to continue, and the Gotrian picked up where he had left off as if nothing had happened. At some length, he caught up to recent history and gave a somewhat distorted view of Thomas' last trip here with his mentor.

Brachi played up the role the Gotrians had contributed to the solution while downplaying their part in the problem that had caused the whole mess in the first place.

Pipien turned to Calla again. "But that's not—"

A harsh hiss from Rana silenced her.

Thomas made notes about the differences between his memory and Brachi's story. The tale then outlined how the evil Olvians had restarted the fighting while the noble Gotrians resisted the temptation to go to war.

"Then, the plague began." Brachi drew a deep breath. "At first we thought we had made the Ancient angry. We had fallen from the true path described in the Book of the Ancient, but when we mended our ways, the plague continued. Before long, we rrealized that the Olvians were rreleasing this sickness on us."

Rana rose up straighter in her chair. "Preposterous!"

Calla held up her hand to stop the tirade. "Could you tell me more about the plague that's afflicting your people?"

Brachi drew his legs up and crouched in the chair. "I can tell you what I've seen, but I'm not a healer, so I don't know how useful my information would be."

"Anything will help." Calla flipped a page in her notebook.

"Children, who are weaker, of course, are worse afflicted. It begins with hair turning brittle and falling out. Then there is a terrible fever and boils. Nothing our healers can do will stop it. Even prayers and intercessions for the sick only slow it down. Eventually all who become ill die when they begin to bleed internally."

"Everyone?" Calla asked.

His eyes narrowed. "Yes, child, as I said, all."

She nodded.

Thomas projected his thoughts. *"Ignore it."*

"Ignore what?" Calla looked up from her notepad.

"You were just insulted." He glanced at Brachi.

"I was?" She followed his glance.

"'Child' is not a term of endearment in his culture. He thinks you're being ignorant by not taking his words at face value. He doesn't like that coming from someone younger than he is."

She scowled and returned her focus to the notepad. *"It's a valid question. Resistant individuals can go a long way toward helping find cures or vaccines."*

"I understand, but that's not your job, remember? You're a negotiator right now. He might react differently if he knew about your training. It doesn't bother me if you ask questions like that as long as they don't reveal your credentials, but be prepared to ignore

an insult." He continued out loud. "How long was it after the last treaty before problems started?"

Brachi drilled a hard look through Rana. "Well, barely a year had gone by when we found evidence that the Olvians were spying on us."

Thomas rubbed his tired eyes and leaned forward. "What kind of evidence?"

Brachi encompassed the room with a gesture. "At first it was just trash. At the base of our trees we would find food wrrappers and things of that sort. Then one of our patrols disappeared. We always knew the Olvians were rresponsible, but we couldn't prove it until after the war started and one of our liberation teams found the corpses of our missing people, or at least what was left of the bodies, at the bottom of the rreef near one of their cities."

Jumping to conclusions, Brachi. To counter that, Thomas needed a higher authority, someone older than Brachi. "Trash and dead bodies could be planted easily enough. Stephanie Davilla taught me that the obvious answer often hid the more insidious truth."

Brachi turned his gaze to the floor and fidgeted with the fur tufts on his wrist. "Wise counsel, yes, but who else could it be?"

That was a reasonable question, but Thomas didn't have the answer. On his last mission to Cordil, other factions had caused all sorts of trouble. Could this be more of the same? Politicians often rose to power on war rhetoric and fell when peace returned. On the other hand, a subversive group might want the war to continue so they could have a sanctioned excuse for murder or even genocide.

"Are there any groups within your people who were not satisfied with the last treaty or who might prefer war for whatever reason?" he asked.

Brachi shrugged. "There are always such dissenters, but even they have had members stricken with the plague."

Rana fidgeted and harrumphed while Pipien sat with her eyes closed. They'd been patient enough. Thomas had to give them the floor soon.

"Okay. If you could have every whim of your heart, what would it take for you to stop the fighting?" Thomas wrote "They want…" on his notebook and underlined it.

Brachi drew himself up straighter. "The plague must stop, and the Olvians must be punished for unleashing it on us. The prisoners they have must be rreleased. The wardens of the prisons must be held accountable for starving all those poor souls. We want rrestitution."

Calla finished a line of writing. "Let's say someone besides the Olvians is responsible for the plague."

Brachi tensed. Fur bristled.

Thomas nodded. Her brain must have been going in the same direction as his. He'd been about to ask the same thing. Was she reaching into his mind? No, of course, not. Even if she were that rude, she'd never be able to enter his mind without him knowing.

"Rridiculous!" Brachi slammed his fist into the arm of the chair.

Thomas exchanged a look with her then pivoted his chair toward Brachi. "Hypothetical question. What if the Olvians aren't responsible? Then what would you need to end the fighting?"

Brachi shook his head and considered his response. "Then the offending party, whoever that is, must pay for their crimes."

"That's fair." Thomas drew a line across his paper and dated a new page. "Rana, thank you for your patience. As I promised, I'll hear whatever you wish to tell me."

Rana nodded, blinking her large eyes, and turning the light gray of amusement before looking at Calla and addressing her.

Calla's thoughts came to him. *"Uh, Thomas?"*

"I can still hear her. Let her go on."

Rana jostled Pipien who startled and opened her eyes. "First of all, as all truly intelligent beings know, the Goddess created the universe then made the first life on Great Sister, who shares orbit with this lesser and younger Ologo."

"Blasphemous frog," Brachi said under his breath.

Thomas shot the Gotrian a disapproving look that convicted his own conscience as well. How was Brachi's insult any worse than calling Calla "Syndromer?" If one was wrong, the other was, too.

Rana threw a hard look at Brachi. "That aside, there is no proof that we ever sent patrols into Gotrian territory. We were perfectly happy to honor the treaty Stephanie helped us secure."

"Stephanie Davilla, you inconsiderate lout," Brachi whispered.

Thomas' weary mind wandered again. Rana went on refuting everything Brachi had said.

For longer than Brachi had spoken, she continued railing about how untrustworthy the Gotrians were as a whole. For as much as she talked, she didn't say anything useful, which didn't do much to help Thomas stay awake. Even Brachi's barely audible but creative racial slurs against the other delegation didn't help.

Thomas scratched his scalp above his ear and pushed his thoughts to Calla. *"Could you wake me up when she's done with the propaganda?"*

A smile flickered across Calla's face. He supposed he shouldn't be surprised to find her unsympathetic. She had offered to solve the problem for him, but he had turned her down flat. He had chosen his course, and now she intended to make him face the consequence, and he couldn't blame her for that.

Finally, when Thomas was moments away from requesting that the meeting be postponed a couple hours for him to sleep and then find some potent coffee, Rana left the diatribe behind and started her own account of the last few years.

Just like Brachi, she had her own sequence of the last treaty negotiation, although she hadn't even been there. Thomas made notes about her departures from the facts before she then went on to tell about the vicious Gotrians' attempts to lure the peaceful Olvians into war again.

Brachi continued to mutter insults and protests barely loud enough for Thomas to hear if he focused on it.

"Then, when they couldn't beat us, they came after us with a disease." Rana quivered and returned to her seat. "I don't know much about the disease, but do you want to know what I can tell you?"

Calla looked up from her notes. "Yes, please."

"The plague only affects the males of our race. Ones who are ready to do their metamorphosis don't. Those who've begun, stall mid-change. They grow lethargic. This illness foul creates lesions on their skin that will not heal. In time, the loss of blood kills them." Her black eyes shimmered with excess fluid.

Thomas looked from Rana to Calla. *"Y'know, I don't think I've ever seen a male Olvian."*

"Unless you go swimming, you won't." Calla finished writing and flipped her pen around her fingers. *"Only females are amphibious. The males are much smaller, and they don't even look like they could be the same species. There's—"*

Thomas interrupted her. *"Race."*

Stephanie had drilled that into his head every single time he'd made that mistake. Some people took major offense to such a simple word slip. If Calla made that mistake out loud, they could have real trouble.

"What?" Calla's brow furrowed.

"Species is for animals and plants, not sentients. Race is for sentients." Thomas pointed at the two delegations with the back of his pen.

"Oh. Okay. There's even some debate in the medical community about whether or not the males are really sentient."

That was all very interesting but not relevant to the current situation. Why did she bother him with trivia?

"Have you been able to isolate the agent causing this disease?" Calla stopped flipping her pen and prepared to write.

Thomas kept his head toward his paper and looked up at Calla. *"Careful. You sound like a scientist when you talk that way."*

Her thoughts came back to him. *"I'm sorry. Old habits."*

Rana turned her chair toward Calla. "No. We even went to Pharmacorp for help, and they weren't able to find anything, either."

Thomas yawned and covered his mouth with the back of his hand. "You mentioned that Gotrians tried to goad you into war. How did that happen?"

"We had some of our people vanish only to show up dead in the swamps at low-tide, including a few males who had suffocated because they couldn't breathe air. Some sections dry of our cities were flooded when they bombed us, and we found a couple soldiers dead Gotrian with breathing devices faulty." Rana pointed at Brachi. "Unlike him, we have proof that they murdered our people to provoke a war. We demand that they pay for the damage they have done to us. We want the treaty to include stipulations that they be forbidden to enter our territory without an escort. Finally, they've abducted and tortured many of our citizens, and we want them back."

"I understand. Pipien, you haven't said much." *Lately.* "Is there anything you wish to add?"

Pipien drew a deep breath. "Yes. My sister oldest was involved in the group who came to Pharmacorp for help. She told me that Pharmacorp had said that they had recently helped the Gotrians set up a lab which could have been used to produce some virus or bacteria that would wipe us out."

"Of course we have a medical lab." Brachi growled and bared his teeth. "How else could we try to figure out what you're doing to us?"

Pipien turned jet black. "We didn't do anything!"

Thomas scowled. "Stop!"

Rana and Pipien turned to Calla in unison. Calla scowled at the younger Olvian for the outburst.

Thomas looked around for a clock and resorted to his watch when he didn't find one. How had three hours passed so quickly? Brachi and Rana must have droned on for over an hour apiece. He didn't care. The hour gave him a valid reason to end this meeting before he did something more stupid than losing his temper. Lunch provided the perfect excuse.

"I think that's enough for one morning." He flipped his notebook closed. "Let's take a break for lunch and meet back here in an hour and a half."

Brachi took a timepiece out of his steel gray tunic. "That will leave us only an hour to meet before I must leave for afternoon prayers."

Pipien snorted. "Miraculous you get anything done."

Brachi's eyes narrowed. "At least I have my priorities

straight."

"That won't be a problem," Thomas said as Pipien started another sarcastic retort. "I'll see you back here."

He stood and gestured to the door. Once he and Calla remained, Thomas dropped into his chair. When he leaned back to stretch, the chair went back much farther than he had expected and showed no signs of stopping. He flailed with his arms to try to regain his balance, but Calla's firm hold on his wrist kept the chair from pitching him onto his head. With her help, he righted himself again. She had a wicked grip.

"That was graceful." He rubbed his wrist.

"Why don't you stay here and sleep?" Calla tossed her jacket to him. "You can use that for your pillow if you wish. I'll go find Patina and see about better space for the negotiations."

Thomas nodded. "That would be great. Thank you."

Her smile belied the hard edge in her thoughts. "I'll be back to get you for lunch in a little while."

As he stretched out on the floor, she turned off the light and closed the door behind her.

Calla clenched her jaw and closed the door more gently than she'd like to. She had offered Thomas the opportunity to be more alert, but he had declined. With his fatigue weakening his natural mental shields, the reason behind his refusal had blared at her.

If his reluctance to accept her help had been because he didn't want to deal with the side effects, which could be pretty obnoxious, she would have understood and respected his reasoning. He had instead decided against her offer because the thought of mental contact with her disgusted him. He only tolerated basic communication because of the necessity for their job.

All she had wanted to do was help him. They both needed him to stay awake. If he chose to think she had cooties like a grade school child, she could do little about his attitude, but his crippling fatigue left her with doing most of his job and hers, which wouldn't have been so bad if she'd had more than a vague guess about what to do.

If he had been more awake, maybe the morning would have gone better than it had. On the other hand, she had never been on one of these trips, so maybe all the useless bickering was normal, but his own explosions of temper could not possibly be in keeping with good arbitration protocols.

Surely, the nap would do him some favors. If he had missed something from this morning, the meticulous notes she had taken would help him come back up to speed without offending him with her PDS-derived eidetic memory.

She didn't need all the reminders. Only the information about the diseases held any real interest for her. Since she had been concentrating on those parts of the conversation, she still recalled the entire discussion word for word, gesture for gesture, all the way down to the whispered insults from Brachi and the subtle color changes in the Olvians.

For the moment, she had other concerns. Patina had offered to help if they needed her, but their liaison had neglected to mention where to find her. Calla went down the hallway until she found a receptionist seated behind a large, half-circular counter. She leaned on the counter and waited to be acknowledged, but a couple minutes passed.

Calla tapped her fingernail on the blue Formica counter a couple times. "Excuse me."

"Yes?" The receptionist kept sorting through her papers. "What is it?"

"I'm looking for Patina Faulks." Calla leaned closer. "Could you help me find her?"

She buried her head further into her paperwork. "I need to stay here."

Calla smiled. "That's fine. Could you tell me where she is?"

"I'm not her secretary, so she doesn't tell me where she'll be."

Calla rubbed her forehead. "Okay. I understand. Where is her office? Maybe her secretary can help me."

The woman looked up at the ceiling. "What floor is she on? Sixth? No, that was only until they needed that floor for the executives. Fifth? No, she moved again when the fifth floor was needed for corporate lodging. Third. I'm pretty sure she's probably on the third floor, unless she had to move somewhere else when the building was reorganized."

Are you sure? It wouldn't possibly be the roof of the building down the street that can only be reached by parachutes during a total eclipse or maybe the fifth sub-basement level where they keep all the left-handed, glow-in-the-dark monkeys? "Third floor. Thank you. I'll try that."

Calla took the elevator upstairs. When she reached the third floor, she walked up to the man sitting behind another blue receptionist's counter.

The man typed information into the console. She gave him a couple minutes to reach a fair stopping place, but he kept going.

Calla leaned on the counter. "Pardon me. Might I ask you a question?"

The man continued typing. "One moment, please."

That moment turned into a few minutes while the man kept right on typing. He reached a section break but blazed past it into the next part of the manuscript.

Rudeness is a prerequisite for receptionists here, I take it. "I won't take but a moment of your time."

The man stayed glued to his keyboard. "One moment, please."

Calla drummed her fingers on the counter and waited. *At this rate, our whole lunch break will pass before I get an answer.* "Could you please tell me where I could find Patina Faulks or Kevin Lithos?"

He didn't even look up. "There's no one here by that name."

"Are you sure? I'm Calla Geisman from Haidar Station. Ms. Faulks is our liaison with Pharmacorp."

"There's no Patina Faulks or Kevin Lithos here."

She glared at the bald spot on the back of the aggravating man's head. "I saw them this morning. Might they be on another floor or in a different department?"

"There's no one who works here by that name," he said again.

"Thanks anyway."

Calla shook her head. *It's a conspiracy, a Waste Calla's Time conspiracy.* Well, she'd have to change the rules on them.

Technically, she should be able to find anyone she wanted in the complex by relying on her telepathy. Mr. Zagruder hadn't taught her how to do a search yet, but the process seemed intuitive enough.

She sat in a chair in the receptionist's waiting area. Leaning her forehead on her fingertips, she dropped her mind's defenses. The cacophony of voices in her head rose to intolerable levels, making her skull pound like a rail gun being discharged. Gritting her teeth, she shut everyone out again.

She couldn't do it. Although Calla dealt with mental noise of all sorts on a normal basis, she couldn't handle the intense conglomeration of voices. How did other telepaths deal with so much unbearable ruckus when they used their powers to hunt for someone?

Sighing, she considered her options. If she continued the merry hunt for Patina, receptionists and other people she might ask could continue to direct her everywhere but where she needed to go. Going door to door would take too long, and she could miss her quarry altogether. She could even go back to Thomas and say that looking for Patina had come up blank.

That would be about the norm for this trip. Nothing had gone quite like it should have, so he couldn't blame her for the problem, but he probably would. Thomas already thought of her as a failure, and her inability to track down one woman would lend proof to his belief. If she were ever going to show him that she could be trusted, she would have to start here.

Calla took a deep breath and lowered her mental defenses again. As the voices crowded around her and the rail gun started in on her skull, she held her breath and eliminated the ones that didn't match her search criteria.

First, she blocked all non-Terrans in the immediate area, but that didn't do much to help. Then she shut out all the male voices, which turned out to be the lion's share of them. At least the volume of all the women's voices didn't make her feel like she would go mentally deaf.

Reaching her thoughts to each one, Calla confirmed that the voice didn't match the one she needed and shut it out. Not quite halfway through the group, Calla found

Patina and blocked all others.

Calla pushed her thoughts outward. *"Patina."*

She felt the woman jump and sensed a surge of fear.

"Don't be afraid. It's me, Calla. I won't hurt you. I need to talk to you. Can we meet somewhere?" She readied herself to hear the other woman's thoughts.

"I'm really kind of busy right now." Patina's thoughts echoed as she spoke them aloud.

"It's important, and I'm sure it won't take more than a minute or two of your time."

"I really can't."

The telltale feel of a lie blared at Calla. No, Patina could meet. She just didn't want to, which amounted to the same thing in practical terms.

"That won't be a problem. I'll ask you this way." Calla felt Patina's apprehension spike. *"Thomas and I are concerned about the conference room we've been assigned to. It's not large enough for the whole group, and the temperature is too warm for the Olvians, but we can't find the thermostat. Is there somewhere else we can move to?"*

"No," Patina said too quickly. *"I'm afraid that's the only space we have. All of our other conference rooms are taken for other meetings. Now I do have to go."*

"All right, thank you." Calla broke the connection.

That couldn't be the end of her quest. She had promised her partner that she would find other arrangements, and she intended to do exactly that.

Pharmacorp couldn't be the only non-native establishment here. Reaching out with her thoughts again, Calla eliminated everyone in the building and all non-Terrans. That left a collection of thoughts nearby. Could that be a town to support the men and women who worked here? There would be shops and restaurants nearby. One of those would have a party room they could borrow for a day or two.

After looking at her watch to confirm that she still had time to do this, Calla got up and left the building, walking as quickly as she could without breaking into a run.

10

Calla looked at her watch again as she entered the Pharmacorp building. She was about out of time, but if she were quick, she could wake Thomas and both of them could grab some lunch. After she hit the up button for the elevator, a couple minutes passed before one showed up. It never failed. When she needed to hurry, technology would slow her down.

When she reached the right room, Calla eased the door open. Thomas lay stretched out on the floor, snoring lightly.

Resisting the urge to flip on the lights, Calla crouched next to him and touched his shoulder. "Thomas."

He inhaled sharply as he rolled onto his side. "Yeah?"

"We have just enough time to hit the cafeteria downstairs and wolf down something before they get back."

His eyes glowed brilliantly in the dark room. "How much time do we have?"

"About a quarter of an hour."

"You let me sleep too long." Groaning, Thomas sat up and stretched.

"That couldn't be helped. I had a very exciting time, and I just got back." She grabbed her jacket and slid it on. "I'll tell you about it while we eat."

He nodded and got to his feet. She grabbed her backpack and led him to the stairs. The exercise would help wake him up, and the stairs would be faster than the terminally slow elevator.

Thomas rubbed the grit from his eyes. "Ever find Patina?"

"Yes, plus or minus some hide and seek." She ran her hand along the banister. "There's no other available space for us to meet."

Thomas scowled. "Do you mean to tell me that every other possible place in the building is in use?"

Calla glanced at Thomas. "That's what she says. She's lying, but that's what she says."

Thomas yawned. "Just once, I'd like a mission where everything works the way the textbook says it's supposed to."

"I do have some good news. Starting day after tomorrow, I found another place in a nearby restaurant." She pointed her thumb in the direction of the nearby town. "It's a private room we can use, but it's reserved for tomorrow. With some fussing and fidgeting, I convinced them not to charge us rent if our food bill exceeds their usual fee for the room. If not, we'll have to pay the difference. With five of us eating at least twice, that shouldn't be a problem. When I checked the menu, I found stuff that would be agreeable to everyone's dietary needs, too."

He nodded. "Good job. I'm impressed. Really."

Maybe now he would start considering her as more than extra baggage on this trip, but that might be wishful thinking after one minor victory.

They reached the ground floor at the same time the elevator did. A group of people exited and headed right. Calla followed the group through the glass doors marked "CAFETERIA." Thomas gestured her on ahead of him.

The cafeteria filled half the ground floor. Windows forming two of the walls lit the place up with sunlight. Real wood tables were scattered around the room with groupings of four or six chairs around them. Stone tile floor and bare furnishings created an echoing collage of voices. She expected the smell of deep fryers and potatoes, standard fare in most institutional food, but she could only get an overpowering stench of tree-scented cleaning products.

Calla led Thomas to the end of a line that snaked around through a maze of cords.

She scowled. *What are the chances of getting to the front before we run out of time?* "So, this morning seemed like a mess. Did anything useful get accomplished?"

Thomas spun toward her. *"Shh. Too many ears around. I hate to say it, but I think some group of Gotrians with a grudge started it and the Olvians retaliated."*

"Really? Is it likely they could both come up with the same bug?"

"What do you mean? They're reporting different symptoms."

Calla smiled. *"I'll let you be the arbitrator. Please let me be the doctor. The symptoms are different because their physiologies and anatomies are different. I'll have to check in the comparative anatomy text and the information Nikk gave me again, but I'm pretty sure they're both getting hit by the same virus or bacteria."*

"You brought your medical books?" He looked at her backpack. *"On an electronic notebook?"*

"No, nothing like that. Expensive doing it that way, and I'm still paying off med school debts. I studied up on Olvian and Gotrian physiology before we left. I have to hunt down those parts of my memory again and reread everything."

Thomas' eyes went wide. *"You remember everything you see?"*

Calla shook her head. *"Not exactly. I have to concentrate on stuff for it to be recorded with that kind of detail. It's a Power Deficit Syndrome feature. How else do you think I could be the second youngest in the history of the station to get medical pins?"*

He nodded and shuffled ahead as the line moved. *"That makes sense, I guess. So that'd be why you were irritated when I told you to keep notes."*

"Um-hm."

"I had no idea Syndromers had perfect recall."

She glared at him for a moment. He'd been using the term so long he'd likely forgotten the implied slur. For the moment, she was happy enough he'd acknowledged his ignorance. *"PDS is not all bad news, but there are many times when I'd like to lose it and be normal."*

Such as, every time someone called her a foul name because of the genetic oddity. She looked ahead in the line. They'd covered about half the distance in the few minutes they'd been waiting. There might actually be time for them to eat.

Thomas ushered her on ahead as the line moved. *"What do you need to prove that the same thing is waylaying Gotrians and Olvians?"*

"In an ideal world, I would need to examine people who have been hit by the disease and run a battery of medical tests." The lists of the procedures and tests she'd perform started building in her mind. She dismissed the information. Direct observation wouldn't be an option.

Thomas snickered. *"That would blow your cover. What's the next best thing?"*

In lieu of seeing someone, she could talk to the doctors who had treated the people, but again, she'd never be able to hide that she was too knowledgeable for a layperson. The information she needed was too technical. There had to be some way for her to get some information without revealing her credentials.

"Some medical records. Very short of perfect but it'll have to do. We could say that we're going to take them to an expert for analysis."

He nodded. *"Sounds good."*

They reached the counter. Pre-prepared foods were lined up on shelves.

Calla picked up a tray and selected a turkey sandwich from the display. *"If we find out that it's the same germ, that means someone is doing it to them."*

Thomas picked out his own sandwich. *"Or it means that one of them developed it for use on the other, and it got away from them."*

"Maybe." She frowned and shook her head. *"So, what's on the agenda for this afternoon?"*

He picked up a sealed container of chocolate pudding and a plastic spoon. *"Oh, more ridiculous arguments and name-calling. I'm going to try harder not to let them irritate me. I'll ask them for information we need to find out who or what is killing them off. I also want to know who the Olvians and Gotrians dealt with when they came to Pharmacorp for help. That should pretty much do it for the hour, then you and I get to do some digging for the rest of the day."*

They arrived at the cash register, manned by a scrawny Terran woman with stringy hair tied back in a ponytail. Her full-length apron had a lifetime of stains.

Calla opened the front pocket of her backpack and fished around for her wallet.

Thomas shook his head and pulled out a money clip. "You brought breakfast. I'll get lunch."

He was actually being nice to her?

Calla smiled. "Thank you."

The cashier punched a few icons on her screen. "That'll be fifteen Pharbucks for the both of you."

Thomas leaned closer. "Fifteen what?"

"Pharbucks. You get them in your paycheck."

Thomas shook his head. "Oh, well, we don't work here. We're here from Haidar for the Ologo peace talks. I have Haidarian, Gotrian, and Olvian currency as well as standard credit, so how does that work out?"

"It doesn't. Check with your liaison for the currency exchange." The cashier set both their trays aside and directed them away. "Next please!"

Calla stepped past Thomas. "And you can't make an exception for us? We can leave the money with you to show our good faith, then go get the exchange from Patina and bring back Pharbucks."

"No. That won't work. If you don't have the right money, I can't help you. Next!"

Calla didn't move. "What would it hurt if—"

The cashier stood and glared. "Do I have to call security?"

Thomas scowled. "No. Thanks a lot." He gestured to the door with a nod. "We don't have enough time to go out somewhere. I don't suppose you have more care packages."

Calla shook her head. "I'm afraid not, but I do have something else that'll do in a pinch."

She led him to a table and opened one of the smaller side-pockets of her backpack. The emergency ration bars she carried were bland and had a weird texture she didn't appreciate, but they would keep her and Thomas going for the rest of the day.

The foil-wrapped bars were so tightly packed in there that when she pulled one out, the other two came flying with it. She didn't remember having so much trouble getting them in her backpack, but then her trauma kit had been empty at the time. Now medicine cases filled in the bottom of the backpack.

Thomas frowned. "Hmm. Tasty. Nutrient-flavored cardboard."

"Not my first choice either but it'll beat listening to our stomachs rumble." She offered him the one with the red wrapper. "This one has enough caffeine to keep you on your toes for a little while anyway."

She kept a second for herself and put the last back in the same pouch it came out of. They ate on the way back up to the conference closet and finished as Rana and Pipien arrived.

Rana loped into the room. "Any luck finding a place better?"

Thomas smiled and gestured for Rana to take her seat. "Let's wait for Brachi before we get started."

She looked at Calla. "I assume we're still going to start here because that's where we all knew to return. Surely Patina had somewhere else we could go."

Calla frowned and draped her jacket over the back of her chair. *"I'm getting tired of her pretending you're not here."*

"That's the nature of this world, Calla. You're going to have to deal with her."

Calla set her backpack next to her chair. "We'll wait for Brachi to get here."

When Brachi came in, Calla was treated to another standoff as both delegations refused to be the first to sit down.

She looked at both delegations and then at Thomas. *"Not again."*

Thomas nodded. *"Yep."*

"Don't they realize how silly they look?"

"Nope." He pulled out his journal and a pen.

Thomas opened his journal to the marked page. "Okay, I'm glad we all made it back. I have some good news and some bad news. The bad news is Patina tells us that all other meeting rooms here are taken."

Pipien croaked, blackened, and flopped into her seat. Calla tensed, ready to spring if the chair dumped the Olvian over like Thomas' had done, but nothing happened. Rana and Brachi continued their stalemate.

"And the good news?" Brachi asked, issuing his query hack at the end.

Thomas glanced back toward the nearby town. "Starting day after tomorrow, we have a room in a restaurant nearby, and tomorrow we'll be busy, so we won't be here much."

Pipien scrunched up into her smallest form. "I don't want to stay here. The room is too hot."

"Ah, poor baby frog," Brachi muttered almost too low for Calla to hear.

"It's only for an hour." Rana reached over and stroked between Pipien's eyes.

"We'll meet here the morning after next then go over to the new site so no one gets lost." Thomas jotted something in his notebook. "Now, on to other business. Calla and I spent some time considering what you told us this morning, and we have some theories about—"

"What do you need with theories?" Rana turned black and her eyes narrowed. "We told you we have proof!"

Thomas pointed to both delegations with the end of his pen. "All either of you have is indirect proof. Everything you mentioned, including corpses, could have been put there by another party for you to find. We need more information from you to prove or disprove that."

"Isn't the matter clear to you?" Rana whirled toward Calla. "They're trying to wipe us out by striking at the males weak, defenseless. Some ailment they planned to let loose on us probably got out of their control, and now it's running rampant through their own people. I wouldn't be surprised if they tested these things on their own first!"

Calla shifted in her seat but didn't have a chance to answer the challenge.

"The Ancient forbids killing one's own kind!" Brachi drew himself up to his full height and stood in his chair. "It is wrritten in the Book—"

"—Book of the Ancient. So you say. Then you admit to infecting our people." Rana hopped into the middle of the room. "Don't you see, Calla? They trap themselves in their own lies. What more could you need?"

Thomas' thoughts came to Calla. *They'll never hear me. You'll have to insist that they play nice.*

Calla sighed and shook her head. "Rana, if your claims are indeed backed with appropriate proof, then the information we're requesting will support you that much more. If you have misinterpreted the data, then it is possible that the Gotrians didn't do it, and I know you wouldn't want to see the innocent punished."

Rana harrumphed. "Gotrians? Innocent? This is insane!"

Thomas blew out a deep breath. "Everything will become clear in time. You'll have to trust us for now. I'm not asking for much. Please sit down, and at least listen to the sort of information we need from you."

Rana turned to Thomas, her quivering wing-like arms raising from her body a little. Her fury pelted Calla's mind like fistfuls of rocks. She would merrily take Thomas' head off, literally if she could. Thomas rose to the challenge and indicated her chair with his hand.

Instead of sitting, Rana lowered her arms and hopped toward Calla. "We are not satisfied with that creature's handling of the situation, Calla. We demand that you take over the negotiations."

In no way would Calla take on that mantle. Medical crises she could handle. Diplomatic ones were too far out of her training.

Calla shook her head. "No. Thomas has my complete trust. I agree with his request and with the questions he has for you. As I told you, we communicate frequently. I'm afraid you'll have to accept that I would not change his approach to this problem. We agreed on it before he presented it to you."

Pipien bolted upright. "You are nothing but the puppet of that man!"

"That's a pretty serious insult." Thomas scowled and glared at the younger Olvian. *"Don't let that go unchallenged."*

Calla ignored Pipien and looked instead at Thomas. *"I thought we were to ignore insults leveled in our direction."*

"They've lost confidence in both of us. That's big enough to end the negotiations. The only way to get us back on track is to answer and reestablish authority."

"Fine by me. Mind if I do something somewhat undiplomatic?"

He cocked an eyebrow. *"I don't think I'd go quite that far."*

"I won't, but I think I know how to get them to stop ignoring you." Calla stood and drew a deep breath.

Thomas watched Calla stand in slow motion. In such a small room, she dwarfed all of them, and he was only a few centimeters shorter. The Olvians, who barely came up to her chest when standing upright, flushed the dark gray of fear as she came closer to them. His partner's face was a mask of contained outrage and frustration, which from what he could sense wasn't entirely faked.

He projected his thoughts to her. *"Hey, I'm all for leaving them guessing, but I need more details."*

She kept her harsh stare on the Olvians. *"Earlier this morning, Rana said these negotiations are critical or the race will die out within two generations. If the Gotrians are also losing their juveniles, then they're likely in similar straits. I'm going to suggest we go home. The Olvians think I make all the executive decisions. They'll have to play nice to convince me to stay."*

Her plan could backfire in the worst possible way. The Olvians might agree to let him and Calla leave. Pipien at least, had made no secret of her displeasure about these meetings. If Calla were right, however, she could shock them all into being more cooperative.

What other choice did he have? Turning control over to her and coaching her from behind the scenes would please Rana and disgust Brachi who would refuse to work with the younger telepath. Brachi would play the professional for now, but as soon as something turned against his wishes, he'd raise his hackles, just like Rana had. They'd be right back in this same mess again and face the same choices.

Thomas sat on the edge of his seat. *"Go for it."*

"I am no one's puppet." The staccato cadence of her words conveyed more anger than yelling could have. "I'm not his and certainly not yours. That's going to work to your disadvantage right now, because I've had it with your childish behavior." She turned to him. "Thomas, these people are not ready for peace. We should leave."

Brachi's mane and the tufts on his wrists and ankles bristled as he leaned forward.

Rana sat up straighter. "What? You can't be serious!"

Pipien paled to match the off-white walls. Ending negotiations would make her happy, would it? Why?

Calla towered over the Olvians like a Terran drill sergeant getting ready to brace a recruit. "Oh, but I am very serious."

"Fine. Then leave," Pipien said.

Rana silenced her partner with an angry stare.

"I think I can pull this together." Thomas projected his thoughts to Calla. *"Don't make it too easy for me."*

"I'm not so sure it's worth the effort." Calla stepped into the middle of the room and gestured to Brachi. "We have this one muttering racial slurs under his breath and these two," she indicated the Olvians with a sweep of her other hand, "who come running to me when you say something they don't want to hear. I have informed them that the negotiations are in your very capable hands and told them several different ways that I have total confidence in your ability, but they still act like you don't exist."

Rana sputtered through several syllables. "But he's male!"

Calla spun toward Rana. "Yes, he is. While among your people, that's a debilitating condition, among mine, it isn't. If you were serious about peace, all three of you would show more effort to reach a consensus. Instead, you hurl insults and baseless accusations when you should be seeking truth. Thomas, they're not ready to do this yet. When they are, we can come back, but until then, our time is better spent elsewhere. There are dozens of other hotspots where our work would be appreciated."

Brachi hopped down from his chair. "Show wisdom. We need your help. Our people are dying."

Rana sat and fluttered her arms. "Don't you care that our races are about to go extinct?"

"Of course I do, but you apparently do not." Calla closed her notebook and stuffed it in her backpack. *"Are you going to contradict me, or are we going home?"*

Thomas nodded. *"Wait for it. Don't give in right away."*

As both delegations looked on in stunned silence, Calla picked up her jacket and trauma kit and let the tense silence hang a little longer.

He drew a deep breath. "Calla, I'm sure I can do this."

She heaved a sigh and shook her head. "You're wasting our time and theirs. They each came with their own agendas, and even the two parts of the Olvian delegation can't agree on what it is they want. If they really—"

He held up his hand to pause her. "The mission is mine, and you're just here to help me."

She put her things down again and sat, crossing her arms over her chest. "You're right. It's your decision, but you have my opinion, and if you fail to pull it together, I'll make sure it's clear in our report to the Magistrates. You know what they'll do."

"I'll take that chance."

Brachi's fur flattened out as he relaxed, and Rana

went pale while Pipien became much darker.

"Did you notice Pipien?" Calla thought.

Thomas ran his fingers through his hair. *"Yes, but I'm not sure if she wants this meeting to end or the whole thing."*

She kept her eyes fixed on him. *"I vote for the latter, and I think you might have something with that faction theory of yours."*

Thomas nodded. *"Maybe. Good bluff, by the way."*

"You think I was bluffing?"

Except for the mild humor he read in her thoughts, he would have thought she meant that.

Brachi settled into his own seat.

Rana crouched in her chair, angling her back to Calla. "What information do you need from us?"

"You did it." Thomas pushed his thoughts to Calla. *"You realize, though, that they're going to bend your ear later and try to convince you that you made the right decision in letting me do this."*

She rolled her eyes. *"Oh, wonderful."*

Thomas smiled. "First, I need to have more information about your mutual charges of abuse of the prisoners of war. I'd like to take a tour of two typical facilities, tomorrow if possible."

Brachi struck his chest with his fist. "I can have that arranged for you by tomorrow morning."

Pipien straightened in her chair. "Since we have nothing to hide and, therefore, nothing to arrange, I'm certain you can tour our main facility tomorrow as well."

The two delegates glared at each other, and Calla threw Thomas an I-told-you-so look. Brachi looked first at Calla then Thomas and quickly schooled his grimace.

Thomas noted the arrangement for the tours. "Rana, if you could set up that meeting for the afternoon, we can avoid interfering with Gotrian customs, and I can still have the chance to verify that the prisoners are well cared for."

She adjusted her red tabard. "Very well."

"Brachi, would you be available after your mid-afternoon devotions to discuss our findings?" Thomas looked up from his notebook. "Say, an hour before sunset. What we have to do shouldn't take long."

The Gotrian nodded once.

"Will that work for you, too, Rana?"

She darkened for a moment and then returned to a neutral color. "Yes, of course."

"Excellent." Thomas smiled and sat back in his chair. "In addition, to address the issue of the diseases, we need some of the medical records for those who have gotten the plague."

Pipien sat upright. "Half of those things stupid are in code. We don't have time to get someone to translate them. How will you read them? Have you ever seen shorthand medical?"

Thomas leaned back in his chair. "No, I haven't, but if necessary, we'll take them to a neutral expert to decipher."

"How many?" Brachi asked, ending with a cough.

"Calla, what do you need?" Thomas looked across the room at her. *"Remember they may have to scramble to get them and you don't have a lot of time to read a million charts."*

Calla nodded and looked up from her notes. *"Five will do. It's not good for a statistical study, but it should give me a clue, provided they don't select odd cases."*

"Let's go for five of the most typical ones." Thomas glanced at both delegations. "I'll also need to know who you contacted when you came to Pharmacorp for help, and if possible, the date of the first outbreak."

"Thomas, you implied earlier that neither of our

peoples is rresponsible for these plagues." He made a wide gesture with both arms. "Whom do you suspect?"

Thomas winced and tapped his notebook with his pen. "I don't know yet."

Rana looked back at Calla. "Surely you have some idea."

Thomas shook his head. "I don't know anything for certain yet, and I don't want to lay blame unfairly. As soon as I have something more substantial than a hunch, I'll let you know. There are still too many ways this can go."

"Anything else we can help you with?" Brachi asked, hacking again.

"If you can get it, some information on organized groups within your people who stand to benefit from continued hostilities." Thomas stared up at the far corner of the room for a moment and thought about other avenues. "That should do it for now."

There was a light knock on the door.

Patina peeked in. "Sounds like I got here just in time. We'd like to invite you all to a reception tomorrow evening."

The idea sounded as interesting as sorting dust particles, but that was probably his uneasiness around crowds. "That sounds wonderful. What time?"

"How about tomorrow evening at sunset?" She opened the door wider and leaned on the door frame. "The invitation is open to anyone in your governments, of course."

"Thank you." Brachi nodded once. "We will attend."

Rana blinked slowly. "As will we."

Patina clapped her hands once and interlaced her fingers. "Excellent. If you'll excuse me, I have a lot to do."

Then she speed-walked down the hall.

"Are you sure she doesn't teleport?" Calla thought.

Thomas smiled and projected his thoughts back to her. *"At this point, I'm not sure of anything."* Then he said aloud, "Brachi, I'll get Calla tomorrow morning so we can go on that tour, and Rana, I'll meet you and Pipien here tomorrow after lunch."

"Are you coming back with me now?" Brachi asked with a loud huff.

Thomas shook his head. "I'll teleport back later. Right now, Calla and I have some work to do."

Once the delegates had left, Thomas sat down, carefully this time to keep the chair from introducing him to the floor head first.

"So, now what?" Calla closed her notebook and put it away.

"We go ask people some questions." Thomas stood and yawned.

She smirked. "Good luck there. I couldn't even get someone to tell me where to find Patina."

"You just don't know who and how to ask."

Calla rolled over on the cot in the Olvian guest quarters. She clutched the blanket around her and sighed. A moment later, the alarm in her watch beeped. She yawned and pressed the button to stop the irritating noise. Calla stretched as much as the tight space would allow and took a chilly bath before dressing in brown pants and a tan and brown floral print blouse.

Thomas' thoughts reached her. *"Calla."*

She startled. *"I'm here."*

"Are you ready?"

She nodded. *"Yes. Remember to duck."*

A few seconds later, the power surge of an incoming teleport heralded her partner's arrival.

Thomas appeared and reflexively hunched over in the claustrophobic room. "I thought you were kidding about the cramped quarters. How can you stand it in here?

"By spending most of my time sitting."

He snorted and set a small bag on the low table near the wall. "I made a quick trip home for breakfast. I hope an egg sandwich is okay."

She nodded and sat at the table. "Thanks. How are you feeling today?"

He talked through a yawn. "Better but I sure could've used another few hours to sleep. The shorter day rotation is an interesting challenge."

"I know what you mean. Rana was here until the wee hours bending my ear."

Thomas pulled out two wrapped sandwiches and handed one to her. "About yesterday's ultimatum?"

"Umhm." She unwrapped her sandwich and took a bite of salty egg and bread. "I think she's okay for now."

Calla speculated on their plans for the day. Would they find nothing but the rumors of problems? Just another excuse to continue killing each other? Would the accusations of the ambassadors prove true? Was each side harming the prisoners of war to spite the enemy? Was this some elaborate trap to snare her and Thomas?

She'd dismissed that last as foolishness. Who needed a complicated plan to get her and Thomas? They weren't keeping a secret of where they were and neither of them were armed for mortal combat.

"What are you anticipating we'll find today?" She took another bite of the sandwich.

Thomas swallowed. "I'm hoping I can prove all the

claims groundless, but I think there's legitimate reason for concern."

Did he realize that he'd cut her out of the mission with his words? An oversight, she hoped, so she didn't push the matter. "How can we prove the claims are groundless if there's legitimate cause for concern?"

"Well, the rumors and accusations had to come from somewhere." Thomas took another bite and talked around his food. "They don't often mysteriously appear on their own."

She leaned toward him. "Both delegations could be lying."

"Yeah, but not necessarily." He pointed at her with his breakfast. "You shouldn't cloud your mind with preconceptions. We'll find out what's happening when we get there."

"Do you think the prisoners are suffering because of their captors' ignorance or because of malicious intent?" She popped the last bite of her sandwich into her mouth.

He sighed. "I don't know, Calla. Telepathy doesn't include precognitive abilities. We'll have to see what we find."

Taking a cue from his tone, she crumpled the wrapper and dropped it in the trash bin near the wall, then left him to eat in peace. She sat on the cot.

Thomas finished. He stood and dusted crumbs off his gray pants and maroon shirt and then threw his breakfast trash away. "Do you have everything you need?"

Calla slipped her backpack over her shoulder. "I'm as ready as I'll ever be." *I don't suppose we can get there without teleporting.*

When Thomas touched her arm, the mass of whirling color brought on a wave of nausea. Calla sagged to the floor, clutching her abdomen.

"You've still got a few minutes." Thomas tentatively patted her shoulder.

She nodded.

The feeling faded while a couple minutes ticked by. As Calla stood, she looked around the room, four, maybe even five times larger than her own. Instead of a cot made from a rough canvas suspended between support poles, his bed consisted of a soft pile of pillows. A large curtained window let in muted sunlight.

She took in the whole room with a sweep of her hand. "Next time, you get to stay with the Olvians."

He shook his head and sat in one of the chairs at the table. "There won't be a next time."

She went to the window. "You didn't say that last time you were here, did you?"

"Well, actually, yes, I did, but their numbers are dropping too low. Either we find a way to stop this war and cure the plague, or they'll kill each other off. If the plague doesn't kill them first, that is."

She hadn't paid much attention to the chanting in the background until the eerie music gave way to the relative silence of chirping bugs and birds.

"He'll be here in a couple minutes." Thomas ducked into the bathroom.

Calla stretched again, now that she had the space to do a proper job of it.

Thomas came out of the bathroom an instant before there was a hard knock at the door. Calla adjusted her pack and watched a flock of birds zip by the cloth-covered opening.

"Haven't you gotten Calla already?" Brachi asked with a cough.

"Don't you see her standing there?" Thomas asked.

Calla turned toward them and found herself only a couple of centimeters from the Gotrian. Only through a supreme force of will did she avoid opening the space between them. Thomas would have gone supernova if she had.

"How is it you haven't drowned over there?" Brachi asked.

She frowned. *Can't even say "good morning" without insulting them?* "What, are you wishing I would?"

Brachi pursed his lips. "Hardly, I'm just amazed. Come. There is much to see."

Following along behind, Calla looked around at more of the of the treetop city. Gotrians with fur in different natural shades crossed rope-and-plank bridges or swung hand to hand along ropes.

For all the marks of battle Calla saw borne by the city itself, the people showed more. Terrible scars devoid of the thick fur anklets and bracelets peeked out from the edges of tunics and pants. Some Gotrians limped on their way, many with canes or crutches. More than a few were amputees, and none of them had the prosthetics that would have made their burden easier to bear.

As they moved through the city, sharp pain, jittery fear, hot anger, and fierce hatred shrieked through her mind. She winced and rubbed her temples before she slammed her mental defenses shut to dim the ruckus.

She looked at the people. There hadn't been such brutal scars and handicaps among the Olvians. Was their medical technology better? She'd forgotten to ask Thomas, and now didn't seem to be a good time.

The creaking boards under her feet drew her attention. How safe were the walkways here? She looked over the edge of the platform. No nets and Gotrians were running at top speed across ropes without hanging on to anything.

Thomas' thoughts intruded on her musings. *"Come*

on, Calla. This isn't the time for sightseeing."

Staring at the back of his head, she jogged to join them again and forced her brain to focus on the matter at hand.

"—taking you to our only facility." Brachi pointed toward the ground in the distance. "We even built it close to the ground to scare the little frogs less."

Calla projected her thoughts. *"I'm not buying that. Wouldn't they build the prison close to the ground because height denotes importance?"*

Thomas glanced at her and nodded. *"A two-for-one deal, I'm sure, but not relevant for our purposes."*

They rode an open-sided elevator to the bottom of its shaft then went across two more wobbly bridges and descended in another car ending at a small platform. Looking over the edge, Calla smiled when she saw Brachi's definition of "close to the ground" still meant some ten meters up. Connected to the small landing was a much larger collection of buildings suspended from the trees. Only a single pair of ropes, one high, one low, joined the distant buildings to the elevator landing. The ropes ran through pulleys on each side. The wood on the far side bore scuff marks as if something attached there. Two steel loops were mounted below the floor.

"I suppose I'll have to teleport Calla and me across." Thomas ran his fingers through his hair. "I'm not sure about her, but my balance isn't up for walking across on the ropes."

"There's a bridge." Calla pointed to the pulleys. "Retracted, I'm assuming. It runs on the cable and pulleys, doesn't it?"

Brachi's blue, hooded tunic rippled in the breeze. "Yes, just so."

He sauntered back to the nearest tree and pressed a button. Calla heard and felt the rumble of a motor under the deck as the pulley played out the rope. A meter-wide bridge crossed the gap. Once locked into place on the other side, the squeal of metal sliding on metal down both sides of the boards made her grit her teeth until the clank of the rods in their support rings signaled the way was safe.

"Stay near me." Brachi stepped onto the bridge and looked back at them. "We have some dangerous troublemakers in our establishment."

Thomas nodded and gestured for their host to lead the way. When they reached the other side, Brachi flashed an ID and barked a countersign to the guard to get them through the razor wire topped gate.

"If you're carrying any weapons, you'll have to leave them here." Brachi gestured to Calla's backpack. "That will have to stay, too."

She pushed her thoughts to Thomas. *"I can't leave this behind. If they open it, they'll find out that I'm not a negotiator."*

Thomas frowned and scratched over his left ear. *"Why did you bring that along anyway?"*

"I have nowhere to lock it up."

"Your room, maybe?"

"Olvians don't believe in door locks, remember?"

"Oh, yeah, forgot about that. Well, I need you with me to give me a medical assessment of any prisoners we happen to see," Thomas thought. Then he said aloud, "Brachi, Calla is carrying a lot of sensitive information. She's legally required to keep it with her or secure it somehow."

Brachi scowled and spoke to the nearest guard in a jumbled mess of grunts, barks, and whistles. "There are lockers. He'll take you to them. We'll wait here."

Calla followed the guard down a maze of halls bordered by offices to a room lined with lockers. A few had open padlocks hanging from them. After locking her trauma kit in one of them, Calla pocketed the key. Was there a master or a duplicate? Even if she had the only key, lockpicks or bolt cutters would make short work of such an easy lock. She couldn't do anything about it now.

When she rejoined Brachi and Thomas, a tan-uniformed Gotrian with silvering brown fur waited with them.

Brachi gestured to the newcomer. "This is the warden. He'll lead the tour. I can communicate between you as needed."

The first building they entered had a harsh, burnt smell to it. Calla's mind sorted through earlier experiences and identified charcoaled rice as the nearest scent. She'd gotten a whiff of that acrid smell five years ago. The night before an exam, she'd gotten dinner going then went back to studying. The smoke alarms had gone off before she remembered to check the stove. Even the apartment fire hadn't matched this.

The Warden grumbled then launched off into some sort of explanation.

Once the Warden finished, Brachi turned to Thomas. "Pardon the smell. The Olvians assigned to cooking duty are often lazy, and they burn their food because they spend all their time in idle gossip. This is, of course, the cafeteria. We provide meals for the prisoners at midday and sunset. We are in accordance with EToP protocols."

"EToP?" Calla thought.

"Ethical Treatment of Prisoners." Thomas walked further into the room and looked around. *"You don't watch the news much, do you? EToP and GATBAC were huge a few years ago."*

"A few years ago, I was still finishing up med school and taking a double course load. Eidetic memory was essential for such an ugly schedule, but I still didn't have

time to breathe."

While Thomas asked about the sorts of foods available, Calla took a deep breath to see if she could identify any other odors, but burnt grain overrode everything else. Then she took a slow look around the hall and estimated that some four hundred to five hundred could be seated along the low tables.

She turned toward Brachi and waited for a break in the conversation. "How many prisoners do you have?"

Brachi conferred with the warden. "Not quite seven hundred."

She glanced around again to confirm her last guess. "So they eat in shifts?"

Brachi got the answer from Warden and shook his head. "That would be chaos. There is room."

Calla projected her thoughts. *"If they're cozy, maybe. You'd think rioting might become an issue."*

Thomas nodded. *"Yeah, you'd think, but where would they go? I don't think Olvians are graceful enough on land to cross those ropes and I didn't see any buttons on this side to extend the bridge."*

The workshop they went to next buzzed with the noise of Olvians hard at work sewing. Noise from all the machines echoing off the bare walls made Brachi's voice indistinguishable, so Calla looked at the workers and their conditions.

Each wore a blindingly bright yellow tabard. Many sported a dark skin tone for their unhappiness, especially after they looked up long enough to see the tour group.

Although Calla had problems reading their body language beyond that, the fear and despair in their minds threatened to bury her. She blocked those perceptions as well as she could, but her efforts were far from perfect.

No matter how much she wanted to help these poor

beings, Thomas would never allow it. They were here not to rescue prisoners from harsh conditions but to assess the problems and verify the accusations. She hadn't seen any signs of the physical abuse Rana claimed, but then the visit had just started.

Calla followed the Warden out to the relative silence of the walkway.

Brachi looked over his shoulder while he walked. "There are similar facilities for laundry and gardening. This prison strives to be self-sufficient, which helps prevent boredom and rrestlessness in the prisoners."

"And what's the average workday?" Thomas asked.

"A total of ten hours."

A little long perhaps but then Calla could honestly say she often worked ten to twelve hours a day herself between her daily medical duties, classes, and emergency calls.

When they reached the barracks, Calla raised an eyebrow and smiled. Not a dust particle was out of place. Her mother must have given them cleaning tips, but did anyone actually live in such severe sterility? There were two rows of cots with folded sheets on the end, not unlike what Calla slept on last night. Didn't Olvians sleep underwater?

An armed guard hovered over a dark gray Olvian female waiting quietly. Did she have a simple case of nerves? Had she and the others been threatened if they said or did anything to raise suspicions?

Brachi paused inside the door. "We arranged for you to speak with one of the prisoners. I'll translate for you."

Thomas gestured her on ahead of him. *"You'd better handle the interview. She'll be more open with you."*

She raised an eyebrow. *"With the guard and the warden here?"*

"She'll trust you more than me. Talking to a male may make her shut down."

Calla nodded and projected her thoughts. *"Fair enough. Aside from questions about her well-being and the conditions, anything I should ask?"*

"If I come up with anything, I'll tell you."

She walked forward with Brachi close behind. *"Should I suggest using telepathy to do this?"*

"Because..." Thomas followed.

"Her answers may lose something in the translation, deliberately or otherwise." She looked back at him.

He grinned as his thoughts came back to her. *"Possible but you'd offend Brachi. He knows from the last visit that telepaths can pick up on such deceptions. He tried it on Stephanie, and she embarrassed him horribly for it. You concentrate on talking to the prisoner. I'll keep an eye out for intentional misrepresentations."*

Could she draw out the information they needed? Although she conducted interviews several times a day, they always had to deal with diagnosing injuries and illnesses. Hopefully the experience would transfer, but what they needed would include more than general health issues.

Calla suppressed a sigh. Best to start with what she knew and go from there. Thomas would redirect her if necessary, she hoped.

She sat cross-legged in front of Olvian. A discontented grumble came from behind her, and she cast a glance back at the Warden's scowl.

She pushed her thoughts to Thomas. *"Now what?"*

"You gave up your height advantage," Thomas thought.

Calla rolled her eyes. *"What do they expect me to do?*

I'm the tallest one here, and Olvians aren't capable of looking straight up. I'm not going to talk to her back."

"I agree. Just don't expect Brachi to join you."

"I have no problem with that."

The female furtively peeked up at Calla but wouldn't keep eye contact.

Calla turned to Brachi. "Please tell her who I am and why I'm here."

"No, not like that. Talk to her, not to Brachi. He'll make the appropriate translation," Thomas thought while Brachi spoke.

Calla squinted up at Thomas *"What good is that going to do? She can't even understand me."*

"I know it feels weird, but that's how it's done. You'll get used to it after a while. Besides, you'll get a more accurate representation of your words to her that way."

"'I'm pleased to meet you,'" Brachi translated.

"And your name?" Calla asked.

Brachi chuckled. "Not pronounceable by your people or mine for that matter."

"We wouldn't even hear all the sounds," Thomas said.

Calla nodded. "I understand. Are you well?"

"Avoid questions that can be answered with one word," Thomas thought.

"'As well as could be hoped,'" Brachi replied.

Calla leaned her elbows on her knees. "Tell me about conditions here."

"Better," Thomas thought.

While Brachi spoke to the female, Calla gauged the prisoner's health.

The Olvian's skin had been scratched raw in a few places and her wrists were bruised. Calla reviewed her memories of the tour so far and noticed there had been several other Olvians with scraped up patches of skin and injured wrists. She looked again at the one in front of her. Some of the skin was flaking, which explained the scrapes and scratches. Amphibians could spend time out of water, but they couldn't stay out indefinitely. At least this prisoner wasn't getting enough time to be thoroughly wet and her skin was drying out.

Behind her, Calla sensed Thomas reaching outward with his thoughts. Then shock and revulsion came from him an instant before he withdrew into himself.

She twisted around. *"What is it?"*

"Not now," he thought.

"I cannot complain," the Olvian said through her translator before Calla could press him further.

"Y'know, if we keep getting these short non-answers, we're not going to learn much of anything," Calla thought.

Thomas shrugged. *"You said it yourself. She's intimidated. What she won't say tells me more than what she will. Keep trying."*

Calla nodded. "What happened to your wrists?"

The prisoner tugged at her bright yellow tabard. "I was punished for my disobedience."

"Don't pursue that," Thomas thought.

Calla looked back at him over her shoulder. *"Why? This might lead to proof of Rana's claim."*

"I already have the answer about where those injuries came from and going farther will either endanger her or cause her to go silent to protect herself. Neither situation would help us."

Her eyes narrowed. *"What's going on? What aren't you telling me?"*

"Later."

"Thomas—"

He held his hand up to stop her. *"For now, trust me and don't open yourself up to mental reception if you can avoid it. Concentrate on the interview."*

How did he expect her to do her part if he continued to hold important data from her? How could she put the puzzle together with huge pieces missing? Calla made a mental note to be sure she got the details later, but for the moment, she considered her next question.

She turned back to the prisoner. "How long do you get to stay submerged?"

The Olvian absently scratched a raw spot on her arm. "For an hour, twice a week."

Calla frowned at Brachi. "Two hours a week, for an amphibian sp—" She caught herself. "Race?" *"Not nearly long enough, Thomas."*

Thomas' thoughts returned to her. *"I'm not surprised."*

"Although, at times, it's better to stay out," the Olvian said.

With all the open wounds, hopping in the water for a swim would really sting. Calla winced.

The warden spoke briefly.

Brachi nodded. "She needs to rreturn to her work soon."

"Okay." Calla projected her thoughts to Thomas. *"Anything else?"*

"I have the information I need," he thought.

She wished she did, but Calla had to end the interview and fell back on her experience. A slight mutation to the question she often used to end her appointments would bring their discussion to a close in a safe way.

"Is there anything you want to ask me?"

For the first time since their arrival, the Olvian's color muted slightly toward light gray, and she looked into Calla's face. "Will the war end soon? Can I go home?"

"Don't promise what we can't guarantee we'll deliver," Thomas thought.

Calla smiled. "We're working on a treaty, and I am hopeful the matter of these camps will be addressed in the agreement. Thank you for meeting with me. You've been very helpful."

She rose and returned to Thomas' side as the guard herded the prisoner out.

"Where to next?" Thomas asked.

Brachi gestured to the door on the far side of the barracks. "The pool and then you will have seen something of everything here."

Calla followed along past gardens patrolled by armed guards and worked by a couple Olvians each. Except for that one workshop, no one seemed to be anywhere for there being some seven hundred in residence. Where was everyone?

As they walked, the few Olvians they saw refused to look up at her. Every one of them had bruises and scratches, some inflamed and needing care they weren't getting.

Calla increased the length of her stride and came even with Brachi. "What do you do if one of the prisoners falls ill?"

Brachi waved a dismissive hand. "We haven't seen an outbreak of plague."

Calla shook her head. "Obviously not. Rana said only males are affected, but there are other sorts of illnesses and injuries."

Brachi scratched his head. "If necessary, we would bring in a physician, naturally."

Oh? How close to dead would someone need to be to meet the definition of "necessary" in your protocols?

The pool, a meter deep if that, had only one prisoner scuttling around under the murky water. The smell of decaying leaves rising from the pond wrinkled Calla's nose.

"There are often many more here," Brachi said. "Today's the day for the work detail to do their weekly cleaning, which always kicks up more debris from the bottom before they get the job done."

Although ocean water could hardly be considered clean, the pool would go stagnant between the visitors. Rather than a pond, the Olvians had a perfect breeding ground for some sorts of insects and quite a few kinds of bacteria and mold. Calla frowned. The earlier comment about going for a swim being unwise at times took on a brand new significance.

Brachi gestured for them to continue along the walkway.

Calla regarded the jailers with a growing dislike. With Thomas keeping secrets from her, he didn't rank too highly on her favorite people list, either. Hadn't he been the one to insist they had to be open with information?

She drifted back to walk closer Thomas. *"All right, enough is enough. I don't appreciate being kept out of the loop. I'm here to lend my expertise, but you aren't even giving me the whole picture to work from."*

He flinched. *"I didn't want to distract you with too much information."*

She turned and glared at him then projected her thoughts. *"Too much information? Do you have any idea who you're dealing with? Never mind. In any case, the tour is over for any practical purpose, so what did you discover earlier?"*

He drew a deep breath between his teeth. *"As nearly as I can tell, a public flogging."*

She stopped, and he bumped into her.

He righted himself and gestured her on ahead.

"Come on. We have to keep up. We can't let on that we know."

She continued after their hosts and drilled a hard look through them. *"They're pretty brave doing that with us here."*

"That's how they handle their own justice."

Calla shook her head then sent her thoughts to him. *"Well, that explains why we haven't seen anywhere close to several hundred. Everyone's where that farce they call justice is being meted out."*

"Yep, with just enough around the rest of the camp to make it look like business as usual. They showed us this small part so we would assume that the rest of the prisoners were in other areas."

She shook her head. *"Unbelievable."*

"Be careful, now. You have to stay neutral."

"How am I supposed to do that, knowing what they're doing?"

He shrugged and thought, *"You have to withhold your judgment until we see the other side. The Olvians may not be any better."*

She looked sideways at him. *"That doesn't make this right."*

His feelings of reassurance washed over her. *"No, it doesn't, and I agree with you, but it's much more humane than some things I've seen in my travels, and we don't have the power to make them stop."*

Calla frowned and projected to him. *"Then what are we doing here—other than ensuring our consciences won't be letting us get any sleep tonight?"*

"Gathering information. If they won't end this, we can present a case to those who do have the power to do something about it."

She sighed and rubbed her forehead. *"Going to a higher authority will take too long."*

"Perhaps, but the two of us, even on our best day, could save only a few, and then the rest would suffer much more in retaliation. We would destroy any chance of ending this war and freeing them all. We're not done here. We're just not ready to act."

She didn't appreciate his answer, but he did have a point. She had no intention of letting him forget what they'd found. Years would pass before the memories faded from her own mind, if they ever did. Hopefully, the Olvian prison wouldn't generate more nightmares.

13

Thomas climbed out of the Olvian sub, grateful for the chance to work out the kinks his body had developed during the half-hour he'd spent tied up like a knot. Had he known the ride would be so unpleasant, he would have requested a picture of the place and teleported. Calla groaned as she likewise loosened up.

Pipien harrumphed and dragged herself out of the sub, grumbling something in her own language.

Rana hopped out and sat back on her haunches. "I hope the ride wasn't too uncomfortable."

Thomas shook out his arms. "We'll be okay, but we'll teleport back."

Calla snickered. *"Equally disagreeable to me in either case."*

Thomas smiled lopsidedly. *"Oh, I don't know. I teleport us, and you feel sick for a couple minutes. If you ride in the sub, you get cramped up for half an hour then spend a few minutes remembering how to move."*

As Rana led them away, Calla smiled at him briefly and then frowned. *"I'm going to have to take the lead on this, aren't I?"*

He gestured her ahead of him. *"We'll see. If Rana does the guiding, she'll probably deal with me because of your ultimatum yesterday. Play it by ear for now."*

They left the docks through the only corridor and came to a huge metal door with a garish red X. A speaker mounted nearby issued a constant, raspy hiss.

Rana stopped in front of Calla and blocked the way. "Don't touch, or you'll get a shock."

She dropped into her smaller, crouched form and pressed an intercom switch. After she spoke for a few moments to someone further removed, the door popped open with a loud click and swung back.

"Follow me." Rana hopped through the door.

Pipien followed, grumbling the whole way. "This is a waste of time. Their accusations are all lies."

Calla's eyes narrowed. "Well, then we should be able to confirm your assertions quickly and be on our way."

As soon as he'd crossed through, the door closed itself with a mechanical whine and locked in place with a loud click. Thomas jumped.

Calla glanced at him. *"It is a little creepy, isn't it?"*

Thomas nodded and tried to gauge her feelings. A blank wall. Hardly surprising. After what he'd discovered at the Gotrian's prison, he had half a mind to protect himself, too. One of them, though, needed to be primed to pick up those sensations again. His greater powers made him the logical choice, and her Syndromer mind might not be able to handle all the input.

All the same, he kept his telepathy on a tighter rein than usual. The memory of the Olvian victim's pain and terror echoed in his thoughts.

After signing in with the gate guard, Rana and Pipien took them first to the barracks, which weren't all that interesting. Ankle-high poles ran the length of the walls. Spaced about every two or three meters, a thin blanket and a small box waited. Not a soul occupied the place.

Calla walked further into the room. *"At least this one looks like someone lives here."* Then out loud, she said, "Where is everyone?"

Rana waved a hand toward the door. "They're working. We would rather keep them busy than make them sit and be bored all the time. No one would like that. We'll go to the work area after we visit the cafeteria."

Pipien led the way down a corridor and through a door low enough Thomas had to duck. The huge dining hall looked like an unadorned quarter-circle with a door in one face and no windows. The decoration, if it could be called that, consisted of stripes painted on the floor at one-meter intervals.

"We used to offer three meals a day, but when we noticed no one partaking of the first, we stopped that one." Rana hopped to the middle of the room and rose to her full height. "They get their trays and sit in their lines to eat before returning either to their work or to their barracks."

She took them through a door and into the kitchen. Five Gotrians worked on cleaning the dirty dishes while they softly sang a strangely familiar song. They didn't even pause long enough to look up. Calla walked closer to the Gotrians. Rana drew a breath.

"You be careful." Thomas stepped between Calla and Rana. "How many prisoners do you have here?"

As one of the Gotrians walked toward Pipien, she shot up to her feet. "About five hundred."

Rana darkened. "It was closer to six hundred, but there was an outbreak of plague last month. We quarantined all those affected, but we could do no more than try to make them comfortable before they died."

"We offered to send them home to see their families, but they refused." Pipien waved a dismissive hand.

Thomas nodded and looked at Calla, still milling around the Gotrians. "Probably afraid of carrying the plague there."

Calla stopped near the stove and stirred a huge pot. "You cook dinner this far in advance and leave it cold?" She ladled out a spoonful of grayish-brown glop and dumped it back into the pot.

Rana croaked and turned a couple shades darker. "No, that was part of their lunch."

Pipien darkened. "They're so finicky!"

"How so?" Thomas asked.

"We make bread and something else for their meals." Rana harrumphed and threw open a pantry containing stacks of crusty bread. "The first day or two they eat everything, but then they have only the bread until the menu changes."

Calla turned away from the stove. "So what do you do with all the leftovers?"

"Package and distribute it for our homeless and poor." Pipien glared at the prisoners. "At least they deserve it."

Rana closed the pantry. "Some have suggested giving the Gotrians only bread, since they like it so much, but hearts humane won't hear of offering a diet deficient. Shall we continue?"

"By all means," Thomas said.

Nothing could be gained here, either. As far as he cared, the tour could end immediately. He'd found no evidence to support Brachi's assertion that the Olvians were starving the prisoners. The Olvians couldn't be held responsible if the inmates refused to eat the food offered them.

He followed Rana to the workshops. The Gotrians worked at either sorting mail or assembling some sort of circuit board while they sang. With so many more voices, Thomas recognized the chants he heard every morning.

Thomas turned to Rana. "May I speak with one of the prisoners?"

Pipien muttered in her own language and turned black. "And how much good will that do? They don't speak your language. Do you know theirs?"

He shrugged. "Not exactly, but if necessary, I can

communicate and receive information telepathically with images and feelings and bypass the whole language issue altogether."

Rana turned a hard eye on her associate and darkened. "It doesn't have to be that complicated. A guard can speak to the prisoner then I'll tell you what was said." She left to talk to a guard.

Calla took a step closer to one of the work benches. *"Translating twice is going to introduce all sorts of interesting errors even if there is no attempt to distort the truth."*

Thomas projected his thoughts back. *"It'll have to do. While I'm waiting for the answer, I can reach out and hunt for the same problems I found last time."*

A guard in a gray tabard moved toward Calla and brought a harpoon up.

Calla showed both hands empty and turned away from the workbench. *"Focus on the conversation and let me handle the other."*

"Nah. Got it covered."

Her disappointment soured his perception in spite of her silence, but then she didn't have to protest. His own memories pleaded her case, reminding him of how Angela had left him out of the loop and withheld information over and over again. Although he didn't intend to exclude her, he could see why she thought he meant to do that. Scanning the rest of the camp himself allowed him to compare his perceptions, but he had to give her something to do if for no other reason than to reduce her frustration with him.

He watched the harpoon-wielding guard as she pursued Calla a few more steps and stopped. *"I need you to watch for any intentional translation errors. That will keep you too busy to search the compound."*

She nodded.

Rana returned. "I'm afraid they won't cooperate as long as they're singing. They do this every day in the morning and afternoon. The Ethical Treatment of Prisoners protocol requires that we respect their duties religious."

Pipien crouched and harrumphed. "Have you ever seen anything so stupid?"

Thomas checked his watch. "They should finish in about fifteen minutes. We'll wait."

Pipien croaked and collapsed into her smallest form. Briefly turning a deep black, Rana shot her assistant a warning look.

While they waited, Thomas extended his mental senses to look for the same brutality he'd found at the other camp but registered nothing. Going farther, he sought out any sort of evidence of maltreatment but came up blank again. Unless the amphibious natives were better at covering their tracks, Thomas would have to accept Rana's claim of innocence.

Calla moved closer to Rana. "Do you ever have outbreaks of non-plague illnesses?"

Rana turned both hands toward the ceiling. "Oh, now and again. Periodically they seem ill for a few days then they're fine again."

Pipien grumbled. "They're faking sickness to get a day off. Gotrians are so lazy."

Calla turned her back to Pipien. "Have you been able to correlate the illnesses with other events?"

"I'll check." Rana stepped away and spoke to a guard.

Thomas studied Calla for a moment then projected his thoughts. *"Fill me in. What are you after?"*

She stayed fixed on Rana. *"Food poisoning."*

Was she that desperate to find something to pin on the Olvians?

He kept an eye on Pipien in case she showed signs of aggression more serious than her typical grouchiness. *"Based on what?"*

"A hunch and a half-remembered fact."

He shrugged. *"No harm in playing it out, I guess, but I don't think you're going to get anywhere."*

Rana rejoined them. "The guard tells me we haven't tried to look for the cause. They become ill for only a time short, then they recover without any trace something had been wrong."

Calla nodded.

"Did you get what you were looking for?" Thomas thought.

Calla returned to him. *"Not exactly. I'm still missing a piece that Rana probably can't give me. I need to check another source."*

Minutes later, the singing ceased and Rana brought a guard and a young male Gotrian over. The prisoner had to be roughly a teenager, which offered confirmation for Thomas' earlier guess about sub-adults being sent into at least some aspects of military service.

Thomas tried to close the distance between himself and the prisoner, but the guard croaked, and Rana's hand restrained him. So much for honoring customs.

"Do you know who I am?" Thomas demanded.

He waited for Rana to translate for the guard who barked a single word to the prisoner while pointing at Thomas with one clawed finger.

Calla glared at the guard. *"Somehow, I don't think that's what you said."*

"So much for even modest accuracy in this relay," Thomas thought. He said aloud, "Rana, I understand that we're going to lose some in the two language changes, but I'd appreciate it if the guard were more faithful to my words."

"What difference does it make?" Pipien stood and pointed to the prisoner. "The male is just going to lie anyway."

Thomas glanced at Calla and pushed his thoughts outward. *"Maybe they'll cooperate if you remind them that you're ready to kill the deal."*

Calla frowned and towered over Pipien before turning to Rana. "The Gotrians were much more helpful. I warn you again. Do not take us for idiots."

Thomas scratched above his ear. "Maybe I could handle the interview myself telepathically."

Rana turned the dark gray of fear. "That won't be necessary. I'll tell the guard to be more careful."

Thomas looked at the teenager, who cast a worried look back to the other prisoners. A graying female Gotrian with a broom moved closer and worked on a patch of floor nearby.

"What are you doing here?" Thomas demanded.

He watched his words pass down the line and waited for the boy's answer to make it back around.

"'Not my choice,'" Rana said.

Calla's thoughts came to him. *"Still a mistranslation. The greeting wasn't finished, so he would have answered with another question, right?"*

He glanced at Calla. *"Yes. I think the gist of it's there, but that's about it."*

Calla shook her head and gave Rana a stern look. "Telepathy does include the ability to discern truth from falsehood. I will not warn you again."

Rana stepped back from Calla. "I mean, 'Do you think I'm here by choice?'"

Thomas leaned forward with his hands on his knees to put him closer to the level of the prisoner. "What are the conditions like here?"

The kid studied the floor. "I work. I eat what I can. I

sleep. I want to go home. I miss my grandparents."

"I understand. Tell me about the food here."

The kid fidgeted with the hem of his black tunic. "The bread is good and the water is okay."

"And the rest?"

"I don't like it."

Thomas shrugged. "Any particular reason why?"

The kid looked over his shoulder at the graying Gotrian female who had contrived to keep sweeping the same spot of the floor. She slowly shook her head.

"I just don't care for it," the boy said.

Calla's thoughts came to Thomas. *"The boy's afraid. The woman is, too."*

Thomas nodded. *"Nervous, probably the same problem you ran into with the Olvian prisoner. This is going to get us nowhere."*

"He's not going to complain with a guard and two Olvians hovering over him. I believe I already have a lead on the answer. I think they—"

"Later." Thomas left the teenager and the guard.

Pipien lightened to a neutral gray. "Finally. I told you nothing useful would come of talking to one of them."

Rana glared at her partner again. "Is there anything else you wanted to see?"

Thomas looked at Calla as if he needed her approval then said, "No, we have what we came for."

Once they'd signed out and passed through the electrified door, Rana took them back to the docks.

"Thanks for the tour." Thomas stepped in front of Calla. "Calla and I will see you an hour before sunset at Pharmacorp."

The two Olvians climbed into the sub more gracefully than Thomas thought possible and disappeared under the water.

Thomas turned toward Calla. "Fill me in on this

theory of yours."

She pulled a dried leaf out of her pocket. "I didn't know I'd need to bulk up on my local botany, and I need to make sure this doesn't contain the compound I think it does. The Gotrians may not be eating the food—"

He pointed to the leaf. "—Because that herb makes them sick?"

Thomas frowned. Given a million chances, he wouldn't have caught that. Thomas put a hand on her shoulder and focused his thoughts on a mental image of her office on Haidar. When the spinning colors faded, he caught Calla as she fell and helped her into a chair.

The lights snapped on.

Calla groaned and rested her forehead in her hands. "Here's hoping I can teleport myself without getting sick someday."

"Worked for me." Thomas perched on the arm of another chair. "The good news is we can get our party clothes for tonight's reception while we're here."

She peeked through her fingers. "Party clothes?"

He nodded. "Receptions of this sort are generally formal dress. Do you have something that will work?"

She stared into the corner of the room. "I believe so. If it's still in Mom's cedar chest and if it still fits." Calla stood and wobbled then caught herself on the desk. She held up the leaf. "Well, let's get this plant figured out. Will you join me, or do you have other errands to run?"

"Actually, I'm pretty curious about what you'll turn up." He smiled and waggled his eyebrows.

"All right. This way."

He followed her out into the darkened hall and then flinched as all the lights came on. "The medical wards close at night?"

"This part does. These are offices and exam rooms, only staffed during typical business hours. The part where our overnight patients stay and the emergency rooms are staffed constantly."

They continued through the winding corridors until they reached a door with an electronic lock.

She pressed one of four green buttons. "Calla Geisman."

His eyes narrowed. "So, what keeps someone from teleporting in?"

She smiled and gestured him in ahead of her. "You'll see."

A creepy tingle raced up his spine. Thomas eyed her suspiciously. "Ladies first."

Calla chuckled and stepped into the room. As soon as she crossed the threshold, he lost mental contact with her.

He rolled his eyes. "Anti-psionic generators."

"Yes, some of the equipment in here is very sensitive." She gestured him in with a nod. "In or out. I can't turn anything on with the door open."

With a deep breath to prepare himself, Thomas joined her. Losing his powers brought an unpleasant recollection of getting high on Minum, but he drove the memory away with a reminder that he'd finished that idiotic chapter of his life ages ago.

The room, maybe three meters on a side, had unidentifiable machines taking every available space on the counters. A small island in the middle of the room held a sink and had enough open surface for a work area.

He parked himself on a stool. "How long will this take?"

"A few minutes." Calla pulled a mortar and pestle out of a cabinet then flipped a switch on a machine with a readout display, a small keypad, and an opaque, sliding panel.

She offered Thomas a bulky set of safety goggles.

They looked no more comfortable than the ones in his high school chemistry labs.

Thomas shook his head. "I'll let you do the fun part."

"Wear them or wait for me outside." Calla donned a pair herself.

Thomas frowned and took the offered eyewear from her. The goggles pressed uncomfortably against his face. Just his luck to meet up with a rules lawyer.

After Calla had crushed the dried leaf into a fine powder, she pulled out an amber dropper bottle of fluid. As she added the odorless, clear liquid, Thomas leaned forward to watch the reaction, but the plant matter only got wet.

He snorted. "Well, that was anticlimactic."

Calla shrugged and scooped the wet plant guts into a shallow glass dish. "If I'd expected a more exciting reaction, we'd be working under the vent hood." She indicated a big boxy compartment built into one wall.

After inserting the glass dish into the machine she'd turned on earlier, Calla set about cleaning up what little mess they'd made so far. Before she'd finished, the test equipment chimed. Thomas followed her and looked over her shoulder at the read-out on a small screen. The symbols and numbers meant no more to him than some list of chemical goo.

"Compounds contained in the leaf." Calla scrolled through the list, scanning faster than Thomas could read, and stopped about four screens down. Calla tapped one line. "That's it."

"What will that do to them?" Thomas asked.

"Nothing fatal. It builds up over a day or two, and then it'll make them sick to their stomachs." She turned away from the screen. "Do you suppose the Olvians deliberately add this?"

Thomas shrugged. "Hard to say but let's hope not. If

the Olvians are that spiteful, we're going to have our hands full. They won't appreciate being caught."

"Better for us if it's accidental?" She hit the button marked "print" next to the screen.

"Umhm. Much better. Meet you back in your office in a half hour? Will that be long enough for you to get your things?"

"If that dress still fits, yes."

"If it doesn't and you can't make other arrangements, pick something significantly less casual than you're wearing and it'll do."

She nodded. "I'll see you soon."

He left her to finish up in the lab. If he could get his own things quickly enough, he could visit with Meiko for a few minutes. Perhaps with him in the same room, she'd be more comfortable explaining the tears he'd seen before he'd left.

Calla preceded Thomas into the tiny Pharmacorp meeting room, going from winter in the hall to summer in a couple steps. The delegations were there already, standing in front of the chairs in their usual posturing. Turning sideways to slip between them, Calla went to her seat and set the bag containing her party clothes nearby. She flopped into her seat and pressed her arm over her stomach. The world around her still spun a bit too quickly. At least the task of explaining the day's findings fell to Thomas, not her.

Thomas settled into his seat. "All right, before we get started, I want an agreement from all three of you to hold commentary of any sort until after I've finished."

She smiled and projected her thoughts to him. *"Good luck with that."*

He quirked a half smile.

Brachi struck his chest. "Agreed."

Rana blinked her huge, dark eyes. "All right, fine."

"Pipien?" Thomas asked.

She turned obsidian and scrunched up in her chair. "Sure. I'll follow the directions of a male."

Rana croaked something stern-sounding at her assistant, who had the good grace to shrink back in her chair.

Thomas shifted position in his seat. "Okay. I'll take them in the order that we visited them. We went to the Gotrian prisoner of war camp in the morning after the Gotrian devotions. For a camp that supposedly held several hundred prisoners, Calla and I were both astonished by how few we saw. We noted that many had bruises and scratches. While Calla interviewed a prisoner, I reached outward to try to find the rest of the population. I found them all right, and I figured out what was going on. We also consulted an expert on Haidar Station about how much time the Olvians are given to spend in the water. I'm sorry, Brachi, but the Olvian claim of mistreatment is valid."

Brachi bristled but kept quiet as agreed.

Pipien raised herself up in her chair. "See! I told you the Go—"

"Pipien!" Calla turned to face the younger Olvian. "You agreed to the stipulation. If your word means anything to you, honor it."

She croaked and squashed back down.

Thomas shifted in his seat and drew a deep breath. "In the afternoon, we went to the Olvian prisoner of war camp. While taking a tour of the kitchen, we noted many of the ingredients. Consulting an expert on Haidar, we learned that aside from the bread, the food being prepared for the prisoners is not safe for them. Preparing food they can't eat is equivalent to preparing nothing at all. Bread alone is not a sufficient diet, so, Rana, the Gotrian claim of starvation is equally valid."

Even before the echo of his voice had faded, both delegations were on their feet spewing accusations, insults, threats, and racial slurs.

While they vented, Calla looked wide-eyed at Thomas. *"Are we going to have to break up fisticuffs?"*

He shrugged. *"Maybe. Get ready to duck furniture."*

She rolled her eyes. *"No, seriously. How do we stop this and get them on track again?"*

"Carefully." Thomas put his thumb and forefinger in his mouth and whistled.

The delegations ignored him.

His second attempt had no better effect.

Calla frowned and sent him her thoughts. *"I think I can make them relax, but I've never done it on three people at once and doing it in series will take too long."*

"Take your best shot at it. I'll warn you if a chair comes your way."

Calla closed her eyes and projected calm feelings outward. The effect on those around her was like emptying a swimming pool with a bucket. Gradually, the volume diminished and the speakers' fury bled away. Calla heard their chairs creak. Only the hum of the overhead fluorescent lights remained.

After taking a deep breath, Calla opened her eyes.

Thomas stared at her. *"Good trick!"*

She smiled. *"Sometimes patients panic. Helping them calm down again is part of the job."*

Thomas looked at each delegation. *"You've got to show me how that works."*

"Later, perhaps. You'd better get going before they remember they're mad at each other."

He nodded and said aloud, "I know the results were not what you wanted to hear, but the fact remains that both sides are guilty of exactly what the other accused them of. The food the Olvians are serving their prisoners is unpalatable, and—"

Pipien harrumphed. "Stupid. We eat food like that all the time."

Thomas glared at her. "—the Gotrians are indeed injuring their prisoners both directly and indirectly."

Brachi bared his teeth. "We must use discipline to maintain order."

Calla turned toward him and pointed her finger at him. "Beating someone senseless whether or not you do it in front of the rest of the population is not discipline."

His fur bristled. "Someone must pay for the deaths

of our people caused by the plagues."

Thomas shook his head. "But the ones you're punishing aren't the culprits, or do you pick one of your citizens at random to be punished for crimes committed in your cities?"

"No, of course not."

Calla leaned back in her chair and crossed her arms. "Then don't try to sell us the idea that you're delivering justice when you're really after revenge."

Now, after the fact, she was glad Thomas hadn't let her sense the torment of the Olvian prisoner. Knowing about the abuse second hand sickened her quite enough.

"Ease up, Calla. It doesn't help if we get grouchy." Then he said out loud, "Think about it this way. Rana, if your warden would stop cooking what Gotrians can't safely eat, the prisoners can work longer instead of needing a day off when they get a bad case of indigestion. Furthermore, you could save money by not buying what they can't eat. To continue serving the poor, you could perhaps assign some prisoners to prepare an extra meal for that purpose and continue giving away any leftovers.

"Brachi, if your warden would let the Olvians get in the water more often—clean water, mind you, not the muck you showed us—and stop punishing people for crimes they didn't commit, you would spend much less money on medical bills. Then they'd be able to work harder or more accurately than when they're wounded."

Calla nodded. If the humanitarian arguments weren't going to work, then maybe the economic ones would. What government didn't look for ways to save a little money here and there?

The delegates grumbled and glared at each other.

Thomas held both hands palm out. "Now, I'm not going to suggest that either of you tried to deliberately deceive us, but for these negotiations to progress, both sides need to make an effort to correct the problems. Otherwise, there's no purpose in continuing. This situation will be a point of contention no matter what else we do. Can we agree to that much at least?"

Rana nodded but turned a deep black. "I cannot promise a quick change to the way the camp is run, but I will use what influence I have."

Brachi struck his chest with his fist. "I am the Speaker for my people. I will make noise about this. They will hear me, but they may be difficult to persuade."

"Fair enough." Thomas smiled and stood. "We'll meet here tomorrow before going to our new meeting site. As for tonight, we should have about enough time to go get ready for the reception."

Calla stood and turned to Rana. "I have my clothes for the evening with me, so I'll remain here and ride back with you afterward."

"I understand." Rana returned to her neutral color. "I'll make sure I bring the records medical that you requested when I come back."

Brachi's eyes widened. "That rreminds me. I need to collect those, too."

Calla watched them leave and turned to Thomas. "Well, that was exciting."

He snorted. "Not as bad as I expected, actually."

She stretched out her stiff muscles. "Think you can manage that party without me?"

"And why aren't you going to be there?"

That should be obvious. Calla froze mid-stretch. "Medical records. They don't analyze themselves, y'know."

He shook his head. "How do I explain your absence? Can't say you're off looking for answers in notes about plagues."

"Make something up. I took the records to an expert

to analyze. I'm making a report to our bosses or off handling some family problem." She shrugged. "How about the perennial favorite: I've got a headache?"

Thomas chuckled. "No good. We show up, get the records from the delegations, then you disappear. Um, I don't think they're dumb enough to miss putting that puzzle together."

I've already pulled my all-nighter for this fortnight. Calla sighed. "Then you'd better get some sleep tonight, because I can guarantee I won't."

He winced. "Sorry. I can bring you some coffee."

"Don't. That's a momentary fix. I have a way that will work better. The side effects aren't any fun, but they pass."

"Okay. Well, what say we go get some dinner? I'm starved."

"They won't have food at the party?" She picked up her backpack and bag.

"Yeah, but I've found that food at these shindigs is either really good or really pathetic. Best to eat something little ahead of time in case the stuff they're serving is of the pathetic variety."

Calla gestured for him to lead the way.

Calla checked herself one last time in the mirror. She rarely had an opportunity to dress up, so the blue, sequined formal felt wrong no matter how she adjusted it. The split up the side from her ankle to above her knee made it possible for her to walk but left her feeling over-exposed. All her concentration would go toward trying not to fidget with the open seam all evening.

She slung her backpack over her shoulder, scooped up the medical records, grabbed her bag, and left the ladies' room. Her heels clicked on the foyer floor and continued alerting the world to her presence all the way across the raised parking lot to the Olvian sub. She twisted the trunk-release and lifted the lid. After dropping the records in, she plunked the bag with her normal clothes on top of that and slid the backpack in last.

Protocol forbid leaving her trauma kit unattended, but she and Thomas had already discussed the matter in aggravating detail. Any heat coming her way for this stupidity would be deflected in his direction. She'd make sure of that.

She slammed the lid down and tugged upward on the lip to make sure the latch worked. That was as secure as she could make it. Calla walked back across the parking lot and snickered at the pixelated version of the company logo formed by strategically lit, colored windows.

Inside, she bee-lined to the reception room. Calla stopped and rested a hand on the knob. She hadn't even opened the door yet, and her pulse had risen several clicks. Rowdy delegates and worried, frightened families of critically wounded patients she could handle. A room full of government officials and diplomats was another matter altogether.

Calla took a deep breath, then opened the door and stepped in.

The huge room seemed less crowded than she'd anticipated even though there were some three or four dozen people on hand. A plush yellow carpet showed some wear near the door. Pictures of company leadership hung on the walls. Padded chairs were arranged in small groups around the edge of the room.

The buffet table along the back wall ended with a bar manned by Kevin Lithos in a gray suit and tie. With all the tuxedos and formal wear in attendance, he looked underdressed.

Calla smiled. *Bodyguard by day, bartender by night?*

Most of the attendants were Terrans, but there were collections of Gotrians and Olvians polarized on opposite sides of the room. They were all safer that way if the delegations were any indication of how cross-species sentiments ran. Gotrian formal attire was cut along the same lines as Brachi's characteristic sleeveless, hooded tunic, but the material was decorated to look like scales, feathers, or fur. Olvians wore brightly colored tabards with patterns of clashing colors.

As Calla scanned through the room with her mind, she found several telepathy voids. That didn't bother her, though, since the owners' paranoia meant fewer sets of thoughts impinging on her own mind. Nowhere in the room did she find Thomas. So much for the common notion that women needed longer to dress.

She projected her thoughts to him. *"Thomas, you're pushing the outside edge of fashionably late."*

"I—I know. I know. I'm—I'm almost ready."

A blurb from his medical records popped into her head. *Mild agoraphobia.*

She turned toward him. *"Do you want the anti-psionic generator from my kit?"*

"You have one? I thought you were kidding about that."

"They're handy sometimes. It won't reduce the number of people in here, but it will kill the noise in your head. Some find that dampening the background thoughts improves the situation to a tolerable level."

She could sense him weighing his options. Telepathy

blockers were disconcerting, but there were enough unshielded people in here to make for a deafening noise in the heads of some sensitives.

"I'll—I'll take it," he thought.

Calla nodded and left the party. As she walked across the parking lot and dodged cars, subs, and little planes, the hair on the back of her neck stood on end.

"This is silly," she mumbled but proved she was alone by scanning the area.

Calla pulled the generator out of her backpack and strode back to the building. Thomas, dressed in a black tuxedo, met her in the foyer.

She leaned close and handed him the generator. "Here's the on-off switch, and this dial controls the radius of the field."

After engaging the device and cranking the radius to its minimum, Thomas pocketed the generator. He shuddered. "Thanks."

She smiled. "Crowds used to annoy me, too. I always found it helpful to stay near the walls."

He patted his pocket. "I'll do that, but this little widget will help tremendously. Shall we?"

Calla nodded and led the way back to the reception room.

"Get some food and a drink. Try to enjoy yourself." He took a step away and then turned back. "You look great, by the way."

She managed a smile as sincere as his compliment felt. "Thank you."

Brachi called Thomas over as Calla wove her way through the crowd.

"Calla!" Patina called.

Quick movement at the perimeter of her vision caught Calla's attention. Patina rushed over.

Patina clasped Calla's hand in both of hers, casting

Calla into a mental void. "I'm so glad you were able to make it."

Calla shook Patina's hand and then backed out of range of the anti-psionic device. "Oh, well, I couldn't miss this party."

Patina flashed her artificial smile. "We have a full bar this evening. Can I get you a drink?"

Calla shook her head. "No, thanks."

Alcohol, she had found the hard way, reduced her telepathic control.

"Later, perhaps, after you've had something to eat." Patina looked back at Kevin. "Why don't I get you something now? Then you'll be all set when you want it."

Calla held up one hand and shook her head. "No, Patina, I don't drink, but thank you anyway."

"Okay, well, that's fine. Let me know if I can get you something." Patina's smile slipped as she turned away.

What was the big deal? Not everyone in the galaxy needed alcohol to have a good time.

Calla blew out a breath. She shook her head, grabbed a plate, and joined the buffet line. What were those tentacle-looking things on shells or what about that stuff that looked like dead bug salad on tree bark? Cheese and crackers and celery sticks looked safe enough, so she took a few of each before finding a group of older Gotrians at the edge of the room to go join. They would ignore her for the most part, which would give her a chance to eat and relax as much as she could without being a wallflower.

She had cleared half of her plate when she sensed a telepathy void coming toward her.

A few times in her youth, she had turned to greet people coming her way because she'd been certain they'd meant to speak with her. When they'd continued on to some other destination, she'd seen the folly of her assumptions. A couple of those embarrassments had cured her of such vanity. Now she pretended not to see the person until he stopped behind her.

"May I have a word with you, D—or rather, Miss Geisman?" an older man said.

What had he been about to call her? If it was "dear," she was glad he'd had a change of heart. Outside of her family and Matt, only some of her geriatric patients could get away with such a familiar address.

Calla turned toward an old man in a gray tuxedo, the president of Pharmacorp according to the company's sales literature. His bio appeared in her mind's eye. Miles Efren founded Pharmacorp thirty-five years ago after graduating from Lunar Agri—

She cut off the growing parade of personal trivia. None of that information would be necessary to carry on a conversation with the man.

Now what had he asked her? Something about a private word?

"Certainly." She followed him to one of the clusters of chairs ringing the room.

He indicated one of the chairs with a sweep of his hand then parked himself in the one across from her. "I understand that you're pushing for these negotiations to end without an official treaty."

She nodded. "Oh, it came up yesterday and again today, but my partner still thinks he can work it out."

He clasped his hands in front of him. "Which one of you makes that decision?"

Calla shrugged. "Both of us. We agree to stay or go. For the moment, I'm willing to trust his judgment."

Efren shifted in his seat. "But if it were up to you..."

"We wouldn't be here now."

He glanced around the room before straightening his already straight bowtie.

Was he interested in keeping things going or not? Why did he even care? Both the Olvians and the Gotrians had made concerted efforts to keep their war to themselves, so she couldn't see why the conflict would affect him either way.

"That's interesting." His smile was somehow less sincere than Patina's. "How did someone like you get into this line of work?"

"Someone like me?" Calla took a bite of cheese and salty crackers to give herself time to figure out what he meant by that.

"Well, with your different skills."

Are you talking about telepathy in general or about Power Deficit Syndrome? She swallowed the cracker. "Oh, the usual way. I trained for my job, just like Thomas."

"Your colleague has a very checkered past, doesn't he?"

Calla studied the weird, old man. *And what would you know about that? Are you fishing?*

Thomas kept his past secret. The only way anyone could know about it would be to get into the medical database. Without being able to get a psionic reading on Efren, she couldn't figure out his game. This conversation needed to end. Now, before she tripped up and said something she shouldn't.

Calla glanced behind her then leaned closer and smiled. "Oh, well, we all have some skeletons in our closets, now don't we?"

He felt around in his jacket pocket. "Yes, I—I suppose we do. If you'll excuse me."

She nodded, not at all upset about his quick departure. If he wanted to go make someone else uncomfortable, she didn't mind. He got a few steps away and took an anti-psionic generator out of his pocket, checked it, and put it back. What was that about?

He joined another conversation, and Calla went back to the buffet table. She unhooked a cup from a crystal punchbowl and filled it from the water fountain in the corner before joining a group of Olvians. Now that she had eaten something, some conversation would be a nice way to pass the time.

Hurried steps raced up behind Thomas. He turned as Calla slowed and stopped. Now out of her gorgeous, blue-sequined dress, she looked more comfortable in pants and a long-sleeved shirt.

Whatever you have to say, make it quick. "What's up?" he asked.

She didn't answer right away. "Are you okay?"

"Yeah, why?" he asked through a yawn.

She shook her head as if she didn't know why she'd asked. "You seem a little off in my perception." She studied him for a moment. "Your mental signature is, well, wobbly. It surges and fades some."

On one level, her concern was touching, especially in light of all the grief he had given her over the last few days. On another, her question annoyed him. The longer they stood here debating how he felt, the longer he would have to wait until he could sleep.

Thomas sighed. "I'm wiped out, Calla. It's late. I've had a long day after a couple of other really long days. I need to go check my eyelids for holes and defects."

She reached her hand toward him but stopped. "Are you sure?"

"I'm fine, you worrywart." He gave her a gentle push.

"Now get out of here. Your ride's waiting."

She nodded. "Okay. See you in the morning."

As she ran off, he went to the plane and shrugged off a wave of dizziness. Good thing he didn't have to drive.

Thankfully, Brachi didn't try to drum up a conversation on the way back to the city. When Thomas leaned back against the headrest and closed his eyes, his guts churned. Bile rose in his throat. He swallowed hard and opened his eyes again. He had never encountered problems with motion sickness before, so why now?

Maybe Calla had been right. He didn't feel like himself, but he couldn't expect to feel normal. The hours of sleep he had gotten in almost three days could be counted on his fingers. Maybe he should've teleported back to his room. He could be curled up on his pallet of pillows already. Brachi wouldn't have appreciated that, though. Taking care of transporting himself was all well and good when Thomas had other business, but otherwise such behavior would be construed as avoidance.

With the dizziness getting worse, the ride back to the treetop city took a couple years or more. Something he had eaten must not have agreed with him, because he hadn't drunk that much. Both of his drinks had been more soda than alcohol anyway. The first had been moments after his arrival at the party and the other right before the end. He was a lightweight, but not that much of a lightweight.

When he got back to his room, he would have a big glass of water before he went to bed. By morning, he would feel fine again.

Sweat ran down Thomas' cheek and beaded on his forehead, so he took off his tuxedo jacket and slung it over his shoulder. Brachi didn't seem to be at all bothered by the heat, but then he was adapted to the climate.

While following Brachi down a few levels, Thomas looked at his watch, but he couldn't manage to keep his hand steady enough to read the numbers. He needed more sleep than he'd thought.

"Can you find your way from here?" Brachi stifled a yawn.

Thomas looked out across the catwalks and spotted a blurry version of his door. "Yes, thank you."

Brachi left.

"Good night," Thomas called after him.

He started across the walkways toward his room. The vertigo's severity continued to increase by the moment, and he considered if he could survive a fall from so far up in the canopy. As hot as he was, he slid the jacket back on to free both hands to hold the rope handrails.

The nausea became more of a pain in his gut. What had he eaten to make him so sick? He hadn't felt this wretched since the time he'd taken two hits of Minum too close together. At the time, he hadn't believed he could feel that bad again, but the previous experience seemed like a vacation. Calla had not been wrong, after all. He felt worse than "a little off."

Thomas made his way across the walkways to the right platform. If he could get to bed, he could sleep this off. By morning, he would be back to normal. All he had to do was take the short set of stairs down, then walk a couple meters to the door. Safety was so close he could feel it.

On the first step, his foot slipped. Thomas grabbed the handrail, but the rope swayed under his weight, and he fell, hitting the deck hard enough to see an explosion of white. Seconds passed while he lay there too stunned to move. He tried to push himself up, but his shaking arms refused to support him, and he collapsed.

Thomas reached out with his thoughts. *"Calla."*

Maybe she had gone to sleep already.

"Calla!"

Stupid Syndromer. Why wouldn't she answer him? This was not the time to hold a grudge.

He reached farther, back toward Haidar. *"Meiko?"*

He didn't even hear the dim echo that came from thought projection.

"August!"

Nothing but the silence of his own mind. Even the minds of the Gotrians around him had gone quiet. He didn't still have Calla's anti-psionic device, did he? He checked his pockets with his trembling hands to confirm he'd given it back to her. His powers were gone.

Calla closed the door of her room after seeing Rana out. Although she was glad they now trusted Thomas to take care of the negotiations, she wouldn't have played that card if she had known ahead of time she would get to listen to two nights in a row of the Olvians begging her to reconsider ending the meetings.

She yawned. Medical records still needed to be reviewed. Hopefully Thomas would get a decent amount of sleep tonight. They couldn't manage well if both of them were incoherent.

Calla looked at the medical records on the table and scowled. The sooner she started, the sooner she would finish and be able to get at least some rest.

"Dr. Geisman," a familiar-sounding thought-voice called. *"Calla, it's Joy Demouchette, the head of the arbitration department. Can you hear me?"*

She frowned and pushed her thoughts back as far as she could. *"Yes."*

"Calla?"

"Yes, I hear you, but I can't project that far. You're going to have to help me out."

She felt the contact form with her mind and flinched as she remembered the attack a month ago.

"Calla? You are there, aren't you?"

She squeezed her eyes closed and rubbed her forehead. *"I'm here. I don't have the power level to project over light-years. If I can get around the back side of the planet, it's a good day."*

"You could have told me."

Calla rolled her eyes. How was she supposed to have explained about the problems with sending her thoughts so far if she couldn't project far enough to tell Joy about it? Calla let the comment go. Explaining the flaw in that logic would take too long anyway.

"I can't seem to reach Thomas," Joy thought.

"He's had a rough couple of days. He's probably sleeping by now. What can I help you with?" Calla grabbed the first medical file.

"Someone hacked into the medical and training databases. Five files were accessed before the system could lock the hacker out again. Yours and Thomas' were among them."

"Why ours?" Calla squinted in the direction of Haidar.

"We don't know, and whoever did it was skilled enough to cover his tracks so well we don't even know how to start searching. Be careful out there. Can you tell Thomas for me?"

"As soon as he wakes up." Calla turned back to the record.

"How's it going?"

Calla leaned her forehead on her fingertips. *"We had a rocky start, but everything should be fine now."*

"How did he have a rough day?"

There wasn't anything like enough time to give Joy a complete mission update, review ten records, and still manage to sleep for a couple hours.

Calla sighed. *"Nothing is going as expected. He had to do a lot of scrambling."*

"I see. How are you holding up?"

"I'm managing. Thomas is giving me a lot of guidance in some matters, and the information Nikk gave me is coming in handy."

"Good, good. Well, have Thomas contact me with an

update," Joy thought.

"I'll do that."

The contact finally ended.

Calla flipped through the paperwork inside the rough, brown folder. She frowned. There were standard protocols in place for how to organize the information, and the Gotrians didn't follow the usual pattern. She picked up an Olvian one and found that they had also ignored the standard arrangement.

Calla sighed and starting sorting through one, making notes about things that felt relevant. At least each race's files had been organized according to a local standard. Once she figured out the first one, the next went more easily.

She had finished with the second and opened the third folder when the door opened. Calla's head snapped up. Rana stood there in a wrinkled tabard hanging askew. She was flushed the same dark gray she had been when Calla had threatened to end the peace talks. If she had returned for another rousing chorus of "Please let Thomas try to complete the negotiations," Calla would have to kick the delegate out even if diplomacy demanded a more courteous response.

"I've received a message from the Gotrians." Rana loped into the room. "Thomas has fallen and hurt himself, apparently pretty severely."

Calla grabbed her trauma kit and the medical records. "I need a ride to the Gotrian city where Thomas is staying. Can you arrange that for me?"

"Already done. I have a driver who will take you to Pharmacorp where a pilot Gotrian will be waiting to take you to Thomas."

"Thank you." She followed Rana into the waiting hovercraft as the Olvian instructed the driver.

Buildings whizzed by, but Calla would have liked to

have gone faster. If her mental calculations were right, traveling from the Olvian city to the Gotrian one would take about an hour. Unless Brachi's physician could treat Thomas, he could die by the time she reached him if his injuries were as severe as Rana had suggested.

"He's yours, isn't he?" Rana's cold, slimy hand landed on Calla's wrist.

Calla turned away from the blurred scenery. "Mine?"

"Is he to be your husband?"

"No." Calla shifted the backpack on her lap. "He belongs to another woman, but she entrusted me with his safety. We never should have separated."

Rana pulled her hand back, leaving a damp spot on Calla's wrist. "Why did you?"

Was she serious? She'd been there when all that confusion had happened.

"Of all the things the people of Ologo have to fight over, we didn't want to become a reason for hostilities ourselves."

Rana turned darker. "This is our fault."

Calla shook her head. "Whether it is or not is irrelevant. The decision is well past."

This discussion could do nothing to help either of them. Rana would continue to find reasons to blame herself or Brachi, and Calla preferred to hear more information about Thomas' condition. The more she had to start with, the better prepared she would be when she got there.

She imagined the worst: broken bones, dislocated joints, massive trauma, head wounds. The only thing she knew she didn't have to worry about was a psionic injury. There weren't any telepaths around except her and Thomas, fortunately for him. He would never let her treat him if he'd been injured in that sort of attack.

Calla drew a deep breath. "Did Brachi's message say

anything about how badly Thomas is hurt or what kinds of injuries he received?"

"He fell down a flight of stairs and had to be carried to his room, but the message didn't give me anything else to go on. Are you going to be able to help him?"

Calla shrugged. "I won't know until I see him."

Rana turned dark gray. "You will continue the negotiations for him, won't you?"

How could she be concerned about that at a time like this? For all Calla knew, Thomas lay bleeding to death while some Gotrian witch doctor stood over him chanting useless nonsense.

Perhaps Rana had seen so many of her own people die that stopping the war became more important to her than the life of one man she only knew professionally. Thomas, a male, wouldn't rate highly after all.

"I'll do what I can." Calla rested her hand on Rana's slimy forearm. "I may have to get him back to Haidar, but I'm sure the Magistrates will send someone else to take over."

They reached the submarine depot, and Rana led her to the sub they had been using. Calla climbed in and felt as much as heard the engines roar through startup. Rana didn't join her, which made Calla happier than would have been safe to express.

The Olvian's concerns about her home world's fate were understandable, but Calla might be able to do something to help Thomas even as far away as she was, provided he would allow her to.

Calla reached out with her thoughts. *"Thomas."*

Nothing. Joy had mentioned that problem, too, but the wounds had to be pretty serious if he couldn't even echo to her. Once they were away from the Olvian city, she lowered the barriers in her mind. The mental noise roared. Closing out all natives and females kept the pounding headache down.

Among all the remaining males, Thomas should have shown like the sun in the sky, but the sole non-local mind she sensed so far removed from the others had to be him, and she could not find his thoughts.

What could have robbed him of his telepathy? A generator would have blocked her perception of him altogether. Drugs maybe? Was Thomas taking Minum again? He had been clean for years, but he wouldn't be the first one to do well for a while then falter.

She couldn't believe that. Thomas kept that one troubled time in his life private, but kicking the addiction made him proud. She had sensed a real regret that he had wasted so much of his life getting high.

Blocking all but the one mind she was certain was him, Calla focused and projected her thoughts again. *"Thomas."*

She reached into the fringes of his mind to be able to pick up his response. The pain, weakness, and fear she sensed there threatened to drag her down.

"Calla." His response was slow and faint.

"Yes, Thomas. How badly are you hurt? They're telling me you fell down a flight of stairs."

He struggled to form his thoughts. Concussions could do that. So could certain illnesses and drugs. Had the Gotrian plague struck him? Impossible. Nikk had assured her their physiology differed too much from the locals. What if the bug had mutated and could now affect telepaths even with their stronger immune systems?

She pressed her fingers against her forehead. *"I'm on my way, Thomas. I'll be there as soon as I can. In the meantime, I'm going to use my powers to help you sustain yourself."*

She felt a dim acknowledgment laced with the same underlying disgust she had felt when she had offered to help him stay awake.

"Don't be afraid." She ramped down the volume she used to project. *"I won't hurt you. I don't have to go any farther into your mind than I am now."*

Calla closed her eyes and read Thomas' vital signs. She sent pulses of psionic energy to steady his pulse and breathing. As the contact went on, he continued to decline. Too much distance separated her from her patient, but her efforts would become more effective as she drew nearer. For now, Calla had to be satisfied with delaying his death by however much she could.

An intolerable half-hour later, the sub pulled into the Pharmacorp lot. As Rana had promised, a Gotrian waited there to finish the trip. Calla left the sub. The Gotrian met her partway and stood entirely too close.

"What do you think you're doing here at this hour?" he asked.

Calla frowned. "Aren't you here to take me the rest of the way?"

"Yes. Please get in. Your friend is very sick."

She supposed that falling down a flight of stairs and being ill didn't preclude each other, but why the different accounts? Perhaps she should be grateful to get anything at all. She climbed into a battered Gotrian plane. As soon as she fastened the seatbelt, the pilot took off.

Calla projected her thoughts to Thomas. *"I'm halfway there. Stay with me, Thomas."*

As before, she received only an acknowledgment, but her sense of him hadn't become any stronger than it had been before. At least he no longer weakened with each passing minute. Her efforts were paying off as the distance separating them closed.

By the time the plane landed in the treetops, Thomas read more stable, perhaps even a trifle stronger. Once she could be with him, she should be able to get him coherent enough to tell her what had happened.

Of course, if he were unconscious, he wouldn't be able to protest if she went into his mind and found the answer on her own. When he woke up later, he wouldn't be happy about her intrusion, but at least he would be alive to be mad at her.

Her pilot led her through a maze of rope-and-plank bridges to a platform but stopped at the end of a short run of stairs.

The guide pointed with a quivering hand. "He's in there." He bolted back the way they'd come.

"Thank you!" Calla called after him.

She ran the short distance and entered. The pungent odor of incense filled the air and candlelight flickered off the walls. Thomas, covered from the waist down by a sheet, lay shaking, doubled over on a flurry of red pillows. A blond-furred Gotrian knelt next to him wringing out a wet cloth. Brachi stood nearby, mumbling a repetitive phrase she couldn't hear clearly.

Both Gotrians looked up as Calla crossed to Thomas' side and went down on one knee. She continued to focus her powers on strengthening him in hopes of bringing him around enough to talk to her.

Calla looked up at Brachi. "What happened?"

"You weren't told?" Brachi scowled.

Right, you're old, so you were supposed to start. This is an emergency. Get over it.

"He fell down the stairs out there." Brachi pointed to the door. "The people who came out to investigate the noise found him and brought him in here."

"They thought it was plague." The other Gotrian pulled on a sweat-drenched lock of Thomas' hair, which made Thomas wince. "Obviously, it's not."

"This is our healer," Brachi said.

Calla slid her backpack off her shoulder and set the records aside. "What has your examination turned up?" She looked at her watch while she counted Thomas' breaths.

The healer glared at her. "Have you no eyes? I know nothing of your people's medicine. I couldn't even find his pulse. All I could do was try to make him comfortable. I would suggest you get a healer from Haidar Station."

Twenty breaths in thirty seconds would make forty in a minute. That was far too fast.

"I am one." She located the pulse in Thomas' wrist.

The healer simply nodded, but Calla picked up the shock in Brachi's thoughts.

The Gotrian delegate stepped back and gave her an incomprehensible look. "You—you're a physician?"

Calla peeked at him. "Yes."

Doing the mental math, she concluded that unless Thomas had finished running a marathon within the last minute or two, he was tachycardic. That confirmed her long-distance assessment.

Brachi bared his teeth. "Why didn't you tell us?"

"I have my orders, but right now Thomas can't afford that secret."

"Is there anything I can do to help?" the healer asked.

Calla shook her head. "No, but thank you."

Brachi hid his teeth. "Let me know if you need anything."

"I will," Calla said.

Right now she wanted the room clear of unnecessary

personnel.

The healer nodded and stood, then ushered Brachi out and closed the door behind them. Once they were gone, Calla pulled Thomas onto his back. Raw scrapes with splinters still embedded marred the side of his face. His eyes were dull. Their natural blue color showed rather than the telepathic glow.

"Calla?" he whispered.

She leaned closer to him. "I'm here, Thomas. Tell me how you feel."

"It's too hot in here." His words ran together. "My powers are gone, and I hurt."

"Where?"

"My head and my stomach. I—I can't stop shaking."

This had all the trappings of a Minum overdose with some unusual complications. Had he downed more of those pills again? He could have gotten them through an old contact when they'd gone home. No, that made no sense. He'd kept her generator armed the whole time. Why would he need the drug? Had he taken it before she'd offered the better solution?

"Thomas, I need a straight answer. Did you take a hit of Minum tonight?"

He frowned. "No, but I haven't felt this bad since the time I took two hits too close together about ten years ago."

"Is this better or worse than that time?"

"Worse. Much worse. You—you have to believe me. I—I—"

Had he been lying, she would have sensed the deception there.

"I believe you." Calla opened the front pouch of her backpack and pulled out a blood analysis kit. "I'm going to check your blood and find out if you have an infection or if you've been drugged. I'm going to have to stick your finger. Okay?"

He nodded convulsively.

Calla took out a lancet and a capillary tube. He winced when she pricked his finger and bled like she'd opened a vein with a scalpel. The capillary tube filled, and she treated the bleeding wound with a styptic then wrapped a small bandage around it.

Agonizing seconds passed between the time she slipped the tube into the analyzer and the time its indicator light showed bright red.

"It found something." She tapped the light.

"What?" he asked.

She set the analyzer aside. "You've been given a lethal dose of Minum."

Thomas stammered a few inarticulate syllables. The sickening terror in his mind spoke for him.

"You're going to be all right. I have what I need to counteract what's happened to you."

She opened the main part of her backpack and pulled out the hard cases stashed in the bottom. The antibiotic one would be useless, but the other would have what she needed. Opening the antitoxin box, she found it empty and bit back the curse that came to mind. Maybe the case had opened up and dumped its contents. She searched the bottom of the trauma kit but found nothing. The antibiotic box contained only the bottles she'd put there herself. She should never have left her backpack unattended. She had thought it would be safe enough in the trunk of the Olvian sub, but she should have known better.

Calla sighed. "Someone stole the antitoxins out of my kit."

Thomas closed his eyes in a futile attempt to hide the despair.

Pharmacorp manufactured what she needed, but she

didn't have enough time to run through their gauntlet to find someone with enough clearance to give her the needed medicines. They'd made a huge production of finding Patina, after all.

Without the drugs or even a way to contact home, she had little choice but to watch Thomas die. Even if she went to Brachi to have him send a message back to Haidar, hours would pass by the time someone came. Thomas didn't have that long.

There had to be something she could do. Could she use his own body to save him?

Thinking back through her classes on pharmacokinetics and the literature she'd read on Minum, she looked for the biological mechanism for detoxifying the drug and found the needed pathway.

The required power level for affecting metabolic functions on such a grand scale lay beyond her comfortable range. She could do it, but the effort would take time. Pushing the limit for so long would give her a skull-exploding headache. During the process, if she made even the smallest mistake or pushed the edge so hard that she passed out, Thomas could die, like his last partner had, when she couldn't find the strength to do what needed to be done.

Succeeding might be no better. Her efforts to treat him would sap her strength even as she empowered him. She knew what he thought of her. Even his own fiancée feared how he would react to finding out she carried one of the Power Deficit Syndrome genes. Thomas professed love for Meiko and only revulsion for Calla.

She shook her head. Thomas was dying. Calla had never given up on a patient. She would try, if Thomas would allow her to, and trust him not to hurt her as he grew stronger and she weakened.

"Thomas, listen to me. I can still help you, but you

have to let me further into your mind. The procedure I would have to use is a hair outside of my power level, but I'm willing to try it."

He didn't answer. He hadn't been thrilled about her poking around in his head the first time. Calla cautiously reached deeper into his mind, feeling a surge of fear from him with the contact. The resistance he put up was negligible, but the intention came through clearly. He did not welcome her presence.

She backed off. "I can't get a message to Haidar myself, and hyperspace radio would take too long. You'll die if I don't do something."

While projecting a calming influence on him, she could hear the turmoil of his unguarded thoughts. He didn't trust her, but she had never harmed him. She was inferior, but he had seen her do things he couldn't imagine doing himself. She was a Syndromer, but he had no one else to turn to. Meiko came to his mind and finalized his decision. He couldn't bear to think of leaving his fiancée alone.

The meager resistance drained away. Calla rested her hand on his feverish forehead and sank deeper into his mind. Thomas gasped and clenched his eyes. Images flashed into his thoughts of a sneering man with greasy black hair and dark eyes, like her own. Pain and terror associated with the image slammed into her mind, not terribly unlike her own recollections the night of the fire. Had he been attacked by whatever lunatic had been killing off disabled Haidarians?

Calla let his feelings wash past her while she returned tranquility to him. *"You're safe. Rest, Thomas. I'll help you."*

The memory faded, and Calla summoned her visualization of his mind-maze. A much younger Thomas wandered out of the maze, trembling. This teenage image of him looked around with darting glances. His ragged clothes were heavily worn and a size or two too small. He had the appearance of someone who had seen too few meals and too many drugs.

Sympathy threatened to drown her. *"You can wait here, or you can come with me."*

With a shake of his head, almost indistinguishable from the tremor, he faded from her inner sight.

Calla nodded. *"As you will."*

She zoomed out and looked at the maze as a whole. No obvious damage appeared, but the whole structure wobbled precariously. Careful not to upset the balance, she continued to support Thomas' failing strength and took the stairs down to the midlevel. There, as above, nothing looked out of sorts, but the quivering columns could come down at any moment.

Passing the final barrier into the deepest level, Calla found herself facing an intense lightning storm. Although some parts of the giant nerve network remained dark, most were sparking at various intervals, and some never quit.

Calla wove her way through the three-dimensional web to find the area she would have to control to speed up the metabolic pathway responsible for detoxifying Minum. When she found what she needed, the sheer enormity of steadily pulsing neurons gave her pause. The responsible structures covered a greater combined volume than she had ever dealt with before, and she had no nurses or other doctors to help her.

The procedure combined with the need to continue supporting Thomas for at least the first phase of her work would tap out every reserve she had, leaving her fragile and weak. He'd made no secret of what he thought of her, but there weren't many options. She'd have to trust him to act like a gentleman as he recovered, otherwise she would be forced to let him die.

Drawing a deep breath, Calla split her attention. While still buttressing his feeble efforts to stay alive, she synced up with his metabolism and gradually encouraged his body to void the unnecessary chemicals.

As she worked, she ignored the headache looming in the background.

Grimacing against the soreness and stiffness of every muscle and joint in his body, Thomas rolled to his back. In the distance, the Gotrians' morning chants filled the air, providing an odd counterpoint to the natural sounds of the singing birds. He felt much better than he had a right to.

Recollections of last night swam in a gray fog, which cleared as he awoke. He remembered falling down the stairs, but how had he gotten from there to his room? Then Calla had come. He couldn't recall what she had found wrong with him, but he knew that someone had stolen part of her medical kit, leaving him with the wretched choice of dying or letting a Syndromer into his head again.

Calla's presence in his mind hadn't been as vile as he'd anticipated. Contrary to his expectations, her gentle and compassionate nature had made him want to draw nearer to that comfort as he'd regained his strength though her efforts. Despite the close contact, nothing about her presence made him feel like he had betrayed Meiko. Calla had simply been a physician doing her job.

He should feel violated on all sorts of levels for allowing a freak like her to have total access to his very being. Syndromers were useless, weren't they? While he didn't take August's hard line about eliminating the ones who already existed, Thomas did advocate trying to make sure there were no more of them. This one in particular had caused someone's death by pretending she could do something she couldn't.

On the other hand, he should be grateful to her for saving his life again. She could have concluded the procedure was too power-intensive for her and left it at that, and no one could have faulted her for making that decision. If she had told everyone he'd refused to let her try, no one who knew him would have been surprised.

The memory of the difficult time she'd had helping him stood out in his mind. She had tried to hide her problems from him, but she'd feared losing him in spite of her best effort. She worried the pain of the headache would become overwhelming. Most of all, she'd been afraid he would hurt her as her efforts restored him and drained her strength. Still, through a sheer force of will, Calla had persisted. The touch of her thoughts had remained with him while he had recovered.

In addition to her mental presence—he still had no idea what she'd been doing the whole time—he vaguely recalled other things she had done. She had mopped the sweat from his face and chest with a damp towel and meticulously pulled splinters from his cheek and palms. When he had become thirsty, she had held him up to help him drink some water and had gently tucked the sheet and pillows around him, even laying her jacket across him when he'd become cold.

All of her ministrations had worked. Aside from sore, stiff muscles, he felt infinitely better than last night. He had survived, and when this mess was over, he could go home to Meiko. He owed his existence to Calla. An inferior person had saved his life again, but should he even think of her in those terms?

Thomas opened his eyes. He lay on his pillow pile, covered with the sheet and Calla's heavy leather jacket. Lying nearby with nothing but a small pillow for her head, he found Calla. Without even connecting their minds, he could feel the pain of an outrageous headache and something even more bizarre.

Although she showed the easy rhythms of sleep, he sensed an alertness, as if part of her were awake. Even in sleep, she still watched over him. He had never seen anything like it before, but then she had been doing all kinds of things he hadn't known were possible.

As Thomas sat up, Calla inhaled sharply and opened her eyes. "How do you feel?"

"Better." His voice sounded more toad-like than human in his ears. Thomas cleared his throat and answered again.

She smiled. "Good."

Reaching over her head, she groped for something. Her fingers came within a centimeter or two of the cardboard-bound notebook she used to record information about the meetings.

Thomas picked it up. "I've got it."

"Information you'll need today," she said.

He flipped through it. "I'll read it, then we can talk about it later. Sleep now, and I don't mean that pseudo-half-sleep business I caught you doing. Really get some rest. I'm all right."

Calla nodded and closed her eyes.

The cold, wooden floor couldn't possibly be comfortable. Thomas crawled over to her and picked her up. She tensed.

"I promise I won't drop you," he said.

Keeping his word proved difficult. As rail-thin as she was, she was heavy, a side effect of both her height and his worn out muscles. Fortunately, only a meter or so separated him from the pillows and he made it without doing harm to either one of them.

After setting her down in the middle of the pile, Thomas covered her with the sheet and sat watching her until she drifted off to sleep less than a minute later.

Thomas picked out tan pants and a dark blue shirt and went to the shower, waiting until he had closed the door to turn on the light. He looked himself over in the mirror while the water warmed up. His eyes glowed even in the bright light of the room. Under the bandage on his index finger, he found the yellowish stain of a styptic and a little blood clot. He didn't recall how that had happened, but then many parts of last night were fuzzy.

The ugly red scrapes on his hands and face sparkled with the liquid bandage that would keep them clean and dry while he healed. Had he gotten that professional case of road rash falling on the deck last night?

Thomas stepped into the spray of almost-too-hot water. His muscles relaxed and his joints loosened up. Although he probably imagined it, the warm water carried away the fog of weariness in his mind as well. He indulged in the shower until the water began to cool.

After he dressed, he grabbed Calla's notebook and sat on the floor in the sliver of light coming from the bathroom where he could read without disturbing his partner's sleep. He opened to the page she had dog-eared. Calla's writing in the front part of the journal had been blocky, laser precise, and readable. In the more recent part, there were more strike-outs. The spacing became erratic. Words drifted above and below the lines. Words were abbreviated with names becoming little more than initials after the first mention. He read Calla's account of the party, including not only Patina's insistence that she have a drink, but also the president's questions.

Thomas' own discussion with the company's president last night had included his odd questions about Calla's power level and the negotiations.

The president had been unwilling to answer even the most harmless questions but equally determined to ask his own overly personal ones. Calla's assessment of "weird, creepy old man" fit perfectly.

Calla's notes went on to describe her hour-long talk with Rana, who was terrified that the negotiations might be called off altogether. His partner conveyed her aggravation in the words she chose, but she didn't seem to regret her decision. He had control of the meetings again, as he should.

Then he got to Joy's warning and Calla's account of her journey to reach him and her work to keep him alive. Whoever had cracked the medical database had learned about his addiction. Even without Calla's explanation, he could tell that the amount of Minum he'd been hit with should have killed him. His drinks had probably been drugged, now that he thought about it. Fortunately for them both, Calla had stuck with water.

Much of her explanation of the procedures she had used to help him was lost in medical jargon and shorthand, but her fears came through clearly. For all of her skills, she had no confidence in those abilities. He had thought she regarded Angela's death with cold nonchalance, but Calla blamed herself for the loss like he had blamed himself for not forcing Angela to leave Cordil IV faster.

As he read on, Thomas reached her analysis of the medical records. She had only gotten to a couple of each race's files, but how had she found the time to do even that much? As he read through the descriptions of her findings, he saw a pattern emerging.

The Gotrians could not have unleashed the bacteria causing the sickness because their labs had been set up months after the first cases of plague. Since the Olvians lacked the technology, they similarly couldn't have developed the germ.

Time and again their doctors referred to a virus

causing the problem. Calla believed bacteria did the dirty work, based on some repeating theme he didn't understand. Her notes ended there, with the last few sentences drifting off the printed lines as her exhaustion took over.

The plagues were no respecter of factions, wealth, or political standing, so dissenters couldn't be the problem. Although he had heard of plenty of groups who were willing to sacrifice most of their members for the great cause, that didn't feel right for this. Both populations were dropping too low. Only one logical solution remained. Someone else had unleashed the sickness on these people.

He turned off the light and sat on the wooden chair by the wall where he could watch his partner rest. The pain of her headache troubled him. Although he wanted to think he hadn't caused the problem, he knew she had gotten into that condition by pushing her limit for hours. Thomas knew about the blinding pain. Stephanie had gotten exertion headaches, too, because of her own power level.

Fortunately, rest did wonders for making them go away. Thomas needed Calla up and running today to help him explain her findings to the delegates.

Pushing the light button on his watch, Thomas confirmed that the time at home was reasonable to contact someone. He should check in with Joy first, then he needed to hear the reassurance brought by talking to Meiko.

Thomas projected his thoughts. *"Joy."*

"Hello, Thomas. Sleep well?"

"I'm feeling much better now."

"I had a hard time reaching you earlier. I told Calla to let you know that someone hacked the medical database and pulled up your file."

Thomas nodded. *"That's what I hear."*

"Oh good. She remembered." She sounded genuinely surprised.

Thomas ran his fingers through his hair. *"Actually, she has a phenomenal memory."*

He was defending her? Well, and why not? Truth couldn't depend on how much he approved of someone.

"Yeah. I forgot that the PDS genes give them that particular quirk. Well, what's going on over there?" Joy thought.

"We think the plague is being caused by an outside influence." He flipped Calla's notes open to that part of the account. *"Calla reviewed some medical records and found that both races are up against the same bacteria."*

"That could still be one race developing it and losing control." Joy thought.

"I believed that, too, but the plague hit before either side had the facilities needed to develop bioweapons. There's only one group here with the needed equipment and expertise."

"You don't think...Pharmacorp? What would they gain?"

"They could develop their bacteria using Ologo for one huge Petri dish." Thomas paused as another thought came to him. *"No, wait. I was going to suggest that it could be used on other worlds to wipe out the Gotrian and Olvian populations, but they're only found here on Ologo."*

"Don't give up on your theory yet. There may be other races with sufficiently similar biology that the bacteria could hurt them, too. The bug could even mutate."

"Possible, I suppose." He'd have to bounce that idea off Calla later.

"All right, so, Ologo is being used as a real-world

laboratory. Please, go on."

Thomas took a moment to regain his momentum. *"Well, both native races are too far behind the galactic technological average and have been at war for ages, so no one would find it all that surprising to see them dying off so rapidly."*

"And given how little they affect other planets' economies, many folks wouldn't afford them a cursory look. Y'know, Pharmacorp could even develop the 'miracle cure' in time to save the locals, which would boost their legitimate sales."

"Exactly. Pharmacorp offered to play host not to be neighborly but to keep an eye on things and sabotage the meeting in small ways like inappropriate rooms, less than helpful liaisons, and confusion about where to stay."

"You've probably been given a bugged conference room." Joy's thought blared a warning.

Thomas nodded and closed Calla's notebook over his thumb. *"Very likely. Calla and I had her threaten to end the talks so I could 'convince' her to let me try."*

"To what end?"

"The Olvians had decreed that they wouldn't work with me."

"If Pharmacorp were listening in, and even remotely believed the bluff, then they'd—" She stopped for several seconds. *"Thomas, have you been attacked?"*

Thomas looked at his scraped-up palms. *"Poisoned last night at a reception, and someone stole meds out of Calla's kit."*

"She told me you were tired."

He turned toward Calla. *"When we parted company, that's what we assumed. When it was obvious something else had happened, the Gotrians sent for her. She used some psionic trickery to help me."*

"But you're all right now?" Her concern tugged at him.

Thomas flexed his hand and felt the odd pressure of the spray bandage. *"Yeah, yeah, I'm fine. I'm sore, but I'm okay. We're moving the meeting today."*

"Good. I hate to admit it, but it sounds like you're on to something. I'll see what I can dig up around here to help you solidify your case."

He checked out his other palm, which wasn't banged up quite as badly. *"Thanks, but I think I'll turn our evidence over to the authorities and let them handle it. As soon as I get the treaty in place, I'm heading out."*

"You may not be able to get the treaty agreed upon without concrete proof of Pharmacorp's role. If you can, that would be wonderful. In case the delegations and their governments don't go for that, you may need to address Pharmacorp directly."

Possible, but not likely. He had planted the seeds already that some outside force had driven them to war. That would be enough. Still, Joy's efforts could speed up the dismantling of the company.

"Let me know what you find out," Thomas thought.

Joy promised to keep feeding him updates, then signed off.

Thomas sat back and rubbed his eyes with his fingers. He'd never been naïve enough to think these missions could ever be completely safe, but this was the first time someone had tried to kill him specifically. The threats always came to Haidar's envoy in general, not to any one person in it.

He wanted to put all his stuff together, get Calla's gear, and go home before Pharmacorp could take another shot at him. The people of Ologo needed him, though, and he didn't feel right abandoning them to their fate, especially knowing where the plague must have come from.

For the moment, however, their problems would keep. He needed to spend some time with more sympathetic counsel.

He projected his thoughts again. *"Meiko."*

No answer came.

"Meiko, my love, my darling, sweetheart, the light of my day, the air that I breathe."

"Thomas?" Her thoughts were hazy with fatigue.

"Uh—oh. I woke you up, didn't I?"

"Don't worry about that. I was taking a nap. Isn't it still dark there?"

Thomas looked at the billowing curtain in the open window. *"Yeah, but almost dawn. Ologo has a weird rotation time relative to Haidar."*

"So, how's it going?" Meiko's drowsiness faded.

"Not so good. I had a tough night. Can't sleep."

"What happened?"

Even though he had contacted her to talk and share his experience, he didn't want to tell her about last night for fear she might panic. Their fight before he'd left still bothered him, and she apparently had too much on her mind already. However, he felt the need to tell someone about the time he'd had, and she listened so well. Of course, the touch of her thoughts and the pleasure of her company didn't hurt either.

"Come on, Thomas. Tell me what's happening."

Thomas looked at the floor for a few moments while he collected his thoughts, then told her everything, feeling her worries grow as he went.

"And you're okay now, right?" Her thoughts wrapped around him like a hug.

He nodded and scratched over his ear. *"Yeah, I feel like I overdid my workout, but I'm fine."*

"I'm glad your partner is a doctor this time."

Thomas looked at the sleeping Syndromer, and the revulsion that always came up when he dealt with one of them bubbled up.

"You're not still nursing a grudge about her having Power Deficit Syndrome, are you?" Meiko thought.

I shouldn't be, and I know that. He stood, padded over to the window, and looked out at the massive tree trunks and platforms of the city. *"Meiko, I—I keep thinking about that guy. Him and Angela."*

"That dealer was not Calla's fault, Thomas. You know that." She offered reassurance through their connection. *"And there was nothing to be done for Angela. She'd been shot twice in the chest. There's a lot of important anatomy around there."*

The cool wind blew in his face. *"In Calla's thoughts last night, I heard her wonder if she could have done something better. I'm not sure why that stuck with me when little else does, but I do remember it."*

"She has doubts. So do you. Or don't you?"

He reluctantly nodded. *"I do."*

"Some things just happen, Thomas, and they're no one's fault. Could be the bullets killed Angela. Could be the teleport strain. Could be the mental damage. It could be some error you, Calla, a nurse, Dr. Petrov, or even Angela herself made. You can't blame Calla on a bunch of ifs and maybes."

"You're right, but it's so hard to trust her. In fact, I almost didn't let her try last night. Stupid, yes, but I was too scared to yield control to a Syndromer, too afraid she'd fail like she'd done before."

He could feel Meiko's fury building, and he was pretty sure he deserved it, but she tamped it back down again.

"Thomas, you have to get past this problem you have with people who have Power Deficit Syndrome." A

hard edge bled through her effort to remain calm. *"You have to take people for who they are, regardless of whatever recessive genes they're carrying."*

"I'm trying. I'm not sure I'll ever get there, but I'm trying."

In the distance, the Gotrian chants drew to a close.

"I have to go. Thanks for listening."

"Yeah, no problem. You be careful out there," she thought.

"I'll contact you again soon. I love you."

"I love you, too. I hope you can learn to appreciate people, even ones who are handicapped. If you can't, there may be no point to all these wedding preparations."

Before he could ask her to explain, she broke the connection. He was inclined to reestablish the link and get her to elaborate on that last ultimatum. She'd mentioned some health-related thing before, but Meiko had insisted on waiting until he got home before they spoke about the problem further. Was her parting comment related?

Thomas walked over to Calla and crouched next to her. When he touched her arm and whispered her name, she startled and shrank away from him.

He sat back on his heels. "Easy, easy, it's me. If you want to go back to sleep, I can make your excuses. Otherwise, you have about fifteen minutes before Brachi gets here."

Calla sat up and got her backpack. "I'm afraid you're stuck with me today." She pulled out another emergency ration bar, the last one as he recalled, and tossed it to him. "It's not much, but it'll keep you going until lunch time."

"What about you?" His stomach growled.

"I'll make it."

He frowned. "How about I split it with you?"

"No." She shook her head and backed a step away from him. "The way I danced around with your metabolism last night, you need it. I'll be fine until lunch."

When he opened his mouth to protest again, she silenced him with a look.

"Don't argue with your doctor. I don't need you passing out in the middle of negotiations, and all that glucose I shot you with earlier should be nearly burned up by now. By the time we get to Pharmacorp, you'll be feeling like you haven't eaten in a week."

With that, she went into the bathroom and closed the door, ending the discussion unless he went in after her or projected his thoughts. He didn't like the idea of leaving her with nothing, but she had a point. He would add this to the growing list of what he owed her on this trip.

When he heard the knock on the door, she still hadn't emerged. He sympathized, remembering his own extra-long shower, but if she wanted to leave with him, she needed to get ready now. He could stall but not forever. Thomas rapped on the bathroom door, then went to admit Brachi.

"Thomas!" Brachi bounded forward. "Are you well?"

He smiled. "Don't I look better?"

Brachi nodded. "Oh, much better. How is this possible?"

Thomas glanced back at the bathroom. "Calla will have to take responsibility for that. Your efforts helped, too, I'm certain."

"She must have wisdom past her years."

Thomas nodded. "She's something. A perpetual surprise."

"Might I ask what happened?" Brachi asked.

Thomas looked at his scraped palm. "I was poisoned."

The shocked look on Brachi's face protested his innocence. "Who? How?" He coughed after each abbreviated question.

"We think someone put something in my drinks last night. We can only guess who at this point." He absently picked at the spray bandage, but it stayed firmly put.

Brachi sighed. "I knew we couldn't trust them. Blasted frogs."

Thomas scowled and shook his head. "It's not the Olvians. You can't assume that they have a hand in everything that doesn't go according to plan. There are hundreds of ways they could have kept Calla from reaching me if they meant my death."

"Then who could—" He cut himself off. His eyes narrowed. "Pharmacorp."

"Perhaps. We have a theory to propose to you and Rana about what's been going on."

As he spoke, Calla came out of the bathroom with still-damp hair and the same wrinkled clothes she'd slept in. Thomas looked around the room and didn't see her dufflebag anywhere. Brachi nodded, and Thomas felt him resisting the urge to insist on knowing the theory immediately.

The Gotrian Speaker stepped past him and closed with Calla. "Were you up all night?"

Calla raked her fingers through her hair. "Could I be coherent if I had been?"

"You brought a man back from death's gate. I suspect you could do many things."

Calla blushed and grabbed her trauma kit. "Well, um, I'm ready to go if you are."

"Let's head out then."

As they left the room, Thomas slowed when he

approached the stairs. Looking at the deck where he had fallen made the side of his face hurt. Butterflies danced in his stomach.

"It's all right. I'm not keen on heights, either," Calla thought.

He nodded and stepped up the stairs. By the time they reached the landing platform, his efforts to fumigate the butterflies had succeeded.

17

Upon landing in the company's parking lot, Thomas spotted the Olvians' sub. He hoped they hadn't been waiting long. If they were running their usual schedule, they'd been there for maybe a quarter of an hour. That didn't sound like much, but the Olvians had been an impatient bunch. He didn't look forward to any further tantrums from them.

Thomas turned to his partner. Calla leaned on the locked door with her eyes closed.

"We're here." He jostled her shoulder.

She startled awake. "Huh? Oh. Right."

Thomas stepped out of the plane, stretched, and then led the way toward the Pharmacorp building. The sooner they collected the Olvians and left, the better Thomas would like it.

Thomas' guts churned as he neared the door.

Calla rested a hand on his shoulder. *"I'll get the Olvians and meet you back here."*

He patted her hand. *"Thanks, but I've got it."*

Thomas opened the door and stepped in ahead of her.

Inside the building, everything looked like normal business. He hadn't been expecting them to do anything radically different, but no one seemed to react to what they must've thought was an animated corpse walking through the lobby. Was Calla's conclusion wrong? Maybe someone else had poisoned him. No. It had to be Pharmacorp. Patina or Kevin had to have slipped the Minum into Thomas' drinks. Nothing else made sense.

Thomas' muscles ached as he jogged up the stairs to the second level with Calla and Brachi behind him.

Patina's voice drifted down the hall from the open door of the conference room. "And you haven't heard anything since then?"

Rana harrumphed. "No, I took her to the submarines and saw her go. We're here now in hopes that someone will come with news."

"Oh, I do hope he's all right," Patina said.

Liar.

Last night wouldn't have happened if not for her.

When he reached the door of the room, Rana and Pipien both went mottled, then paled to match the fluttery joy in their thoughts. Patina's electric pink skirt and sparkly silver blouse clashed outrageously with the Olvians' blue tabards.

"Thomas!" Rana leapt out of her chair.

"Hi, we made it." Thomas stepped further into the room. "I'm sorry we're late. Thanks for waiting."

Pipien sat straighter. "You're sounding well."

"I'm feeling much better."

Patina stood and offered a grin that wouldn't win her an acting award any time soon. "Calla must be an amazing doctor."

Thomas smiled at his partner and projected his thoughts. *"Who'd you tell about your credentials?"*

"Brachi and the Gotrian healer. That's all. Sorry, I know that was against our orders, but I didn't have time to be graceful." She said out loud, "Doctor? Where did you get the impression I was a doctor?"

Patina wrung her hands. "Well, what I mean is you must have some medical training to treat such a difficult, um, poison without any medical supplies."

Thomas' jaw clenched. Although Brachi could have told Patina about Calla's background, he couldn't have said anything about a poison or the missing gear in Calla's kit. Given the suspicions about Pharmacorp's involvement in the local plague, Joy wouldn't have mentioned Calla's real purpose even if Patina had thought to call Haidar Station.

"Poison?" Rana's coloring turned mottled. "I thought he fell!"

Calla nodded. "The poison made him ill and that caused him to fall."

"How did you help him?" Patina asked.

"Just following procedures. I had to be a little inventive at some points, but I've seen worse." Calla managed to sound like she dealt with patients who'd been unwillingly drugged as a matter of course.

Last night was anything but routine. Thomas gestured to the door. "If you'll excuse us, Patina, we have a lot to do today."

She nodded. "Sure. Well, it's good to see you up and around again, Thomas."

Once she was gone, Rana darkened. "She knows too much. I could hear the guilt in her voice."

Brachi bared his teeth. "She frowned when she first saw you, Thomas. Be careful of that one."

"I will," he said.

"Are you really a doctor, Calla?" Pipien asked.

Thomas caught Calla's eye and the unspoken question. *"No sense hiding it now. Whoever we were trying to hide your background from got it from your medical records."*

"Yes, I have certification for psionic and physical medicine." Calla adjusted her backpack on her shoulder.

Pipien rose to her full height and fluttered her arms. "You lied to us!"

Calla shook her head. "I never said I was or wasn't a doctor. I said I was here to advise Thomas, and I am."

"We made assumptions. She simply didn't correct us." Rana darkened even more than her associate.

Thomas ushered Calla out before the Olvians could press the matter further. "Let's go to the restaurant, and I'll suggest an explanation for all our troubles."

Pipien blackened and flopped into the chair. "Changing sites will not make the Gotrians more trustworthy."

Rana turned obsidian and spoke her native language to her protégé. Whatever words passed between them made Pipien flush the dark gray of embarrassment and shrink back in the chair.

Thomas agreed wholeheartedly with the decision to move but probably for a different reason. If he could avoid being a "guest" of Pharmacorp again, he would be ecstatic. He set a hurried pace down the stairs and out the door. Once outside, he faded back to let his partner lead the way.

She headed through a flower garden that brought up mental images of Cordil IV's failed negotiations. Pathways of dark gray gravel wove through brilliantly-colored flowers growing in ordered rows.

Exiting the far side, they entered a shopping center. A one-kilometer stretch of road had restaurants, a grocer, and a few clothing stores. Calla walked across the street and stopped in front of a quaint restaurant advertising "Good Home Cooking."

Whose home did the eatery try to emulate? Meiko's mom made stuff he couldn't even pronounce on the first try. The red-checked sign said, "Mangiare," which conjured up images of noodles and tomatoes.

Thomas stepped ahead of Calla and opened the door for everyone. The smell of marinara sauce confirmed his guess about the dominant cuisine. Calla walked up to a podium and spoke to a hostess who then showed them to a small room already set for them.

A rectangular, real wood table stained a dark, reddish brown occupied the bulk of the space. Ten wooden chairs with vinyl padding ringed the table. The windows along one wall had red-checked curtains over white sheers. The rest of the room had been decorated with prints of wine bottles and olive trees.

Thomas found his seat and directed the others to places similar to where they'd been in Pharmacorp's closet. The two delegations played their usual dominance game.

Calla yawned and thought, *"You'd think they'd get tired of this."*

"Kids," Thomas thought. Then he said out loud, "Well, this is cozy. I hope this arrangement is more acceptable than our last."

"Will you tell us your theory now?" Brachi asked.

The room took on a spin to the left. He gripped the arms of the chair. "Actually, Calla put most of the pieces together last night, so I'll let her explain."

She could handle that, couldn't she? He needed a few minutes to put his head back together. Calla's glazed, heavy-lidded eyes drifted closed. He didn't envy her, remembering how he'd felt the day before yesterday while functioning on nearly no sleep.

Rana adjusted her tabard. "You mean she helped you recover and put a theory together?"

Calla blinked a few times, and all traces of weariness fled from her. Was that the trick she'd offered him to help him overcome the terminal fatigue?

She drew her chair closer to the table. "I simply recorded my observations, and the theory became too obvious to ignore."

Calla launched off into a description of her information and the data from the medical records, following the description from her notebook with unnatural precision. While she spoke, Thomas looked inward for the source of his unsteadiness. Visions of the previous night, what he could remember, anyway, came to mind. He'd felt woozy then, too.

Had Patina found some way to drug him again? Impossible. Minum had to be injected or swallowed, and they hadn't even shared a handshake.

As Calla's description wore on, Thomas became acutely aware of the thoughts around him. The waiter lamented how tired he felt. The cook grumbled about some customer who had sent an order back. The proprietor worried about the slowing business climate and hoped these negotiations dragged on for a while to generate some steady income. The two delegations listened to Calla with sincere interest, but each ambassador hunted for evidence in her words to prove the other side had caused the problems and framed Pharmacorp.

The doctor's mind, though, was the worst. Although highly structured, Calla multi-tasked uncountable pieces of information about her surroundings, the movements of people, some telepathic perceptions like his own, words, gestures, appearances, smells, sounds, and even strange minutiae like the length and width of the crack in the vinyl on her chair's arm. If that weren't enough, her brain subconsciously made connections to prior experiences.

The medical records she had reviewed and the pages in her notebook where she had written her findings came vividly into her thoughts as if she had the folders and book open in front of her. The words, sketches, and even defects in the paper were clearly visible.

In her feelings, he picked up the tension that came with public speaking and deep concern for someone who was ill. In the stream of medical-ese running through her mind, enough words registered for him to realize he was the object of her worry.

How could she process all that? He'd expected Syndromers to be incapable of dealing with even a fraction of that volume of data. He couldn't keep it all straight, and he couldn't remember how to shut the intrusion out again.

His hands shook and he hid them under the table. Information swamped him like a tsunami. All the images, thoughts, and words jumbled together. He pressed his fingers against his forehead.

Then, without warning, the incoming flood ceased. He couldn't even hear the typical background noise. The lack of thought-impressions unnerved him, but the silence helped him focus again. What had made the telepathic world go quiet?

Thomas opened his eyes. When had he closed them? The delegates were focused on Calla and her ongoing explanation.

The edge of her napkin and the plate hid a small anti-psionic generator. Without missing a beat, she'd seen his distress, recognized it, and enacted at least a temporary solution.

Now, able to think clearly again, Thomas understood. Minum withdrawal. He'd gone through the same thing in rehab. He'd fought his way through the ruckus, hoping he could die and get over feeling helpless and hearing intolerable noise. He could not go through that torture again. Calla could probably fix the problem like she had taken care of him last night. Could he swallow his pride and ask her?

Calla stood. "This would be a good time for a break. I've given you a lot of information to digest. Take a few minutes to stretch or go for a quick walk and think the matter over. When we meet back here in...say...fifteen minutes, Thomas and I can then field your questions and hear your ideas."

The Olvians went mottled and Brachi glowered, but all three delegates walked out.

When the two of them were alone, Thomas scooted back from the table and leaned his elbows on his knees. "Thank you."

Calla perched on the table across from him. "What happened? You seemed to be in a fugue."

"How do you do it?" He ran his fingers partway through his hair and leaned his head on his palm. "How do you keep up with so much incoming stuff?"

She shrugged and pointed to her dull eyes. "I grew up with it. I've never had to deal with anything else for more than a few minutes at a time, and I automatically filter out the unnecessary data, not unlike concentrating on the person you're talking to in a crowded room or ignoring the hum of an air conditioner. Do you often lose control like that?"

"Not since rehab. It's part of the withdrawal. Can— can—" He stopped and took a deep breath before he started again. "I need a hit. Can you help me?"

There. He'd said it.

She frowned and shook her head. "No. Not even if I carried Minum in my kit. The anti-psionic generator is less dangerous."

He leaned away from her. "What? No, no, that's not what I meant. Maybe I said that wrong."

Calla crossed her arms over her chest. "Okay, try again."

He looked away and took a deep breath. "Can you stop my brain and my body from demanding more Minum?"

Calla blew out a sigh. "There is a way, yes, but you

probably don't want me to do that."

"Why not?"

She paced to the window and looked out. "The process is invasive, Thomas. It involves going very deep into your mind and adjusting some things. The good news is that I only have to do it once in most cases. The bad news is I know how much you'd rather avoid contact with me."

Thomas studied the floor while he considered his options. He'd have to let a Syndromer in yet again. He couldn't get away from allowing Calla to meander through his head. He could ask to borrow Calla's generator, but that solution wouldn't last. At some point, he'd have to give the device back to her and face his problems head on.

Once he'd been through rehab, he'd learned to rely on his abilities for information. He'd seen how much Calla received, and he knew she'd give him updates if he asked, but too much time would pass. He needed his telepathic impressions to arbitrate this dispute.

Similarly, he couldn't teleport home to see another doctor. To do that, he'd have to turn off the generator and all the noise would crash down around him. Focusing enough to teleport or even call out to someone on the station would be impossible. Thomas couldn't even ask Calla to contact someone for him. Her powers didn't let her project that far.

Only Calla's option remained.

Thomas nodded. "Do it."

"Are you sure?" She retrieved the generator.

"Yes."

Calla knelt next to him and touched his cheek with her cold fingers. "Okay. Just relax. I won't hurt you."

His innards fluttered.

"Ready?" she asked.

He swallowed. "Yeah."

"If this becomes too uncomfortable, tell me, and I'll break the connection." Calla thumbed the switch to the generator.

All the thoughts flooded his mind again. Closing his eyes tightly, Thomas clenched his fists against the sheer volume. Another presence impinged on his mind, and he flinched, trying to push away his unwanted memory of that drug dealer so many years ago.

"I'll be as careful as I can." Calla's icy fingers pressed lightly on his temple and on the back of his head. "Please don't fight me, Thomas."

"I'm sorry. I'm not trying to, really." He spoke through his teeth.

"Okay. I understand. This will take a few moments."

All at once, he looked forward to the connection with her and yet dreaded another close contact with the Syndromer. She could make both the noise and the craving stop, but maniacal laughter and terror from the last Syndromer he'd encountered kept churning up through his recollections.

Violently loud minutes came and went.

Sweat poured from Thomas' face. "Either do something or—"

He felt a curious shift in his mind. The unbearable noise dropped to the normal background voices.

Had he lost his powers again? No. Calla's thoughts were clear. That could be part of a link with her, so he reached farther and ran into the staff and patrons of the restaurant.

Thomas pulled away from Calla's touch and studied her for a moment. "What did you do?"

She perched on the edge of the table again. "There's a power level below which most people won't perceive a threat, and one less than that below which most people won't even acknowledge contact."

He arched an eyebrow. "You can restrict your power usage that much?"

She nodded. "When you don't have much to start with, turning it down so far isn't that hard. Control, though, that's the tricky part because I can't use visualizations. I have to know exactly what I'm facing. What did you think I was going to do?"

Thomas shook his head. "I was expecting you to blast through the interference."

She gave him a lopsided smile. "I couldn't overpower you that way even if I wanted to. Given your history, more force would have exacerbated the problem, anyway. Not all obstacles can be overcome with the application of a larger hammer."

He leaned back in the chair. "You must get a lot of kids in your practice."

Calla shrugged. "Kids, elderly, and assault victims combined make up about seventy-five percent. They all have some fears to overcome."

He pulled his handkerchief out of his back pocket and mopped the sweat from his face. "I can see why they come to you. I didn't even know you were there."

"I'm glad it worked. Now, sometimes, the adjustment slips." She handed him the generator. "I'll leave this in your care in case you need it. You probably won't, though. Breaking the cycle didn't take much of a nudge."

Behind her, the door opened and Brachi entered.

He looked past her to acknowledge Brachi then projected his thoughts to Calla. *"We're on."*

"Are you okay, Thomas?" she asked.

"Yes, thank you." He tucked his handkerchief into his pocket.

"You're welcome."

As Calla went back to her seat, Thomas pocketed the anti-psionic generator. She really wasn't a genetic freak or a waste of space. She was a doctor who happened to have Power Deficit Syndrome.

18

Dillon swept his hand over the door sensor for the pool area on Deck Seven, where he usually met Calla, only Calla wouldn't be there. Both Dad and Calla would kill him if they found out he was swimming without a buddy, but if he went to martial arts class without smelling like the pool, the other kids would make fun of him and say Calla had left just like Mom had. Only Calla really was coming back. She promised she would.

If Dillon's hair were wet and smelled like the pool, then he could tell the others that Calla had gotten busy with a patient and wouldn't be there, which had happened a couple times before. The partner thing was okay, but going alone just this once wouldn't be so bad.

The odor of pool chemicals wrinkled Dillon's nose.

Someone was splashing in the water. Dillon smiled. He wouldn't be alone after all. He jogged down the short hall. A lady he recognized from other Tuesdays swam laps down the length of the pool. She had long black hair tied in a tight braid and a bright green bathing suit. Maybe she could be his swimming buddy.

Dillon went up to the pool's edge and tried to ignore the turning in his stomach as he waited for the lady to get close enough to hear him. "Miss? Excuse me, Miss."

She stopped and hung onto the concrete lip of the pool. "Hi."

"Hi. I'm Dillon."

"Nice to meet you, Dillon. I'm Meiko."

Dillon studied the tiles at his feet. "Calla is my usual swimming buddy, but, um, she's gone this week."

Meiko nodded. "My swimming buddy is, too."

"We always go swimming on Tuesdays." Dillon peeked at her.

"You need a buddy, don't you?" she asked.

"Yeah, um, I mean, yes, ma'am. I mean, if it's okay." He frowned. *I sound like a dork.*

She smiled. "What a coincidence. I need a buddy, too. Go get your suit on. I plan to stick around for a while yet."

The creepy crawlies in Dillon's gut went away. "Thanks!"

Dillon darted into the locker room and counted down the rows to the right one then found his own locker. He had the combination entered in record time and changed into his red and white swimsuit as fast as a laser bolt. In seconds, he was ready to do battle with the evil water monsters in the pool with his super strength. First, though, he had to put his clothes in his locker.

Dillon heard a loud scream which sounded as though it was suddenly cut off. Dillon freeze in place. He waited to hear some other sound, but even the splashing noises Meiko had been making were gone now. Had his would-be swimming buddy run into trouble?

Dillon crammed the rest of his clothes into the locker and slammed it shut. It bounced back open and spewed half his clothes. He picked up his shoe, socks, and shirt from the floor and stuffed them into the locker, then held the door shut until he heard and felt the latch click. He ran out to the pool. The lady was floating face down near the steps.

Maybe she was playing like Dillon did for Calla sometimes.

Dillon crouched at the edge of the pool. "Come on, you faker, stop messing around."

Meiko didn't move. He waited for her to give up the

game.

Unless she could hold her breath for a seriously long time, she should've come up for air by now.

A queasy pain settled in Dillon's gut. *Is she hurt?* "Miss? Miss, are you okay? Please, don't play with me right now. Miss? Please?"

He stretched as far as he could to tap her shoulder. When she didn't react, he tapped harder. Still nothing.

Something was wrong. Something had to be wrong. Meiko didn't look hurt, but maybe she'd been hurt some way he couldn't see. He had to pull her out. When he tried to grab her hand, his foot slipped. Cold enveloped him, driving a shock through him as he half-inhaled some water. Dillon surfaced quickly. Chlorine stung the back of his throat and nose while he coughed and tried to breathe again.

As he made his way back to the steps, he pulled Meiko with him and made her roll over onto her back to keep her face out of the water. Dillon dragged her as far up the steps as he could, but she was too big for him to get her onto the mats at the top of the steps.

"Don't move, okay?" Dillon backed away, keeping an eye on Meiko.

He ran around the pool to the red emergency call box. He smacked the button and waited for the dispatcher to answer. After forever with no answer, he hit the button again. Dillon looked back at Meiko still lying where he'd left her. He pushed the button and held it down, but no voices came out of the speaker.

He didn't want to leave Meiko alone in case she slid back into the water, but he had to get help. Calla! She'd know what to do. She was a doctor. Dillon wasn't supposed to think to her while she was working, but she'd said she'd be stuck in meetings all the time, not treating patients. Still, she'd gotten pretty mad the last time he'd mentally called her while she was on duty. Who else could he get to help? He didn't know any other doctors.

Concentrating on his mentor, Dillon closed his eyes and pushed his thoughts out as hard as he could to make Calla hear him, even if she'd gone far away. He hoped she wouldn't be too angry.

Thomas sat back in his chair with his hand resting on the anti-psionic generator in his pocket. Having the device so close soothed away the memory of his earlier mental collapse.

"I see what you're showing us, but what rreal evidence do you have that Pharmacorp is the source of our problems?" Brachi ended his question with a dry hack.

"Again? This is the fourth time we've had that question. Can't he accept the idea that neither of their races is to blame?" Calla blew out a breath. *"Hasn't he been listening?"*

Thomas smirked. *"Not likely. Probably been too busy coming up with his next Olvian insult. I walked them through it last time. Your turn."*

While she launched off in the description of the evidence against Pharmacorp again, Thomas plastered on his this-is-fascinating look and let his mind drift.

He should be disgusted by his recent close contact with the mind of a Syndromer, but he found himself grateful for her help. Although insulted by his attitude, she continued to treat him with professional courtesy and at least tried to respect his wishes. Thomas found himself liking her.

Angela died because of her.

No matter how kind and compassionate she could be, that fact remained. Had she not been a Syndromer, Angela would still be alive. Wouldn't she? Had the gunshots really killed her like Calla had suggested? Once, he had it all figured out. Syndromers were to be shunned because of what they were. Now Calla had come along and upset everything he thought he knew.

As Calla's explanation wound down, Thomas banished his musings. If he didn't move this meeting along, Brachi or Rana would find yet another way to ask about proof of Pharmacorp's involvement.

Thomas leaned forward with his arms crossed on the table. "The next step, of course, will be for each of you to go back to your governments with our theories. Find out if they will consider signing a treaty that we'll draw up tomorrow to end the fighting."

Pipien darkened. "You have a theory that sounds good, but no proof real of Pharmacorp's involvement. Without something tangible, the Matriarch will never agree."

Rana glared at her protégé before turning to Calla. "If the Matriarch hears the case from a negotiator, she might consider extending the ceasefire until proof tangible is found."

"That could be arranged." Thomas scratched above his ear. *But let Calla do it. I've had enough excitement on this trip.*

Pipien grumbled in her own language then spoke in the tongue they all shared. "Males aren't permitted to address the Matriarch and her Advisors."

Calla drew a breath between her teeth. "I'll have to present the information then."

Yes! I'm safe! Calla can— He frowned and rubbed

his chin.

Calla didn't show her fatigue anymore, but she had to be spent after last night. Worse, addressing the whole Olvian ruling body would be no walk in the park, even if she knew what to say and do. He'd have to coach her and pray she could pull this off. Maybe he could write the speech for her and have her memorize it. Her phenomenal memory would work to their advantage.

"Brachi, do I need to go before the Elders with you?" Thomas asked.

The Gotrian struck his chest. "I am the Speaker of my people. I will be heard."

Thomas nodded. "Then perhaps I can return to Haidar to look into arranging medical help. If there are no other concerns, then we can go, and I'll see you all here tomorrow. Calla and I will return to the cities this evening. We have some other matters to look into."

Rana pushed back from the table and stood. "I'll have the meeting arranged for the end of the workday. In an hour, if possible. I'll meet you in your room."

"I'll be there." After both delegations left, Calla groaned and shook her head. "Y'know, Olvians don't see all that well on land. With a little make-up and a dress, you might pass for a female."

He walked to her end of the table and sat in the nearest chair. "One who gets five o'clock shadow in the evening? Don't worry. You'll be ready."

"I'll have to be, unless we can con Joy into visiting." She turned her chair toward him. "How are you feeling now?"

Thomas shrugged. "I'm fine. Whatever you did worked like a charm. Pity they couldn't do that seven years ago."

Calla winced. "They could. It's an old, easy trick."

Thomas raised an eyebrow. "Then why do they have

rehab clinics anymore?"

"The theory is falling out of favor, but they believe that if they make the recovery unpleasant enough the first time, you won't be eager to do anything to get yourself back in there again. Addictions aren't just physical."

He rolled his eyes and snorted. "That's some deterrent. How are you holding up?"

She rubbed her belly. "Oh, I'm hungry enough to eat a whole house for dinner, and I'm not looking forward to the exhaustion I'll feel when I undo the metabolic change, but I'll manage."

"Well, I'll order us a snack." *Mozzarella sticks and marinara sound good.* He stood and went to the door. "Then we'll get going on your public speaking crash course."

Hardly a step out of the room, nearby telepathic activity buzzed in his mind. Behind him, Calla drew a sharp breath between her teeth. He turned. She held her head and rocked forward and back, eyes tightly closed. Memories of the Cordil attack and the mercenary telepath haunted Thomas. No Syndromer would be up to fighting a battle on that front.

He reached out with his mental senses and came up blank. "Calla, what is it?"

"Dillon, the kid I mentor," she said through clenched teeth. "He's panicked about something, and he's not controlling his volume."

He crouched in front of her. "What's his problem?"

"He hasn't gotten that far yet." She leaned forward in her chair. "He's still on why he went swimming without me. I can't project far enough to tell him to ease off."

Thomas sat in the nearest chair. "Dillon, huh? I'll tell him for you."

She shook her head. "He's so frantic I'm not sure

he'd listen to you. Finally. We're getting to the point."

"What's going on?"

Calla reached for him. "It's Meiko. She's hurt."

Thomas jumped to his feet, knocking the chair back. "Where?"

"Pool, Level Seven."

He knew the place well. Meiko sometimes went there to swim a few laps after work.

After pulling Calla up with one hand and grabbing her backpack with the other, Thomas teleported back to Haidar Station. When they appeared, the smell of chlorine assaulted his nose. Calla doubled over. He helped her to the floor and spun, looking for Meiko. She lay half in the water on the steps. A kid in a red and white swimsuit, Dillon probably, knelt next to her holding her head up. Dillon's dark, wet hair clung to his head.

Thomas raced around the pool. Dillon left Meiko and blocked the way.

"Get out of my way." Thomas took a step aside and the kid moved with him.

"Meiko's hurt, and you're not a doctor." Dillon settled into a horse stance. "You have to leave her alone until the doctor is finished."

Maybe if Meiko had been sitting up or at least awake, Thomas wouldn't have worried so much. Looking past Dillon, Thomas teleported and appeared next to her.

He knelt on the blue and white tile and gently shook her shoulder. "Meiko? Honey, can you hear me?"

"Leave her alone!" Dillon screamed. "You're not a doctor!"

"Dillon, stop!" Calla commanded in a firm tone.

As she continued to give Dillon directions to back off, Thomas leaned over Meiko, checking for a pulse in her neck. The weak heartbeat slurred under his fingers, but he couldn't feel her breath on his cheek.

He looked across the pool at Calla. She came to her feet, staggered, and fell back to one knee.

"Calla!" He reached for her. "Calla, she's not breathing!"

She pushed off from the floor and stayed upright. "Does she have a pulse?"

"Yeah, but not much of one."

"I'm coming. If you know how to do rescue breathing, get started."

Thomas went down the pool steps. Cold water cramped his calf muscles. He carried Meiko to the rough mats at the water's edge. Eons had passed since his CPR course, but he knew enough and followed the instructions. While Calla staggered around the water's edge, Thomas watched Meiko's chest rise and fall with each forced breath and felt keen disappointment when she didn't resume breathing on her own.

Calla dropped to her knees across from him and dug in her trauma kit. "Dillon, how long has it been since you heard her scream."

The kid scooted half a step closer. "I—I don't know."

She fished a plastic bag and a facemask from her trauma kit. "It's important, Dillon. A couple minutes? Ten? Twenty? An hour? About how long?"

"A couple minutes, I think." Dillon shivered and crossed his arms over his chest. "I ran out and—and then I found out she wasn't joking and—and I got her to the steps and—and then I found the box broke and—and then I called you."

Calla nodded and attached the facemask to the bag. "All right. Thank you."

"Can you help her?" Thomas asked.

"I'll do everything I can, but we're running out of time." Calla handed him the rig she'd assembled.

"Breathe for her. Let me know if there's any change. Every few times, check to see if she's breathing by herself and check her pulse while you're at it."

With trembling hands, he fitted the mask over her face, squeezed the balloon, and watched her chest rise and fall. How could this happen? Meiko swam like a fish.

Calla closed her eyes, rested a hand on Meiko's forehead, and whistled. "She's been attacked, Thomas. There's a large section of the maze in pieces."

He shook his head. "Who? Dillon?"

She kept her eyes closed. "No. He doesn't have half the control needed for this. When I correct the damage, maybe she'll be able to tell us. Whoever did this probably timed the attack so we'd think she'd drowned."

He squeezed the bag and watched Meiko's chest rise and fall. "She'll be okay, right?"

Calla nodded. "Yes, but the longer it takes for her to breathe on her own, the greater the chance for a collapse. What you're doing will buy her some time, though."

Thomas wished someone else were available to take over Meiko's care. Calla might be good at rearranging metabolisms and directing the body to detoxify drugs, but a few days ago, she'd lost a patient who, like Meiko, had mental damage and had stopped breathing.

He looked up at Dillon. "Dillon, I need you to go find a working call box and phone in the emergency."

Dillon stood there watching Calla. His bottom lip quivered and his eyes teared. Confusion and fear had replaced all the bravery now that Calla had taken over.

"Did you hear me?" Thomas reached back and jostled the kid's elbow.

"Dillon, this is Meiko's friend, Thomas," Calla said.

"Hi, Thomas." Dillon sniffled and wiped his nose on the back of his hand.

Thomas forced a smile. "Hi, Dillon. Can you go find a

call box that works and call in the emergency?"

Dillon nodded. "Sure."

"Would you do that right now?" Calla kept her eyes closed but turned her head toward the kid. "Go out the door, then turn right and go until you find a red emergency box. Then call Dispatch to send help here."

"Okay." Dillon ran out.

He continued to operate the airbag. *You've got to live, honey. You've got to.*

Finally, he heard an unsteady gasp as she drew a breath of her own.

Thomas pulled the mask away. "Calla, she's breathing without my help."

She smiled but didn't look up. "I heard. That helps. Keep an eye on her, and watch for Dillon to return with the paramedics."

Thomas held Meiko's hand in both of his. Telepathy buzzed nearby.

"Not now, Dillon." Calla's eyes clenched shut and her hand shot forward, grabbing his wrist in a painfully firm grip.

"What?" He pried her hand loose. "What's wrong?"

"Remember what I said about how delicate this kind of work is?" Her words broke the lightspeed barrier. "The communication from Dillon started a collapse, and it's a fast one. You'll have to help me. I can only slow these things down on my own."

His brow furrowed. "What do I do?"

"Either give me control of—" She cut herself off. "Skip that. Join me and I'll show you where to push until I can stabilize her again."

Letting his eyes close, Thomas reached into Meiko's mind and sensed the tension of the doctor's efforts. A maze made of pictures painted on glass walls appeared with one huge area showing the damage Calla had mentioned. An image of Calla stood in the blasted section trying to brace against a pane threatening to come down.

In spite of her best efforts, the wall inexorably fell, and she went to stop the next. "Push exactly where I am hard enough to halt the collapse but not too hard."

He nodded and obeyed her directions. As he took over the work, he felt an uncomfortable weight on his mind.

"Got it?" Calla asked.

He shifted the force he applied to go for better leverage. "Yeah, but hurry."

"I'll be as quick as I can, but it'll be a few minutes."

Those minutes felt like hours while the pressure bearing down on him rose from uncomfortable to painful.

He shook with the effort. "Calla? Calla, I'm losing it!"

"Just hold on." Her voice sounded distant. "I'm almost there."

When the first panel fell, the pain in his head grew exponentially. A second threatened to topple.

Thomas felt his fingernails digging into his palms. "Calla! I can't do this!"

She touched his arm. "You're doing fine. This isn't easy. Slow the decline as much as you can. I'll repair the damage later."

Using every bit of power he could muster, Thomas fought to hold the wall segment up but couldn't prevent the inevitable fall. The third wall went faster than the first two as his control slipped. The fourth and fifth walls came down. What was taking Calla so long?

"When I say 'go,' release your hold," she said with supernatural calm. "Ready? Go!"

He let go as something he couldn't see shifted in Meiko's mind. The headache faded, and Thomas watched, expecting to see the glass walls fall like dominoes. Nothing happened.

Calla's image appeared next to his own.

He released the breath he'd been holding. "That was harder than I thought it'd be."

She peeked from the corner of her eye. "If you think that was tough, try bracing against two simultaneous collapses of a similar intensity using a tenth of your current power."

He stared at her and remembered what little she'd told him about his previous partner's death. "Is that what happened to Angela?"

"In her case, there were two collapses, a full arrest, and two sucking chest wounds." She counted off the problems on her fingers. "The collapses were my problem to deal with, though."

Two of them? He'd barely held one up long enough for her to do her work. No wonder she'd been furious with him for blaming Angela's death on her. Calla hadn't failed because of Power Deficit Syndrome. She'd been given an impossible task. Now that he'd had a try at the same job, he wondered if even August could have managed.

He looked down at his feet. "I—I didn't realize what you were up against."

She nodded. "I have to finish healing the damage in Meiko's mind. Dillon should be back with the paramedics shortly. Tell him not to think to me for at least the next twenty minutes, okay?"

"Yeah. I can do that." Thomas gripped her shoulder. "Thanks, Calla."

She smiled. "I'm glad you were here."

He withdrew from Meiko. How could he have been so wrong about Calla's incompetence? Could he be equally wrong about other things?

19

After pulling away from her patient's mind, Calla drew a deep breath and opened her eyes. She looked at her watch. So late already? She'd have to get back to Ologo soon and meet Rana.

"Dr. Geisman?"

Calla looked up at the emergency medical technician in a white shirt and black cargo pants squatting nearby. "She'll be fine. There were no further complications." Pulling out a prescription pad and a pen from her kit, she wrote orders and read them back to the paramedic. "I want her under observation until she wakes up. A guard needs to be posted at her door and an anti-psionic generator is to be armed in her room with sufficient radius to protect her if her assailant makes another attempt."

Once assured of their comprehension, Calla gave the note to the two paramedics and led Thomas aside while they loaded Meiko onto a gurney. Worry and traces of self-recrimination lined his face.

"You did everything you could, Thomas." Calla started to grip his arm but stopped and pulled her hand back. "You couldn't have known she would be attacked."

He stared past her at the paramedics. "She could have died because I couldn't stop the collapse."

"Fast collapses are hard to deal with." Calla stretched the stiffness out of her muscles. "When your patient is telepathically stronger than you are, the job is even more difficult. The difference between your powers and Meiko's is more than I had expected. When those domino effects go so quickly, the best you can do is slow it down until the imbalance can be corrected."

He nodded but bit his lip.

"You did fine, Thomas." Calla pivoted to see the emergency medical staff securing Meiko to a gurney. "If you hadn't been there, she would be dead now. Because of your help, Meiko will recover."

An awkward silence passed between them until a sniffle from Dillon broke in.

She glanced back at him sitting against the wall and then turned to Thomas. "Go on ahead with the paramedics. I'll be along shortly." She recalled a mental image of the duty roster to remember who had charge of the nearest ward. "Xava Vandamir is a good doctor. She'll take over Meiko's treatment so I can return to Ologo in a little bit. Thanks for your help."

Thomas gave her a small, tight smile, then left.

Calla gathered her supplies into her backpack again and joined Dillon at the wall. "Are you okay?"

He turned away from her.

She sighed and crouched next to him. "Don't be like that, Dillon. What's wrong?"

"You're mad at me!" He glared at her.

"Why do you think I'm mad at you?"

"I thought to you twice while you were working." He wiped his nose with his hand. "You were mad at me the last time I did that."

She twisted around and sat next to him by the wall. "Well, the first time was okay. You were worried about Meiko and had to get help. I may not have been your best choice for—"

"Who was I supposed to get?" He hugged his knees to his chest and stared at the water.

"How about your dad, Matt, or Mr. Zagruder?"

"They're not doctors."

"True, but they could've gotten help for you while you stayed with Meiko." She turned his chin to make him look at her. "The second time, you knew I had a patient to help. You know it's dangerous to think to me when I have a patient."

He shrugged away from her. "I just forgot cuz I was excited that a call box worked. I didn't mean to hurt Meiko. I really didn't."

"I realize that, but try harder to remember next time, okay?"

He nodded.

She pointed at the pool. "Do you understand now why you shouldn't go swimming alone?"

"But I wasn't alone. Meiko was there. She was my buddy."

Calla frowned. "You didn't know you would have a buddy when you left home. I think you meant to go swimming in any case. True?"

He stared at the water.

"Dillon, am I right?" she asked.

He plopped his chin down on his knees. "Yeah."

"Not a good idea, squirt. Even I don't go alone."

"Meiko was alone before I got here."

She nodded and looked at the mats where the rescue work had taken place. "And look what happened. If you hadn't been here to pull her out of the water, no one would have known to get help until too late. If she hadn't been here and you had gone alone, you could've been the one who got hurt."

Dillon sniffled. "Is it okay if I don't want to swim anymore today?"

Calla nodded. "That's fine, since I have to go back to work again and that would leave you without a buddy. Go get dressed and I'll see you home before I go back to work."

He groaned. "Do you have to go back to work?"

She stood and pulled him to his feet. "Yes. We're not finished yet, but we're close. I'll be home again soon."

He frowned and hugged her too tightly. "I really don't want you to go."

She wormed an arm free to return his hug. "I know you don't, and I really wish I could stay, too. The meetings haven't been much fun. Just a little longer, that's all. You can handle it. I still need you here to water my flower."

He sighed and held on a moment longer before he sulked off to the locker room.

While waiting for him to return, she grabbed her backpack and went to the call box. The red panel built into the wall had a speaker, microphone, and a large, black button. Everything appeared to be intact. Calla pushed the button down for five seconds to start the autotest, but nothing happened. Awfully convenient, wasn't it? Meiko got waylaid in the pool area that just so happened to have a defective emergency call system. Who would want to hurt Meiko? Calla recalled case after case of disabled Haidarians being injured, attacked, or killed by an unknown assailant. Did carrying a PDS gene make Meiko a target?

Maybe the police would turn up more in this investigation than they had on Calla's apartment fire a month ago.

After seeing Dillon home, Calla went to the medical ward nearest the pool. The smell of antiseptics and cleaning solutions were more welcoming than the nose-blistering chlorine of the pool. The guard at the door and the red tape marking the edge of the null-telepathy area cast by the generator gave away Meiko's location. Calla showed the guard her identification then lightly knocked on the door before stepping in.

Meiko lay on the bed covered by light blue blankets, and Thomas, fingers buried in his red hair, sat in the nearby chair staring at her.

"Who would do this?" He kept his gaze on Meiko.

"I don't know." Calla leaned against the wall. "Maybe this is another not-terribly-creative way to get you off Ologo before securing the treaty. If they got into your records, finding that you and Meiko have applied for a marriage license wouldn't take much more effort."

"If that was their plan, it didn't work." His blue eyes narrowed. "I'm more determined than ever to put an end to them now. Coming after me is one thing but hurting Meiko?" He shook his head.

Calla nodded. "I'll help if I can."

To feel more useful, Calla retrieved the chart and scrolled through the entries, then added her own notes about the poolside rescue to the end. There was no mention of a disability, but then carrying a single PDS gene wouldn't be recorded. She'd just turned the chart off when another knock on the door preceded the entrance of a police officer in a dark blue uniform. His hair was cut close, and his eyes were dark. After Thomas fielded some basic questions, Calla gave her clinical assessment, and she and Thomas related how they'd found Meiko and their efforts to revive her.

"Does she have any disabilities?" the officer asked.

Calla went to Meiko's side. "So you also think she might be a victim of the bizarre mishaps targeting the handicapped?"

She thought back over the last few years to a blind woman in the park who had fallen to anaphylactic shock for no apparent reason. A man with a prosthetic arm had nearly died when his recently re-certified space suit had developed a leak during a spacewalk. Then, of course, there had been the fire in her own apartment. There had been other strange occurrences, too, like random, untraceable attacks. Many had looked accidental but almost too perfect, like an over-conceived plan.

The officer jotted on his notepad. "It's too early in the investigation to speculate on that."

Calla nodded. The non-answer hid a "yes" within.

Thomas shook his head. "There's nothing to it. She has no disabilities."

Meiko hadn't told him, but then, how could she have? There hadn't been time.

"Can I speak with you outside, officer?" Calla indicated the door with a nod.

She followed the gentleman out. Her powers returned as she crossed red tape on the floor. They ducked into an empty exam room.

"What is it?" he asked.

"The day I left for Ologo, she came to see me. She told me her father had been affected by Power Deficit Syndrome, and she wanted to know if she carried one of the genes. She was awfully upset when I told her she most likely did." Calla paused and recalled an old case. "Two years ago, when I was finishing up my medical training, her father died of a heart attack, which wouldn't be strange except that he had no risk factors. His physical two weeks before had found him in excellent health. His wife, Meiko's mother, said he'd been threatened several times in the previous few weeks."

He wrote line after line on his notepad. "Do you know if Meiko has been threatened?"

Calla replayed the conversation with Meiko just before the Ologo mission had started. "She gave me no such indications. Then again, when I was hit last month, I hadn't been threatened, either."

"Thanks."

She walked with the officer as far as Meiko's room

then left him and went in.

Thomas stood and glared at her. "What do you know?"

"I can't answer that." Calla held both hands palm out and backed away a step.

"Don't try to hide behind confidentiality!" He came toward her. "Tell me! What do you know?"

She ran into the door behind her. "Confidentiality doesn't just apply when you want it to."

"If you know anything about who did this to her and you don't tell me..."

"Thomas?" Meiko whispered.

After a quick double-take, he rushed back to the bedside. "Meiko? Honey? I'm here."

Love overcomes so much. Calla smiled.

Meiko reached for Thomas' hand. "I told Dr. Geisman not to tell you. I made her promise."

He clasped her hand in both of his. "Promise not to tell me what, Meiko?"

Meiko looked around. "Why am I in the hospital?"

"You had an accident at the pool."

"How did you get here?"

"Calla's friend, Dillon, pulled you out then called her for help. You scared me half to death." He leaned over and kissed her forehead. "How are you feeling?"

"Tired." She managed a weak smile.

"Yeah, I can imagine. What don't you want Calla to tell me?"

Feeling more like a voyeur than a doctor, Calla tapped Thomas' shoulder. "Thomas, I'm going to hitch a ride back to Ologo. It should be getting about time for me to meet with the Matriarch, and I need to figure out how to say what I need to say. If I don't hear from you sooner, I'll see you tomorrow morning at the restaurant."

Thomas nodded but kept his eyes on his fiancée.

Calla quietly stepped out and hoped Meiko wouldn't regret telling Thomas about her father. Surely his prejudice would lose the fight against his love. For both their sakes, she hoped so.

As Calla left, Thomas remembered that he hadn't had a chance to give her the speed course in diplomacy. She'd have to wing it, and he hoped she could handle the situation. She'd shown remarkable instincts with the Olvians before, and he'd have to trust her to continue relying on those skills.

He needed to keep his focus on Meiko. Although typically honest and direct to a fault, she'd been dancing around some unpleasant matter since before he'd left for Ologo. Between some kind of secret meeting with Calla, the weird explosions of temper, an unknown medical thing, and now her reluctance to answer so simple a question, he feared she would tell him she had some terminal disease. Had he helped her back from the brink of death just to lose her again?

"What is it, Meiko? What's wrong?" He held her hand in both of his.

She touched the scrapes on his face with her cold fingers. "What happened?"

He sighed and pulled away. "I fell down some stairs last night. I told you about that earlier. Stop avoiding the question and tell me what's going on."

Her arm fell back to her side. "You have to go back to Ologo, don't you?"

Thomas grimaced. *Don't get mad. That's not going to help.* "Yes, but not for several hours. Tomorrow should be it. Either we'll have a treaty or the parties will demand more proof of Pharmacorp's involvement. That could take a while for law enforcement to dredge up. Either way, I'll be done at least for the moment. Why are you stalling?"

He wished he could get a sense of her emotions, but the generator protecting her from another attack stopped him.

"Will you stay with me?" Tears formed in her eyes.

What kind of question is that? "Until I have to go back. You're driving me nuts with your delays."

She forced a smile. "It's a short trip."

He nodded. "And getting shorter by the second." After lowering the rail on one side of the bed, Thomas sat next to her. "You're giving the impression you're afraid of me. I'm not sure I like that."

She pulled her hand out of his grip. "I am, and there is cause."

A knife in the chest would have hurt less. He stared at her, unable to find any words for longer than he'd like. "Why?"

Meiko faced the wall. "After seeing how you and August talked to Calla and about her, I just..."

"What does this have to do with Calla?" His spine stiffened.

Meiko sighed. "If everyone with PDS were forced out an airlock—"

He crossed his arms over his chest and glowered. "That was August, not me, who said that."

"—Or sterilized, then I wouldn't be here." She sat up and glared at him. "My dad had Power Deficit Syndrome."

Thomas' heart stopped for a moment. Her dad had died from a heart attack not two weeks before Thomas had met her. Now, with the wedding coming up, she mourned him all over again because he wouldn't be there. No wonder she wouldn't say anything.

Meiko was a Syndrome carrier. He repeated the words to himself over and over, trying to gauge how he felt about the news, but his mind wouldn't focus.

"Say something." She flopped back onto the bed.

Say something? Like what? Thomas didn't know a lot about genetics, but he knew enough to realize that if she carried that glitched gene, she might pass it on to their kids. He could become the parent or grandparent of a waste-of-space Syndromer, a never-ending drain on the resources of the station, a kid with weak powers who could only pretend to do a job as well as everyone else.

On the other hand, Calla was a Syndromer. Although he had made no secret of what he thought of her for having that disorder, she had put herself at risk to help him. Although she'd been terrified that he would hurt her as she grew weaker, she had set her own feelings aside and helped him anyway. To save his life, she had allowed herself to be vulnerable. She'd saved Meiko's life, too, and helped him get past his body's demands for a drug he didn't want.

Not only that, Calla could do ridiculously complex things he couldn't even dream of. She could handle an enormous influx of information that would have made him dizzy even without the Minum withdrawal, and she could calm a room full of angry delegates just by thinking hard enough. Without her help, he'd still be floundering around trying to make sense of the situation on Ologo. Then, too, Meiko's Syndromer dad had produced her, and among the people Thomas knew, only August could beat her power level.

Thomas couldn't lose Meiko. She brought light into the darkness of his world and didn't even care that he'd made major mistakes in his past. She'd been a carrier from the day they'd met, so why would that matter now? He'd fallen in love with her, not the genes she carried.

Tears streamed from her eyes. "Thomas?"

"Why didn't you tell me?" He ran his fingers through his hair.

"I didn't know what you thought about people with PDS until you started pestering Calla." She twisted around and grabbed the tissues off the table near the bed. "Then, the day you guys left, I went to talk to her about it and found out that I have one of those genes from my dad. The one from Mom's obviously normal."

He slumped. "And you thought I wouldn't love you if I found out? You thought I'd find you inferior, too."

She slowly nodded. When she blinked, tears rolled down her face.

Thomas' guts knotted. She was right. He would have. Years ago, he had broken up with a girlfriend for the same kind of offense. Could he do that again? Did he even want to? Meiko was his life.

Thomas squeezed her hand and kissed her fingers. "I won't stop loving you because one of your several gazillion genes is weird. I was just shooting off at the mouth."

"No, I don't believe that. You hate people with PDS." She wiped her eyes with a tissue. "I could feel that when you guys were giving Calla a hard time."

She had him there. Last night, he had feebly tried to push Calla away, and she had only been guilty of the horrible crime of trying to help him survive an overdose. "That was true, but now that I've had a chance to see one in action, I know I was wrong. I'm feeling pretty stupid for how I behaved."

Awkwardly, Meiko pulled him down for a hug. Given all of eternity, he never would have guessed that she could be afraid of him for anything. He wouldn't have thought he could be the source of her pain. He wanted to protect her from harm, not cause it.

"I'll talk to August and tell him to lay off the anti-Syndromer talk." Thomas sat up and scooted closer to her.

She shook her head. "He's not going to like that. You know how he is."

"Well, he's going to have to deal with it." He brushed her hair aside with his fingers. "Friend or not, he's not getting away with being disrespectful to the father of my wife."

Meiko beamed a smile at him, and he enjoyed a few minutes of peaceful silence while the tension between them vaporized.

"I wish you didn't have to go back," she whispered.

He stroked her arm. "Me, too, but I think we're almost done there."

"What about Pharmacorp?"

He shook his head. "I'm not going to take that on. Whether there's a treaty or not, I'll give everything I have to the authorities and let them handle it. Calla found somewhere else for us to meet so we don't have to deal with them anymore. Everything will be fine. You'll see."

She tossed the used tissue on the bedside table. "You'd better come back in one piece this time. I'm not putting up with my mom's wedding lunacy for nothing."

"So what's the latest?" he asked.

Professionally, with Meiko out of danger, he knew he should head back to Ologo. There might not be time to bring Calla up to speed on what she had to do, but he should be there to give her support if nothing else. His partner had, however, clearly told him in her own gentle way that she didn't expect to see him back there any time soon, another of her gifts, which he accepted with gratitude. Once the doctors released Meiko, he'd return to the war zone.

After working all day on a computer, August wanted nothing more than dinner and a few rounds on the new *Menace in a Cape,* a first-person-shooter he'd picked up on the game rack yesterday. All those run-around-and-blow-things-up games were pretty much the same, but after leading computer-illiterate people through troubleshooting problems for several hours, he needed to destroy something.

He entered his apartment. It was decorated in monochrome and silver with Escher prints covering most of the wall space. The smell of this morning's breakfast of toaster waffles and hot syrup still permeated the place and reminded his stomach that lunch had been a long, tedious six hours ago.

The message light on the communication board blinked. With his luck, Joseph would have another favor to ask. Although August liked his mentor, Joseph's never-ending list of tasks could try the patience of even the most stalwart superhero.

Grabbing a notepad and pen, August smacked the play button and tapped the pen on the desk while he waited for the date and time to go by.

"Hey, August, it's me." Weariness weighed down Thomas' voice. "I'm back, for a couple hours anyway. Meet me in Medical Ward Seven, room one-oh-five. Someone tried to kill Meiko."

August stared dumbstruck for a moment. Then, he ran out of the apartment and consulted the computer in the hall to get the location. Teleporting into a medical ward was only permitted in emergencies, but he was tempted to do it anyway. Who would want to take Meiko out? Was this some random crime or did someone really have it in for her?

Dodging other pedestrians, he ran through the corridors until he reached the right place. After finding her name on the board over the nurse's station, August walked down the hall, scanning the room numbers.

When he found the place, a security officer posted outside the door rose to meet him at the edge of the red tape on the floor. "This room is restricted to medical personnel and family."

August glanced at the door. "I'm a close friend of Meiko's."

The officer flipped open a notebook. "Name?"

"August Cantor."

"Nope, you're not in here. You'll have to go to the waiting room."

"But Thomas McCrady is a friend of mine. He called me down here."

"Sorry, Mr. Cantor, but outside of family, only those cleared by one of the attending physicians can go in." The guard propped his hands on his hips.

"Who are the attending physicians?" August asked.

The guard went back to his notebook. "Xava Vandamir and Calla Geisman."

Geisman? Thomas really let a Syndromer near Meiko? Maybe he hadn't been given a choice.

"You'll have to go to the waiting room." The guard pointed down the hall.

Scowling, August went to the nurse's station. "Can you tell me where I can find Dr. Vandamir?"

Given his earlier interactions with Geisman, August couldn't hope for a favor from her.

A brunette nurse built like a teenage boy looked up

from her computer screen. "She's seeing other patients. Is this an emergency?"

August shook his head. "I just want to see my friend, and the officer at the door says I need Dr. Vandamir's permission."

"If you'll go to the waiting room, I'll let her know."

"Yeah. Thanks."

August went two doors down the hall and walked through a door marked "Visitor's Lounge."

He flopped on a cool plastic chair and waited, trying to work out who would have gone after Meiko. Maybe there'd been a mistake. Not one possible suspect came to mind. After he'd been staring at the red-and-purple-checked carpet for a few millennia, the waiting room door opened to admit Thomas.

August squinted at the scabbed-over scrapes marring Thomas' face. "What happened to you?"

Thomas brushed the scrapes with his fingers. "Fell down the stairs."

"Klutz."

"Wasn't my fault." Thomas sat in the nearest seat.

"It never is. So, what's going on?" August turned to face Thomas. "I came as soon as I got your message, but I couldn't get in."

"What?" Thomas frowned and looked toward Meiko's room. "Oh, sorry. I forgot to have you put on the list."

August indicated the room down the hall with a nod. "Is Meiko all right?"

Thomas nodded. "Yeah. She'll be fine now. Got a little scary for a few minutes, but she'll make it."

"What happened?" August asked.

Thomas scratched above his ear. "Meiko says she was doing laps in the pool when she was attacked."

"By what?"

Thomas leaned forward. "Remember that shadow-warrior I told you about?"

August thought back through the snippets he could recall of their recent conversations. "The one with the fiery knives who came after you on Cordil? Yeah, I thought you took her out."

"Yes, but Meiko says it was a man with a flaming sword." Thomas hesitated and lowered his voice. "Didn't you say your boss used an avatar like that?"

"Sure, but it wouldn't be him." *At least I can't imagine why he'd have it in for Meiko.* "Could be another ex-student. I'll look into it for you. Do the police have any leads?"

"There are a couple possibilities." Thomas counted off the options on his fingers. "They think there might be someone behind all the accidental deaths of handicapped people lately. Then, too, Pharmacorp may have sent someone to hurt her so I'd leave the negotiations on Ologo to Calla so she could shut it down."

August shook his head. "Neither of those make any sense. She's not crippled and why would Pharmacorp want to stop your meetings?"

"She's not crippled herself, but Meiko is carrying a genetic glitch, and Pharmacorp already tried to kill me once because Calla and I think they're behind all the biological warfare wiping out the natives."

August pointed to the scrapes on Thomas' face. "Is Pharmacorp the one who, uh, helped you down the stairs?"

"Yeah. Was it yesterday or the day before? Yesterday I think." Thomas shrugged and rolled his eyes. "My mental clock is out of whack again, but someone hacked the medical computer and got Calla's records and mine. They found out I was a recovering addict and drugged my drinks at a reception. Then we found out someone had stolen some stuff from Calla's medical kit, but she pulled me out of the overdose using some sneaky psionic trick she knows."

August felt the color drain from his face. Surely Joseph hadn't been the one who'd supplied Pharmacorp with the information used to make the attempt. Could he also be behind Meiko's poolside misadventure? Had he lied about checking the system's integrity? August should've known there was something funny about seeing Thomas and his partner on the same "security check list."

"Hey, August, I'm okay." Thomas gripped August's arm.

August laughed it off. "Yeah, but you had to let that Syndromer into your head again."

Thomas frowned. "Look, that's another thing. I'd appreciate it if you'd put a stop to the anti-Syndromer thing at least when Meiko's around."

"Why?"

"Her dad had Power Deficit." Thomas stared at the checked carpet. "Because you and I have been so hard on Calla, Meiko was afraid to tell me she had one of those genes from her dad. She thought I'd break off the engagement."

"Are you?"

"Of course not!"

August held both hands palm-out. "Just asking. Just asking. What are you going to do if you have grandkids who turn out to be Syndromers?"

Thomas smiled. "Spoil them rotten, what else?"

August shook his head. "Who would've thought Meiko had a Syndromer for a dad. She's not that far off from my power level. See, and Joseph said the gene weakened future generations."

"Apparently not." Thomas glanced in the direction of

his fiancée's room. "Meiko's stronger than I am, and Calla's been a perpetual surprise on this trip. I keep underestimating her. Did you know the PDS genes give her eidetic memory? She remembers whole conversations and pages of medical documents perfectly."

August snorted. "Watch it. You're starting to sound like you actually like that freak."

"I do. She's a good partner, and honestly, a good friend. Even when I treated her badly, she growled at me, but she did what she had to do to help me out. She even let herself get hurt to save my miserable butt."

"Did that trip down the stairs trash your memory?" He squinted and pointed his finger at Thomas. "She killed your last partner."

Thomas shook his head. "No, she didn't. I had to try to stop just one collapse in Meiko's mind. I had no idea how hard it was, and Meiko didn't have physical injuries to complicate the situation. Angela had two collapses going. I don't think you could've stopped two with or without cardiac arrest and other mortal injuries."

They had been friends for a long time, but August didn't like this change in Thomas. August would dig up the information to prove Syndromers were useless after he'd checked out the business with Joseph and Pharmacorp. Once armed with irrefutable facts, Thomas would have to admit he was wrong.

"Well, whatever." August waved his hand back and forth to clear the air. "Hey, ya think you can get me past the security goon so I can go pester Meiko?"

"She's sleeping." Thomas glanced that way again. "I'll get with Dr. Vandamir or Calla to get you clearance for later, though. I'll be staying with Meiko until she's released, if I can. I can tell her you stopped by."

"Okay." August stood up. "Are you all right?"

Thomas rose and backed a step away. "Sure. I have to go back to Ologo, but I should be done before this time tomorrow."

"See ya when you get back, then." An impulse to offer to join Thomas on Ologo surfaced, but August pushed it aside. He had other things to do, like prove Syndromers were worthless. "Hey, and watch out for stairs."

He visualized his apartment and teleported back. The whirl of colors from such a short trip lasted no longer than a heartbeat. He dug through the papers in one of his desk drawers. Fortunately, he hadn't cleaned his desk in months and managed to dredge up several of Joseph's "security check lists" to crosscheck against the obituaries and police reports. Maybe the attempt on Thomas had been a bizarre coincidence, but August wouldn't rest until he knew.

Dimly aware of anything but her churning stomach and spinning head, Calla leaned into Matt's embrace, but affection only played a small part this time. If she didn't hang on to him, the post-teleport disorientation would have left her on the floor. Matt held her more tightly. His strong presence in her mind staved off the worst of the queasiness.

The nausea passed a few minutes later, and she knew they both had work to do, but she didn't want to see him go so soon. She needed someone reliable near at hand, a refuge in the midst of the intrigue and squabbling. Even the coarse fabric of his white uniform shirt seemed peaceful compared to what waited for her. Unfortunately, he'd only secured a few minutes away from his job.

She pulled away from him and flopped on the cot in her Olvian guest quarters. "You'd better head back."

"Are you sure?" He crouched in front of her.

She crossed her arms over her stomach. "Yes. You need to get back to work, and I need to figure out how to tell the Matriarch about the Pharmacorp theory."

"You've explained it at least twice already." He shrugged. "Do it again."

"I hope it's that easy."

"Piece of cake." He waved his hand dismissively. "I don't like the idea of leaving you here alone, though."

Calla shook her head, which briefly intensified the pending revolt of her stomach. "I'll be fine. Pharmacorp isn't on the guest list, and all the attempts have been against Thomas anyway. The Olvians are pretty harmless. You'd be bored. All I'm going to do is talk to the Matriarch and her Advisors then curl up for a nice, long nap."

"When's Thomas due back?" He ran his fingers through her hair.

"We didn't actually set a time. I assume he'll stay with Meiko until she's released, which would probably put him back here in a few hours, but I won't likely see him until morning."

"I don't like it, but if you're sure you'll be okay, I'll take off." He kissed her cheek. "Take care of yourself. I'll see you soon."

"Real soon, I'm hoping. Thomas seems to think we'll be done with this mess by tomorrow." As he stood, she caught hold of his hand.

"Good, because I still owe you that dinner for taking that emergency case." He squeezed her hand.

Matt stepped away and disappeared, leaving a sharp sense of loneliness in his wake. Calla stared at the space Matt had left and then sighed. She had work to do and no idea how to get it done.

Maybe Matt had a point. She'd explained her ideas once on paper for Thomas and repeatedly out loud for Brachi, Rana, and Pipien. Surely telling the Olvian ruler and probably about a dozen or so advisors wouldn't be so hard.

Calla pulled out her notebook and read back through her information to look for errors and awkward phrasing and make sure she came across as if she had authority, not as if she were a complete moron or, worse, a desperate fanatic.

She'd gotten a third of the way through the notes when the door opened to admit Rana. Why couldn't they knock like normal people?

Rana stepped in and clasped her hands in front of her turquoise tabard. "Oh, good, you're back."

"Hello, Rana. Is it time?" Calla flipped her notebook closed.

"Yes. Everything's been arranged."

Calla stuffed the cardboard-backed notebook back into its space in her backpack and shouldered her bag. "Is Pipien not joining us?"

Rana darkened. "No. She has been more interested in ending the talks than ending the war, and she won't tell me why, so I dismissed her."

No shock there.

Calla followed her hostess out and climbed into the gold and turquoise hovercraft waiting for them. Instead of heading for the fringe of the city, the driver took them farther into the interior. They passed roads arranged in concentric rings. Farms and fisheries dotted the roadsides as they drove by a collection of modest homes like the one Calla stayed in.

After going through a slime-green and orange archway, they entered an area of larger, more elaborate homes. Shops were painted in bolder schemes than the drab breakfast shop they'd stopped at every morning. When they'd stopped for traffic once, announcements being made from the speakers mounted by the door frames grew louder. She supposed the comments were advertisements of some sort, but she couldn't make out any of the Olvian words.

They passed another textured archway painted purple and neon yellow. Sprawling mansions, each with their own surrounding swamp or lake, were laid out for kilometers.

Finally, a gateway of red and silver admitted them to a swamp. Here and there, brilliantly-colored obelisks stood upright.

She pointed to one as they passed. "Rana, what are those structures?"

"Sculptures." Rana paled several shades as pride resonated in her thoughts. "They tell the story of our people. There's one near the entrance to the Advisors' Hall. I'll show you."

When the hover car pulled into a parking space, Calla climbed out and followed Rana to the edge of the paved road. The Olvian walked out into the swamp along a muddy trail, paying no heed to the muck sticking to her bare feet.

Rana stopped and looked over her shoulder. "Come. You won't feel anything from there."

Calla pulled off her shoes and socks then rolled up her pants before stepping out into the squishy trail. She sank a few centimeters into the mud and gingerly made her way out to her host. *Eww. Almost as much fun as fingerpainting with Dillon.*

The obelisk had an inlaid picture covering the entire surface. Bright, high-contrast colors combined with the textured surface to relay some sort of message, but the symbols meant nothing to Calla.

"What does it say?"

"The sculpture does not speak." Rana ran her four, equally opposable fingers across the surface. "This tells the story of the creation of the world and the fall of the males."

Calla let her vision blur so she could see like an Olvian then traced her hand over the patterns, feeling the swirls that condensed into two round planets, undoubtedly Ologo and the co-orbital planet, dubbed Partner by the Terran stellar cartographers and Great Sister by Rana earlier in these talks. She would have to learn its original, untranslated name someday. "Interesting."

"Each obelisk tells another part of the story. Perhaps later we can take a full tour." Rana stepped away from the obelisk. "We shouldn't keep the Matriarch waiting."

Calla followed Rana back along the path to the paved road. Shoes and socks in hand, Calla accompanied the Olvian delegate along the tracked mud trail giving evidence that others had visited the monuments on the way in.

Within, the floors were flooded with cool, ankle deep water flowing from a central ridge toward drains in the sides. The gently moving water washed the accumulated mud off Calla's feet as she continued down the vast corridor decorated with more of the same sort of artwork as she'd seen in the swamp. The interior of the building smelled like a chemical version of the swamp muck outside.

Rana hesitated outside a gold-gilt door. "When you're giving your report, please speak slowly and remember to pause from time to time so I can provide the translation necessary."

Calla frowned. She'd forgotten that of all the Olvians she'd met, only Rana, Pipien, and a couple at the reception knew anything but the local language. The earlier troubles with Thomas' interview of the prisoner didn't inspire much confidence.

"I'm sorry, but there is no other way." Rana's skin tone went mottled. "I promise I'll give as accurate a rendition of your words as I can."

Calla pasted on a smile. "I'll keep the discussion as non-technical as possible. That should help."

Rana's coloring solidified to a somewhat darker gray, clashing with her turquoise tabard. Stretching out with her thoughts, Calla picked up the other delegate's jittery nervousness, which hardly came as a surprise. Her own guts were practicing for a gymnastics tournament.

Calla stepped into the room. Aside from the ruler, over a hundred Olvians had gathered. They were dressed in a riot of clashing colors that threatened to give Calla a migraine.

She froze a step inside the door. "Who are all these people?"

Rana pointed. "That's the Matriarch there on the dais." She took in the rest of the room with a sweep of her hands. "The rest are her Advisors. There are a handful who had other commitments unbreakable, but most of them are here."

"Why so many?"

"We do have a democracy representative." Rana started for the steps up to the dais. "This is our capitol."

Calla drew a deep breath and blew it out.

Rana stopped and turned around. "Is there a problem?"

Calla shook her head and joined Rana on the steps. "No, no problem but this isn't what I had expected."

"Should I try to reschedule? Perhaps then all the representatives would be here."

With the delay, she could get those pointers Thomas had promised. Then again, they both wanted to be done with this fiasco much sooner than later. To do that, he expected her to give the presentation so they could move ahead to the actual writing of the treaty in the morning.

Rana leaned closer. "I can hear the tremor in your voice."

"I do that when I'm nervous." Calla gestured for Rana to lead the way. "I've never spoken to such a large collection of people."

Rana's chuckle sounded like a rasp on metal. "It gets no easier if you speak before groups large more often."

Calla wished she could use one of her procedures to quiet her nerves, but she couldn't focus on them right now.

On the raised platform, Rana introduced Calla to the Matriarch, a wrinkled prune of an Olvian with sagging bags under her wide eyes. Another Olvian in a purple tabard banged a jeweled stone on a metal plate. All the noise in the room petered out. With the purple-tabarded one's help, the Matriarch rose from a shallow pool and addressed the group before stepping aside for Calla to begin her report on a stage so bare she didn't even have a podium to hide behind. Feeling every eye on her, Calla drew another deep breath and reminded herself of Matt's reassurance. She'd already presented the data a time or two. One more shouldn't be a big deal.

Calla looked out at the sea of colorful tabards and waiting faces. All of Thomas' instructions about Olvians and everything she'd discovered about them played through her mind at rapid speed. *Simultaneously maintain authority without downplaying Thomas too much. I can do this.* "Good evening. I am Doctor Calla Geisman of Haidar, here to help the people of Ologo find the source of the plague. I believe we have tracked down the cause of your trouble." Once she started, the words came more easily and her nerves subsided somewhat.

Rana finished the translation and the Matriarch's aide in the purple tabard grumbled something the elderly ruler cut off with a sharp croak.

"At first, I believed that one of the two races of Ologo had developed the bacteria responsible and released it only to infect themselves at the same time. That's not possible." She drew a breath to continue.

Rana gripped Calla's arm. "I need a moment to translate."

"Oh, I'm sorry."

While Rana made the translation, Calla recalled her explanation in her notebook, rereading the pages in her mind.

"Very simply, Olvians lack the specific technologies needed to genetically engineer and then weaponize bacteria effectively; and, while the Gotrians do possess the knowledge, they did not have the laboratories set up early enough to account for the first cases of plague in either race."

Across from her, the Advisors changed from a neutral gray to the mottled shades of confusion.

At least they haven't rejected my suggestion out of hand yet. "Only one group on Ologo has the capacity to design and weaponize bacteria fatal to both races: Pharmacorp."

The moment Rana finished the translation, the mottled gray of confusion became the dark hues of rage. Shrill pings rang out from all around the room. Nearly three-quarters of the population rose.

Rana darkened. "So many questions!"

Calla blew out a breath. "Well, let's answer the ones we can."

"How can you be sure the Gotrians aren't responsible?" Rana translated the first question.

"The same way I'm sure you aren't. There are issues with the timing and the availability of technology. The Gotrians did not have the capability until after the first reported cases of plague."

When about half the group sat down, Rana leaned closer. "They all had the same question." She picked the next person. "What does Pharmacorp gain?"

"That's trickier." Calla mentally scanned back through her notes and found the pertinent part. "We believe they are using Ologo as a testing ground for either a bioweapon or to test cures for bioweapons."

Another huge chunk of the group sat down and a few others popped up. Calla squelched a sigh. At this rate, they'd never finish.

"Do you have evidence direct they're responsible?" Rana relayed.

"Not yet but we have people working on that. We need time, and that's why we are requesting an enforceable treaty. There are many specialists Haidar will not send into a war zone." *Including doctors, usually.*

Rana chose another Advisor. "Have they done this elsewhere?"

Calla pressed her lips together. Nothing in her notes addressed that, and if there had been clear evidence, the event would have been all over the news. *Cordil IV, maybe?* "There have been other sabotaged negotiations. The negotiator Thomas McCrady was recently assisting on Cordil IV when they came under attack. That one also had to do with illnesses spreading through the population."

The Advisor shouted something over Rana's translation.

Rana rose up to her full height and expressed her aggravation with the interruption by fluttering the membrane under her arms. "That is evidence circumstantial."

Calla nodded. "Yes, it is, but I've already told you that we do not have all the answers. The situation on Cordil IV is similar to here."

Only a few Advisors sat down.

"Challenging Pharmacorp will invite war with Earth," Rana translated.

"Earth tends to shy away from controversy. If you or the Gotrians accuse Pharmacorp of causing this plague, Earth will get caught up in rhetoric and debate. History suggests they'll get loud, but they won't do much. In that gap, we can search for evidence to prove or disprove their involvement."

"Do they already know you suspect them?" Rana turned to Calla and clasped her arm. "They attacked Thomas, right? So you would leave and not investigate?"

"Yes."

"I will tell them."

While Rana related the previous night's trauma, Calla rubbed her eyes. Her hands shook. This was going to have to end soon. Even her endurance had limits.

Rana picked someone. "Will Haidar help with the investigation?"

I already answered that. "With an enforceable treaty in place, specialists can be sent to handle investigation. Detailed investigation is outside my skill set."

Many of the Advisors sat, and just as many stood up.

"What about treating the plague?"

Calla blew out a breath. *Variation on the same theme.* "An enforceable treaty will need to be in place before other doctors are sent. My arrival here was an unusual breach of protocol."

Rana was only half-finished with the translation when the Matriarch tapped her assistant. The purple-clad assistant smacked the jeweled stone on the metal plate three times.

The grumbling assembly sat down.

Rana directed Calla to a cushion on the dais. "The Matriarch has called an end to the presentation. She's heard enough and believes the others have, too."

Thank you, Matriarch!

Now, with her part of the evening finished, Calla's weariness weighed her down. The metabolic shifts had kept her going strong all day, but now her body demanded real sleep. She couldn't rest until after this meeting, which she hoped would end soon.

Rana flopped into a crouch nearby and leaned closer. "She's telling the advisors to consider their votes carefully. We need help to deal with the plague before our population drops too low, and Haidar won't send help medical while there is war here. She does not, however, want another treaty doomed. She'll allow debate now."

If Olvian debates went like the news reports of the senate on Earth, the assembly wouldn't be voting any time soon. Calla suppressed a groan.

When Calla seriously believed she could fall asleep sitting up, the votes were entered into small computers.

A mechanical voice from a loudspeaker declared the results.

Rana faded to a pale gray. "Seventy-two percent in favor of considering a treaty. Twenty percent opposed. Eight percent absent or abstaining."

Calla didn't know whether to be happy or not. Some government systems required a seventy-five percent vote to get anything new done.

After a long bout of croaking from the Matriarch, Rana grabbed Calla's arm. "Good news! She'll consider a treaty if one is presented."

Calla patted Rana's hand. "Excellent. We'll have to be sure to get a good one hammered out tomorrow."

The Matriarch shuffled out, followed by many of the advisors. Some approached the dais instead of heading for the doors.

After a long hour of dealing with all the stragglers who insisted their questions required immediate answers, only Rana remained with her.

"Do you think they'll sign the treaty after we put it together?" Calla stifled a yawn.

"Yes, I think so." Rana paled and hopped down the stairs.

Calla descended to the ground floor. "It would be pity if they don't."

"You were very convincing." Rana gestured for the door. "There will be some concern if the treaty doesn't address the disease."

Calla followed her hostess through the halls. "Well, like I said, Thomas and I will petition the Magistrates to send medical assistance."

"And if they refuse?"

"It has happened before." *Only not during my tenure.* She reached back through her memory of news reports to one that had been posted just before she'd graduated high school and another a couple years before that. "The last couple times it has, though, as much as a third of the medical staff put in to take their vacations at the same time to go help. The department head approved. One way or another, someone will come to investigate this mystery and treat the sick."

"You'll come, won't you?" Rana led her through the outer doors.

The dark sky was lit up by a scattering of stars and a crescent of Partner.

Calla shook her head. "If it came down to going on vacation, I couldn't do it. I haven't been around long enough to have that much leave, but don't worry. There are folks who specialize in contagious diseases, and one gentleman who has dealt with a community hit hard by biological warfare. You'll get the help you need, even if I can't be here. You may, however, have to overcome this notion that men are inferior. With Haidarians, males and females are biologically different and have different strengths, but they're neither one inferior to the other."

Rana darkened slightly but didn't answer. That idea would take some time to adjust to, but Rana had accepted Thomas, so the rest shouldn't be too big of a stretch.

When they reached her room, Calla bid Rana goodnight and went inside. Sliding her backpack off her shoulders, Calla dropped it by the door and then flopped on the bed. The technique she had used to keep from dozing off during the meetings today had worked well for the bulk of the day, but she had to pay the piper now.

She was both physically and mentally exhausted, and she hadn't even corrected the shifts she had made in her body's natural rhythms yet. Without even bothering to undress, Calla undid those changes, and within moments, dropped off to sleep.

Pipien paced the length of a flower garden in the park behind the Pharmacorp building. A sound like a scratchy reed whistle thrummed behind her. Pipien whirled but made out only dull shadows that she'd already verified were vegetation. Being here at night had her jumping at every shadow and terrestrial bug noise, but what choice did she have, really? If she didn't follow Pharmacorp's bidding, she would never see her little sister again. Mother had said to do whatever was necessary to secure the release of Tyra, which meant seeing the Pharmacorp liaison at odd hours of the night.

Footsteps approached. Pipien spun to face them and made out the profiles of two humans and a third, human-like creature with glowing eyes. A Haidarian? Was there a fourth person? There were too many footfalls for three.

"Ah, Pipien, so good of you to come." Patina sounded like they had gotten together for a cordial swim.

Pipien squinted and tried to make out more detail in the figures. "Where is Tyra?"

"When you finish what you were told to do, then you'll be reunited." Kevin's voice carried menace.

She lifted her arms slightly and sent the membrane quivering. "I've done everything you've asked!"

"Have you?" Kevin's boots crunched on the gravel path. "The meetings continue. The treaty could come any day now, couldn't it?"

Pipien slapped her arms back to her sides.

"Well, there is a limit to—" Patina said.

"Not one more word, Ms. Faulks, or you may be joining dear little Tyra yourself." The Haidarian's voice was several pitches lower than even Kevin's.

Hearing the male address Patina so shamefully made Pipien's skin darken, but she didn't dare say anything, not with Tyra being held captive.

The unknown one came forward, but there was something odd about the way he walked. Something seemed to be attached to his hand and two different footfalls happened at once. "You will follow my instructions carefully."

Pipien backed away from the voice and the uncomfortable pressure in her head.

Calla awakened to the disconcerting feeling of wrongness, but she couldn't say for certain where the uneasiness came from. Although the terminal fatigue had lessened, weariness still weighed on her. More than anything else, she wanted to roll over and go back to sleep, but the nagging sense of danger grew.

Unwilling to give in to the paranoia, Calla listened for some sound that could be triggering her feelings. Back home, she'd awakened a time or two with the same danger sense because the people in the next apartment had been quarreling. This night, nothing came to her. In fact, even the mental background noise was gone.

In one move, Calla rolled onto her back and sat up. Less than a meter away stood an Olvian female. A blade glinted in the dull light coming from the room's one window. As the knife descended, Calla leaned back and raised her arms to protect her face. The blade cut her not far below the elbow sending a sharp pain through her arm. Calla scrambled away from her attacker and rushed to the door, but the Olvian beat her there in one quick hop.

"You can't leave." The creature drew up on her back legs.

Pressing her hand against the stinging wound, Calla backed away. She knew that gravelly voice. "Pipien? What are you doing?"

Pipien loped forward. "I want my sister back."

"I don't have your sister." Calla's heart pounded.

"Tyra is only ten years old. She wanted no part of this war." Pipien lunged.

Calla darted aside. "Why do you think I know anything about this?"

"She went for a swim and never returned!"

Calla felt the wall at her back. "Put down the knife. Turn off your anti-psionic generator. I'll help you look for her."

"They won't give her back to me until you're dead!"

"Who? The Gotrians? Pharmacorp?" Calla edged her way toward the door. "Who kidnapped your sister, Pipien?"

If she could just get out the door and clear of the

telepathy blocker, she could try calling out to Thomas to retrieve her from the Olvian city. She had to coax Pipien away from the door.

"I—I don't want to do this." Pipien's voice burbled in her throat. "I have to."

"There are other ways. Let's sit down over here at the table, and we'll look at what we can do." Calla sidestepped closer to the door.

"I have to!"

With a rage-filled cry, Pipien jumped, leading with the knife. Calla dodged aside and ran for the door.

"I want my sister!" Pipien screamed.

Calla tore out of a room and collided with a tall Terran.

There were four of them, all armed with blasters and wearing the extra bulk of body armor. A red Pharmacorp logo was stitched above the pocket of their black shirts. The one she'd run into pushed her back into the room and hurled her at the cot. Two others trained guns on her as the last watched the door. When he turned on the lights, Calla squinted and saw Pipien cowering in the corner. The first man, with his blond hair cut in a severe military style, stood over Pipien.

Blond confiscated the knife and threw it aside. "What's this? You were not told to kill, vermin. Our orders were to take her alive."

"If—if she's dead, Thomas will go home. He's just a male. He relies heavily on her for information." Pipien turned the dark gray of fear. "They said if I make the negotiations stop, I can have Tyra back."

The bald man by the door, Doorman, laughed.

"What? That's what they said back when Tyra first disappeared." Pipien scrunched further into the corner.

Blond snorted. "You'll join her soon enough."

Calla didn't need telepathy to figure out the subtext

of that comment. She gasped and made a move to rise. "No, don't—"

One of her guards, whom she dubbed Scarface in honor of the line below his right cheekbone, aimed a gun at her. "Don't even breathe, freak."

"Wait!" Pipien scrunched down into a tiny ball.

Blond fired a bolt at Pipien's back. She screeched a higher pitch than Calla had ever heard from an Olvian.

"Let's go." Scarface gestured with his gun. "Don't try anything. We have to bring you in alive, but you could be hurtin' pretty bad and still be breathin'. You get me?"

Calla scowled. "I get you." *If I could access my powers for half a minute, I'd really get you.*

As they led her out, Doorman picked up her backpack. Pipien groaned. The Olvian made a feeble, useless effort to push herself up. She was still alive after a point blank blaster shot? Pages of medical texts came to mind showing what organs would be in that area of a female Olvian's body. If the shot didn't go too deep and if she received medical help in time, she could live through this, but she would likely never have children of her own.

They climbed into a van with Doorman taking the driver's seat while Blond, Scarface, and Number Four stayed around her with their guns aimed. Number Four's bloodshot eyes suggested fatigue. Could she find a way to take advantage of that? She'd have to keep her eyes open.

If only they would encounter an Olvian on the way. Surely, someone would find something amiss in seeing their friendly negotiator being held at gunpoint. Sounding the alarm might be dangerous for her, but she doubted she could escape alone. Calla stole a look at her watch and frowned as she did the mental calculation to figure out local time. No one would be up at this hour, and the water they slept in would muffle any airborne sounds. There would be no salvation here.

A larger ship emblazoned with the Pharmacorp logo waited in the sub depot. Calla glanced at the edge of the pier and considered diving into the water. She could swim well, but could she hold her breath long enough and avoid hypothermia?

Scarface grabbed her arm and pressed his gun to her ribs. "Don't even think it."

Blond chuckled. "No, no, let her try. How many predators are there in these waters?"

She conceded the point. There'd be another, maybe drier, option.

The leader flung her into a corner of the sub as the goons took the four real seats and congratulated each other on a job well done. The Pharmacorp sub was larger than any of the Olvian ones, but she enjoyed the ride even less while her mind conjured up frightening things they might do to her.

To stop that flood, she turned her thoughts to Thomas. If these goons had been sent for her, what would they send after him? In the Gotrian's open city, he would be even more vulnerable. Instead of running through a maze of streets to get him, they could simply find the right tree and climb ropes to reach his room. If he had been sleeping like she had been, he wouldn't even see the attack coming until they were on top of him.

No, his stronger powers should give him fair warning. They had to. Her biggest problem had been the depth of her sleep caused by her sheer exhaustion. Without that, he would sense the attack coming. Even if all other routes of escape were cut off, he could teleport home. He would be safe. Maybe he hadn't even come back to Ologo yet.

She sat under the eye of three of her guards. Number Four dozed a couple times only to be roughly jostled by Blond. Perfect. A quick nap might have given him a second wind.

Calla twisted her arm around to inspect the cut. Coagulated blood closed the wound. It shouldn't hinder any escape efforts but what about Pipien? Had someone discovered her before the gunshot had killed her? In spite of the attack, Calla hoped so. She couldn't help feeling sorry for the young Olvian.

In the end, all Pipien's efforts to appease Tyra's kidnappers had gone for nothing. The young female, barely an adult, had already been murdered. The tragedy outweighed the shallow wound from the knife.

They slowed to a stop without transitioning to land. That would make her getaway harder. She had to get free from her captors and find a way to get up to the ground floor, then make her way to the door before she could get to safety.

Blond towered over her. "We're here. Remember, no funny business. Understand?"

Calla nodded. She understood all right, but if they thought she would meekly follow along until they put her in a cage, they were dumber than she already thought. The leader jerked her to her feet and pushed her out of the sub. Blond led the way through the cramped, musty depot into another, more hospitable part of the building. Doorman followed, and Scarface and Number Four flanked her.

The colors and the basic decorations were the same as the levels of the Pharmacorp building she had seen. Carpet had muffled their steps above ground, but here the clack of boots on the tile echoed in the empty hall. The corridor widened in front them. Elevators were set in one wall.

The door pinged and slid open. At the same moment, Number Four yawned mightily.

Calla darted past him. Scarface's hand brushed her sleeve. She caught the arm of the lab-coated scientist exiting the lift and flung herself into the car while sending him crashing into the guards. She hit the Close Door button repeatedly and flattened herself against the wall before punching the ground floor button.

As the car ascended, she left the influence of the guards' generator. Her telepathy popped into focus. Before she could do anything useful, another device took over and plunged her back into mental silence. The elevator chimed for the ground floor. When the door opened, she expected a hail of bullets, blaster bolts, or even tranquilizer darts, but nothing happened.

"Come out, Calla, I know you're there. I've been expecting you."

She'd heard that voice in the recollections of the wounded students who came to ER every week sporting combat-type "training accident" injuries. They'd all had the same instructor.

Joseph Pearce? Here? While no steps had been taken to keep the Ologo mission a secret, how could he have known to expect her here at Pharmacorp? Could he be allied with the company? Given his star pupil's attitude toward people with PDS, she couldn't trust him to help her. She let the doors slide closed again as if the car were empty. A quick ride up a level or two and she could use a different elevator, stairs, or even a fire escape, if there were such things, to make her way back down to the ground floor again.

When the doors had closed, she heard another chime

and they reopened. This time, a cane held them there. Could she push past him, too? If she could get clear of the generator, she could try calling for Thomas.

"You're more resourceful than I thought." Joseph stepped into the doorway and grinned. "But, it's time for this little game to end."

"Not yet." Calla pushed past him and bolted for the outside doors.

Joseph laughed.

The void went away.

Calla projected her thoughts *"Thomas!"*

Even as she sent out her plea for help, a malevolent presence pushed into her mind, taking on the guise of a shadow warrior armed with a sword of fire.

Thomas snapped awake with every physical and mental sense on alert. Someone, a woman, had called his name, and he'd heard real fear in that voice. Before he'd left Haidar, he'd walked Meiko to her mom's place. Had something happened to her again?

He projected his thoughts. *"Meiko, are you okay?"*

"Me? Sure, Thomas, I'm fine. You sound tense. Is everything all right?"

He got up and went to the window. *"I don't know. I heard a scream, and it woke me up. I'm fine, but if it wasn't you, who could it have been?"*

Meiko's jittery thoughts radiated fear. *"Calla. Thomas, it must have been her."*

Thomas struck the window sill with his palm. *"Gotta go."*

"Please be careful."

He nodded. *"Yeah. Treaty or no treaty, I'm getting her, and we're getting out of here. See you soon."*

He broke the connection and sought for Calla's mental signature among the Olvians. Even with Power Deficit Syndrome, a Haidarian woman should have been obvious, but he came up with nothing but Olvians.

"Calla." He pushed his thoughts outward. *"Calla!"*

His guts clenched. Where was she and what was going on? Maybe he had missed her.

A conglomeration of four small, telepathic voids headed quickly toward him. They would arrive in minutes, and he didn't plan to stick around to find out why. They wouldn't be using anti-psionic generators if they weren't coming for him, and he didn't suppose they wanted to sell him a magazine subscription. When it came to fighting without his abilities, he knew just how pathetic he was.

Thomas stuffed his things in his bag and recalled the image of Calla's room with the Olvians. As he focused his thoughts there, his room dissolved into a swirl of color and righted itself as hers. Suddenly aware of the low ceiling, he hunched over but then remembered he could actually stand up without hitting his head. A weird smell like burnt meat filled the air. He went to the door and flipped the switch near the wall. Bright light flared on. A low groan came from behind. He spun. In the corner, Pipien lay face down, colored solid, dull black. A blaster burn marred her gray tunic.

He rushed to her side and went down to one knee. "Pipien?"

"Thomas," she whispered.

He reached for her but withdrew his hand before making contact. "You need a doctor. How do I call for one?"

"They won't answer you."

He rolled his eyes. "Right, because I'm male. Where's Calla? She can help you."

She looked at him with glazed eyes. "They killed her. Thomas, Tyra was just beyond her metamorphosis, but they killed my sister little." Her words slurred together. "I'm sorry. I was such an idiot. They had promised to give her back. I should have known I could never trust them."

Thomas lightly gripped her slimy hand. "I'm sorry, Pipien. I had no idea anything had happened to your sister. Please, tell me where Calla is."

"Everything I tried to do was useless. Tyra was already dead. I made a mess of everything."

The pain and grief in Pipien's mind threatened to swamp Thomas, but he reached out to the dying being and tried to impart calm.

Thomas stood. "I'm going to go find help."

He started for the door, but as he reached it, her mind faded to nothing. Thomas froze in place and sighed. Looking back, he saw her lying too still. Her transparent skin had changed to a dull gray not much darker than her tunic.

Closing his eyes to aid his concentration, Thomas sat on the cot and sorted through all the minds in the city to hunt down Rana. When he located her in close proximity with three other females and the dimmer, smaller presences of two males, Thomas isolated her and projected his thoughts with minimal power. *"Rana, Rana, it's me, Thomas. Wake up."*

He felt her bolt awake in spite of his efforts and readied himself to read her response.

"Thomas, what is the meaning of this?" Her voice echoed as she spoke aloud. *"Do you have any idea what time it is?"*

He scooted to the edge of the cot. *"In truth, I have no*

idea of the current local time. We have an urgent situation. Can you meet me in Calla's room?"

"I will not! The hour is too unreasonable. I'm going to have to—"

"Pipien is dead." He squeezed his eyes closed and pictured the younger delegate's body.

"What?"

He leaned his elbows on his knees. *"I'm in Calla's quarters. Pipien's been shot. She died a few moments ago as I was going for help."*

In Rana's mind, he sensed the turmoil of emotions running amok, confusion chief among them.

"I'm sorry, Rana. I wanted to find a kinder way to say that."

"You're wrong. You don't know where to find a pulse," Rana snapped at him.

Thomas studied the rough floor. *"I'm reading no brain activity, but I hope you're right. Nothing would make me happier than for you to show up and find Pipien is still alive."*

"I'm on my way. Stay there."

Breaking the connection, Thomas searched the room. At first, nothing stood out, but there had to be some clue to Calla's whereabouts. Judging from the wrinkled but still closed sheet, Calla had slept on rather than in her bed.

There were no clothes piled on the floor or draped over a chair or table, but she didn't strike him as someone so meticulously neat. Her office was a qualified disaster, after all.

Chances were pretty good she'd returned from the meeting with the Matriarch, reversed the metabolic changes that had kept her going all day, and then promptly collapsed. She had mentioned that changing the body's rhythms to stay awake invariably brought hunger and greater exhaustion later.

Conducting a thorough search of the room, he found her ever-present backpack missing. Under the table near Pipien's body, he turned up a knife with blood laced along one edge. Seeing the knife, he recalled the scream that had jolted him awake.

Was Calla dead, too? Had Pipien answered his question before going on to mention Tyra? No, Calla had to be alive. He couldn't say why he knew, but he knew.

Thomas continued looking, this time seeking newly dried, dark red blood. A few drops stained the floor near the bed, and a few more near one wall. A smeared handprint marked the dark brown door frame.

Had Calla escaped? Thomas opened the door and expanded his hunt to the streets beyond. Nothing. If she had gotten away from the knife wielder, she'd been recaptured probably about the time she'd called out to him.

All told, however, even combined, there wasn't nearly enough blood to suggest a fatal wound. Of course, blasters cauterized their wounds, but the shooters had left Pipien for dead. Why would Calla be taken but not Pipien? Why had Pipien been in Calla's room in the first place? Rana would be the one handling official business, and Calla didn't seem too excited about spending more time with the locals.

Thomas turned to head back into the room as a hover car stopped nearby. Rana clambered out and frogjumped the rest of the way, covering a meter or two for every thrust of her powerful legs. Her black and gray, splotchy coloring confirmed the confusion he sensed in her.

He waited for her and gestured her in ahead of him. "Pipien is over there against a wall."

As Rana hopped toward her assistant's body,

Thomas watched the splotched coloring give way to dark gray fear, which darkened to the black of grief. Rana pressed quivering fingers between Pipien's eyes. The older delegate's hand fell away.

Thomas stepped toward her. "I offer you my condolences, Rana."

She came up to her full height and turned on him, remaining an inky black. "Where was Calla? Why didn't she help Pipien? What good is telepathy if you people can't do anything when you're needed?"

Oh, is that how it is? Telepathy makes Haidarians undesirable until you need us, huh? Thomas killed his defensive response, remembering how unreasonable he'd been upon learning of Angela's death and confronting Calla. "I don't have all the facts, Rana. What I can say is that the blood on the knife under the table and in a few places around the room isn't pale enough for Olvian blood or orange enough for Gotrian. Very likely, it's Calla's. She was hurt. For all we know, she was trying to help Pipien when she was injured."

Rana glowered.

"Calla is missing." Thomas took in the room with a sweep of his hands. "When I searched for her, I came up blank here and in the Gotrian city. There are anti-psionic generators blocking my ability to read some parts of the Pharmacorp building. I think she's there. Can you help me?"

She gestured to Pipien. "My assistant is dead! I need to make sure there are no more intruders!"

"It would take me less than fifteen minutes to scan this and every other Olvian city either to confirm that I'm the only non-Olvian or to find any invasion force."

"Thomas, although I begin to see the strength Calla wishes to nurture in you—" she began.

He shook his head and set about gathering what

remained of Calla's things. "Save it. I'm not up to another round of 'You're just a guy. What would you know?'"

She lifted her arms slightly and vibrated the membrane. "You have to understand."

He stopped and glared at her. "No, you understand. My partner is in trouble. All I'm asking for is a little help from you. I'll check the security of your cities for you to make sure this isn't a full-blown invasion. I would think you would feel at least some gratitude for Calla's work here. If she hadn't come to help me make sense of this plague business, she'd be safe at home. Even if you felt no sense of duty toward Calla, I would've thought you'd be concerned about finding Pipien's killer. I was wrong on all counts, it seems. Goodbye, Rana, and good luck writing the treaty tomorrow."

She blackened. "You won't be there to help us?"

He shouldered Calla's duffel bag. "I'm going after Calla. If I can reach her, I'm taking her home. She's probably hurt."

Rana reached for him. "You'll be back to finish what you started, won't you?"

Thomas shrugged and shifted backward. "You don't need me. I'm just a male."

She shrank away from him and lightened to dark gray to match the embarrassment he sensed.

He sighed. "I'm sorry. That was harsh. I'll be back if I can, but I'll be bringing more backup. I'm sorry about Pipien, but right now, I'm more worried about the living."

He teleported away. After dropping his and Calla's things in his room on Haidar, he returned to the platform outside his assigned chambers in the Gotrian city. If the intruders were still there, he intended to get the jump on them for a switch. All senses alert, he heard movement within and sensed three distinct presences: Brachi and two others but no anti-telepathy devices.

Thomas stepped into his room and looked at the debris. Furniture had been overturned and smashed. The pillow pile had been shredded. White fluff littering the room reminded him of a trip to Peregrine II in the dead of their winter to assist with negotiations to set up food convoys and trade.

The two uniformed Gotrians with Brachi were taking notes and surveying the wreckage.

Brachi looked up and then stormed over, coming toe to toe with Thomas. "Where have you been?"

Thomas raised an eyebrow. "You think I did this?"

Brachi reopened the space between them. "No, witnesses saw the four men fleeing into the night. They got up here using cables shot into the lower surface of the platform. I wonder, though, how did they know this rroom was yours?"

Thomas shook his head. "I have an idea, but I don't like it."

"Fortunate you were not here." Brachi adjusted the lay of his green, hooded tunic.

"Yeah." Thomas blew out a breath. "I was dealing with another tragedy."

"Oh? Tell."

Thomas brought the Gotrian Speaker up to date on Pipien's death and Calla's disappearance. Brachi listened attentively and managed to avoid his usual stream of quiet insults.

"Unfortunate that Pipien didn't live long enough to gain her wisdom." Brachi fidgeted with the hem of his tunic. "At least her community doesn't lose much with the death of one so young."

"I'm not sure they see it that way. I'm certain Pharmacorp has kidnapped Calla, which would explain how they knew where I was." Thomas pointed in the direction of the Terran company's headquarters. "They could have forced her to reveal my exact location."

"Yes. Pipien obviously betrayed her." Brachi stared at the floor while he paced. "Have you considered something more final happening to Calla?"

Thomas shook his head. "No, no. She can't be dead."

Now that he'd begun to understand her, he couldn't think of losing his second partner in as many missions. The two of them had been a good team, taking or giving control and support as needed. For all their early squabbles, the mission hadn't disintegrated half as much as Cordil had. How much better would things have been if they had trusted each other from the start, if he hadn't let misconceptions cloud his judgment?

"No." He rubbed his forehead like she so often did. "Calla can't be dead. I would have sensed it. I would have known."

Brachi paused in his pacing. "Not if one of those generators hid her from you."

"I need your help to go get her out of their hands." He drove away thoughts of her death.

Brachi resumed his restless movement. "If we have some assurance that she's still alive, then yes, of course."

Thomas tried to stare a hole through Brachi's morbid head. "She's not dead."

"You don't know that, and I can't rrisk any of my people on a mission to possibly rretrieve a corpse. She's old for her youth, yes, but those I would send are older yet; and therefore, they are more valuable. I'm sure you understand."

Thomas glared at Brachi. "No, I don't. She came here to help you, and now that she's in danger, you would abandon her."

He wanted to say more, wanted to tell them how

foolish they were. He wanted to convince Brachi that the real cruelty would be to leave Calla to suffer. Nothing would come of it, he knew. Brachi and Rana were both as deeply entrenched in their own prejudices as Thomas had been less than a week before.

Thomas focused his thoughts on home and teleported. His head still reeled from the refusals he had encountered so far. Someone had to help them. The people of Ologo wouldn't, which left two options.

He could try Haidar Security Forces, or he could attempt the rescue himself. Everything he knew about such missions came from Terran movies, not an encouraging prospect. Haidar Security had to help. They were duty-bound, weren't they? Thomas rushed out, hoping Calla had the strength to hold on.

August completed his last entry into the spreadsheet he had created then printed the file. The results were not encouraging, but they confirmed what he had set out to prove. Over the last three years, Joseph had asked for help conducting "security checks" eighteen times. Each request had involved five people. Of the ninety, all had some kind of disability or a less-than-pristine past. Eighty of them had died inside of a few weeks from some sort of accident or unexplainable phenomenon. Of the other ten, including Thomas, tragedy had been averted by the intervention of outsiders.

Along the path to gathering his proof, August had come across a number of other stories involving bizarre events happening to people with odd handicaps. The fire in Calla's apartment typified those cases.

His guts turned. Joseph had turned his philosophy of cleansing the station into action. Unwittingly, August had helped plan the murders. In his ignorance, he had nearly killed his own best friend. Now he had a Syndromer to thank for saving Thomas from an unexpected overdose.

Thomas had spoken of Calla's strengths. Did Joseph's lies extend to the effects of Power Deficit Syndrome? August called up a search engine. He'd find out, and then he'd do the hardest thing he had ever done. He would take all this evidence to security and turn himself in.

Calla's head throbbed with her pulse. A rough cord bound her wrists and ankles. The smell of old wood and dust suggested some kind of storeroom. She lay on a hard, flat surface. If she could gain some purchase on her powers, she could battle the fog of pain and correct the damage Joseph had done.

How had he come to ally himself with genocidal maniacs like Pharmacorp? Although she wanted to hope he had been duped or coerced into cooperating, she knew better. He'd been far too pleased about knocking her down with more force than he'd needed, and the injuries she often treated in his students spoke volumes of his character.

Joseph's psionic attack had sent her to the ground hard, and the pain had subsided a trifle since then. Worse, she knew his avatar. He'd been the one who had attacked her and torched her apartment a month ago. The man had no soul. He must have joined Pharmacorp with full knowledge of what his allies were up to.

His motives were less important to her than her other big concern. Her call to Thomas had gone unanswered. She hadn't seen him, heard him, or heard about him, and her brain came up with hundreds of reasons why.

Joseph might have blocked the effort. He certainly had the power to do so. Thomas might not have been on the planet. If he hadn't returned from home, he never would've heard her. Maybe he had been captured, too. If he had been caught already, then their only hope to get out of this mess would be the Gotrians and Olvians. Would Pharmacorp's superior technology destroy both races? Could they even manage to overcome their differences long enough to attempt a rescue?

Of even greater concern, Thomas led the mission. One attempt had already been made on his life. If they had him now, they could do whatever they liked to him. This time, she wouldn't be able to help him.

More than anything else, she feared she had been abandoned. Thomas' growing understanding for her and her condition could have been all for show. He had needed her help to solve the problem on Ologo and might have thought she would hold out on him because of his attitudes. With his stronger powers, he could have easily hidden deception from her if he'd tried.

Would he consider risking himself to save her to be worth his time and effort?

When a nearby door opened, Calla stayed still, partly to avoid drawing attention and partly to avoid aggravating the pain in her head. Footsteps and the periodic thud of a cane came closer.

"It wouldn't take you two minutes," Kevin said.

Joseph snorted. "Should I chew your food for you, too?"

"Look, you're being paid to do a job!" Kevin hollered.

"And I've done it." Joseph kept his voice level. "I arranged with the Magistrates to send two inexperienced, weak negotiators. I gave you all the information on those two that you could have possibly needed to do anything your hearts desired. I only helped capture Calla because the idiots you sent after her let her escape. That was a bonus."

Kevin growled. "You got your money for it."

"In that generator's influence, she's a helpless little girl. Anyway, she should still be too weak from my earlier attack to cause you any trouble. I have to go teach my class or at least inform my assistant that I have other business before someone wonders where I've gone. I'll be back shortly. If I find that your people botched the attack on Thomas or didn't get the information he collected, then we can work out another deal."

As one set of footsteps and the sound of the cane retreated into the distance, Calla felt a slight measure of relief. Thomas hadn't been captured. Provided he considered coming for her important enough to try, she had hope for a rescue now, but maybe Thomas should stay away. Joseph had far more power than either one of them could take on, and her partner had no way of knowing to prepare for a fight with such a strong telepath. As much as she hadn't liked Thomas before, she didn't want to see him hurt.

Kevin grabbed her chin and shoved her head back. Calla gasped and closed her eyes when the pain in her head raged.

"What do you want?" Calla glared at the unclear image of him and tried to make her eyes focus.

"We know why you moved the negotiations away from here." He sneered.

Yeah, something about you poisoning my partner and being oh so helpful. "The accommodations weren't working out, and Patina had said there was no other space."

He pulled out a silver rod with a couple buttons on the end. "I wouldn't advise you to play games. Your boss told the Magistrates you had proof of our involvement in the plagues, but we've gone through all your things and found no sign of it. Where did you put the evidence, and who did you tell about it?"

Well, if that concerned him, she could end this in a hurry.

Calla blinked hard. "We had no evidence. We only had a hunch."

"You expect me to believe you'd present information to the delegations based on a hunch?" He flipped a small switch and the device hummed.

"That's exactly what we did. We had a theory that fit the facts. That's all."

"How stupid do you think we are?" He adjusted a dial on the rod.

Do you really want me to answer that? "I'm serious. We had no hard evidence."

Kevin pressed two prongs on the end of his weapon against her chest. "Tell me. Where did you put the evidence? Who did you tell?"

She tried to shrink back from him, but the wall behind her gave her nowhere to go. "The medical records of afflicted Olvians and Gotrians were returned to them. Everything else was speculation."

He pushed the button on the side of the rod. Fierce pain tore through her and set her nerves on fire. Calla tensed so hard her muscles hurt. Her lungs seized up, and she couldn't draw a breath.

He shook his head. "I don't believe you."

Calla panted to catch her breath. "Everything we knew was written in my notebook."

"I've read it."

"Then you know we had nothing! Nothing for certain."

"I know you wanted me to think you had nothing." He adjusted a setting on the rod.

Calla closed her eyes. How could she convince him?

He grabbed her by the front of the shirt and hauled her halfway to a sitting position. "Joy Demouchette told the Magistrates you had proof Thomas planned to take to the cops—not speculation, not guesses, not even a good hunch, but real, tangible proof. Where is it?"

"She's mistaken. There's no real proof."

He shoved her down again. "Wrong answer."

The hot electrodes on the rod pressed against her chest.

"Thomas McCrady?"

Thomas looked up at the sound of his name. An officer in the Security Forces beckoned. He joined the woman and followed her back to a small cubicle. The space had half-height walls on three sides and a plastic surface for a desk. The computer was a few models out of date.

The officer gestured to a plastic and metal chair. "I'm Lieutenant Effinger. You wanted to report an abduction?"

Thomas took the offered seat. "Yes, my partner, Calla Geisman. We've been on Ologo all week negotiating a treaty. Pharmacorp, who has a corporate office there, tried to kill me a couple days ago and now they've abducted Calla. I need help to get her back."

Lt. Effinger frowned. "I'm sorry, Mr. McCrady, but even if we did that sort of raid, Ologo is out of our jurisdiction."

Thomas sighed. *So much for another brilliant idea.* "There's nothing you can do to help her?"

"I'll be happy to take all the information and refer it up to the Galactic Law Enforcement office, but it could be a few days before they respond." She took out a notebook and pen.

Thomas struck the arm of the chair. "She won't be

alive in a few days. These guys aren't exactly patient."

"Understand, sir, bringing an armed force into a region beyond our sphere of influence would be an act of war." She flipped to a blank page of the notebook. "Now, if you'll begin when you first noticed her missing."

Thomas stood. "Thanks anyway."

Lieutenant Effinger caught his arm. "Don't do anything rash, Mr. McCrady. If you try going in there yourself, you'll be killed."

He pulled away from her. "I appreciate the advice."

As soon as he'd cleared the security area, he focused his thoughts on Joy's office and teleported. The colored swirls faded in moments. Her door stood open. Thomas knocked on the doorframe.

She looked up and smiled. "Come in, Thomas."

He entered and leaned against the inside of the doorframe. "Calla's been kidnapped by Pharmacorp."

Joy's jaw dropped. "Are you sure?"

Thanks for having the decency to look surprised. He bit his lip and nodded. "She called out to me with a clear note of panic in her voice. When I went to her room, I found one of the Olvian delegates dying and Calla's blood in a few places. She's nowhere to be seen, but there are huge voids in Pharmacorp, and she can't leave by herself. She's got to be there. Haidarian Security gave me some out-of-jurisdiction noise and wouldn't do anything except refer the case to Galactic Enforcement."

Joy winced. "That's all they can do in a situation like this, Thomas. You're not thinking about trying your hand at a rescue, are you?"

"Yes, and I could use some backup."

Joy shook her head. "The Magistrates will never approve. Pharmacorp is a Terran company. They won't risk open hostilities with the Terrans."

"I can't leave her there!" He gestured in the general

direction of Ologo.

Joy came around her desk and perched on the edge. "I know how you feel, but all we can do is apply political pressure on the Terrans and get them to force Pharmacorp to yield up Calla."

Thomas rolled his eyes. "That could take months. You know how slow their government is. If Calla is lucky, she has hours."

"I'm sorry, Thomas, but I can't authorize what would amount to an attack on a Terran company."

"Are you serious?" He pushed off from the doorframe. "Between abducting Calla and the attempt on my life, Pharmacorp has effectively declared war on us. We're in our rights to get our people back, and then we can be terribly magnanimous by not pursuing war with the Terrans."

"Nice in theory, but that's not how it works in practice. The politics are much more convoluted, and we can't afford a major conflict with Earth right now."

"So we'll sacrifice our own to keep the Terrans happy?" History lessons about the Haidarian slave revolts on Earth came to mind. "Isn't that why some of their folks helped our ancestors flee Earth in the first place?"

She scowled. "That's an oversimplification. Come with me, Thomas, and we'll go talk to the Magistrates and see what they're willing to do. They almost certainly won't authorize a raid on a Terran company, but let's see what they'll consider acceptable."

"They're the ones who got us into this mess in the first place. I'm not wasting any more time." Thomas walked out. "I'll be back later."

Before Joy could say anything else, Thomas teleported back to his apartment. What else could he try? He had no idea where to find Calla's family or boyfriend, if she had one. Meiko had learned hand-to-hand combat from her father, but Thomas couldn't bring himself to involve her. The blaster burn Pipien had sustained made a strong argument for striking from a distance. August, however, would be a great help.

Thomas projected his thoughts. *"Hey, August."*

"Busy."

Thomas frowned. *"This is serious, August. I need your help. Calla's in trouble."*

"I've got a bigger problem."

Thomas flopped onto his rust-colored couch. *"Could you forget she's a Syndromer? I need your help!"*

"I told you. I'm busy. I gotta talk to a judge."

Thomas sat up straighter. *"A judge?"*

"The bailiff's calling me. See ya later."

He broke the connection, leaving Thomas facing another dead end. He was going to have to retrieve Calla himself or resign himself to her death while he carved up red tape. He would not leave her, not when he'd come to understand her and especially not when he considered all she'd done to help him.

Thomas concentrated on the park in the middle of the block of shops near Pharmacorp. Colors of his apartment swirled and righted themselves as flowers and trees. He found a bench and sat. Thomas reached out toward the building with his mental senses and found the voids right where they had been before.

Calla had to be somewhere in the middle of that psionic black hole. He couldn't teleport into a void, and walking straight up to the building's front door would bring resistance if they even guessed at his purpose. There had to be a service entrance for shipping. He headed out of the trees and made for the near side of the corporate building.

"What are you doing back here, Thomas?"

Spinning toward the call, he found Brachi and Rana outside the restaurant they used for a conference room. Thomas resolutely turned his back on the pair and continued onward. Something grabbed his pants leg. He fell forward, catching himself on a convenient light pole.

Thomas wrenched himself free and stared at Rana then at Brachi rushing to catch up. "What?"

"Where have you been?" Rana brought herself up to her full height. "We've been waiting for you at the restaurant for over an hour."

"I told you I wouldn't be there." He crossed his arms over his chest. "My partner needs me. She's been kidnapped by the people who already tried to kill me once."

Rana darkened. "Such is the thinking of males. By helping us complete the treaty, you could save millions of lives. Instead, you want to go after one person. Don't you realize you will probably die in there? You're one male against an entire building of males and females both. You don't even know Calla is still alive."

He jabbed his finger at Rana. "Then I'll bring her home for a proper funeral."

Panting hard, Brachi joined them, blocking Thomas' intended path. "Listen to greater wisdom. Our governments won't even consider a treaty if the Haidarian arbitrator is not there to ensure fairness."

Thomas spoke slowly. "Until my partner is safe, I am not available. Discussion over."

He did a quick line-of-sight teleport to get around them and started walking again.

"We'll go to your supervisors!" Rana yelled.

Thomas looked back over his shoulder. "Go right ahead."

Brachi bared his teeth. "Someone so young is that important to you?"

Thomas stopped and spun toward them. "For the last time, listen to me. I used to hold an inherited disability against her, and I wrongly blamed her for the death of a previous partner. Hating her for that made me the worst hypocrite for condemning your prejudices while indulging in my own. If not for her, I'd be dead twice. I'm going after her, alone if I must."

"Creature impossible!" Rana lifted her arms and sent a ripple through the membrane. "Haidar won't send in physicians to treat the plague, will they?"

Thomas shook his head. "Not until there's an enforceable treaty in place. Training doctors costs Haidar a lot, so they're usually protected. Calla is the only one I've ever heard of who was permitted to go into an active war zone. In fact, after the recent kidnapping and murder attempts, there won't be any arbitrators coming back to Ologo, either, unless they come with military forces."

Rana rubbed between her eyes. "Your chances of rescuing Calla would be improved if we distracted their personnel."

"They might at that," Thomas said.

Brachi struck his chest with his fist. "You could use a small force to forge the path to her. The maps we made while the building was being constructed will help, too."

"That's also true."

Brachi beckoned. "Come. There's much to plan."

Thomas followed the delegates back to the restaurant.

If Thomas had known an hour would pass for

preparation, he would've gone after Calla without them. Her terrified cry kept echoing in his mind. Whatever they had done to her to make her scream like that, they'd had another hour to do more of the same or worse. Even a week ago, when he had hated Syndromers for having the dumb luck of bad chromosomes, he wouldn't have wished such fear and agony on one.

Hang on, Calla. It won't be much longer.

The voids he sensed in the Pharmacorp building would keep her from hearing his simple reassurance.

Brachi's mental signature came up behind him. Thomas faced the older Gotrian.

"Are you rready to go?" Brachi ended the question with a hack.

Thomas snorted. "You think this delay was my doing?"

"No. Everything is rready." Brachi lowered the hood of his tunic. "The Olvians have already begun their assault through the underwater tunnels, and they're meeting rresistance. As soon as your team is in, we'll start our attack and split their forces. They should be too busy to trouble you."

He nodded. "Thank you."

Brachi pursed his lips. "Get Calla to safety and don't worry about us. Leave the battle in more experienced, wiser hands. Do you have everything you need?"

Thomas checked himself over. The modified, light body armor he'd borrowed from the Gotrians protected his chest. A Gotrian projectile gun in a hip holster would give him a means to fight in the telepathy blackout areas, and the four Gotrian fighters assigned to him would help even out any bad odds.

He nodded. "I'm ready. Give me about a minute after I teleport us in, then begin your attack. That'll give my team time to recover from teleportation."

"May the Wisdom of the Ancient guide you." Brachi hesitated. "Do not let the age of those we have assigned to you fool you. They are experienced in battle, and the young female knows the ways of their computers."

Thomas gathered his little team into a circle and concentrated on the lobby of Pharmacorp. As the entryway solidified around him, the members of his party staggered.

Steadying the two nearest him, he ushered them all into the ladies' restroom as planned, since it was closest to the passage heading to the downward stairs displayed on the Gotrian map. He hoped they wouldn't find anyone, and he was right.

All four of the Gotrians plopped on the pink tile floor and groaned.

Although he hadn't been officially timing, Brachi seemed to take a lot longer than sixty seconds to start the attack.

What were they waiting for? Pharmacorp held Calla, suffering who knew what torment, somewhere in the bowels of this place.

Thomas ran his fingers through his hair and sighed. He had to be patient. If he rushed out before the Pharmacorp mercenaries were engaged, he would have a much more difficult fight ahead.

A couple of the members of his team still looked green from teleporting. Thomas had Brachi's assurance this was a skilled group, but pushing them too soon would get them killed. Even after the first explosion rattled the building, and Thomas felt the presences of all the fighters responding to the attack, he paced for another minute or two while the last of his people overcame the teleport disorientation.

Reaching out with his powers, Thomas impressed upon all the minds out in the lobby that they did not see the one Haidarian and four Gotrians making their way to the stairs. Once certain he had the humans under his control, Thomas led his band out of the bathroom.

One of the mercenaries turned and looked straight at them. Thomas froze and held his breath. He had never forced his will on so many before. The process should be the same as for a smaller number of people, but if he had missed some of them, this could get awfully messy.

Turn around. There's nothing here.

The goon returned his attention to the front of the building.

Thomas followed his team the down the corridor and out of the reception area before he released his hold on the minds of those men.

They reached a dead end. Had the Gotrian map been incorrect? The trained force with him fanned out and began a search of the walls and floor. One, looking intently at a plant, made a clicking noise with his tongue and pointed out a hidden keypad.

Another came forward and studied the buttons, then pointed out the three that looked more worn than the others. She snapped a small computer onto the keypad then flipped a switch. Within moments, a door slid open.

The computer went back into a hip pouch then one soldier forged ahead alone while two stayed back with Thomas and the fourth took a position to keep watch the way they'd come.

As they headed down the flight of stairs, Thomas' mental perceptions vanished. Drawing his borrowed gun, he slowed. The Gotrian in the lead hopped up onto the banister and ran on it as easily he took the stairs.

Thomas raised his left eyebrow.

The door closed behind them with a hiss. Thomas glanced back at the female computer operator. She waved him on ahead. From time to time, a muffled gunshot came from ahead of them or behind them. One of the two with him would bolt off in that direction, then return seconds later with the pursed lips of a Gotrian smile.

He came to a stair landing. A man in a black uniform embroidered with Pharmacorp's logo lay slumped against the wall with a bullet hole in the middle of his forehead. From that point on, similar corpses appeared every few dozen steps.

They finally reached the bottom, and Thomas took a deep breath. A huge, bright red SL-2 had been painted on the gunmetal gray door. According to Brachi's notes, the submarines were on this level, and although Calla could be anywhere in the building, Brachi had insisted on starting the search for her on the second sublevel. As far as Thomas cared, the bottom floor was as reasonable a place to begin as any other.

Putting his ear to the door, he listened for some sign of life on the other side. He felt strangely disappointed when he heard nothing. As odd as it seemed, he listened longer, hoping to hear Calla's cries. He didn't want anything to happen to her, but her scream would let him know that she still lived. Silence brought unbidden images to his mind of finding her mutilated body. How could he ever explain her death to her family? He would rather die than lose a second partner.

He pushed all worries aside. She was alive. She had to be alive. No sound came from the other side of the door, but that didn't necessarily herald her death. Instead, the silence meant they weren't hurting her for the moment.

Thomas inched the door open. As soon as the door cleared the frame, an alarm sounded. He slammed the door closed again, but the klaxon continued.

Pushing him out of the way, two of the Gotrians

rushed out the door and took up a position in the hallway while the other two set themselves up in the door frame. The door looked out into an L-shaped intersection. Another door loomed in the right-hand wall a short sprint down the corridor.

Terran voices coming from the direction of the sub depot grew closer. One of his team members gestured for him to go on without them. Thomas nodded and ran across the intersection toward the door.

Gun held at the ready, Thomas stepped into another corridor then through the nearest door on his left. This took him into another room and away from the elevators the map said were located further down. Unlabeled crates stacked three deep floor to ceiling lined the walls leaving a narrow corridor. Smeared, dried blood stained a few boxes about hip high on one side. Calla's blood from the same knife wound she'd sustained in her quarters? Possibly, and the best lead he had so far.

He went to the door at the other end of the room and listened. Soon, very soon, he'd find her.

Calla awoke again. Nerves tingled and muscles ached. The headache still shrieked at her. She had no way to judge how much time had passed since then, but the pain in her head and in her body hadn't changed much. She tried not to show that she was awake again. If they thought she had regained her strength, they would be back for another round of asking her questions she had already answered.

The door opened, and Calla peeked at the newcomers. Joseph led Kevin in.

"Let me get this straight." Joseph's hard stare pierced Kevin through. "She's as weak and helpless as a blind kitten, and you still couldn't get the information out of her?"

Kevin gestured toward Calla with a sweep of his hand. "If you think you can make her talk, you go right ahead and do it."

Joseph pushed past Kevin. "What did you people do before I came along to solve all your problems?"

"We avoided encounters with you freaks. Just find out what she knows. You'll be compensated."

"Very well." Joseph rolled his eyes. "Give me the generator shielding her."

Calla closed her eyes. Hard steps and the dull thud of his cane approached her. Joseph's reputation and the details of the students she'd treated came back to her. No matter how creatively she tried to set up her defenses, she wouldn't be able to keep her assailant out of her head.

"Look at me." His last footfall landed a hand's-breadth from her nose. "There's no sense in pretending you're still out cold. I'm not a Terran to be fooled that easily." His hands pressed against the sides of her head and tilted her back to look up at his snarky smile. "You know what will happen if you resist me. Don't you?"

Joseph reached into his pocket. His and Kevin's thoughts came into her mind. She sensed Kevin's fear and Joseph's anticipation. She tried to reach beyond the room and found a bumpy ring of voids blocking the way. A second later, a hard pressure burned into her mind. Her headache flared, like getting a rod rammed through her skull. Calla clenched her eyes and jaw.

The silhouette with its flaming sword appeared. Calla envisioned herself across from him.

Her mental self looked as battered and beaten as she

felt. She hadn't the energy to be creative. *"I don't have the information Kevin wants. We had no evidence, no matter what Joy implied."*

"I don't care." He shoved her aside.

Her convoluted mental maze took form, looking much denser than a normal person her age. She didn't stick around to admire the complexity or assess the damage. Twice already, Joseph had proven how one-sided a fight between them would be. She form-shifted to a small bird then zipped down a stairwell and ladder to the inner level. There were no severed axons, but many swollen dendrites and bruised cell bodies needed to be repaired.

As she approached the nearest, a shock of pain made her cringe. Joseph was adding to the injuries he'd already caused. Focusing through the agony, she healed the inner level as quickly as she could and darted back to the midlevel.

Joseph struck again and again as she struggled to realign damaged columns. She'd finished once only to have him cause another to shift with his attacks. Darkness closed in on her.

Calla half-fluttered, half-fell back to the lower level. She disconnected some axons and re-linked them to other dendrites and cell bodies, rerouting some of her body's energies to renew her strength. The pain didn't change, but she felt more alert.

She returned to the maze.

Joseph made his way back through the straight path he'd made by wrecking any panes blocking him. "What a pity. You really didn't have any evidence, but it won't change how we deal with you. You know too much now."

With that, the shadow warrior left. The stabbing pain receded back to the intolerable headache. She relaxed the tension in her muscles. Rivulets of sweat, or maybe tears, pooled in the corner of her eye. The generator was still off, and she took full advantage of her powers.

Calla went to the nearest broken pane of her mental maze and grabbed two smoky shards. The more damage she fixed, the better her chances.

"Well?" Kevin asked.

Joseph snorted. "They know nothing. Well, that is, they knew nothing until you brought her here. Now she has your admissions, and she knows about my involvement. Do I need to dispose of her, or do you think you can handle that much?"

Kevin growled. "I'll get your payment for you in a moment after I take care of Geisman."

"Well, get on with it."

"I don't need you hovering over my shoulder."

"As soon as the job's done and I've been paid, I'll leave."

Kevin's hard step came closer. "Well, whaddya know? You were telling the truth all along."

Calla gathered all the power she could in preparation to shoot a bolt of psionic energy right into Kevin's mind. The make-up lesson in her room nearly a week ago came to mind. Mr. Zagruder had mentioned in their training session that the first stage of teleporting was much like a telepathic punch. She could use that.

Thomas neared the door leading out of the third cramped storeroom. He listened, expecting to hear the same silence he had before. The gun battle he'd left behind in the corridor barely registered now.

Two male voices came from within the room. One said something about being paid and leaving. A mercenary? The other, obviously Kevin, mentioned something about telling the truth all along. Was he talking to Calla?

Thomas opened the door and felt a sympathetic ache in his chest. Calla lay bound on the floor. If not for the tension in her face, he would've thought her unconscious. A cut in one sleeve of her black jacket leaked bloodstained coat stuffing.

Kevin stood over her aiming a gun at her head. The other man, a Haidarian, looked familiar, but Thomas couldn't place why he knew the guy. Thomas brought his borrowed gun to bear.

His hand shook. He'd only ever blasted holes in targets. If he fired now, someone would die.

Kevin turned, leading with the gun.

Thomas steadied one hand with the other and aimed the pistol at Kevin's chest. "Drop it!"

"You stupid junkie." The Haidarian laughed while he spoke. "If you meant to fire, you would have already."

A smile crept across Kevin's face. "True enough. Thanks for coming. You spared us the aggravation of having to hunt you down."

The Pharmacorp hitman reeled back like he'd been

kicked in the head, and his gun clattered to the floor. Falling hard, he pressed a hand to the side of his skull. The second man looked first at Thomas, then Calla. The stranger scowled, and Calla cried out, as chilling a sound physically as it had been mentally.

Thomas pushed past the Haidarian and dodged a swipe of the man's cane. He went to Calla's side. As he cleared the effect of the anti-psionic generator, Thomas felt a surge of pain from Calla and anger from her attacker. Thomas projected his presence into Calla's mind.

An image of her struggled to rise amidst the wreckage in part of the glass-walled maze. A huge, shadowy figure held a sword ringed with fire hearkening back to the knife-wielding shadow woman who had attacked him during the final negotiations on Cordil IV. Whether they were somehow related or not, Thomas would drive the intruder out, just like he had the female on Cordil. Shifting to his gray wolf form, Thomas tackled the swordsman.

Watching Thomas' initial attack as a massive, gray wolf surprised Calla as much as his arrival. Joseph had power and training Thomas couldn't hope to match. Then again, his best friend had been Joseph's protégé for years. Perhaps August had given some unofficial lessons.

In any case, Thomas would need help to defeat Joseph. Calla knew too little about mental martial arts to be any good even if she hadn't felt so weak after taking a physical and mental beating. If she could distract Joseph without drawing attention to herself, Thomas might be able to take advantage of the opening.

Having a tiny power signature would work to her advantage for a change. Expending as little energy as she could, Calla sent herself outward. She contacted Joseph's mind and waited for one of Thomas' successful attacks to create microscopic cracks in the defensive shielding.

She crept through. Calla didn't dare summon the maze or a visualization of herself for fear of tipping her hand, but she could use Joseph's own body against him just like the paramedic Mr. Zagruder had described during her lesson. Struck by a sudden inspiration, Calla wove her way to the deepest level of her opponent's mental structures. The sharp sting of injury clearly reported in Joseph's mind.

Nearby, she heard Thomas draw a sharp breath. Joseph reveled in the pain he'd caused.

"After I kill you both, I'll go finish the job I started with that Syndromer's brat you love," Joseph said.

Thomas' rage flared to be replaced by another stunning hit against him. *"Calla? Calla, I need you!"*

Joseph laughed, but Calla didn't dare answer. He'd recognize where she was hailing from.

She reached her destination but didn't call up the images of the neuron network. She didn't have to. The brain was a chaotic place with little electrical jolts carrying information every which way. If she could impose a pattern, she could bring the whole system crashing down.

Calla sent short psionic pulses. Before long, she felt her patterns echoing back to her from small groups of neurons. Those recruited the ones near them, which in turn affected their neighbors. She kept up her efforts until convinced the cascade would be self-propagating then withdrew to go lend Thomas more direct help if she could.

Thomas limped hard while circling with the swordsman. The few good strikes he'd landed foamed but he hadn't been faring too well himself. He'd gotten several searing nicks from his opponent's blade. The last comment about Meiko had driven him to attack rashly, earning a hard hit on his flank.

Nothing he tried gave him the upper hand, and given Calla's lack of response to his plea, Thomas couldn't count on help from her. He was fresh out of ideas.

"You might as well give up." The opponent twirled his sword in a loop over his hand. *"Leave the Syndromer and save yourself. By the time I catch up to you, you might have—"*

He cut off mid-taunt. His avatar's hand quivered, becoming more violent by the moment. Calla's image appeared, horribly bruised and battered, on the verge of collapse. A triumphant smile came to her face.

"What—what is this?" The shadow warrior's sword fell from his hand and vanished.

His whole arm had taken up the intense tremor, which started up in his other hand, too.

Calla crossed her arms over her chest. *"Come on, Pearce. You were a paramedic. Surely you recognize a seizure when you see it. The kind I started won't cause any lasting harm, but it will leave you incapacitated for a while if it continues. I'll make it stop if you get out of my head and quit attacking us."*

Pearce? As in August's mentor Joseph Pearce? No wonder Thomas hadn't gotten far in that fight. In fact, he'd done better than he could've hoped against a man who specialized in mental combat.

The shadowy image vanished.

Calla's form fell, as if nothing but the tension of the moment had been keeping her up.

Without withdrawing his support from her, Thomas opened his eyes and blinked hard to force his blurry, double vision to straighten up. His head throbbed. Nearby, Joseph dropped as the tremors became coordinated twitches of his arms and legs.

"Calla, what do I do?" Thomas fished his little knife out of his pocket.

She squinted in Joseph's direction. "He'll be out for a while."

Gradually, the jerky movements calmed until he lay still.

Thomas flipped open the largest blade. "Sneaky trick. How'd you get past his defenses?"

"Smaller hammer." Her thin voice rasped.

He nodded. She'd used the same thing to slip past his unintentional resistance to her treatment. Nearby, Kevin moaned but stayed still.

Thomas used his pocketknife to cut Calla free of the cords binding her. "We've got to get out of here. There's a fight going on not so far away."

Teary-eyed, she looked up at him. "Go."

"Not without you." He cast the cords aside.

She rubbed her forehead. "Teleport strain will be too much."

He flipped the blade closed and returned it to his pocket. "Not if I support you."

"You're hurt, too."

He leaned closer to her. "I'm not leaving without you. You're going to have to let me further into your head, though."

She clutched his hand and closed her eyes. "I trust you."

He smiled. "I knew you were brave."

Thomas grabbed Joseph by the ankle and then gently reached deep into Calla's mind. Without the preoccupying stress of battle, he got a clear sense of the heart-wrenching effects of her ordeal. He shared his strength with her to help her tolerate the coming teleportation. Visualizing the medical ward he'd become too familiar with lately, Thomas projected his powers. The storeroom disappeared into a whirl of colors.

The waiting room took form around them. The nauseating stress of near-instant travel slammed into Thomas through his connection to Calla. He took as much of the effect as he could onto himself to protect her and stubbornly resisted the urge to retch. Her grip on his hand slackened as she wilted. Even with his support, he could feel her slipping away, just as Angela had before he'd teleported her to safety.

He pulled her closer to him. "No you don't. We're home. We're safe. You've gotta stay with me."

People rushed up behind him, and a flash of a white lab coat at the edge of his vision solidified into the balding, overweight doctor who had released him from here less than a week ago. He knelt next to Joseph. Dr. Xava Vandamir, who'd treated Meiko yesterday, crouched near Calla. Dr. Vandamir had her long brown hair pulled back into a pony tail. The glitter in her eyes was noticeable over the room lighting but not by much.

"You again?" Dr. Vandamir pressed her fingers against the side of Calla's throat. "You're getting to be a regular around here."

Thomas returned a wry smile but didn't appreciate the joke. "Is she going to be okay?"

Dr. Vandamir nodded and picked Calla up. "Come with me, and don't let her mind go until I tell you. It'll be less traumatic if we don't switch until the teleport stress wears off.”

Thomas nodded and rose, weaving unsteadily as the red and purple checked floor seemed to spin to his left. Keeping a hand pressed to his temple, he followed the woman bearing Calla into the emergency room where the doctor laid Calla out on a bed and checked her pulse, blood pressure, and breathing.

“Calla, can ya hear me?” Dr. Vandamir’s thoughts echoed in Calla’s mind.

“Xava?” Calla’s answer was so soft. Had he imagined it?

“Yeah, it’s me. I’m going to take over supporting you. That means your friend is going to let you go. Understand?”

Thomas felt more than heard an affirmative response.

Dr. Vandamir’s presence in Calla’s mind grew as the physician took over Thomas’ self-assigned job. His sense of Calla stopped sliding away, and he marveled that a woman with a lower mental signature could do more with less power.

“All right, Mr. McCrady, I have her. Withdraw, slowly.”

As Thomas complied with those directions, he saw structures that looked like glass panes arranged in a maze. Many of the walls were burnt or cracked, several others were broken in a wide path.

“I’m listening even if I don’t look like it. What happened?” Dr. Vandamir pulled a stool up to the bed and closed her eyes.

Thomas leaned against the bed. “I don’t know anything specific. I got the impression that before I got there, she was tortured for information she didn’t have. Joseph Pearce had a hand in it.”

“I thought this mess had his trademark on it.” Dr.

Vandamir blew out a breath. "I'll get the details of how she was injured from her memory. How'd you stop ol' Pearce?"

"I fought him, and he had me on the ropes until Calla caused some kind of seizure."

Dr. Vandamir smiled. "That's our girl. You look a little unsteady yourself. Are you hurt?"

He nodded, which made the headache surge. "I was hit pretty hard a couple of times."

"You're lucky there. You must be pretty quick or resourceful to get off that lightly against someone of Pearce's caliber." She pointed to the empty bed behind her. "Hop up on that bed right there until someone can check you out."

Thomas eased himself up onto the bed, and his headache pounded with his pulse. He cringed as he lay flat.

The other doctor walked over. "Xava, third patient is stable and can keep for a little bit. Cops will be here momentarily. Do you need me here?"

"Yes, I've got Calla. See to Mr. McCrady." Dr. Vandamir indicated Thomas with a nod. "He went ten rounds with Pearce."

The doctor whistled. "That's a trick not many can tell about." He walked up to the bed. "All right, remember me? I'm Dr. Andy Hale. I need to take a peek into your head for a few minutes to see what needs to be put back together."

Thomas nodded and his guts clenched. *I don't suppose there's a way to do this without you getting into my head?*

"This won't hurt." Dr. Hale smiled.

Thomas had heard that before and hoped this doctor was as gentle as Calla. He closed his eyes. The physician's hands rested on either side of Thomas' head as a new presence pushed into his mind.

Unlike the softness Thomas had come to expect from Calla's contact, Dr. Hale's mental touch communicated an almost uncomfortable pressure, making Thomas tense involuntarily. Feelings of peace washed over him in the same way Calla's efforts had stopped the raucous word war back on Ologo. His muscles slowly loosened up.

"That's better," Dr. Hale said.

The glass-walled maze appeared showing a number of cracked and blackened panes and one section of broken ones.

An image of the doctor appeared. "Not too bad, actually."

One by one, each damaged glass wall sealed and cleared up. The slight dizziness and headache faded. Once the doctor had reassembled the last wall, Thomas felt a little tired but fine otherwise.

Dr. Hale stepped back. "There we go. That should do it. How do you feel now?"

Thomas opened his eyes and sat up. "Better. Thanks."

"Good." Dr. Hale clapped Thomas on the shoulder. "Now if that dizziness comes back or you get a headache in the next couple days, you need to come back in." He went to Calla's side. "Xava, how's it going in there?"

"Slowly. Who's handling physical injuries today?"

"That'd be Nikk. I'll get him. Better get her parents and Matt here, too."

Nikk, Thomas supposed, would be Dr. Nikolai Petrov, who had treated Angela after the mishap on Cordil IV, but who was Matt again?

Dr. Vandamir nodded as Dr. Hale left. "You'll have to go to the waiting room, Mr. McCrady. I'll let you know when I have more news about Calla."

Thomas squeezed Calla's hand and then started away.

"Hey," the doctor said.

He turned back. "Yeah?"

"She wouldn't have made it back without you. Good job."

He smiled, then took one last look before going to the waiting room. If Calla survived this, then he would feel better about how he'd done.

$$\backsim$$

After reading the same paragraph in her book for the fifth time and still not understanding what she saw on the page, Meiko closed the anthology and set it aside. She had nothing left to do.

She had given up on sewing, having stuck her shaking hands with pins too many times. Although she usually ate dinner around this hour, food didn't interest her at all. When she felt nervous, eating always made her sick. Even concentrating on her lesson plans for next week had been a total bust. Fortunately, she'd been teaching teenagers trigonometry long enough to wing it when she had to.

Thomas had said he would get Calla and come home. Hours had passed since then and still no sign of him. If Calla had been in trouble and he had gone to help her, he might have found himself in over his head. Why hadn't he gotten in touch again?

Maybe the next call she received would be from a doctor telling her to come to the medical ward if she wanted to see Thomas. That would be better than having to report to the morgue to identify his body.

Maybe some company would help keep her mind off of her worries.

She pushed her thoughts outward. *"August."*

He didn't reply. She scowled. Ever since he had found out how Thomas had almost died on Ologo, August had ignored her and everyone else.

Whatever your problem is, get a grip, will you? She stood up and paced the length of the apartment. *"August, I need to talk to you. Thomas isn't back yet, and I'm worried about him."*

The lack of response ratcheted her aggravation up another notch.

If she knew more about Thomas' location, she might try teleporting to him. He might need help, and although years had passed since the class she'd taken, she didn't do half bad in a telepathy fight.

In reality, though, appearing in the middle of whatever he had to deal with might be a catastrophically rotten idea. She could appear in the crossfire and get hurt or be such a major distraction for Thomas that he made a stupid mistake and got himself killed trying to protect her.

Pacing a hole in the floor wouldn't help, either. Meiko sat down at her computer and loaded a mindless card game. Thomas had once accused her of being able to play this one in her sleep, and right now, she happily let her mind go on autopilot.

While she played through several rounds, her brain conjured up worst case scenarios. Thomas was strong and skilled. He would be fine, and she had to keep reminding herself of that until it sunk in.

"Meiko." Thomas' thoughts echoed in her head.

She leaped to her feet and projected her thoughts back to him. *"Thomas! Where are you? Are you okay? How's Calla?"*

"I'm in Medical Ward Seven. I'm fine. I'm tired, but I'm fine. I'm waiting for news about Calla."

"Then it was her who called for you?"

"Yeah. Care to come join me? I can fill you in on the details."

She nodded. *"I'll be there in a second."*

Meiko smiled and left without bothering to turn the computer off. At least this time when she went to see him in the medical ward, she wouldn't have to ask the receptionist for the number of the room he slept in.

She reached the waiting room. Red and purple plastic chairs were lined up around the edge of the room. Pictures on the walls showed happy kids racing around the Level Seven gymnasium nearby.

Thomas sat with another man about their age. The man's dark hair was almost long enough to cover his fiercely glowing eyes.

"When Joseph attacked, I held him off until Calla took him out," Thomas said.

Meiko hung back, not sure if this was a good time to intrude on their conversation.

"I wish you'd gotten in touch with me." The other man rested his elbows on the chair's armrests and interlaced his fingers. "Even if it wasn't a good idea to go through official channels, I'd've helped you."

Thomas nodded. "I understand, Matt. Believe me, I wanted the help. Things happened so fast for us out there, we didn't have time to chat about anything like family, fiancées, or boyfriends. Looking at it now, I suppose I should've gone to her office and asked there."

"Yeah, well, thanks for bringing her back."

"Least I could do." Thomas looked toward the emergency ward. "She saved my life on that trip, too, even though I wasn't the most cooperative patient. Then when she called out to me earlier, she woke me up. If she hadn't, I may not have seen the goon squad coming for me. I sleep so solidly that I'd never have known they were there until too late. I wish I could have gotten to her sooner."

Matt shook his head. "Going in unprepared would have gotten you captured. Then where would you two be? Calla will be all right. She's much stronger than people give her credit for."

With the lull in the conversation, Meiko joined them. Thomas met her part way and embraced her. Meiko leaned against him and closed her eyes, listening to his heartbeat. Having him back was almost too good to be true.

"Miss me?" He held her out at arm's length and looked her over.

Except for his chest, his clothes were brushed with gray dust. Here and there, bits of sawdust stuck to the material.

She smiled. "Who, me? Why would I miss you?"

"Because you need to practice your aim." He conducted her over to the other man and introduced her to Matt.

After shaking hands, they sat and talked more about the mission. All the while, Matt kept looking up at the clock on the wall. Meiko sent him feelings of reassurance. Calla would be okay. If she could put up with all the insults and verbal abuse people with PDS received, she had too much persistence not to be.

Thomas' story about the mission had reached the end of the first full day when a man in a lab coat came out.

Matt bounded to his feet and met the doctor. "Nikk! How is she? She okay?"

The doctor nodded, and Matt's tense muscles loosened.

"She'll be fine." Nikk pulled a chair over and sat with them. "She has a few minor injuries, and there are raw patches on her wrists and ankles from the cords she was bound with. She'll heal without a problem."

Matt scooted forward to the edge of his chair. "Thomas said she was attacked by Joseph Pearce."

Nikk winced. "I wasn't involved in treating any of the psionic injuries. Xava is still at it, but she told me that everything is progressing well. She can tell you more when she finishes."

"When can we see Calla?" Matt asked.

Dr. Petrov stood. "Once Xava is done, she'll come talk to you about going in to visit."

Matt nodded. "Thanks, Nikk."

Meiko slipped her hand into Thomas' as he returned to his description of the Ologo disaster.

Calla felt rested but continued to lie in bed with her eyes closed. The pain had left a dull ache behind. The mental fog caused by Joseph's torment had gone, too. Only the unpleasantness of the IV needle in her arm remained, and that would be easily remedied. She could take on the world again.

She turned her perceptions outward. There, near enough to be in the same room with her, stood someone with a mental signature too powerful to be her parents, Matt, Dillon, or anyone else she could think of who might come to wish her well.

Her eyes snapped open. August stood by the bed, looking down at her. The restaurant conversation between August, Meiko, and Thomas replayed in her mind. He'd emphatically insisted people like her deserved to be spaced. August was Pearce's disciple from start to finish.

Calla sat up and backed as far away from him as she could then pushed outward with her thoughts. *"Matt!"*

She looked at the nurse's call button built into the bed's opposite rail and then up at August's face. Could she hit the switch before he could stop her? As she reached across the bed, August's hand shot toward her.

"No, wait!" He caught not her hand but the tube in her arm.

She felt a pull on her skin as the tape came loose and the IV needle came out at an awkward angle. Calla retracted her arm and used her other hand to put pressure on the new injury.

August gasped and stepped back. "I'm sorry, Calla."

A surge of power preceded Matt's appearance. Grabbing August by the arm, her boyfriend flung her assailant into the far corner of the room. August hit the wall with a loud groan but didn't return the attack. She registered the mental buzz of telepathy in use nearby. Was that Matt or August who'd called someone?

Matt clenched both fists. "You here to finish what your boss started? Bad enough you harass a disabled woman, but to come after her while she's in the hospital is pathetic."

"You don't understand." August came to his feet and showed both hands empty.

Matt rose to his full height. "What's to understand?"

Another power surge heralded Thomas' arrival. He had rescued her and helped her escape, but he was August's friend. Where would his allegiance lie?

Thomas turned his back on Matt. "August, what are you doing here?"

"I told you last night I wanted to talk to Calla." August massaged his shoulder and moved it through the range of motion.

"Yes, I remember." Thomas scratched above his ear. "I also remember saying something crazy about how I would set that up because if you came in here alone she would do what?"

August sighed. "Panic."

Thomas indicated her with a wave of one hand. "Yes, and I was right, wasn't I?"

"I don't want to hurt her."

"She doesn't know that, and even when she knows it here." Thomas pointed to his temple. "It'll be a good long while before she knows it here." He pointed to his heart. "That's where it counts."

August growled. "I don't want an audience. This is a

private matter between her and me."

"Tough. She doesn't trust you enough to be in the same room with you alone." Thomas stepped aside and pivoted to where he could see all of them. "You scare her, and considering everything that's happened lately you really can't blame her, can you?"

Matt opened his fists as tension bled away from his muscles. "Wait, then this wasn't an attack?"

August's brightly-glowing eyes widened. "No, it wasn't. It—I—" He stopped and clenched his jaw, then groaned in frustration.

What had happened to the cocky, self-assured bully? Could what he said be true? Had she misunderstood his intentions? The events had occurred so quickly she couldn't rightly say. This had to be a trick. What could August possibly want to talk to her about in private?

Calla felt Thomas' eyes on her and looked up at him.

"While August takes a minute or two to put his thoughts together, let's deal with the more critical problem." Thomas walked over to the bed. "Calla, you're hurt."

She looked down at the blood on both her arm and the fingers of her other hand. "Yes, but I don't think it's as bad as it feels."

"It was an accident!" August took a step forward. "My fingers got caught in—"

"Later." Thomas silenced his friend with a raised hand. "You'll have a chance to explain later. First, we need to help Calla."

August glared at Thomas but didn't continue.

Calla lifted her fingers away from the wound. The bleeding had stopped, but there would be a bruise all right. Faint edges were already showing. "I need to clean this up so I can see the injury more clearly."

After a quick trip to the bathroom, Thomas returned

with a damp towel.

She gingerly cleaned her arm, wincing when she saw the extent of the damage resulting from her scuffle with August. The skin near the needle's original puncture was torn a couple millimeters on each side.

August bit his lip. "Calla, I'm sorry. I didn't mean to do that."

"What did you mean then?" She set the towel aside but kept her arm protectively cradled. "Why were you hovering over me when I woke up?"

"Can we talk about this alone? I promise I won't hurt you." August looked at Matt and Thomas, then back to her.

Matt snorted. "You're Joseph Pearce's assistant. I know about you and your mentor and what you two think about people who don't fit your tight definition of 'normal.'"

August waved his hand back and forth to clear the air. "Things are different now."

"If you think for one microsecond that I'm going to leave her alone with you..."

Thomas stepped between them. "Matt, I understand how you feel, but Calla must be the one to make the decision."

"Fine." Matt came to her side and pulled her into a one-armed embrace. The coarse material of his white uniform shirt was like a fine grain nail file. "Don't let anyone coerce you into being alone with him if you don't want to be, hon. I'm here for you."

Calla nodded.

With everyone looking at her for the answer, she felt like she sat facing the business end of a blaster. August seemed sincere enough, but was this another ploy or did he mean what he said? Thomas had taken neutral ground, but given his relationship to August, the arbitrator might not stay there. Matt was the only one she knew for certain had her best interests in mind. Until she could clear her head again, she would trust his instincts.

She shook her head. "No. If you want to talk to me, Matt or my dad will be there with us."

August rolled his eyes. "This is hopeless!"

"You knew this was coming." Thomas leaned on the purple countertop along one wall. "We talked about it last night. She wasn't there, so she doesn't know about your discovery. Having Matt here will work to your benefit. He clearly has a bad opinion of you. Your explanation may change that."

August flopped into the red plastic chair by the wall. "I don't even know where to start."

"She asked you to explain why you were here when she woke up. That might be the best place to start."

He looked up at Matt. "It was a big misunderstanding."

Thomas turned August to face Calla. "Tell her. She's the one you have to deal with. If she's convinced by what you have to say, then Matt will let it go, too. Won't you?"

Matt nodded. "If she doesn't feel threatened."

August looked down for a moment. "I had another meeting with the station attorney and a judge this morning. When I left there, I came by here to see how you were doing. Thomas told me coming here alone would be a bad idea, but the doctor said you weren't supposed to be up and around until this afternoon at the earliest, so I didn't think it'd be a problem. I just meant to come in and sit with you for a few minutes then leave. In fact, I'd just gotten up to go when you woke up."

That sounded plausible, but she couldn't shake the gut feeling he had ulterior motives.

She looked down at her arm. "Why did you rip the

needle out, then?"

"All I wanted to do was stop you from hitting the panic button." He shook his head and sighed. "I got tangled up. That's all. I shouldn't've tried to grab your hand. I didn't think that far ahead, and you didn't give me a chance to explain."

Matt's eyes narrowed. "Explain what?"

August frowned and shook his head.

What was the big secret? Why couldn't he come up with a way to say what was on his mind? August was the same guy who had insisted that everyone with PDS had to be crammed out the airlock. Only a few days had passed since he'd said that. Still, he clearly struggled with some internal demon. Had he changed his mind?

August blew out a breath. "Calla, could it be just you, me, and Thomas? Thomas won't let anything happen to you."

Thomas shook his head. "She's already set her condition, and it's not unreasonable. Since you were the aggressor, you'll have to abide by it."

"I can't do this." August struck his forehead with his palm. "Telling you was hard enough."

Thomas gripped August's shoulder. "Tell her the same way you told me."

He stared at the red, white, and purple tiled floor for several seconds. "All right. Here goes. I know where Pharmacorp got the personal information they used to attack you guys on Ologo."

Calla shrugged. "It's not a great mystery. They're the ones who hacked the database."

"They didn't. I did."

Calla felt the blood drain from her face. "You? You got the information for them? I know you hate everything about people like me, but they nearly killed Thomas with the records you gave them."

"I didn't know what Joseph intended to do with the data." August stood and paced to a picture of a grassland before he turned back to face the group. "He said he'd been asked by the Magistrates to test the security of the medical and training databases. He'd had me do similar stuff before, and with his brother on the tribunal, the frequency of the requests didn't seem all that unusual. I had no idea Joseph was working with Pharmacorp."

She shook her head. *You almost got your own best friend killed. How could you not know what you were doing?* "What did he do with the data all the other times he asked you to do similar things?"

August looked up at the corner of the room. "When Thomas told me he'd been drugged after the database had been hacked, I got suspicious and compared all the names Joseph's given me to the news, obituaries, and police reports. Within a week or two of the hacking he had me do, every one of the people on those lists died or had some nearly fatal accident. There are bunches of others I think he had a hand in, too, but I can't prove those. I had no idea. I really thought he was having me check security for his brother. How am I going to tell Meiko her dad's heart attack wasn't natural?"

Calla made a clicking noise with her tongue. "That'll be a tough one."

Thomas nodded. "We'll deal with that one later. Just do us both a favor, August, and don't go off half-cocked again."

"Yeah. Anyway, when I realized what I'd done, I went to the authorities." August took a tentative step closer. "Thomas told me about that fight you were in. It's a good thing you two stopped Joseph. He would've killed you if you hadn't. Believe that. You were worse than useless in his eyes."

"What about in your eyes?" Calla asked.

Matt squeezed her tighter. "Is making sure she gets spaced still the best thing for the galaxy?"

August's face flushed. "That's something else I checked into. When I realized Joseph had played me for a fool, I looked up information on everything else he'd said. Know what I found out? The Terran geneticists who designed our ancestors made the PDS gene on purpose. It was a military contract. Espionage. There was a trade-off. Low power levels to escape detection in exchange for enhanced memory and increased drug resistances, and when I realized Meiko's dad was a Syndromer—"

Thomas held up a hand to stop August. "You may want to find a less insulting way to say that."

"I, uh, yeah. When I found out Meiko's dad had PDS, I figured out that the gene doesn't weaken our future generations. I fell for all of Joseph's lies. I should've checked him out."

"You weren't the only one he got," Calla said.

"Yeah, but at least I'll be the last one. He's in jail now awaiting trial on a variety of counts: murder, attempted murder, assault, arson, and who knows what else."

"So what now?" Matt asked.

August shrugged and shook his head. "I don't know. I haven't thought that far ahead. I went to Security with the information I have on all the people Joseph killed or tried to kill. I offered to testify against Joseph. I won't be tried as an accomplice, but I'm on probation and can't leave the station until I finish the community service I was assigned. And, Calla, I don't expect you to be my friend, and I'm not even sure I deserve your forgiveness, even if you are in a forgiving mood. Just know I'll leave you alone. Thank you for saving Thomas from my stupidity, and I'm sorry I was such an idiot."

She gripped Matt's hand. "I understand. Thank you."

Calla wanted to believe him. She really did. He

sounded so sincere, but her brain still cried warnings. Maybe in time his actions would prove his words.

Standing in front of the Pharmacorp building waiting for Rana and Brachi gave Thomas a feeling of déjà vu. Once again, Calla was right there with him, sitting on a broken piece of curb while she recovered from being teleported halfway across the galaxy.

The landscape around them had drastically changed from two weeks ago. Much of the glass on the building had been broken. Blackened holes pockmarked the parking lot and some of the platform had fallen to the swamp below. The smell of the sea competed with the stench of burnt materials.

Galactic Law Enforcement personnel in their gray and white uniforms were crawling all over the area, accompanied by Gotrian and Olvian troops.

When the Olvian sub pulled up, Rana emerged.

Calla groaned as she stood. "We're on, aren't we?"

Thomas steadied her. "Yeah, are you ready?"

"Close enough for any practical purposes."

Thomas patted her on the shoulder and sent her feelings of strength and reassurance.

Rana frog-hopped over and rose onto her haunches. "Calla! You're all right!"

She nodded. "Thanks to everyone who had a hand in getting me out of that place."

Thomas glanced at the building. "I got there just in time. A couple minutes more could have been deadly."

Rana straightened her brilliant orange tabard. "Calla said you were clever for a male."

Not sure how to answer that sort of back-handed compliment. Thomas smiled. "Um, thanks."

The Gotrian plane landed at the far end of the parking lot. Brachi exited and lowered his hood.

Thomas indicated the plane with a nod. "Looks like everyone is here."

Brachi came over and stood toe to toe with Thomas. "Were you successful or not?"

Thomas looked down at the Gotrian Speaker. "Don't you see her standing there?"

"I do." Brachi approached Calla. "Shouldn't you be in bed?" He coughed.

She shook her head. "Do I look that bad?"

"I suppose not." Brachi left Calla and went to Rana. "Rrana, did you tell them the news?"

"I thought it would be better if we were all here." She hesitated and stammered a few syllables. "Don't you agree?"

Thomas nodded. Rana was at least trying to honor Gotrian customs. Was Brachi also adapting?

"Shall I tell them?" Rana asked.

Brachi's fur bristled then lay flat as his lips pursed. "By all means."

Apparently he was. The old Brachi would never have trusted someone younger with news of any significance.

Rana hopped forward. "During our raid on Pharmacorp, we came across a lab and proof absolute that they both started and perpetuated the plague."

Brachi reached into his dark green tunic and pulled out a hand-sized, leather-bound notebook. "We gave the original to the proper authorities already."

Calla took the notebook and flipped through. "If we can complete the treaty, Nikk's team will need this. It'll shortcut finding the cure."

"We thought so." Brachi struck his chest with his fist.

"That's why I had a scribe make a copy for you."

"Yes. On the matter of the treaty, there is news as well." Rana's coloring went a few shades paler.

"We drafted one for your approval." Brachi held his hand out toward Rana. "Not everyone is pleased with all the provisions, but all of us can live with it. The governments have agreed to rratify once we have the signatures of our arbitrators."

Thomas smiled. "You've been busy."

Rana produced a watertight case from a pocket of her tabard. "This is a copy you can read. If you'll come with us, we have set up a shelter on the beach near here for the meeting."

Thomas gestured for them to lead the way.

Calla leaned on the back of the couch with Matt. Thomas and Meiko stood hand in hand looking over August's shoulder as he typed furiously on Matt's computer. Calla knew how to do basic computer tasks, but watching him flip from screen to screen so quickly made her wonder how he had enough time to make sense of what he saw.

August tapped the screen. "Got 'em!"

Meiko leaned closer. "You found Pharmacorp?"

"Not exactly." He spun the chair to face the rest of them. "I found a supply company who picked up a new order for goods to be delivered to a new location. The manifest shows enough stuff to take care of a group about the size we're guessing Pharmacorp is. The initials on the record match Pharmacorp's president."

Thomas whistled. "Not bad but can we find out for

sure?"

"Yeah, I should be able to confirm it with some long-distance snooping." August shrugged and turned back to the screen. He looked at the computer for a moment, then zipped through several screens until he had called up a star chart. "President's name was Miles Efren, huh? Lemme look." He leaned back in the chair and closed his eyes.

Meiko looked up at Thomas. "He's going to search for him from here?"

Thomas nodded. "Scary, isn't it?"

Now that's some range. Calla whistled appreciatively. "I can't even get around the other side of a planet."

"Shh." Matt placed his hand over her mouth. "Hard enough without the peanut gallery."

She silenced the random thoughts in her mind. For long seconds, nothing happened. August made no movements, and the soft even rhythms of his breathing didn't change. Telepathically, she sensed him reaching outward but couldn't follow him far enough to tell where he was headed. She would have to be patient and wait for August to finish his task.

Two minutes turned into ten, and August's brow furrowed as he leaned forward to rest his forehead on his fingertips. His breathing became labored as he continued the effort.

Meiko put her hand on his shoulder. "Wish I could help."

"You're a sweetie, Meiko, but I don't need the distraction," he said through clenched teeth.

"Sorry." She took her hand away.

He put his head down on the desk a few minutes later, and the tension in his body ebbed away. "Ow."

Thomas winced. "I've never seen you push it that

hard."

"First time for everything." August sat up and pressed his palm against his forehead. "Searching for one man in a crowd light-years away is harder than I thought."

"Find anything?" Meiko asked.

"Gimme a minute."

Calla pushed away from the back of the couch and took a tentative step toward him. She could help him deal with the overexertion headache. She'd certainly experienced more of them than he ever had, but reaching into his mind would make her vulnerable. Even in his weakened state, she didn't doubt he could overpower her. Before Matt would be aware of the problem, August could do incredible damage. If he were fast enough, he could even kill her.

Would he do that, though? Ever since he'd found out about Joseph's ultimate plan, August hadn't intentionally done anything to hurt her. Although he could have been biding his time and waiting for her to lower her defenses, she didn't believe that. He would gain nothing from such a ploy, not with the sheer difference in their powers. He'd been as good as his word about keeping away from her except for these prearranged meetings.

What was wrong with her? He was in pain. She had the means to ameliorate the headache. If nothing else, she had an obligation to help him. The oath she'd taken to become a doctor said she'd help the sick and injured when she could, not when she wanted to.

Shoving her fear into the background, Calla perched on the edge of Matt's desk. She looked up at her boyfriend. He smiled and nodded.

"I can help you." She rested her shaking hand lightly on August's head. "I can't make the pounding stop completely. Only sleep will do that, but I can make the rail gun beating on your skull less obnoxious until you get somewhere to lie down."

He blindly reached up to pat her hand. "You don't have to do it if you don't want to, but I won't refuse any help I can get right now."

"Are you really okay with this?" Thomas' thoughts came to her. *"I was much worse off than he is, and you were convinced I'd hurt you."*

She looked up at him. *"I can't watch him suffer if I can do something about it."*

"He's a good guy. I'd trust him with Meiko and our kids, if we had any."

Calla nodded and reached into August's mind. "Just relax. I won't hurt you."

August managed a tight smile.

After visualizing the structures of his mind as a glass maze, Calla sought out the masses of panes that had cracked under the stress. Finding and repairing them all took a few minutes, and as she worked, his pain faded.

When she'd done as much as she could, Calla withdrew. "You'll have to sleep to get the rest to go away."

August took a deep breath, then sat up and rubbed his forehead. "Thanks. I don't understand why people always tell me how much they hate seeing psionic doctors."

Matt snorted. "Most of the doctors aren't so gentle."

Calla's cheeks warmed. "Well, more to the point, the procedures are pretty invasive. That makes people nervous."

August chuckled. "If you're that way with all your patients, you must have a busy practice."

"Did your search turn up anything?" She returned to Matt's side.

He turned back to the computer and pointed to one of the star systems marked on the map. "Jackpot. Found Miles Efren and a bunch of other folks who work for Pharmacorp. They're in a cave or underground complex of some sort on Chrysal."

Matt nodded. "No doubt waiting in the shadows until it's safe to return."

"Well, we've got 'em, and they don't know that."

"I'll call the officer in charge of this case." Thomas went to the message board. "We should move quickly in case they plan to be mobile for a while."

Calla grimaced. "Does it fall to us to personally go up against them?"

Thomas shook his head. "Nah. We'll leave catching them to the experts. With Pharmacorp's specific whereabouts, putting the company's leadership under arrest should be the easy part. Then all we have to do is turn over all our data and depositions of our experiences. They'll handle Pharmacorp from there."

Calla winced, but she understood. August had done the hard part of finding Pharmacorp again. If she and Thomas didn't start the wheel turning against the drug company, they'd move on, and some day another race, or even she and Thomas, would have to face a new threat from them. The company's leaders would remember who had stopped them.

As much for herself as for Thomas and the next planet Pharmacorp would infect with plagues, Calla would do her part to put an end to the company.

Originally from Michigan, Cindy Koepp combined a love of pedagogy and ecology into a 14-year career as an elementary science specialist. After teaching four-footers – that's height, not leg count – she pursued a Master's in Adult Learning with a specialization in Performance Improvement. Her published works include science fiction and fantasy novels, a passel of short stories, and a few educator resources. When she isn't reading or writing, Cindy is currently working as a tech writer, hat collector, quilter, crafter, and strange joke teller.

Looking for more? Find excerpts, links to interviews, guest blogs, and other content at http://ckoepp.com

Connect with me at http://facebook.com/koeppc

Other titles by Cindy

Novels
Condemned Courier
Like Herding the Wind
(Urushalon Book 1)
Remnant in the Stars
Lines of Succession
The Loudest Actions

Teacher Guides & Educational
Finished? Now Get Busy!
Writing Prompts for
Intermediate Grades
Crunchy Word Problems &
Other Brain Challenges

Anthologies
Mythic Orbits, Vol 2
Medieval Mars
Aquasynthesis Again, Vol 2
Victorian Venus

Hero's Best Friend
Avatars of Web Surfer
A Chimerical World:
Tales of the Seelie Court

And coming soon!
Into the Open (Urushalon Book II)